好萊塢 A 咖教你

電影英文
Film
Everything

U0012405

CONTENT

CONTENT

電影類型 A to Z

看電影相關報導時，免不了要讀到各種電影類型（film genre）的字眼，如本文中就出現了 drama（戲劇）、sci-fi（科幻）、comedy（喜劇）這幾個字。

其實電影並沒有標準的區分法，我們經常可以看到一部片的類型長得像這樣：action/adventure/fantasy/sci-fi（動作／冒險／奇幻／科幻），簡直跟食品成分表一樣，只能讓人大約猜想男主角應該有打鬥戲或飛車追逐、劇情大約跟尋寶有關，片中可能會出現巫師或機器人。

這樣的分類看起來似乎沒什麼意義，但對挑選想看的電影很有幫助，像上面這部片一看就知道不會有男女主角親親抱抱，是第一次約會的安全選擇。所以大家還是來認識一下這些字吧。

- **action** 動作片
- **adult** 成人電影
- **adventure** 冒險片
- **animation** 動畫片
- **art film / art house film** 藝術電影
- **biography** 傳記片
- **comedy** 喜劇片
- **black comedy / dark comedy** 黑色喜劇

- **rom-com（romantic comedy）**愛情喜劇片
- **crime** 犯罪片
- **disaster** 災難片
- **documentary** 紀錄片
- **drama** 劇情片
- **family** 家庭溫馨片
- **fantasy** 奇幻片
- **horror** 恐怖片

- **musical** 歌舞片
- **mystery** 推理片
- **romance** 浪漫愛情片
- **sci-fi（science fiction）** 科幻片
- **thriller** 驚悚片
- **war** 戰爭片
- **Western** 西部片

其他電影類型字彙

上面這些字是以電影內容為分類標準，還有一些字則是在描述電影長度及發行方式：

feature film 劇情長片
根據各大電影獎項報名分類，一個小時以上的電影即為「長片」。

short film 短片
短於四十分鐘的電影被視為「短片」。

made-for-TV 電視電影
由電視公司製作，只在電視上播出的電影，通常製作經費及拍攝水準較一般電視劇高。

made-for-DVD 直接出 DVD 的電影
這種電影拍攝完成之後就出 DVD 發行，不在電影院播出，也稱作 direct-to-DVD movie 或 straight-to-DVD movie。

電影獎項

BAFTA Awards 英國影藝學院獎

BAFTA 為 British Academy of Film and Television Arts（英國影藝學院）的縮寫，同時也能表示英國影藝學院獎這個獎項，相當於美國的奧斯卡獎，設立於一九四七年，從二〇〇〇年開始在歐登電影院萊斯特廣場旗艦店頒發。成立之初頒獎儀式於四月或五月舉行，二〇〇一年為了趕在奧斯卡之前而改成二月。

Golden Globe Awards 金球獎

金球獎頒獎典禮是美國一年一度的電視及電影盛會，由近百位外籍娛樂記者組成的好萊塢外國記者協會（Hollywood Foreign Press Association，簡稱 HFPA）所舉辦，由協會成員投票選出得獎者。與電影奧斯卡金像獎 (Academy Awards) 和電視艾美獎 (Emmy Awards) 不同的是，金球獎因受限於缺乏專業投票團，故略過技術方面的獎項，只頒發普通獎項。頒獎日為每年的一月中旬，距離三月的奧斯卡頒獎典禮頗近，故被稱為「奧斯卡的風向球」。

Academy Awards 學院獎

通稱為奧斯卡金像獎或奧斯卡獎 (Oscars)，每年由美國電影藝術與科學學院頒發，設立於一九二九年，於每年的二月下旬舉辦頒獎典禮。奧斯卡獎的評選委員是由學院中的會員和學院邀請的貴賓產生。若是要說獎項本身而非指頒獎典禮，英文最後的 s 則須拿掉，變為 Academy Award 或是 Oscar。

Razzies 金莓獎

全名是 Golden Raspberry Awards，簡稱 Razzies。這個名稱源自於 blow a raspberry 這句俚語，raspberry 原意是「覆盆子」，不過在倫敦東區的同韻俚語中，raspberry tart 是指放屁 (fart)，簡稱為 raspberry，後來 raspberry 就被用來指模仿放屁的聲音，而這樣的動作也有「喝倒采、發出噓聲」的意思，也可以說 make a Bronx cheer，因此金莓獎即是頒給那種令人想發出噓聲的「最糟」電影。

首屆金莓獎於一九八一年開始，每年都選在奧斯卡提名揭曉前一天宣佈入圍名單，由來自各國的電影專業人士組成的金莓獎協會 (Golden Raspberry Award Foundation，簡稱 GRAF) 成員以及影迷和媒體公開投票選出得獎者，並在奧斯卡頒獎典禮前一天揭曉得獎名單，目的就是為了反諷好萊塢商業電影，還把原本的獎項 Best（最佳）改成 Worst（最糟），實在是酸到最高點。

Leonardo DiCaprio 李奧納多狄卡皮歐

李奧納多狄卡皮歐

©s_bukley / Shutterstock.com

SHOWBIZ WORD

star 主演

有些電影常因為某些大明星來主演、當主角而名聲大噪。star 除了是名詞「大明星」之外，還可以當動詞「由…主演」star (in)。

- *Star Trek* features Leonard Nimoy and Zachary Quinto as the old and young Spock.
  《星際爭霸戰》由倫納德尼莫伊和塞奇瑞昆托分別飾演年老以及年輕的史巴克。
- In *Revolutionary Road*, Kate Winslet plays the role of a dissatisfied 1950s housewife.
  在《真愛旅程》一片中，凱特溫蕾斯蕾飾演一九五〇年代不滿現狀的家庭主婦。

MP3 001

Born in Los Angeles in 1974 to an Italian-American father and German mother, Leonardo DiCaprio received his name because his [1)]**pregnant** mother was looking at a Leonardo Da Vinci painting at a museum when he first kicked. His parents [2)]**divorced** when he was a baby, and he was brought up by his mother in a poor, dangerous L.A. neighborhood. The young DiCaprio looked to acting as a way out, and his [3)]**blond-haired** good looks were soon winning him parts in commercials and then a small role in the [9)]**sitcom** *Growing Pains*.

DiCaprio first appeared on the big screen in the 1991 low-budget horror movie *Critters 3*, but his [11)]**break** came when he was picked by Robert De Niro to star [4)]**alongside** him in *This Boys Life*. This serious role proved he was more than just a pretty face, leading to other challenging roles in independent films like 1993's *What's Eating Gilbert Grape*, where he plays a mentally [5)]**handicapped** boy, and 1995's *Total Eclipse*, in which he appears as the French poet Arthur Rimbaud.

DiCaprio's starring role in the 1996 [6)]**hit** *Romeo + Juliet* brought him to wider audiences, but that was just a warm-up for 1997's *Titanic*. The highest [7)]**grossing** film to date, *Titanic* turned the young actor into an international superstar. DiCaprio [8)]**retreated** into smaller roles over the next few years, but returned to the top of his game in the 2002 Spielberg crime drama *Catch Me if You Can*. Also that year, he starred in Scorsese's *Gangs of New York*, which marked the beginning of a long-term [10)]**collaboration** with the director that has included *The Aviator*, *The Departed* and most recently *The Wolf of Wall Street*.

6

©danzden / flickr.com

1) **pregnant** [ˈprɛgnənt] (a.) 懷孕的
The woman is pregnant with twins.
這個女生懷了一對雙胞胎。

2) **divorce** [dɪˈvors] (v./n.) 離婚
Mark's wife refuses to divorce him.
馬克的太太拒絕與他離婚。

3) **blond** [blɑnd] (a.) 金髮的
Many Swedish people have blond hair and blue eyes.
許多瑞典人都是金髮藍眼。

4) **alongside** [əˈlɔŋˈsaɪd] (prep./adv.) 跟某人一起，在（某人事物）旁邊
Australian troops fought alongside the British in World War I.
澳洲軍隊在第一次世界大戰時與英軍並肩作戰。

5) **handicapped** [ˈhændɪˌkæpt] (a.) 殘障的
Rob got a ticket for parking in a handicapped zone.
羅伯得到一張殘障車位的停車券。

6) **hit** [hɪt] (n.) 成功、受歡迎的事物
The clown was a big hit at Timmy's birthday party.
蒂芬妮生日派對上請來的小丑非常受歡迎。

7) **gross** [gros] (v.) 獲得…總收入
The movie grossed 20 million dollars but didn't make a profit.
這部電影總收入兩千萬卻沒有獲利。

8) **retreat** [rɪˈtrit] (v./n.) 撤退，後退
When our troops attacked, the enemy was forced to retreat.
當我方軍隊進擊時，敵方只好撤退。

進階字彙

9) **sitcom** [ˈsɪtˌkɑm] (n.)（電視）情境喜劇，為 situation comedy 的簡稱
Friends is my favorite sitcom.
《六人行》是我最喜歡的情境喜劇。

10) **collaboration** [kəˌlæbəˈreʃən] (n.) 共同合作（的作品）
(v.) collaborate [kəˈlæbəˌret]
The building is a collaboration between two famous architects.
這座建築物是兩位名建築師共同合作的作品。

口語補充

11) **break** [brek] (n.) 大好機會，幸運的轉折
The band is still waiting for its big break.
這個樂團還在等待成名的機會。

一九七四年生於洛杉磯，雙親分別為義大利裔美國人和德國人的李奧納多狄卡皮歐，會取名為李奧納多是因為他第一次在媽媽肚子裡踢的時候，她正在一間博物館欣賞李奧納多達文西的一幅畫作。雙親在他還是嬰兒時就離婚了，而他由母親在洛杉磯一個貧窮、危險的地區撫養長大。年輕的狄卡皮歐把演戲視作出路，而他金髮的漂亮面孔很快為他贏得拍攝廣告的機會，以及情境喜劇《歡樂家庭》的小角色。

狄卡皮歐在一九九一年的低成本片大恐怖片《外星通緝者 III》初登大銀幕，但當他獲勞勃狄尼洛欽點，和他一起主演《男孩的生活》後，演藝生涯就此突破。這個嚴肅的角色證明他不只臉蛋漂亮，為他帶來其他具有挑戰性的獨立電影角色，例如一九九三年的《戀戀情深》和一九九五年的《全蝕狂愛》，他在前者飾演弱智男童，後者則詮釋法國詩人韓波。

狄卡皮歐領銜主演一九九六年賣座片《羅密歐與茱莉葉》，讓他知名度大開，但這只是暖身，好戲還在後頭：一九九七年的《鐵達尼號》。這部當時史上票房最高的電影使這位年輕演員搖身一變成國際巨星。接下來幾年，狄卡皮歐轉回琢磨於小角色，但在二○○二年藉由史匹柏執導的犯罪片《神鬼交鋒》重返顛峰。同年，他也主演史柯西斯的《紐約黑幫》，開啟他與這位名導的長期合作，包括《神鬼玩家》、《神鬼無間》和最近的《華爾街之狼》。

與黑幫電影大師的師生情緣

©Everett Collection / Shutterstock.com

談到李奧納多，就不得不想到與他長期合作的名導演馬丁史柯西斯 (Martin Scorsese)。史柯西斯的大師級地位因黑幫電影而屹立不搖，如《殘酷大街》(*Mean Streets*)、《四海好傢伙》(*Goodfellas*) 等，而他與李奧納多的緣分也是從黑幫電影開始萌芽。二○○二年的《紐約黑幫》是李奧納多和史柯西斯的首度合作，再來的《神鬼玩家》、《隔離島》(*Shutter Island*)、《神鬼無間》，到第五度合作的《華爾街之狼》。李奧納多曾公開表示，十五歲的他曾夢想有天能和史柯西斯合作，就算只有一次也很滿足。由此可知，這位大師在李奧納多心中的地位無人可及。

The Wolf of Wall Street 《華爾街之狼》

🎥 電影介紹

喬登貝爾福（Jordan Belford，李奧納多狄卡皮歐飾）是一名華爾街股票經紀人，因其獨特行銷口才，靠著炒股、內線交易甚至洗錢，年紀輕輕就賺進大把大把的鈔票，曾經是叱吒華爾街的證券之王。喬登帶領工作夥伴唐尼（Donnie，喬納希爾 (Jonah Hill) 飾）等，虛度荒淫的享樂，喝酒吸毒嫖妓樣樣來。只是大難臨頭各自飛，喬登最後怎會淪到涉嫌詐欺罪行入獄，身邊卻連一個挺他的人都沒有？

MP3 003

the name of the game 重點，成功關鍵

the name of the game 可不是在說什麼電玩名稱喔。這裡的 the game 意思是「某活動或行業」，整句俚語是在形容做某方面的成功祕訣。

A: What's your secret to success in sales?
你當業務的成功祕訣是什麼？

B: **The name of the game** is getting customers to trust you.
成功的關鍵在於如何讓客戶信任你。

🎬 電影對白

喬登第一天到華爾街上班，老前輩馬克漢納（Mark Hanna，馬修麥康納 (Matthew McConaughey) 飾）請他吃午餐。喬登說他很榮幸可以來這間公司上班，因為這裡的客戶都是大咖。沒想到漢納卻告訴他，其實客戶是誰根本不是重點，客戶口袋裡的錢才是重點。

Mark: You got a girlfriend?
你有女朋友嗎？

Jordon: I'm married. I have a wife. Her name is Teresa. She cuts hair.
我結婚了，娶老婆了。她叫泰瑞莎，在幫人家剪頭髮。

Mark: Congratulations.
恭喜。

Jordon: Thank you.
謝謝你。

Mark: Think about Teresa. **Name of the game**: move the money from your client's pocket into your pocket.
想想泰瑞莎。最重要的是，如何讓客戶口袋裡的錢流進你的口袋裡。

🎬 電影對白

喬登追求財富不擇手段，且縱情於聲色狂歡，這讓喬登的爸爸非常擔心。不過喬登覺得他老爸太過度緊張了。

Jordon's dad: How can I not get stressed out? Look at the knuckleheads you got working for you.
我怎麼能不緊張？你看看那些幫你工作的蠢貨。

Jordon: I know they're knuckleheads, but I need them to want to live like me, you get it? To live like me.
我知道他們都是蠢貨，但我必須讓他們想要過著像我一樣的生活，你明白嗎？和我一樣的生活。

Jordon's dad: Jordy. One of these days, **the chickens are gonna come home to roost**.
喬迪，總有一天會有報應的。

Jordon: You're looking at me like I'm crazy.
我知道你覺得我太瘋狂。

Jordon's dad: Crazy? This is obscene.
瘋狂？你這是荒淫無度。

MP3 004

(chickens) come home to roost 自食其果，自作自受

root 當名詞時，有「歇息處」的意思。在英文中，用小雞一定也要回巢休息這樣的循環定律，來形容人如果做了壞事，最後一定會得到報應。(chickens) come home to roost 就是在說人家惡有惡報、自作自受。

A: How can he make money by cheating his customers?
他怎麼能利用欺騙客戶來謀利？

B: Don't worry. The **chickens** will eventually **come home to roost**.
不用擔心，總有一天會得到報應的。

A: Do you think the president will be reelected?
你覺得現任總統還能連任嗎？

B: No. All his bad policy decisions are **coming home to roost**.
不會，他的不良施政一定會讓他自食其果。

「搶心肝」拼影帝

三次角逐奧斯卡影帝的李奧納多，這次演出《華爾街之狼》雖然獲獎呼聲極高，但最後還是讓給了馬修麥康納，抱憾而歸。很巧的是，馬修麥康納也有參與《華爾街之狼》的演出，飾演帶領李奧納多進入華爾街的啟蒙師。有趣的是，片中的麥康納為了紓壓所唱的捶胸歌曲原創正巧就是他本人，這是他開演前讓自己放鬆的熱身運動，正巧被李奧納多看到，安排在電影橋段之中。沒想到，這次「搶心肝」的居然變成李奧納多，讓這次的影帝爭霸戰，增添更多話題。雖然這次李奧納多未能如願將小金人給抱回家，但二度奪下金球獎影帝，應該能稍稍彌補他心中的缺憾。

©Debby Wong / Shutterstock.com

©Debby Wong / Shutterstock.com

Blood Diamond
《血鑽石》

 電影介紹

本片背景設定在一九九〇年代表內戰和為社會動亂所苦的獅子山共和國。故事主要由南非籍傭兵丹尼艾奇（Danny Archer，李奧納多狄卡皮歐飾）、門德族漁夫索羅門梵迪（Solomon Vandy，迪蒙杭蘇 (Djimon Hounsou) 飾）以及一位懷抱理想的美國際記者麥蒂鮑恩（Maddy Bowen，珍妮佛康納莉 (Jennifer Connelly) 飾）所串連。他們的生活背景全然不同，卻在命運安排之下，展開一場危險的冒險旅程，追尋那顆足以換來自由、家人以及真相的稀有紅鑽。

電影對白

麥蒂厭倦了幾張瘦弱的小孩、頭上一堆蒼蠅的老套非洲難民照片，想藉由索羅門的故事，讓世人了解挖鑽背後剝削非洲人民的事實，遏止大家購買鑽石。而丹尼則潑她冷水，告訴她不要以為幾篇報導就能夠改變非法採鑽的現況。

Danny: You know Solomon thinks his son will be a doctor someday? Maybe his baby dies in that camp, maybe his daughter gets *raped. Who knows, maybe both. Do you realize that that diamond is his only chance of getting his family out of here?

妳知道索羅門覺得他兒子將來會當醫生嗎？也許寶寶會在難民營夭折，女兒會被強暴，誰曉得，也許都會。妳知道那顆鑽石是他救回家人的唯一機會嗎？

Maddy: You **don't give a rat's ass** about his family!

你才不在乎他家人的死活！

*rape   [rep] (v./n.) 強姦

MP3 005

not give a rat's ass 一點都不在乎

在口語上，rat 常用來形容「不值錢的東西」。一整隻老鼠都不值錢了，更不用說只有牠的屁股。這麼不值錢的東西你都不想給，就表示這人事物的發展對你來說不痛不癢，not give a rat's ass 就用來形容「不在意、不在乎」。你也可以說 not give a damn 或是 not give a shit，不過這三種說法都不是很禮貌的用法，在用的時候要小心一點。

A: I think you should go on a diet.

我覺得你應該要減肥。

B: I **don't give a rat's ass** what you think!

我才不在乎你怎麼想咧！

Shutter Island
《隔離島》

📷 電影介紹

隔離島是一個精神病院的所在地,美國聯邦法警泰迪(Teddy,李奧納多狄卡皮歐飾)和他的新夥伴查克(Chuck,馬克魯法洛 (Mark Ruffalo) 飾)到此來調查一位女精神病患失蹤事宜,不過事情似乎並不像他們想像的那麼簡單……。

🎞 電影對白

船剛抵達隔離島上唯一的碼頭,泰迪和查克下船並出示他們的聯邦法警警徽給副典獄長麥法遜 (Deputy Warden McPherson) 先生看。

McPherson: Never seen a *Marshal's *badge before. I'm *Deputy Warden McPherson, gentlemen. Welcome to Shutter Island. I'll be the one taking you up to Ashecliffe.

從未見過聯邦法警的警徽。我是副獄長麥法遜。歡迎來隔離島,由我帶你們上去亞殊崖醫院。[泰迪和查克上了副獄長的車子,此時周圍的獄警全程備槍緊盯著他們]

Teddy: Your boys seem a little **on edge**, Mr. McPherson.

麥法遜先生,你的手下看來有點緊繃的。

McPherson: Right now, Marshal. We all are.

警長,我們現在都是這樣。

*marshal [ˈmɑrʃəl] (n.) 聯邦法警,警察局長

*badge [bædʒ] (n.) 徽章,警徽

*deputy [ˈdɛpjəti] (a.) 副的

MP3 006

on edge 緊張

edge 除了「邊緣」,還有「刀口」的意思。因此 on edge 正是形容被人用刀尖上脅迫的那種緊張、焦慮的感覺。

A: You look a little **on edge**. What's wrong?

你看起來有點緊張,怎麼了嗎?

B: I have a job interview today.

我今天有一個工作面試。

J. Edgar 《強艾德格》

🎞 電影對白

在酒吧裡,胡佛跟同桌的女子們談論起被撕票的小林白綁架事件,胡佛原本說不能透露太多情報,但後來又向她們透露另一個重要的機密。

Hoover: The gold notes from the ransom money have surfaced. And can you guess where?

贖金支付的金子憑證已經出現了,妳們猜得到在哪裡嗎?

Woman: Tell us. Please, Mr. Hoover.

拜託告訴我們,胡佛先生。

Hoover: In the Bronx, on three occasions. And each one of the shop owners claim they received them from a man with a pointed chin and a German accent.

在布隆克斯區,有三次。而且每個店主都聲稱那些錢全來自一名有德國口音的尖下巴男人。

Woman: **Take my word for it**, Mr. Hoover. All the admiration in the world can't fill the spot love goes. Or keep your bed warm.

相信我,胡佛先生。全世界的讚美也無法填補愛的空缺。或者溫暖你的床。

The Great Gatsby

📷 電影介紹

故事背景設定在經濟如日中天但道德淪喪的美國一九二〇年代,以一名未成名的作家尼克卡拉威(Nick Carraway,陶比麥奎爾 (Tobey Maguire) 飾)到紐約追逐美國夢所經歷的一切,進而帶出神秘富豪傑蓋茲比(Jay Gatsby,李奧納多狄卡皮歐飾)的故事。蓋茲比對已婚黛西(Daisy,凱莉默里根 (Carey Mulligan) 飾)的迷戀與執著,這段無緣愛情終將為其帶來毀滅。尼克目睹所有的事情,對這紙醉金迷上流社會的謊言大失所望,決定寫下這個悲慘故事。

MP3 008

take one's breath away 令人嘖嘖稱奇

在英文中,用 take one's breath away (把呼吸拿走) 來形容令人驚訝的樣子。可以因為和自己所預期的不同而驚訝,或是看見令人傾倒、讚嘆人事物時的那種驚艷感受。

A: How was your trip to Nepal?

你的尼泊爾之旅怎麼樣?

B: Wonderful. The mountain scenery **took my breath away**.

超棒的,那山景令人嘖嘖稱奇。

🎥 電影介紹

此為首任聯邦局局長約翰艾德格胡佛 (J. Edgar Hoover) 的傳記電影，由李奧納多狄卡皮歐主演同名角色。描述年輕僅二十四歲的胡佛如何大刀闊斧，帶領他一手建立的聯邦調查局成為美國最有權利的司法機關。

MP3 007

take sb's word for it 相信某人

word 除了表「字」的意思，也可以指「說的話」，take sb's word for it 把人家說的話拿去，那就表示你聽進去了、相信了。

A: Pig intestines are really tasty.
豬腸很好吃。

B: Uh…I'm just going to **take your word for it**.
呃……我就姑且相信你說的吧！

《大亨小傳》

🎞 電影對白

喬丹貝克（Jordan Baker，伊麗莎白戴比基 (Elizabeth Debicki) 飾）告訴尼克，蓋茲比和他的表妹黛西在五年前曾有過一段情，卻因種種因素兩人未果。現在他想請尼克幫忙找黛西出來，讓他能和她碰一面。喬登還說蓋茲比會舉辦這麼多盛大的宴會都是有原因的。

Jordan: He threw all those parties, hoping she would wander in one night. He constantly asked about Daisy. I was just the first person that knew her.
他辦了這麼多的晚會，就是希望有天晚上黛西會突然出現。他不斷地向人問起黛西。我只是第一個他問到認識她的人。

Nick: All that for a girl he hasn't seen in five years. And now he just wants me to invite her over to tea. The modesty of it....
一切都是只是為了一個已經五年沒見的女人，而現在他希望我能邀請她一起喝茶。真是夠含蓄了……。

Jordan: Kind of **takes your breath away**, doesn't it?
有點難以置信，是不是？

Gossip Box

李奧納多的 old sport！

有看過《大亨小傳》都知道，電影中的蓋茲比總是喜歡稱尼克為夥伴，也就是英文的 old sport。現實生活中，李奧納多跟陶比麥奎爾也真的是一對好兄弟。李奧納多和陶比在童星時期因常爭取同一角色因而結識，種下深厚的兄弟情。李奧納多曾說過若不是有陶比麥奎爾和他一同參與《大亨小傳》的演出，他可能沒有自信能夠擔下飾演蓋茲比這個大角色。

Matthew McConaughey 馬修麥康納

©Joe Seer / Shutterstock.com

MP3 009

The youngest son of a gas station owner and a teacher, Matthew McConaughey grew up in a small Texas town. He [1]**excelled** at sports in high school, and was voted "Most Handsome" by his senior class. McConaughey originally planned on becoming a lawyer, but changed his major from law to film at the last minute.

First appearing in TV commercials, McConaughey made the leap to the big screen when a chance [2]**encounter** with a producer at a bar led to a role in Richard Linklater's 1993 comedy *Dazed and Confused*. His first leading role in a Hollywood film came in 1996, when he starred alongside Sandra Bullock in *A Time to Kill*. More big roles followed in 1997, including Jody Foster's love interest in the sci-fi film *Contact* and a young lawyer in Steven Spielberg's historical drama *Amistad*.

After heating up the screen with Jennifer Lopez in the 2001 hit *The Wedding Planner*, McConaughey became one of Hollywood's most popular romantic leads. It didn't hurt that he was named *People* magazine's "Sexiest Man Alive" for 2005. But by the end of the decade he began to [3]**crave** more [4]**challenging** roles.

McConaughey [5]**reunited** with Linklater for the 2011 black comedy *Bernie*, and played a male [6]**stripper** in 2012's *Magic Mike*. But his most [7]**demanding** role yet was playing [8]**real-life** AIDS patient Ron Woodroof in 2013's *Dallas Buyers Club*. McConaughey had to lose 47 pounds for the part, but winning the best actor Oscar made it worth the effort!

©cinemafestival / Shutterstock.com

馬修麥康納是加油站老闆和教師的小兒子，生長在一個德州小鎮。他在高中時是運動健將，並被他那屆畢業班同學票選為「第一美男子」。麥康納原本計畫要成為律師，但他在最後一刻改變主修，從法律換成電影。

一開始都拍些電視廣告的麥康納，在酒吧巧遇一位製作人，因而接演理查林克萊特一九九三年喜劇《年少輕狂》的一個角色，一舉躍上大銀幕。他在一九九六年首度於好萊塢電影擔綱主角，和珊卓布拉克合演《殺戮時刻》。一九九七年更多大角色接踵而至，包括在科幻電影《接觸未來》飾演茱蒂福斯特的心上人，以及在史蒂芬史匹柏的歷史劇《勇者無懼》扮演年輕律師。

在二〇〇一年賣座片《愛上新郎》與珍妮佛洛佩茲在銀幕打得火熱之後，麥康納成為好萊塢最炙手可熱的愛情片男星之一。二〇〇五年獲《時人》雜誌評選為「當今最性感的男人」更是錦上添花。但到了二〇〇〇年代晚期，他開始嚮往具挑戰性的角色。

麥康納在二〇一一年的黑色喜劇《胖尼殺很大》和林克萊特團聚，又在二〇一二年的《舞棍俱樂部》扮演脫衣舞男。但他至今最困難的角色是在二〇一三年《藥命俱樂部》飾演真有其人的愛滋病患朗恩伍德夫。麥康納必須為這個角色減重四十七磅，但贏得奧斯卡最佳男演員獎，讓一切努力都值得了！

VOCABULARY BANK

1）**excel** [ɪk`sɛl] (v.) 擅長於，表現突出
Lisa excels in math and science.
麗莎的數學和理化成績優異。

2）**encounter (with)** [ɪn`kaʊntɚ] (v.) 偶然遇見
Laura was surprised when she encountered her ex-boyfriend at the mall.
蘿拉很驚訝會在大賣場遇到前男友。

3）**crave** [krev] (v.) 渴望
Pregnant women often crave pickles.
孕婦常常會很想吃酸黃瓜。

4）**challenging** [`tʃælɪndʒɪŋ] (a.) 具有挑戰性的
The problems on the test were quite challenging.
這次考試的題目很有挑戰性。

5）**reunite** [͵rijuˋnaɪt] (v.) 重聚，再次結合
The family was reunited after the war.
這家人總算在戰後團圓了。

6）**stripper** [ˋstrɪpɚ] (n.) 脫衣者
The star once worked as a stripper before she became famous.
那個明星成名之前曾經去當脫衣舞孃。

7）**demanding** [dɪˋmændɪŋ] (a.) 要求很高的
Teaching is very demanding work.
教學是要求非常高的工作。

8）**real-life** [ˋriəl͵laɪf] (a.) 真實的，真人實事的
The stars in romantic movies often become real-life couples.
演出愛情電影的明星經常成為真正的情侶。

TONGUE-TIED NO MORE

it doesn't hurt... 只有好處，沒有壞處

常用的形式還有 it couldn't hurt、it wouldn't hurt 或 it can't hurt。hurt 有「損傷」的意思，這句字面上是「不會有傷害」，表示一件事做了雖然不見得會有什麼大的效果，但只會更為加分，不會有害處，可以去試試看，用來表達一種建議。經常見到的用法是 it doesn't hurt to do something 或 it doesn't hurt to have something。
A: I seriously doubt my boss will give me a raise.
我強烈懷疑我的老闆會給我加薪。
B: Well, it doesn't hurt to ask.
反正，問一問也無妨。

worth the effort 付出都值得了

worth 是指投入的金錢或心血「有得到對等的回報」，effort 是「努力」的意思。這個形容詞片語表示努力有得到應得的回報，一切都值得了。
A: Doesn't it take a long time to cook a turkey?
烤火雞不是非常耗時嗎？
B: Yeah, but it's definitely worth the effort.
是啊，但你的付出絕對值得。

SHOWBIZ WORD

make the leap to the big screen
躍上大銀幕

因為舞台劇、電視廣告及電視影集的演出機會較多，許多演員都是從出身劇場或電視影集，稍有名氣之後才進軍電影，躍上大銀幕。這句常出現的形式還有 make a leap from small screen to big screen。

love interest
（戲劇或電影中的）另一半，伴侶；曖昧對象

love interest 這個字常出現在電影或小說相關的文章當中，是指在故事中與主角有浪漫關係的角色。 love interest 這個字在一般生活中很少使用。

heat up the screen 在戲中大談戀愛

heat up 有「提高溫度」的意思，在口語中可表示「引發強烈的情緒」。浪漫電影中男女主角熱烈的愛情，讓觀眾無不受到感染，因此 heat up the screen 就是指一對主角在片中的愛情戲不是純純的愛，而是成年人式的交往，甚至有令人血脈賁張的床戲。

13

Dallas Buyers Club 《藥命俱樂部》

🎥 電影介紹

郎恩伍德夫（Ron Woodroof，馬修麥康納飾）生活糜爛，終日吃喝嫖賭，直到有一天意外住院，被告知罹患愛滋病，只剩下三十天的壽命，終於展開為生命奮戰的旅程。

🎬 電影對白

伍德夫當組頭賭輸還不出錢來，眼看就要被債主追上，只能使出下下策，跑去找警察塔克（Tucker，史提夫詹恩 (Steve Zahn) 飾）把自己關進牢裡。伍德夫坐上塔克的警車卻不是去警察局，原來他們倆是親兄弟，塔克開始勸伍德夫不要執迷不悟，但伍德夫不把他的話當一回事，塔克更加苦口婆心起來。

Tucker: Handle your business, huh? **Get your shit together.**
你要好好過日子，好吧？別再胡搞瞎搞了。

Woodroof: Shit, Tuck, you're starting to sound like a goddamn old man.
糟糕，塔克，你講話越來越像個討厭的老頭了。

MP3 011

get one's shit together 把生活、事情料理好

這句話的用途很廣，如果有人腦筋不清楚、生活散漫，或是做事笨手笨腳，都可以用這句話叫對方振作起來，把生活／事情料理好。因為 shit 是個髒字，有些人會把這個字換成 stuff，變成 get one's stuff together，也可以說 get one's act together。

A: I just got my report card, and I'm failing half my classes.
我剛剛拿到成績單，有一半的科目不及格。

B: You better **get your shit together**, dude!
你最好開始振作，老兄！

如果有人房間髒亂或東西沒收好，也可以用這句話叫對方「快點收拾」。

A: What time do we have to be at the airport?
我們幾點一定要到機場？

B: We need to be there in an hour. Hurry up and **get your shit together**!
我們必須一小時內到那邊。快點收拾行李！

另外，get 帶有採取行動產生改變的意味，若要說一個人的狀態是「把生活／事情料理好」，就將動詞改為 have，例如 He really has his shit together.（他的生活井井有條。）

A: Is Aaron still living in his parents' basement?
阿倫還住在他爸媽家的地下室嗎？

B: No. He got a job and moved out, and he even has a girlfriend. He really **has his act together** these days.
沒了。他找到工作搬出來了，還交了個女朋友。他現在的日子過得井井有條。

🎬 電影對白

伍德夫不接受醫院治療，循非法管道取得試驗用藥亂吃一通，最後昏倒住院，醒來又簽字自願出院。他大搖大擺走出病房時，被依芙薩克斯醫師（Dr. Eve Saks，珍妮佛嘉納 (Jennifer Garner) 飾）撞見，並警告他不准出院。

Woodroof: Worst-case scenario being what?
最糟的情況又能夠怎樣？

Dr. Saks: We can make you comfortable.
我們能讓你舒服一點。

Woodroof: What? Hook me up to the morphine drip, let me *fade on out?
幹麼？幫我吊點滴打嗎啡，讓我失去知覺？

*fade out 就是影像慢慢變淡，聲音漸漸變小至無法分辨。在一般用語中引伸為「昏睡過去」。對白中 fade on out 的 on 只是加強語氣。

MP3 012

worst-case scenario 預估最糟的情況

scenario 原本是「劇本情節」的意思，引伸為事情發展下去可能的局面。worst-case scenario 即「預估最糟的情況」，而相反的情況就是 best-case scenario（預估最好的情況）了。

A: What's the **worst-case scenario**, doctor?
最糟的情況會有多糟，醫生？

B: Well, if the filling doesn't hold, we may have to pull the tooth.
嗯，如果牙齒填充物撐不住，我們或許得拔牙了。

Gossip Box

為戲減重，真要命！

為了飾演愛滋病臨終患者，馬修麥康納拍片前減重二十一公斤（83 → 62），到最後因營養失衡造成視力衰退，虛弱到連五個伏地挺身都做不來！為了讓自己變得蒼白瘦弱，還待在家中足不出戶達六個月之久。馬修這段期間因為不能運動，必須找其他方法打發時間，他自嘲因此變得「聰明不少」。

本片三位主要演員：馬修麥康納、珍妮佛嘉納及傑瑞李圖（Jared Leto，飾演變裝皇后Rayon）。兩位男演員分別因本片獲得第八十六屆奧斯卡最佳男主角及最佳男配角獎。

電影對白

伍德夫受傷入院意外得知自己染上愛滋病，開始瘋狂收集醫療資訊，希望能幫自己找到解藥。他得知一款藥物即將在美國展開人體試驗，就跑到醫院要求薩克斯醫師讓他參與試驗。

Dr. Saks: That isn't how it works. For about a year, a group of patients gets either the drug or a *placebo. It's totally left up to chance, not even doctors are allowed to know.

試驗不是那樣進行的。在大約一年期間，一群病患有些會拿到那種藥，有些會拿到安慰劑。完全隨機，連醫生都不得而知。

Woodroof: So, you're giving dying people *sugar pills?

那麼，你們會發安慰劑給已經一腳進棺材的人？

Dr. Saks: It's the only way to know if a drug works.

唯有如此才能知道藥物是否有效。

Woodroof: Can you get some for me? I got cash. I can go a month, a week, however you want to do it.

你能幫我弄到一些藥嗎？我有錢。我可以每個月、每個星期買一次，隨便妳要怎樣都可以。

Dr. Saks: I hear you. Unfortunately, no.

我了解。很不幸的，不行。

*placebo [plə`sibo] (n.) 安慰劑，不具療效只是讓人以為是藥，吃了心安的東西

*sugar pill 糖做的藥丸，即「安慰劑」

MP3 013

I hear you. 我了解。

I hear you. 這個句子隨著前後文及語調可以有許多意思。字面上是「我聽到（你說的）了」，可以表示「我同意」、「我聽到了」，甚至「我了解你的意見但我不能同意」，跟「嗯哼」差不多。另一種說法 I hear what you're saying 則表示「我聽到了」、「我了解」，但沒有同意的意思。

A: I think it's time for us to get a new car.

我覺得我們該換輛新車了。

B: I hear you, but our old car's still running fine.

嗯哼，但我們原本這輛車還很好開。

EDtv 《艾德私人頻道》

🎥 電影介紹

真實電視台決定要開播一個真人秀，在沒有導演和完全不剪輯的情況下轉播一個人的生活。在企劃案定下來後，製作單位四處尋找合適人選試鏡，最後透過一位試鏡者雷（Ray，伍迪哈里遜（Woody Harrelson）飾）找到他們的最佳男主角艾德（Ed，馬修麥康納飾），他的世界從此發生天翻地覆的變化。

MP3 014

have one's back 保護某人

人的眼睛長在前面，可以隨時注意危險保護自己，但是背後（back）可就是安全的死角了。美語中常用 I've got your back. 來代表我已顧好你看不到的地方，也就是「我會保護你」的意思。這個句子常在戰爭片或警匪片中聽到，因為無論作戰或對付歹徒時，都可以告知夥伴自己能夠掩護他的行動。

A: This is the police! Come out with your hands up!
我們是警察! 舉手出來!

B: Go on in and get him, Bob. I**'ve got your back**.
衝進去捉他，鮑柏。我掩護你。

📽 電影對白

家庭會議上，，艾德擔心上真人秀會給家人帶來麻煩，讓想藉機出名發財的雷幻想破滅，於是連忙鼓起三寸不爛之舌，要艾德無後顧之憂地參加節目。

Ray: You didn't have to worry about anything. You know why? Huh?
你根本不用擔心。知道為什麼嗎？啊？

Ed: No, why?
不知道，為什麼？

Ray: Because big brother's **riding shotgun**. I**'ve got your back**. Did anything ever happen to you when you were a kid? Anything ever bother you?
因為有哥哥挺你。我會保護你。你小時候有人敢欺負你嗎？

Ed: Just you.
只有你。

Ray: Just...just me.
對……只有我。

How to Lose a Guy in 10 Days 《絕配冤家》

🎥 電影介紹

安蒂（Andie，凱特哈德森（Kate Hudson）飾）是時尚雜誌專欄作家，她這次要寫的文章為「如何在十天之內甩掉男人」的親身體驗，她計畫先讓一個男人愛上她，然後做出各種女人在戀愛時常犯的錯誤，讓對方落荒而逃。於是安蒂挑上廣告公司的帥哥主管班（Ben，馬修麥康納飾）……。

MP3 015

Touché! 說得好！一針見血！

touché [tuˈʃe] 這個字源於西洋劍，表示自己被對方擊中。跟人鬥嘴或辯論時，對方的話「一針見血」擊中你的弱點，就可以說 touché 稱讚對方，表示你無可辯駁了。

A: You think I should be more independent? At least I don't still live with my parents!
你覺得我應該更獨立？至少我沒有到現在還跟爸媽住！

B: Touché.
我認輸。

📽 電影對白

第一次約會，班跟安蒂開玩笑，說她只能寫些鞋類的小報導，安蒂也諷刺班接的也只是酒和運動器材的案子。

Andie: My boss loves me, and if I do it her way for a while, I can write about anything I want.
我老闆喜歡我，而且如果我先寫一陣子她要的東西，之後我就能寫我想寫的。

Ben: Like shoes?
像是鞋子？

Andie: No, no. Like alcoholic beverages and athletic gear.
不，不。像是酒和運動器材之類的。

Ben: Touché. Very nice.
哎喲。厲害喲。

The Lincoln Lawyer

《下流正義》

ride shotgun 幫人壯膽；坐助理座

這個說法源於美國西部時代的驛馬車經常要幫銀行送錢，為了趕走土匪，驛馬車的駕駛旁都會坐一個持槍的保鑣。

A: I'm gonna go confront that guy and tell him to stop flirting with my girlfriend.
我要去找那個傢伙，叫他不要跟我的女朋友勾勾搭搭。

B: Want me to **ride shotgun**?
要我一起去壯膽嗎？

但現在 ride shotgun 最常見的用法，是引申為坐在助理座（司機旁的座位）的意思。

A: Do you want to sit in the front or back?
你要坐前面還是後面。

B: I wanna **ride shotgun**.
我想坐前面助理座。

電影介紹

刑事律師米奇（Mickey，馬修麥康納飾）行事風格亦正亦邪，即使明知委託人惡貫滿盈，他為求勝訴不擇手段，回過頭來再狠敲惡人一筆，卻又經常不計代價為社會最底層的弱勢者打官司。這次他接到的案件看似天上掉下來的禮物：委託人家財萬貫又絕對清白，他不但穩操勝券還能有大筆進帳。卻沒想到……。

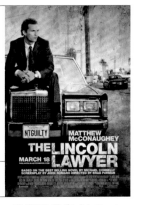

電影對白

米奇到收容所去探望他的老客戶葛蘿莉（Gloria，凱瑟琳莫寧 (Katherine Moenning) 飾），這個妓女一再因吸毒及賣淫被捕，這次的新罪名是持有毒品，米奇知道自己再怎麼神通廣大，葛蘿莉都得入獄服刑了。

Mickey: You may have to do some jail time, Gloria.
妳可能得坐牢了，葛蘿莉。

Gloria: Mickey, I can't.
米奇，我沒辦法。

Mickey: Yes, you can. Hey. They have programs in jail, too. Now, look, you've had a long run. Maybe after this, you can get out of the life.
行，妳辦得到。嘿。監獄裡也有戒毒計劃。聽著，妳下海很久了。或許這次坐牢之後，妳可以脫離這種生活。

Gloria: Yeah. Housewife of the year, that's me. Maybe I can **turn some tricks** with the PTA.
是啊，我還可以當上年度最佳主婦呢。或許我可以跟家長會代表搞援交。

MP3 016

turn a trick 接客

trick 在美國俚語有「（為錢）上床」及「嫖客」的意思，turn a trick 就表示「從事性交易」。

A: Do the hostesses at that club **turn tricks**?
那間夜店的女服務生可以帶出場嗎？

B: Not that I know of. But you could ask, ha-ha.
據我所知不行。但你可以問問看啊，哈哈。

Gossip Box

Alright, alright, alright!

馬修麥康納獲得二〇一四年奧斯卡最佳男主角獎的得獎感言中，用了他著名的口頭禪 "Alright, alright, alright!" 這是源自他在演出第一部電影《年少輕狂》(Dazed and Confused) 的第一個鏡頭開拍時非常緊張，當時他坐的車上正在播放門戶樂團 (The Doors) 的現場演唱專輯，主唱金莫里森 (Jim Morrison) 大喊了四次 "Alright!"，他心裡想自己跟莫里森有哪些相似之處：

一、汽車：莫里森四歲時目睹一場嚴重車禍，對他造成很大的陰影，影響他日後多首創作。馬修想：Alright! 我現在正在車子裡。

二、吸毒 (getting high)：莫里森吸食海洛英。馬修想：Alright! 我現在很亢奮 (I'm high as a kite.)。

三、搖滾樂：莫里森被《經典搖滾》雜誌 (Classic Rock Magazine) 評選為五十位最偉大搖滾歌手第二十二名。馬修想：Alright! 我正在聽搖滾樂。

當他還沒數到第四，也就是「很會把妹」時電影開拍了，他當時喊那三聲 Alright! 就一直跟著他到現在了。

Cate Blanchett 凱特布蘭琪

SHOWBIZ WORD

bit part 小角色

bit 有「微量、一點點」的意思;part 在這裡解釋為「角色」,也就是指所有角色或人物的通稱,也可以説 role 或 character。所謂 bit part 就是指在劇中完全不起眼,甚至沒有台詞、只出現兩秒鐘的小角色。

其他常見的角色種類説法如下:

- 主角:leading role、main character、protagonist
  男主角:leading actor、lead actor、male lead、hero
  女主角:leading actress、lead actress、female lead、heroine
- 配角:minor role、supporting role
- 反派角色:villain [ˋvɪlən]、bad guy、baddie

trilogy 三部曲

trilogy [ˋtrɪlədʒɪ] 是指三組一套的作品,可被視為三個單獨的故事,但由同樣的人物或是主題背景貫穿,常見於文學、戲劇或電影,其中又以科幻類和奇幻類作品最常出現,最具代表性的三部曲電影有《魔戒》三部曲 (The Lord of the Rings trilogy) 和《教父》三部曲 (The Godfather trilogy)。

相關字彙

- prequel [ˋprikwəl] 前傳
- sequel [ˋsikwəl] 續集
- tetralogy [tɛˋtrælədʒɪ] 四部曲
- finale [fɪˋnælɪ] 完結篇

biopic 傳記電影

biopic [ˋbaɪoˏpɪk] 也可稱之為 biographical [ˏbaɪəˋgræfɪkəl] film,是以戲劇的方式演繹一個真實人物的一生,與 autobiopic(自傳電影)不同之處在於自傳電影是由本人親自在片中飾演自己,如穆罕默德阿里 (Muhammad Ali) 主演的《拳王阿里》(The Greatest) 就是一例。

另有兩種演繹真實人物的電影類型:historical film(歷史電影)及註明 based on a true story(改編自真實故事)的電影。傳記電影與這兩者不同之處在於傳記電影刻畫的是一個人的一生,或是此人對歷史影響至深的關鍵年代裡發生的事,及此人的轉變。

MP3 017

Catherine Elise Blanchett was born in Melbourne to an Australian mother and an American father, who died of a heart attack when she was just 10. She studied [1]**economics** and art at the University of Melbourne, but became [2]**dissatisfied** with her studies and left on an overseas trip to find herself. After playing a bit part in an Egyptian movie [3]**aroused** her interest in acting, she returned to Australia and [4]**enrolled** in the National [5]**Academy** of Dramatic Art in Sydney.

Blanchett later joined the Sydney Theatre Company, where she won [11]**acclaim** for her performances in [6]**productions** of Shakespeare's *Hamlet* and *The Tempest*. This [7]**exposure** led to a supporting role as a nurse in the 1997 war film *Paradise Road* and a leading role opposite Ralph Fiennes in *Oscar and Lucinda* that same year. Her next role, as Queen Elizabeth I in 1998's *Elizabeth*, brought her to the attention of Hollywood, earning her an Academy Award [8]**nomination** for Best Actress.

Already an [9]**established** actress, Blanchett won international fame as the [12]**elf** queen Galadriel in Peter Jackson's Lord of the Rings films, the highest grossing film trilogy of all time. And in 2005 she won her first Academy Award—for Best Supporting Actress—playing Katherine Hepburn in the Howard Hughes biopic, *The Aviator*. Now free to choose her roles, she made interesting choices, including a teacher who has an [10]**affair** with a student in *Notes on a Scandal* (2006) and a young Bob Dylan in *I'm Not There* (2007). In 2013, Blanchett starred in Woody Allen's *Blue Jasmine* as a wealthy woman who loses her fortune, a role that earned her a second Academy Award, this time for Best Actress.

©Featureflash/ Shutterstock.com

凱薩琳艾莉絲布蘭琪生於墨爾本，父母分別為美國及澳洲人，父親在她十歲時因心臟病過世。她在墨爾本大學修習經濟學和藝術，但逐漸對其學業感到不滿足，於是遠赴海外旅行，尋找真正的自我。在客串一部埃及電影引燃她對演戲的興趣之後，她回到澳洲，進入位於雪梨的國家戲劇學院就讀。

布蘭琪後來加入雪梨劇團，在莎士比亞《哈姆雷特》及《暴風雨》等劇中演出精湛備受好評。這樣的曝光讓她得以在一九九七年戰爭片《天堂之路》演出護士配角，進而在同年的《奧斯卡與露辛達》擔綱女主角，與雷夫范恩斯演對手戲。她的下一個角色，一九九八年《伊莉莎白》的伊莉莎白女王，使她吸引好萊塢的關注，並獲得奧斯卡最佳女主角獎提名。

已為知名女星的布蘭琪，繼續在史上最賣座的三部曲電影：彼得傑克森的《魔戒》系列飾演精靈皇后凱蘭崔爾而贏得國際讚譽。二〇〇五年，她在霍華德休斯的傳記電影《神鬼玩家》巧扮凱瑟琳赫本，贏得第一座奧斯卡獎──最佳女配角。現在，已可以自由挑選角色的她，做了有趣的選擇，包括在《醜聞筆記》（二〇〇六）大談師生戀，以及在《巴布狄倫的七段航程》（二〇〇七）飾演年輕的巴布狄倫。二〇一三年，布蘭琪在伍迪艾倫的《藍色茉莉》演一個原本富裕，後來失去財產的女性，這個角色為她贏得第二座奧斯卡獎，而這一次，是最佳女主角。

TONGUE-TIED NO MORE

bring sb./sth. to the attention of sb.
使某人注意某人事物

這個用法是在形容人事物讓某人注意到。你也可以說 bring sb./sth. to sb.'s attention。
A: Thanks for bringing the error to my attention.
謝謝你讓我知道有這個錯誤。
B: Not at all.
不客氣。

VOCABULARY BANK

1 ） **economics** [ˌɛkəˋnɑmɪks] (n.) 經濟（學），經濟狀況
(a.) economic
William wants to pursue a major in economics.
威廉想要主修經濟學。

2 ） **dissatisfied** [dɪsˋsætɪsˌfaɪd] (a.) 不滿的
(n.) dissatisfaction [dɪsˌsætɪsˋfækʃən] 不滿
Most of the workers were dissatisfied with the new contract.
大部份的工人都對這份新契約很不滿。

3 ） **arouse** [əˋrauz] (v.) 激起，喚起
The man's strange behavior aroused the suspicion of the police.
這名男子怪異的行為引起警方的懷疑。

4 ） **enroll** [ɪnˋrol] (v.)（註冊）入學
How many students are enrolled at the college?
那所大學有多少學生註冊入學？

5 ） **academy** [əˋkædəmi] (n.) 學院，藝術院
Pauline is studying at an art academy in France.
寶琳在法國的藝術學院讀書。

6 ） **production** [prəˋdʌkʃən] (n.) 戲劇演出
The Drama Department is putting on a production of *King Lear* this fall.
戲劇系今年秋天要演出《李爾王》。

7 ） **exposure** [ɪkˋspoʒəˋ] (n.) 曝光，暴露
The two candidates are competing for media exposure.
這兩位候選人都在搶媒體曝光。

8 ） **nomination** [ˌnɑməˋneʃən] (n.) 提名
The actress has received many Oscar nominations.
那位女演員多次得到奧斯卡提名。

9 ） **established** [ɪˋstæblɪʃt] (a.) 事業有成的，建立已久的
We only do business with established firms.
我們只和老字號公司做生意。

10 ） **affair** [əˋfɛr] (n.) 婚外情，戀情
Roger divorced his wife after he found out she was having an affair.
羅傑發現他太太有外遇後就和她離婚了。

進階字彙

11 ） **acclaim** [əˋklem] (n./v.)（尤指對藝術成就的）稱譽，高度評價
(a.) acclaimed [əˋklemd] 受到讚揚的
The director's films have earned international acclaim.
這位導演的電影獲得國際上高度讚賞。

12 ） **elf** [ɛlf] (n.) 小精靈（複數為 elves）
The elves in the story had magical powers.
這故事裡的小精靈具有魔力。

The Aviator 《神鬼玩家》

🎥 電影介紹

含著金湯匙出生的霍華休斯（Howard Hughes，李奧納多狄卡皮歐 (Leonardo DiCaprio) 飾）是美國第一位億萬富翁，事業版圖擴及航空業和好萊塢電影業。他曾與奧斯卡影后凱薩琳赫本（Katharine Hepburn，凱特布蘭琪飾）有一段情。本片述說美國傳奇人物霍華休斯精彩的一生。

MP3 019

out of the blue 突然地，毫無預警

從藍色出來的東西究竟是什麼？這裡的 blue 指的是 blue sky，而 out of the blue 正是說天空突然有東西掉下，表示令人出乎意料、難以捉摸。

A: I hear Allen got in touch with you recently.
我聽說艾倫最近有和你聯絡。

B: Yep. I hadn't heard from him in years, and he just called me **out of the blue**.
對啊，已經好幾年沒聯絡了，他突然就電話給我。

🎞 電影對白

凱瑟琳為了霍華在報章雜誌上的緋聞和他起了爭執。吵架過後，霍華並沒有發覺凱瑟琳的傷心及異常，只專注在自己的事業上。這天她回家告訴霍華，她已經愛上別人，要離開他了，霍華卻大發霆霆……。

Howard: Actresses are cheap in this town, darling. And I got a lot of money.
這裡女演員隨便買都有。而且我有的是錢。

Katharine: Howard, please, this is beneath you.
霍華，拜託，你是在作賤自己。

Howard: No, no. This is exactly me. You're coming here **out of the blue** and tell me you're leaving me just like that and you have the nerve to expect graciousness?
不不，我就是這樣。妳突然跑來跟我說妳要離開，還敢要求我不要惡言相向？

Katharine: I expected a little *maturity, I expect you to face this situation like an adult....
我只希望你成熟一點，像一個大人來面對這件事……

Howard: Don't **talk down to me**! Don't you ever talk down to me! You are a movie star, nothing more!
別把我當成三歲小孩！別把我看扁了！妳不過就只是個電影明星罷了！

*maturity [mə`tʃʊrəti] (n.) 成熟

The Curious Case of Benjamin Button 《班傑明的奇幻旅程》

🎞 電影對白

到紐約去看黛西芭蕾舞表演的班傑明，還一同去參加黛西的慶功宴會。只是看見黛西與男友親密的模樣，讓班傑明待不下去，默默走出門口。黛西追了出來，並告訴班傑明，這就是她的生活，甚至邀約班傑明一同去續攤。

Daisy: Come on. Have a good time. There'll be musicians, interesting people....
來嘛，你會玩得很開心，那裡有很多樂手和有趣的人……。

Benjamin: You don't have to do that. It's my fault. I should've called. I thought... I'll come here and **sweep you off your feet**, or something.
你不必應付我，這是我的錯。我應該先打電話給你，我以為……我可以到這裡來把你迷倒之類的。

🎥 電影介紹

班傑明巴頓（Benjamin Button，布萊德彼特 (Brad Pitt) 飾）出生在一個不尋常的情況下，一生下來就是個八十多歲的老嬰兒，但隨著年紀的增長，身體卻越來越年輕。這樣返老還童的特質卻成為他和黛西（Daisy，凱特布蘭琪飾）感情間最大的阻礙。電影圍繞著班傑明巴頓的傳奇一生，帶領我們經歷他奇幻的生命旅程。

MP3 020

sweep sb. off one's feet 使人神魂顛倒

sweep off 有「吹走、席捲」的意思，把人從腳吹走，不就整個人都飛過去了嗎？ sweep sb. off their feet 這個慣用語就是在形容一個人魅力非凡，把人家的心都佔據，迷得神魂顛倒。

A: You and Brett are getting married so soon?
你和布雷特就快結婚了？

B: Yeah. I'm surprised too. He really **swept me off my feet.**
對阿，連我自己都很驚訝。他把我迷倒了。

Gossip Box

影后心目中的赫本

©Jvstin flickr.com

布蘭琪因扮演好萊塢不朽女星凱薩琳赫本而奪得她人生中的第一座小金人。在《神鬼玩家》開拍之前，布蘭琪反覆研究赫本數十部影片來揣摩她的神韻，還找來語言練習師，練出一口標準的新英格蘭腔調，因將其語態和姿態都表現得唯妙唯肖，讓她拿下最佳女配角獎。雖然有部分批評聲浪反駁她演得不夠像，布蘭琪曾說每個人心目中都有屬於自己的「赫本」，她也知道她的演出一定會有正負兩極的評價。雖然早知道會有出現這樣的情況，布蘭琪始終不願意放棄演出赫本的機會。

`MP3 019`

talk down to sb. 以居高臨下的態度跟人說話

對人說話要面向下方，顯然你站在比較高的位子囉！talk down to sb. 就表示用高姿態的方式和口氣對人講話，尤其是對那些你認為太年輕或太幼稚的人。

A: I wish the manager wouldn't **talk down to us** all the time.
我希望經理不要老是對我們頤指氣使。

B: I know. He treats us all like idiots.
真的，簡直就是把我們當笨蛋。

©Featureflash / Shutterstock.com

Notes on a Scandal
《醜聞筆記》

🎥 電影介紹

年輕女老師希芭（Sheba，凱特布蘭琪飾）和學生之間禁忌的愛戀無意間被同校女老師芭芭拉（Barbara，茱蒂丹契 (Judi Dench) 飾）給發現了。芭芭拉非但沒有舉發她，反而成為她秘密的守護者。芭芭拉鉅細靡遺地將這段禁忌愛戀記載在日記裡，當她對希芭的愛意與佔有慾日漸增生時，她發現這個會讓希芭失去一切的秘密，成為她操控她的最佳武器。

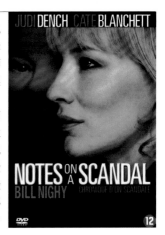

🎞 電影對白

芭芭拉發現希芭和學生之間的不倫戀，便去找她，要她講清楚情況。希芭解釋那位學生很有畫畫的天份，且課餘時間常去找她指導，這種向學精神讓她很開心。

Sheba: Barbara, he came every day for two weeks. Yes, I was *flattered, but more than that, I was excited to find someone who wanted to learn.
芭芭拉，這兩個星期他天天都來報到。沒錯，他的愛慕讓我受寵若驚，但更讓我興奮的是，我找到一個想學習的人。

Barbara: But surely you must have suspected his *motives?
難道妳都沒懷疑過他的動機？

Sheba: I sensed he **had a** little **crush on** me, but so what? It was innocent.
我有察覺到他蠻喜歡我的，但那又怎樣？這是純純的愛。

*flattered [ˋflætəd] (a.) 受寵若驚的

*motive [ˋmotɪv] (n.) 動機，目的

`MP3 021`

have a crush on sb.
迷戀某人，對某人動情

crush 在口語中也有「迷戀」的意思，因此 have a crush on sb. 就是在說熱衷到某人、對某人有心動的感覺。你也可以說 get a crush on sb.。

A: I hear Cindy **has a crush on** our history teacher.
我聽說辛蒂很迷戀我們的歷史老師。

B: Eww, gross!
唷，好噁喔！

21

Blue Jasmine 《藍色茉莉》

📹 電影介紹

茉莉（Jasmine，凱特布蘭琪飾）曾是擁有一切的紐約貴婦，穿金戴銀，出入於豪門富貴的上流社會。遭逢巨變之後，無依無靠的茉莉前往舊金山投靠妹妹金潔（Ginger，莎莉霍金斯 (Sally Hawkins) 飾）。本片以茉莉記憶中的紐約生活和現實裡的舊金山生活穿插呈現。身無分文的茉莉無法擺脫名媛貴婦的習性，對於眼前的一切都無法適應，一步步走向憂鬱。

🎞 電影對白

茉莉與丈夫哈爾 (Hal) 帶朋友們到郊區別墅度假，這時有位男性友人和哈爾討論起生意的事，哈爾建議他需更改公司名稱，讓政府查不著。

Friend: Whenever I hear them, they're one step ahead of the Justice Department. Just hope your house is not *bugged.

據我所知，他們總是能比司法部搶先一步，但願你的房子沒被監聽。

Jasmine: Oh, I never pay attention to Hal's business affairs. **I have no head for** that sort of thing.

噢，我從不過問哈爾的生意，我對這些事情一竅不通。

*bug [bʌg] (v.) 監聽

MP3 022

have a head for sth. 對做某事很有天分

這裡的 head 解釋為腦袋。have a head for sth. 從字面意思來看，很有腦袋去做某件事情，就是在形容對於做某件事情很有天分。相反地，have no head for 就是對某件事情毫無天分、一竅不通。

A: Why did you decide to study accounting?
你那時決定讀會計的理由是什麼？

B: I've always **had a head for** figures.
我對數字一直都很有天份。

🎞 電影對白

茉莉和朋友一同去逛街，但卻一副有心事的樣子……。

Friend: What's the matter? Your mind is a million miles away.
怎麼啦？瞧妳心不在焉的。

Jasmine: Oh, I'm sorry. No, I... I just got a call from my sister, Ginger. Oh, God, she's coming to New York for a week with her husband, Augie. He is **a piece of work**. I just... I don't know, I guess I have to see them.
噢，抱歉，我剛接到我妹妹金潔打來的電話。天哪，她和她老公奧吉要到紐約待一個禮拜。她老公超難纏的，我只是……看來我非得和他們見面不可了。

Friend: The one in San Francisco, the builder?
舊金山的那個建築工人？

Jasmine: Yeah. Oh, no, he's a contractor. I mean, he's.... No, he's a handyman.
對啊。喔，不是，他是承包商。我的意思是……不對，他只是個維修人員。

Jasmine: No, **don't get me wrong**. I love Ginger, I do. She's a dear.
不，別誤會我的意思，我很愛金潔，真的，她很可愛。

MP3 023

Don't get me wrong. 不要誤會我

get 表示「理解」，get sb. wrong 就是指「用錯誤的方式理解某人的意思」，不過這個片語幾乎只會用在 Don't get me wrong. 的情形。

A: You don't think David should get the promotion?
你不認為大衛應該被升職嗎？

B: **Don't get me wrong.** I think he has management potential—he's just not ready yet.
不要誤會我的意思。我覺得他有擔任主管的潛力——他只是還沒準備好。

a piece of work 難搞

work 不只代表工作，也有「費工夫、耗心神」的含義，如果用來形容人，跟他相處還要這麼耗力，這個人一定很難搞。a piece of work 就是在說人家不好相處。

A: Did you know that Charlie and his wife are getting divorced?
你知道查理要跟他老婆離婚了嗎？

B: Yeah. It's about time. His wife is **a real piece of work**.
是啊。也該離了。他老婆超難搞的。

Hanna
《少女殺手的奇幻旅程》

🎥 電影介紹

十六歲的漢娜（Hanna，莎雪羅南（Saoirse Ronan）飾）和曾擔任中情局特務的父親艾瑞克（Erik，艾瑞克巴納 (Eric Bana) 飾）生活在芬蘭野地，相依為命。父親將漢娜調教成一名專業的殺手，並指派她去殺女特務瑪麗莎（Marissa，凱特布蘭琪飾）。在執行任務的同時，漢娜意外發現自己的秘密……。

🎞 電影對白

瑪麗莎到退休特務艾薩克 (Isaac) 的俱樂部找他，告訴他艾瑞克跟漢娜都沒死，她需要他幫忙善後。當時俱樂部正在做表演的彩排，艾薩克和瑪麗莎談到一半，突然大吼要重新彩排。

[回頭向瑪麗莎說]

Isaac: **The devil is in the details**, isn't it? It's the girl or Erik?

別讓一粒老鼠屎壞了一鍋粥嘛，是不是？要殺女孩還是艾瑞克？

Marissa: She is in Morocco. It's all in the envelope. Let me worry about Erik.

她在摩洛哥，任務全在信封裡，艾瑞克就交給我。

MP3 024

the devil is in the details
魔鬼都在細節裡

這個諺語就是在講一件偉大的事業都是由每個完美的小細節所組成，因此想做好某件事情，最困難的部分就藏在小細節裡，這些小細節如果沒處理好，可能會導致失敗，正如同「一粒老鼠屎壞了一鍋粥」的意味。

A: Do you think the two sides will sign a peace treaty? 你覺得這兩方會簽署和平協定嗎？

B: I hope so, but who knows? **The devil is in the details**.

希望如此，但是結果誰知道？任何小差錯都能毀了整個協定。

Gossip Box
中生代演技女神

六度入圍奧斯卡金像獎的凱特布蘭琪，因茉莉一角首度奪下奧斯卡影后。不僅將貴婦的優雅高傲完美呈現，就連落魄後的崩潰情緒也都精準詮釋。布蘭琪曾表示這個角色很難演，起初她因為沒辦法認同茉莉，還差點走不進去這個角色，而且崩潰的情緒尺寸也要拿捏好，不能太多也不能太少。求好心切的凱特還常常要求導演要再來一次，甚至在開拍前提早到紐約生活，讓自己能完全融入角色心境及情境。

Anne Hathaway 安海瑟薇

©Horustr4n / flickr.com

TONGUE-TIED NO MORE

take a/one's cue from (sth./sb.)
學……的樣

這個用法是從劇場表演引申來的。台上演員常需要藉助工作人員的提示來得知出場和講話的時間，或模仿工作人員指引的動作，這樣的提示就叫做 cue。現在則可表達受到別人的指引而「模仿，照著做」。

A: I don't know when to use the different spoons and forks.

我不知道什麼時候該用不同湯匙和叉子。

B: That's OK. Just take your cue from me.

沒關係。只要跟著我做就好。

MP3 025

Anne Jacqueline Hathaway was born on November 12, 1982 in Brooklyn, New York and grew up in [1)]**suburban** New Jersey. She showed an interest in acting from a young age, taking a cue from her mother, Kate, who starred in the first American traveling tour of *Les Misérables*. In high school, Hathaway both acted and sang, and it was after a 1999 [2)]**chorus** performance at Carnegie Hall that she [12)]**landed** her first job, a role in the [11)]**short-lived** TV [3)]**series** *Get Real*.

Early in her [4)]**career**, Hathaway was seen as a [5)]**role model** for kids due to family-friendly roles like Mia Thermopolis in *The Princess Diaries* (2001) and its sequel *The Princess Diaries 2: Royal Engagement* (2004). *People* magazine named her one of its [6)]**breakthrough** stars of 2001. As the young actress matured, however, so did her characters. She had [7)]**nude** scenes in the drama *Havoc* (2005), and played the long-suffering wife of a [8)]**gay** cowboy in *Brokeback Mountain* that same year. Next, Hathaway got to act alongside her [9)]**idol**, Meryl Streep, in *The Devil Wears Prada* (2006).

While she rose to fame as a princess, Hathaway once admitted that growing up, her dream was to be Catwoman. This dream came true when she was chosen to play the sexy cat burglar in *Batman: The Dark Knight Rises* (2012). Later that year, she [10)]**tackled** Fantine—the same role played by her mother—in *Les Misérables*, for which she won the best supporting actress Oscar. It's likely the first of many gold statues for the talented and beautiful Anne Hathaway.

©Horustr4n / flickr.com

VOCABULARY BANK

1) **suburban** [sə`bɜbən] (a.) 郊區的，近郊的
The family lives in a quiet suburban neighborhood.
這家人住在寧靜的近郊社區。

2) **chorus** [`korəs] (n.) 合唱（團）
Kathy sang in her high school chorus.
凱西高中時曾參加合唱團。

3) **series** [`sɪriz] (n.) 系列，連續
J.K. Rowling is the creator of the Harry Potter series.
J.K. 羅琳創造出哈利波特系列小說。

4) **career** [kə`rɪr] (n.) 職業，生涯
After a long career in journalism, James will be retiring in August.
投效新聞業多年的詹姆士，八月將要退休。

5) **role model** [rol `mɑdəl] (phr.) 楷模，好榜樣
Daniel wants to be a good role model for his children.
丹尼爾想當他孩子的好榜樣。

6) **breakthrough** [`brek͵θru] (n.) 突破性進展
Police are still waiting for a breakthrough in the investigation.
警察仍等待調查有所突破。

7) **nude** [nud] (a.) 裸體的
The movie has several nude scenes.
電影裡有好幾幕裸露的鏡頭。

8) **gay** [ge] (a./n.) 同性戀的；同性戀
Do you have any gay friends?
你有同性戀朋友嗎？

9) **idol** [`aɪdəl] (n.) 偶像
Korean idols are popular all over Asia.
韓國偶像風靡了全亞洲。

10) **tackle** [`tækəl] (v.) 著手處理，對付
The government has promised to tackle inflation.
政府承諾要打擊通貨膨脹。

進階詞彙

11) **short-lived** [`ʃɔrt`lɪvd] (a.) 短暫的，短命的
The peace between the two nations was short-lived.
這兩個國家間的和平很短暫。

口語補充

12) **land** [lænd] (v.) 弄到，贏得
Who landed the leading role in the play?
誰爭取到那齣戲的主角？

安賈桂琳海瑟薇在一九八二年十一月十二日出生於紐約布魯克林，後於紐澤西郊區長大。她從少女時代就展現對演戲的興趣，繼承母親凱特的衣缽：她曾擔綱《悲慘世界》在美國的第一次巡迴演出。高中時，海瑟薇既演戲又唱歌；一九九九年，在卡內基音樂廳表演合唱後，她獲得第一份工作：短命電視影集《認清現實》的一個角色。

在演藝生涯初期，因為常飾演全家大小都愛的角色，例如《麻雀變公主》（二〇〇一）和續集《麻雀變公主（二）：皇家有約》（二〇〇四）裡的蜜雅塞摩波里斯，海瑟薇被視為孩童的榜樣。《時人》雜誌評選她為二〇〇一年的突破新星之一。但，隨著這位年輕女演員年歲漸長，她的角色也逐漸成熟。她在《玩命派對》（二〇〇五）一片中有裸露鏡頭，同年也在《斷背山》飾演同性戀牛仔長年備受折磨的妻子。接下來，海瑟薇接演《穿 Prada 的惡魔》（二〇〇六），和她的偶像梅莉史翠普同場飆戲。

雖然是以扮演公主成名，海瑟薇曾經坦承，從小到大，她的夢想是當貓女。當她雀屏中選，在《黑暗騎士：黎明再起》（二〇一二）飾演這位性感貓賊，她的夢想成真了。同年稍後，她接演《悲慘世界》的芳婷——和她母親扮演同樣的角色，藉此贏得奧斯卡最佳女配角。這是才華洋溢、美麗動人的安海瑟薇獲得的第一座小金人，但可望不是最後一座。

©s_bukley / Shutterstock.com

25

Rachel Getting Married 《瑞秋要出嫁》

🎬 電影對白

回到家的金，遇見了同在勒戒中心戒毒的基蘭（Kieran，麥瑟濟凱爾 (Mather Zickel) 飾），沒想到他居然是瑞秋婚禮的伴郎。突然來電的兩人就這樣發生了關係。

Kym: I think that we have started a new tradition. I think it's the best man and the maid of honor sneaking off to **get it on**, while the rest of the wedding party very happily and furiously plans for the big event.

我想我們開啟了新傳統，就是伴郎和伴娘趁著婚禮籌辦小組正熱心籌備盛事的時候，溜出去親熱。[兩人接吻]

Kieran: But I thought that was Emma's role.

但我以為是艾瑪擔任的。

Kym: What?

什麼？

Kieran: The maid of honor. I mean, I heard that that was the plan.

伴娘啊。 我是說，我聽說是這樣安排的。

📽 電影介紹

金（Kym，安海瑟薇飾）從勒戒所回家參加姐姐瑞秋（Rachel，羅絲瑪麗德維特 (Rosemarie DeWit) 飾）的婚禮。這次的回家，讓原本看似幸福美滿的家庭，重新面對金和家人心中的那道陰影，他們能夠一起走出來嗎？

MP3 027

get it on 發生關係

get sth. on 意思是「做某件事情」，而在這裡 it 是指「性事」，因此 get it on 就是在說「跟人家發生關係」，是較粗俗的口語用法。

A: I didn't see Stan at the frat party last night.

在昨晚的兄弟會派對上，我沒看到史丹。

B: He was there. He was probably **getting it on** with some chick upstairs.

他有去，他大概在樓上跟一個妹在打炮吧。

The Devil Wears Prada 《穿著 Prada 的惡魔》

🎬 電影對白

離職後的小安撥了通電話給艾蜜莉，問她願不願意接收從巴黎帶回來的衣服。

Emily: Well, I don't know. It's a huge *imposition, and I'll have to get them taken in. I mean, they'll drown me. But I suppose I could help you out. I'll have Roy pick them up this afternoon.

嗯，我不知道。這樣很麻煩耶，我得把它們改小，我是說妳的尺寸太大了。但我想我可以幫妳這個忙，今天下午我會請洛伊過去拿。

Andy: Thanks, Em, I appreciate it. Good luck.

謝了，小艾。很感激妳，祝妳好運。[掛掉電話的艾蜜莉微微一笑，轉頭向新助理說]

Emily: You **have** some very **large shoes to fill**. Hope you know that.

妳還有很大的障礙要超越呢，希望妳知道這一點。

*imposition [ˌɪmpəˈzɪʃən] (n.) 不公平的負擔

📽 電影介紹

安德莉亞（Andrea，安海瑟薇飾）是擁有漂亮學歷的社會新鮮人，一心想進入知名雜誌社擔任記者。為獲得媒體工作的資歷，她應徵成為時尚雜誌的編輯助理。對時尚一竅不通的安德莉亞必須達到惡魔總編米蘭達（Miranda，梅莉史翠普 (Meryl Streep) 飾）種種無理的要求，還得忍受來自各方的冷嘲熱諷。然而就在她的工作漸有起色，開始受到肯定時，即將崩解的感情生活和人際關係卻讓她思索起這一切的意義，使她明白，自己終究得在這份華麗工作與人生初衷之間做出抉擇。

MP3 028

have large/big shoes to fill 很難取代

穿著太大的鞋子要人家怎麼走路啊？這個俚語中沒人能穿的鞋子來形容前面的人做得太好了，導致後面接手的人要達到相同標準很難。那如果要說和上一任表現地一樣棒，英文就可以說 fill someone's shoes。

A: Do you think Tim Cook will be able to replace Steve Jobs?

你覺得提姆庫克可以代替賈伯斯嗎？

B: I don't know. He **has** some pretty **big shoes to fill**.

不知道耶，他實在太難取代了。

Valentine's Day
《情人節快樂》

🎥 電影介紹

由傑西卡艾芭 (Jessica Alba)、布萊德利庫柏 (Bradley Cooper)、安海瑟薇、艾希頓庫奇 (Ashton Kutcher)、茱莉亞羅勃茲 (Rulia Roberts)……等好萊塢眾星主演的一部浪漫喜劇。背景設定在洛杉磯,以交錯糾葛的故事線,述說一群人在情人節這天各自經歷的浪漫故事,也讓他們找到愛情的真諦。

🎬 電影對白

麗茲(Liz,安海瑟薇飾)原本和傑森在床上纏綿,突然發現自己快遲到了,便急急忙忙起身梳妝換衣,準備出門。

Liz: Thank you so much for last night, I had a *blast, and there is fresh coffee for you in the kitchen.
昨晚真謝謝你,真的很痛快。廚房裡有新煮好的咖啡。

Jason: I think I'm out of coffee.
我以為我的咖啡粉沒了。

Liz: Yeah you were, but I borrowed some from your neighbor. By the way she was very surprised that you had female company, she thought that you were gay. Don't worry, I **set her straight.**
是啊,所以我跟你的鄰居借了一些。她非常驚訝你有女伴,她還以為你是同性戀,但不用擔心,我解釋清楚了。

[親了傑森一下,並走出門]

Jason: Bye.
拜拜。

*blast [blæst] (n.)(玩得很)盡興,狂歡

MP3 029

set sb. straight 糾正某人

這裡的 straight 解釋為「正確的」,set sb. straight 就是指告訴別人正確的資訊,糾正別人錯誤的理解。你也可以說 put sb. straight。

A: I told him I have a boyfriend, but he keeps asking me out.
我跟他說過我有男朋友了,但他還是一直約我。

B: Don't worry, I'll **set him straight**.
別擔心,我會跟他說清楚。

Gossip Box

唱作俱佳的美國甜心

安海瑟薇早期接演的角色大多甜美可人,例如她的成名代表作《麻雀變公主》(The Princess Diaries),但為了證明自己的實力,她努力接演各種不同角色,擺脫甜美印象的牢籠。在《瑞秋要出嫁》中,海瑟薇飾演一個情緒緊繃、敏感脆弱且嗑藥的女子,完全顛覆形象,精湛演出讓她因此入圍奧斯卡女主角獎。海瑟薇演技突破可不止於此,她在《悲慘世界》(Les Misérables)中展歌喉,為戲落髮、減重 11 公斤來詮釋悲慘苦情的妓女芳婷,完美演出在當時被預測為得獎大熱門,果真憑著此角讓她將奧斯卡最佳女配角獎抱回家。

The Dark Knight Rises 《黑暗騎士：黎明昇起》

🎥 電影介紹

此片為《黑暗騎士：開戰時刻》(Batman Begins) 和《黑暗騎士》(The Dark Knight)，時間背景設定在《黑暗騎士》的八年後。蝙蝠俠因背負殺死哈維特的黑名而消失八年，布魯斯韋恩 (Bruce Wayne，克里斯汀貝爾 (Christian Bale) 飾) 也將自己封閉在家裡。隨著末日化身班恩 (Bane，湯姆哈迪 (Tom Hardy) 飾) 的出現，蝙蝠俠決心再出江湖，拯救高譚市。

MP3 030

(Has the) Cat got one's tongue?
你舌頭打結了嗎？

這個俚語用來表示一個人因緊張而結巴，舌頭就像被貓咪咬走了一樣，說不出話來。

A: Uh…, I don't know what to say….
呃……我不知道該怎麼說……。

B: What's wrong? **Cat got your tongue**?
怎麼了？舌頭打結了？

🎬 電影對白

聽見班恩搶劫證券交易所的任務成功，約翰達格特欣喜若狂，準備要開香檳找女人來大肆慶祝。但裝扮成貓女的瑟琳娜 (Selina，安海瑟薇飾) 埋伏在此，準備逼迫他之前答應她的洗刷前科記錄軟體。

John Daggett: Can we get some ladies in here?
可以找些女孩來開心一下嗎？

Catwoman: Careful what you wish for.
不要隨便亂許願喔。

[貓女揍了達格特，並將他壓制在牆]

Catwoman: What's the matter, **Cat got your tongue**?
怎麼啦，說不出話了？

John Daggett: You dumb bitch.
你這個蠢貨。

The Princess Diaries II 《麻雀變鳳凰 2》

🎬 電影對白

婚禮當天，緊張的蜜雅在屏風後面偷偷地跟喬說話，一方面紓解自己的緊張，一方面也安慰被奶奶拒絕的喬。主僕倆一來一往，道盡心中感受。

Joe: Well, the heart does things for reason that reason cannot.
嗯，有時候心會做出一些不成理由的決定。

Mia: You're **preaching to the choir**.
你說的我有同感。

Joe: Then you should know that Nicolas did not set you up at the lake.
那妳就該知道，尼可拉斯並沒有在湖邊設計妳。

🎥 電影介紹

擁有公主身份的蜜雅 (Mia，安海瑟薇飾) 大學畢業後，回到父親的祖國學習治理國家，準備繼承王位。不料有人肖想她的王位，甚至出「奧步」，表示蜜雅必須在一個月內結束單身身份，否則將取消王位資格。於是蜜雅和女王奶奶便展開一連串相親大會，蜜雅能順利解決這次的危機嗎？

MP3 031

preach to the choir 不必多費唇舌；有同感

preach 有「傳教、講道」的意思，choir 是指「教堂的唱詩班」，preach to the choir 字面意思為「對虔誠信仰的唱詩班傳教」，你想想他們都已經是虔誠的信徒了，何必在向他們傳教呢，這樣不是很多餘嗎？因此這個俚語就是在說對已有相同理念的人鼓吹同樣的想法，有「多費唇舌」的意味。不過，因為這句有「你不必說服我」的含義在裡頭，有時也會單純用來表達「我和你有同感」的意思。

A: Do you know how much car exhaust contributes to global warming?
你知道汽車排放的廢氣會造成地球暖化嗎？

B: Hey, you're **preaching to the choir**. I drive an electric scooter.
喂，不必多費唇舌，我騎的是電動機車。

©Horustr4n / flickr.com

Bride Wars
《新娘大作戰》

🎥 電影介紹

莉芙(Liv,凱特哈德森 (Kate Hudson) 飾)與艾瑪(Emma,安海瑟薇飾)兩人自小情同姐妹。婚期相近的兩人,喜孜孜地一起策劃彼此的婚禮,相約在全紐約最頂級的飯店披嫁紗步紅毯,但因飯店的錯誤使其中一人被迫取消場地,讓這對肝膽相照的好姐妹,為了各自的夢幻婚禮,不惜反目並千方百計要破壞對方的婚禮。

🎞 電影對白

艾瑪的膚色變回來,這讓她非常開心,又提起在莉芙的告別單身派對上大出風頭這件事情。

Emma: It's like I was up there, and there's this spotlight, and when I hit that rope, oh, my God.

我在台上聚光燈下,拉著繩索大跳特跳,簡直……。

Fletcher: Hey! Enough, enough, enough! I've heard this story 10,000 times, Emma. You've been acting a little wild lately. Okay? And I'm tired of it. So **knock it off**.

夠了,夠了。艾瑪,這件事我已經聽你說過無數次了。妳最近太囂張了,很煩人,別再鬧了。

`MP3 032`

knock it off 夠了

當你覺得某人的所作所為或是言語讓你心神不寧、感到厭煩,就可以用 Knock it off! 請對方「閉嘴」、「住手」、「別再鬧了」!

A: Will you **knock it off**? I'm trying to get some sleep!

你可以到此為止嗎?我要睡覺!

B: But I have to practice for my violin recital tomorrow.

但我得為明天的小提琴獨奏會加緊練習。

Gossip Box

奧斯卡魔咒纏身

憑《悲慘世界》抱走奧斯卡小金人的安海瑟薇,人氣不增反減,負面傳聞不斷,愛裝模作樣、犯大頭症等全都來,甚至入選美國《明星》(Star) 周刊評比最討厭好萊塢明星的第九名,彷彿中了奧斯卡魔咒一般。日前她在美國脫口秀上與主持人合唱 "Bitch don't kill my vibe",幽默風格深獲觀眾好評,希望能一掃近來纏身的負面批評。

©s_bukley / Shutterstock.com

Hugh Jackman 休傑克曼

SHOWBIZ WORD

revival 重新搬演

有些經典戲劇、電影廣受歡迎歷久不衰,但隨著物換星移,難免有些不合時宜,這時就會有人以新時代的角度重新詮釋,再度搬上舞台或銀幕,這樣的做法就是 revival [rɪ`vaɪvəl],而這個字的動詞 revive 即表示進行重新搬演的行動。

LANGUAGE GUIDE

Tony Award 東尼獎

Tony Award 全名 Antoinette Perry Award for Excellence in Theatre(安東妮裴瑞劇場傑出表現獎),是為了紀念二次大戰時期的紐約劇場名人瑪麗安東妮裴瑞女士(Mary Antoinette Perry, 1888-1946)對百老匯戲劇的貢獻而成立。

東尼獎於每年六月初頒獎,創辦之初只是紐約地區劇場界的內部慶祝活動,但因百老匯引領全球劇場業的地位,加上一九六七年開始電視轉播,逐漸成為比擬奧斯卡金像獎的重要演藝獎項,專門頒發給在百老匯商業演出的的劇場作品及工作人員。

MP3 033

Star of stage and screen, Hugh Jackman is one of the more [1]**versatile** actors working today. From comic book superhero to charming 19th-century [8]**duke** and even a [9]**flamboyant** gay singer, Jackman is known for [2]**taking on** [3]**diverse** roles and delivering [4]**critically** acclaimed performances. Of course, his [5]**rugged** good looks, which in 2008 earned him the title of *People* magazine's "Sexiest Man Alive," only add to his [10]**stardom**.

Born in Sydney, Australia in 1968, Jackman discovered drama in his final year of university. A [11]**communications** major, he chose to pursue a career in acting and continued his studies at the Western Academy of Performing Arts in Perth. Shortly after graduation, he made his Australian television [6]**debut** on *Corelli*, a 1995 prison drama. A London theater producer soon noticed Jackman and gave him his first big break: the leading role of Curly in a 1998 West-End revival of the musical *Oklahoma!*

Today, Jackman may be best known for playing the [7]**muscular** [12]**mutant** Wolverine in the X-Men [13]**franchise**, first in 2000 and most recently in *X-Men: Days of Future Past* (2014). However, leading roles in *Australia* (2008) and *Les Misérables* (2012), also [14]**showcase** his Hollywood appeal. And he's no stranger to Broadway either, winning the leading actor Tony for his role as the Australian singer Peter Allen in *The Boy from Oz* (2004). And at just 45, Hugh Jackman should continue to impress movie and theater audiences for years to come.

©Joe Seer / Shutterstock.com

舞台劇及大銀幕雙棲的休傑克曼，堪稱當今戲路最廣的男星之一。從漫畫超級英雄到迷人的十九世紀公爵，甚至浮誇的同性戀歌手，傑克曼以接演多樣化的角色和廣獲好評的表演著稱。當然，他粗獷帥氣的外貌——曾於二○○八年為他贏得《時人》雜誌「當今最性感男人」的頭銜——更添他的明星光環。

休傑克曼一九六八年生於澳洲雪梨，到大四那年發現自己熱愛戲劇。主修傳播學的他選擇從事演藝事業，於是進入伯斯的西澳表演藝術學院深造。畢業後不久，他以一九九五年的監獄劇《科雷利》首度登上澳洲電視。一位倫敦的劇場製作人隨即注意到傑克曼，為他帶來第一次重大機會：在一九九八年倫敦西區重新製作的老牌音樂劇《奧克拉荷馬！》飾演主角柯利。

今天，傑克曼最為人熟知的角色或許是《X戰警》系列的壯碩變種人金鋼狼，該系列第一集於二○○○年上映，近期則有《X戰警：未來昔日》（二○一四）。然而，他在《澳大利亞》（二○○八）及《悲慘世界》（二○一二）領銜主演的角色，也展現他的好萊塢魅力。而百老匯對他也不陌生，曾以《綠野星蹤》（二○○四）澳洲歌手彼得艾倫一角拿下東尼獎最佳男演員。現年才四十五歲，休傑克曼應該能在未來多年繼續讓電影和劇場的觀眾驚豔。

TONGUE-TIED NO MORE

no stranger to sth. 對……並不陌生

stranger 是「陌生人」，這個句子表示一個人常常聽説、處理某事物，有很多相關的經驗。若説「no stranger to + 某個地方」，則表示「常光顧某個地方」。

A: Kevin built his own PC from scratch?
凱文從無到有組裝出自己的電腦？

B: Yeah. He's no stranger to computers.
是啊。他很懂電腦。

VOCABULARY BANK

1) **versatile** [ˋvɝsətəl] (a.) 多才多藝的，多功能的
The versatile writer was most famous for his novels and short stories.
這位多才多藝作家最有名的是他的小說和短篇故事。

2) **take on** [tek ɑn] (phr.) 接受、承擔（挑戰、責任、任務等）
We're looking for employees who are willing to take on new challenges.
我們在尋找願意接受新挑戰的員工。

3) **diverse** [dɪˋvɝs] (a.) 多種的，不同的
The company manufactures a diverse range of products.
這家公司製造多種不同類型的產品。

4) **critically** [ˋkrɪtɪklɪ] (adv.) 評論上
Most of the director's films have been critically successful.
這位導演的大部分電影皆獲好評。

5) **rugged** [ˋrʌgɪd] (a.) 粗獷的，強健的
The action star has broad shoulders and a rugged face.
這位動作派明星有寬闊的肩膀和粗獷的面龐。

6) **debut** [deˋbju] (n./v.) 處女秀，首度演出
The singer made her debut on a TV talent show.
這位歌手在電視選秀節目演出她的處女秀。

7) **muscular** [ˋmʌskjələ] (a.) 肌肉發達的
Bike racing will give you muscular legs.
自行車競速運動會使你腿部的肌肉發達。

進階字彙

8) **duke** [duk] (n.) 公爵
Prince William is the Duke of Cambridge.
威廉王子是劍橋公爵。

9) **flamboyant** [flæmˋbɔɪənt] (a.) 浮誇的，炫耀的
The singer always performs in flamboyant outfits.
這位歌手總是身穿豔麗的服飾表演。

10) **stardom** [ˋstɑrdəm] (n.) 明星地位
The young actor seems destined for stardom.
這個年輕演員似乎註定要成為巨星。

11) **communications** [kəˏmjunəˋkeʃəns] (n.) 傳媒，通訊
Paul hopes to work in the communications industry after he graduates.
保羅希望畢業後進入傳播通訊業工作。

12) **mutant** [ˋmjutənt] (n.) 突變體，變種人
The mutants in the movie all have special powers.
這部片中的變種人都有特殊的能力。

13) **franchise** [ˋfræntʃaɪz] (n.) 系列授權作品、商品
What's your favorite movie in the Star Wars franchise?
你最喜歡星際大戰系列裡的哪一部電影？

14) **showcase** [ˋʃoˏkes] (v.) 展示
The singing contest showcases talented young singers.
歌唱比賽是年輕歌手展示才華的場合。

31

X-men Origins: Wolverine
《X 戰警：金鋼狼》

🎥 電影介紹

金鋼狼／羅根（Wolverine / Logan，休傑克曼飾）被威廉史崔克（William Stryker，丹尼哈士頓 (Danny Huston) 飾）招攬前，跟哥哥劍齒虎／維克多（Sabretooth / Victor，李維薛伯 (Liev Schreiber) 飾）經歷患難與共的漫長歲月。兩人分道揚鑣之後，維克多為史崔克少校效力，到處獵捕變種人汲取基因，打造無敵變種人來消滅變種人。

©Chesi - Fotos CC / flickr.com

🎞 電影對白

為了遠離自己的過去，羅根隱居在山林之間，以伐木為生，最終還是被史崔克少校找到，他警告羅根陸續有變種人被獵捕，為了安全起見，要羅根跟他回去。羅根斷然拒絕之後不久，心愛的女友被殺。沒想到那個痛下殺手的人就是自己的哥哥維克多，激憤的跑去找史崔克少校。

Wolverine: Why didn't you tell me it was Victor?
你為什麼不跟我説是維克多幹的？

William Stryker: I didn't know!
我不知道！

Wolverine: You lie!
你説謊！

William Stryker: I swear on my son's life! I didn't.... Victor's appetites were becoming too public. I had to lock him up. He felt I betrayed him. He **went AWOL**. He said he was coming for all of us.
我用我兒子的命發誓！我不知道……。維克多嗜殺成癮危害大眾。我必須把他關起來。他以為我背叛他，不告而別。他説他要追殺我們每一個人。

MP3 035

go AWOL 不告而別

AWOL 是 absent without leave 的縮寫。go AWOL 原本是軍隊用語「擅離職守，不假外出」的意思。在一般生活中引申為「不告而別，不見蹤影」的意思。

A: How did Josh's blind date go?
喬許的相親怎麼樣了？

B: When he saw how ugly the girl was, he **went AWOL**.
當他看到那個女生有多醜後，就不見蹤影了。

MP3 036

take sth. for a spin
騎車／開車兜風

spin 是「（輪子）轉」，當我們説 take sth. for a spin 或是 go for a spin，就是騎車或是開車去兜風或試車的意思。

A: Can I **take** the scooter **for a spin** and see how it handles?
這台可以讓我騎一下，看看好不好騎嗎？

B: Sure. You can ride it around the block.
好啊，你可以繞這個街區回來。

Van Helsing 《凡赫辛》

📽 電影介紹

凡赫辛（Van Helsing，休傑克曼飾演）是在群魔亂舞年代中的怪物獵人，對於妖魔鬼怪毫不留情。這次他前往吸血鬼德古拉公爵（Count Dracula，李察若思博（Richard Roxburgh）飾）的領地——德蘭斯斐尼亞，在那裡他遇見了身負殲滅吸血鬼使命的吉普賽公主安娜（Anna，凱特貝琴薩（Kate Beckinsale）飾），且與他並肩作戰。只是在決一死戰的同時，凡赫辛的身世之謎也即將揭曉。

MP3 037

so be it 那就這樣吧
這句話有同意對方提議的意思，也用來表達「不同意但只能接受」的語氣。

A: I tried to talk Sally into going to college, but she insists on getting a job.
我是著要說服莎莉去唸大學，但她堅持要找工作。

B: Well, if that's her decision, then **so be it**.
嗯，如果這是她的決定，那就這樣吧。

🎞 電影對白

羅根為了報女友被殺之仇，答應史崔克少校要接受強化手術，將一種強力金屬與全身骨骼結合。他熬過手術之後發現受騙逃出實驗室，被一對老夫婦收留住在穀倉裡，裡頭還停著一輛重型機車，這天老先生崔維斯 (Travis) 來找他。

Travis: This was my son's jacket. Try it on.
這件是以前我兒子的外套。穿上看看。

Logan: Thank you.
謝謝。

Travis: Yep. You **take** the bike **for a spin**, test the suspension.
沒什麼，騎這輛車去兜一兜，試試懸吊系統。

Logan: Sixty-four, huh?
六四年出廠對吧？ [坐上機車]

Travis: Man you're heavy.
天啊你好重。

Logan: Yeah, I put on a little weight recently.
是啊，我最近重了一點。

🎞 電影對白

德古拉公爵想利用科學怪人的生命能量，讓自己的孩子活下去，於是把科學怪人抓走。

Count Dracula: You're too late, my friend! My children live!
你太遲了，我的朋友！我的孩子們都活下來了。

Van Helsing: Then the only way to kill them is to kill you.
如此一來殺死他們唯一的辦法就是殺死你。

Count Dracula: Correct.
完全正確。

Van Helsing: **So be it.**
那就這樣辦吧！

Gossip Box

全能巨星

一向武勝於文的休傑克曼，可不只是肌肉有看頭！他在《悲慘世界》(Les Misérables) 中，演技歌喉並具，表現令人驚艷！從小就喜歡跳舞的休傑克曼在成名之前，其實是個著名的百老匯演員。休傑克曼曾說很慶幸自己是從舞台劇出身，因為這樣的他能夠對角色有更深刻的理解，畢竟在幾千人面前做表演，感染力一定要夠強，但如果在攝影機面前就可以收斂一些。

The Prestige 《頂尖對決》

🎥 電影介紹

勞勃安吉爾（Robert Angier，休傑克曼飾）和艾佛瑞波登（Alfred Borden，克里斯汀貝爾 (Christian Bale) 飾）原本是與魔術師合作演出逃脫術的助理，在一場表演當中，波登誤殺了安吉爾的妻子，兩人結下不共戴天之仇，從此在魔術世界展開永無止境的復仇。

🎞 電影對白

安吉爾跟他的道具師約翰卡特（John Cutter，米高肯恩 (Michael Caine) 飾）討論魔術。安吉爾嫌把籠中鳥變不見，只是將鳥壓扁在道具裡的手法太老套。

Robert Angier: The birdcage can't be our climax. Everybody knows it.

籠中鳥不能當我們表演的壓軸。大家都知道是怎麼變的。

John Cutter: Not like this they don't.

這次這種他們不知道。

Robert Angier: I don't wanna kill doves.

我不想殺鴿子。

John Cutter: Then stay off the stage. You're a magician, not a wizard. You gotta **get your hands dirty** if you're gonna achieve the impossible.

那就不要登台。你是魔術師，不是巫師。就算是髒活兒也得幹，如果你想成就非凡。

MP3 038

get one's hands dirty 什麼髒活兒都得幹

最低階的工作經常又髒又累，別人要你幹嘛就得幹嘛，明知不對甚至不法，也得硬著頭皮去做，get your hands dirty 就是表示「從事勞力工作」，或是「不計較工作內容」。

A: Why did you decide to become a mechanic?

你決定要成為修車師傅的理由是什麼？

B: The money's good, and I don't mind **getting my hands dirty**.

薪水很好，而且我不介意做勞力工作。

A: How come the crime bosses never get caught?

為什麼那些黑幫老大都不會被抓？

B: They never **get their hands dirty**. They have other people to do their dirty work for them.

他們從來不會弄髒自己的手，那些壞事都叫別人去做。

🎞 電影對白

為了破解仇家波登的魔術秘密，安吉爾從英國遠赴美國追查。回國之後，他又把道具師約翰找來預備復出。

John Cutter: You're back.

你回來了。

Robert Angier: It's good to see you, John.

真高興見到你，約翰。

John Cutter: Good rehearsal space. Blind stagehands, I like it. You always **had a good eye for** publicity.

很棒的預演場地。盲人舞台助理，我喜歡這個主意。你一直都很懂得如何吸引群眾。

Robert Angier: I need your help, John. It's my last show. A limited engagement.

我需要你幫忙，約翰。這是我的最後一場表演，限量演出。

MP3 039

have a (good) eye for 對⋯很有鑑賞能力

eye 在此指鑑賞事物的「眼光」。當我們說一個人 have a (good) eye for...，就表示他有某種事物的眼光很準，或是對某種事物的品味卓越。

A: I'm thinking of applying for a job at an art gallery.

我在考慮去應徵畫廊的工作。

B: That's a good idea. You really **have an eye for** art.

這個主意不錯，你對藝術很有鑑賞力。

Real Steel 《鋼鐵擂台》

🎥 電影介紹

西元二○二○年，傳統拳擊已無法滿足觀眾，更刺激的機器人拳擊蔚為風潮。前拳擊手查理（Charlie，休傑克曼飾）開始訓練機器人拳擊，希望奪得冠軍以彌補自己在拳擊生涯的遺憾，只是一切計劃隨著兒子麥斯（Max，達科塔哥雅 (Dakota Goyo) 飾）的出現被打亂。查理和麥斯找到一個被遺棄的舊型機器人亞當，亞當是訓練專用的機器人，不會任何拳擊技巧，查理決定把自己的拳擊技巧都傳授給亞當。而在這過程中，查理和麥斯也越來越親密，查理能不能在鋼鐵擂台上一舉成功呢？

🎬 電影對白

麥斯問貝莉（Bailey，伊凡潔琳莉莉 (Evangeline Lilly) 飾）和查理認識多久了，貝莉告訴麥斯他們從小到大就認識，她的爸爸還訓練查理成為拳擊手。貝莉拿出查理和頂尖拳擊手對決的報導給麥斯看。

Bailey: I have this newspaper article from Phoenix 2007 when Charlie fought Nico Tandy, the top *contender.
我收藏了這篇二○○七年鳳凰城拳擊賽的報導，查理對戰尼克坦迪，他是頂尖高手。

Max: You were at the Nico Tandy fight?
尼克坦迪那場拳擊賽妳在現場？

Bailey: I was. Charlie was supposed to be a warm-up fight, an easy win. Nico wasn't even supposed to **break a sweat**, but... nobody told Charlie that, so he just kept coming and coming at him. Check this out.
是啊。查理那場原本應該只是熱身賽，很容易贏的那種。尼克輕輕鬆鬆就能解決才對，不過……沒人告訴查理這個事實，所以他步步緊逼。你看這張照片。

***contender** [kən`tɛndə] (n.)（冠軍）競爭者

`MP3 040`

break a sweat 使勁費力

break a sweat 原本只是「開始流汗」的意思，引申為在某件事情上「費心費力」。這個片語經常用在否定句。

A: How was your history final?
你歷史期末考得如何？

B: Easy. I didn't even **break a sweat**.
輕輕鬆鬆，不費吹灰之力。

Jennifer Lawrence 珍妮佛勞倫斯

珍妮佛勞倫斯
Jennifer Lawrence

SHOWBIZ WORD

talent agent 經紀人

talent agent 是專門幫娛樂業（如演員、職業運動員、模特兒）或傳播業（如主播、作家）相關人才尋找工作機會、安排合作機會的人。在美國，一般經紀人的收費行情是收入的 10%，因此也被戲稱為 ten percenter。

talent scout 星探

scout 這種行業一般出現在運動界（球探）或演藝界（星探）。球探的工作是到處看運動比賽，評估球員的能力及發展性，推薦給球隊。星探的工作則是發掘新人，將其送進演藝界。

independent film 獨立電影

提到獨立電影，就會讓人想到導演毫不掩飾的傳達特定想法、具強烈個人風格的電影，這種電影不容易受大型電影公司青睞，也可能是導演不想受到出資電影公司的壓力而改變做法，因此只能以低成本獨立製作，小規模發行。這類電影經常靠參加影展（如日舞影展）爭取電影院上映或 DVD 發行的機會。

box office 電影票房

box office 最先是指戲院的售票窗口，現在則是指一部電影的銷售狀況。box office success 意思「（電影）票房大賣」。

©alien_artifact / flickr.com
CÉLINE
Alpaca-blend shrug and dress.

MP3 041

At the tender age of 23, Jennifer Lawrence is already well **on her way** to becoming one of Hollywood's biggest stars. She not only has a best actress Oscar on her [1]**résumé**, but is also the highest grossing female action hero ever. How has she [2]**managed** all this at such a young age? "Even as far back as when I started acting at 14," she says, "I know I've never considered failure."

Growing up in Louisville, Kentucky, Lawrence persuaded her parents to take her to New York to find a talent agent when she was just 14 years old. But a talent scout [3]**spotted** her first on a Manhattan street, and the offers began [13]**rolling in**. Eager to start her acting career, Lawrence studied hard and graduated from high school two years early. She first appeared on a TV sitcom before her [4]**breakout** performance in the 2010 independent flim *Winter's Bone*. Her [5]**portrayal** of a young woman caring for her younger [11]**siblings** and mentally ill mother earned Lawrence her first Oscar nomination.

Lawrence didn't have to wait long for her first Oscar win. In 2012, she starred in David O. Russell's *Silver Linings Playbook*, impressing [6]**moviegoers** and [7]**critics** alike as the sexy yet [8]**vulnerable** Tiffany Maxwell. The Academy was also impressed, awarding Lawrence the best actress Oscar. And her performance as heroine Katniss Everdeen led *The Hunger Games* to huge box office success that same year. In 2013, Lawrence **teamed up with** Russell again for *American Hustle*, earning a third Oscar nomination and [9]**cementing** her [10]**status** as a [12]**bona fide** Hollywood star.

©Featureflash / Shutterstock.com

年僅二十三歲的珍妮佛勞倫斯，已經穩穩步上好萊塢巨星之路。她的履歷表上不但已經有奧斯卡最佳女主角，還有史上最具賣座能力的動作片女英雄。她怎麼能夠年紀輕輕就有如此成績？「早在我十四歲剛開始演戲時，」她說：「我就知道我沒有考慮過要失敗。」

在肯塔基州路易斯維爾長大的勞倫斯，十四歲便說服雙親帶她到紐約找經紀人。但第一個發掘她的，是一個在曼哈頓街上看到她的星探，此後合作提案便開始湧入。急於開啟演藝生涯的勞倫斯用功念書，提早兩年從高中畢業。她一開始出現在一部電視情境喜劇，後於二〇一〇年獨立電影《冰封之心》有突破性的演出。她詮釋一個照顧年幼弟妹和精神病母親的少女，首度贏得奧斯卡提名。

勞倫斯不必等太久，就拿到首座奧斯卡金像獎。二〇一二年，她主演大衛羅素的《派特的幸福劇本》，以性感但脆弱的蒂芬妮麥斯威爾一角技驚觀眾及影評人，讓勞倫斯獲得奧斯卡最佳女主角獎。同年，她飾演的女英雄凱尼絲艾佛丁讓《飢餓遊戲》票房大獲成功。二〇一三年，勞倫斯在《瞞天大佈局》再次與羅素合作，為她贏得第三次奧斯卡提名，也鞏固她的地位：成為真正的好萊塢巨星。

TONGUE-TIED NO MORE

(well) on one's/it's way (to) 即將成為、達到

on the way 就是「上路」，(well) on one's/it's way (to) 字面上的意思就是已經朝某個目標穩穩走去，也就是如無意外一定會到，引伸為「即將達成」的意思。

A: How is your team doing this season?
你那一隊本季情況如何？
B: They're well on their way to the championship.
他們正朝著冠軍之路邁進。

team up (with sb./sth.) 與…合作

team 當動詞時是「組隊」，team up with... 就是「跟……組隊」，以合作達成目標。

A: Who are you teaming up with for the science fair?
科學展覽時，你們要跟誰一隊？
B: Nobody yet. Do you want to be my partner?
還沒有人。你要當我的搭檔嗎？

VOCABULARY BANK

1) **résumé** [ˌrɛzuˋme] (n.) 履歷
An internship will look good on your résumé.
實習經歷能為你的履歷增色不少。

2) **manage (to)** [ˋmænɪdʒ] (v.) 設法做到，能應付（困難）
How did you manage to finish that task so quickly?
你怎麼有辦法這麼迅速就完成那項工作？

3) **spot** [spɑt] (v.) 看見，發現，注意到
The police spotted the suspect driving a stolen car.
警察發現嫌犯開著贓車。

4) **breakout** [ˋbrɑkˌaut] (a.) 突破性的（表現、作品等）
The actor's breakout role in the film launched his acting career.
這位演員在片中突破性的角色讓他的演藝事業起飛。

5) **portrayal** [porˋtreəl] (n.) 飾演，詮釋，刻畫角色
The actor won several awards for his portrayal of Hamlet.
這位演員因飾演哈姆雷特贏得多座獎項。

6) **moviegoer** [ˋmuviˌgoə] (n.) 看電影的人，電影愛好者
The film festival attracts thousands of moviegoers each year.
這個影展每年吸引成千上萬名電影愛好者參與。

7) **critic** [ˋkrɪtɪk] (n.) 評論家，持批評態度的人
The new restaurant is popular with critics.
這家新開的餐廳頗受評論家歡迎。

8) **vulnerable** [ˋvʌlnərəbəl] (a.) 易受傷的，脆弱的
The neck is a vulnerable part of the body.
脖子是很脆弱的身體部位。

9) **cement** [səˋmɛnt] (v.) 加強、鞏固（地位、關係等）
The couple decided to have children to cement their relationship.
這對夫妻決定生孩子來鞏固他們的感情。

10) **status** [ˋstætəs] (n.) 地位，身分
Luxury cars are status symbols.
名貴汽車是身份的象徵。

進階字彙

11) **sibling** [ˋsɪblɪŋ] (n.) 兄弟姊妹，手足
It's normal for siblings to fight.
兄弟姐妹之間打打鬧鬧是很正常的。

12) **bona fide** [ˋbonɑ ˌfaɪd] (phr.) 真正的，名副其實的，真實的
Theodore Roosevelt was a bona fide war hero.
羅斯福總統是名符其實的戰爭英雄。

口語補充

13) **roll in** [rol ɪn] (phr.) 大量湧入
When the weather gets warm, tourists start rolling in.
等天氣一熱，遊客就會蜂湧而至。

The Hunger Games: Catching Fire

《饑餓遊戲：星火燎原

🎥 電影介紹

凱妮絲（Katniss，珍妮佛勞倫斯飾）和比德（Peeta，喬許哈奇森（Josh Hutcherson）飾）從上一屆飢餓遊戲生還，返回家鄉發現自己已變成叛變的精神象徵。為了除掉凱妮絲，史諾總統（President Snow，唐諾蘇沙藍（Donald Sutherland）飾）假藉次年飢餓遊戲適逢二十五年一次的「大旬祭」，宣布全新遊戲規則，凱妮絲因此必須重返遊戲戰場，與比德和自己的導師黑密契（Haymitch，伍迪哈里遜（Woody Harrelson）飾）決一死戰。

REMEMBER WHO THE ENEMY IS

🎞️ 電影對白

凱妮絲拜託黑密契比賽時幫助比德，這等於是要自殺，黑密契沒有答應。

Katniss: Come on, Haymitch. Nobody decent ever wins the Games.

拜託，黑密契。溫文有禮的人贏不了這場遊戲。

Haymitch: Nobody ever wins the Games. **Period**. There are survivors. There's no winners.

沒有人贏過這場遊戲，就這樣。只有倖存者，沒有贏家。

MP3 043

period 言盡於此

period 是「句號」，句號表示句子結束，話已經講完。因此當你陳述完意見或決定之後加上 period 這個字，就是在強調「我不想再討論了」。

A: But dad, all my friends are going to the party.

可是老爸，我的朋友都會去那個派對。

B: No means no. You're not going, **period**!

不行就是不行。你不准去，沒得商量！

這句話也可以用來強調自己的意見。

A: Italian food is the best in the world, **period**!

義大利菜是全世界最棒的，毫無疑問！

B: It's good, but I like Japanese better.

是不錯啦，但我更喜歡日本料理。

🎞️ 電影對白

「大旬祭」的訊息公佈之後，凱妮絲只想跟愛人蓋爾（Gale，連恩漢斯沃（Liam Hemsworth）飾）遠走高飛，蓋爾以身負革命大業為由拒絕她。黑密契則在屋裡借酒澆愁。

Haymitch: Ah. There she is. Finally **did the math**, huh? And you've come to what? Ask me to...die?

啊，她來了。終於想清楚了，是吧？妳是來幹嘛？拜託我去……死嗎？

Katniss: I'm here to drink.

我是來喝酒的。

Haymitch: Oh. Finally, something I can help you with.

喔。終於，是我能幫得上忙的事。

MP3 044

do the math 盤算，推敲

當面臨抉擇時，心中一定會計算不同決定的利弊得失，所以 do the math 就是在心中「盤算優劣」。也可以表示真相不明的時候，在心中「推敲何者為真」。這句話常用在答案其實很明顯的情況。

A: Do you think Connie will stay together with me when she goes off to college?

你覺得康妮去上大學之後還會繼續跟我交往嗎？

B: **Do the math**, man! She's gonna be surrounded by hot, smart guys every day.

想也知道，先生！到時候她每天身邊環繞的都是聰明帥哥。

©lilinal91.flickr.com

Winter's Bone
《冰封之心》

📹 電影介紹

芮（Ree，珍妮佛勞倫斯飾）的毒蟲父親將房子抵押交保後便不知去向，十七歲的她被迫扛起家庭重擔，負責照料患有精神疾病的母親和年幼的弟妹。眼看法院即將查封他們的房子，急於找出父親下落的芮四處尋求親友們的協助，卻沒人願意伸出援手。堅強的她並沒有因此放棄，獨自一人踏上尋找父親的旅程……。

📽 電影對白

芮和友人蘇妮亞（Sonya，雪莉華格娜 (Shelley Waggener) 飾）開車回家，發現屋外站著一位陌生人，旁邊還停了一台車。

Ree: Who the hell is he?

這人到底是誰啊？

Sonya: Judging by that car, he ain't from our **neck of the woods**.

從那輛車看來，他不是當地人。

`MP3 045`

neck of the woods
某一區，某一帶

neck 除了是「脖子」，也指「連接兩端的狹窄區域」，neck of the woods 原本是通往另一大片林地的狹長林地，引伸為城市、國家等的「某一區」、「某一帶」，經常的說法為 this neck of the woods 或是將 this 換成所有格，例如 my、your 或 our 等等。

A: Feel free to visit me anytime.

只要你想隨時都可以來找我。

B: OK. I'll drop by next time I'm in your **neck of the woods**.

好啊，我下次有到你那附近，再順道去看看你。

Gossip Box

《饑餓遊戲》身高比一比！

珍妮佛勞倫斯在《饑餓遊戲》中周旋於兩位男星之間，一位是大帥哥連恩漢斯沃也就是《雷神索爾》(Thor) 男主角克里斯漢斯沃 (Chris Hemsworth) 的弟弟；另一位就是很可愛，但是個子很矮小的喬許哈奇森。哈奇森到底有多矮哩？這個問題很沒禮貌，所以沒人敢問，請大家看照片自己推算吧。（提示：珍妮佛勞倫斯身高 172 公分，連恩漢斯沃身高 191 公分）

X-men: First Class 《X 戰警:第一戰》

📽 電影介紹

本片為 X 戰警成軍的前傳,回溯 X 教授／查爾斯查維爾(Professor X / Charles Xavier,詹姆斯麥艾維(James McAvoy)飾)及萬磁王／艾瑞克藍歇爾(Magneto / Erik Lensherr,麥可法斯賓達(Michael Fassbender)飾)的童年和青年時期,一度被美國中央情報局(CIA)收編的經過,及兩人對於變種人在人類社會的生存方式意見相左而分道揚鑣的故事。

🎞 電影對白

有變形能力的魔形女／瑞雯達克霍(Mystique / Raven Darkholme,珍妮佛勞倫斯飾)從小被查爾斯收留,兩人青梅竹馬。但查爾斯上研究所之後開始利用他對變種人的研究到處把妹。這天查爾斯又在酒吧找一個兩個眼睛不同色的漂亮女生搭訕,説她也算是變種人,應該要以自己變種為傲,這讓暗戀查爾斯的瑞雯非常不爽。兩人回家後,瑞雯開始質問查爾斯,想知道他對自己是否有感覺。

Raven: "Mutant and proud"? **If only.** [to Charles] Would you date me?
「以變種自傲」?最好是啦。[對查爾斯説] 你會跟我約會嗎?

Charles: Of course I would. Any young man would be lucky to have you. You are stunning.
我當然會啊。哪個男生追到妳是他好命。妳超迷人。

Raven: Looking like this?
長這樣?

Charles: Like...what? Blue?
哪樣?藍色嗎?

`MP3 046`

If only. 是這樣就好了。

這個説法是在回應對方的説法,意思是你根本不認為事情是這樣,或所説的事情會發生,但你非常希望他説的是真的,表示「真的能那樣就好了」。

A: Wouldn't it be great if our company gave us summer vacation?
如果公司給我們放暑假不是很棒嗎?

B: Yeah. **If only.**
對啦。最好是。

也可以用在句首,表示「要是……就好了」。

A: Don't you hate having to always do what the boss tells you?
老是要照老闆説的去做,你不覺得很討厭嗎?

B: Totally. **If only** I were rich. Then I'd be the boss.
的確如此。要是我發財就好了。那樣我就能當老闆了。

Gossip Box

變種人不簡單!

拍攝《X 戰警:第一戰》時,珍妮佛勞倫斯都要站著化妝六、七個小時,因為她所飾演的變形女 (Mystique) 要變上藍色皮膚,因此上戲前她都必須穿一件極薄的緊身衣!為了保持身材,拍戲前及拍戲期間她不但要節食,還要每天健身運動兩個小時。好消息是續集《X 戰警:未來昔日》(X-Men: The Days of Future Past) 她有制服可以穿,這讓她開心不已,因為她終於可以縮短化妝時間了。

電影對白

查爾斯知道瑞雯喜歡他，無奈落花有意流水無情，他被問煩了，只好把話講明。

Charles: I'm incapable of thinking of you that way. I feel responsible for you. Anything else would just feel wrong.

我沒辦法把妳當追求對象。我有責任保護妳。除此之外感覺就是不對。

Raven: But what if you didn't know me?

但如果你不認識我呢？

Charles: Unfortunately, I do know you. I don't know **what's gotten into you** lately. You're awfully concerned with your looks.

很不幸，我認識妳。我不知道妳最近哪根筋不對。妳太過在意自己的長相了。

What's gotten into you?
你哪根筋不對？

當我們問 What's got into sb.? 時，表示這個人最近有情緒困擾、行為反常。這句的 What's 其實是 What has，也可以說 What got into you?

A: What's gotten into Harry? He's been acting strange lately.

哈利到底怎麼了？他最近表現怪怪的。

B: Ha, you noticed too. I think he's in love.

哈，你也注意到了。我覺得他戀愛了

Silver Linings Playbook 《派特的幸福劇本》

電影介紹

派特（Pat，布萊德利庫柏（Bradley Cooper）飾）進精神病院八個月後終於出院回家與爸媽同住，他最想做的事就是與離異的妻子重修舊好。始終深信烏雲背後總會有一線光芒的派特，對於逆境的不屈撓，他不斷改變自己，努力讓自己成為妻子心目中的理想對象。就在此時，他認識了好友的寡婦小姨子蒂芬妮（Tiffany，珍妮佛勞倫斯飾），朝夕相處之下，兩人之間的關係開始產生了微妙的變化……

MP3 048

pin sth. on sb. 怪罪某人

pin 是用圖釘把東西釘上的動作，當我們說 pin…on someone 時，就是把錯怪在某人頭上，常常是構陷無辜的人，羅織莫須有罪名的意思。

A: Did the woman really murder her own daughter?

那個女人真的謀殺親生女兒嗎？

B: Yeah. She tried to **pin the crime on her husband**, but later admitted the truth.

是啊。她想要賴到丈夫頭上，但後來從實招來了。

電影對白

派特的前妻妮琪 (Nikki) 是正經的英文老師，瘋癲的派特很愛妮琪，一直過著壓抑的生活。蒂芬妮則是葷腥不忌，什麼都敢講，她告訴派特她在新寡時跟辦公室裡所有人都上過床，包括女性。這樣的話題讓派特覺得既新鮮又罪惡。

Pat: Oh, my God. Nikki hated when I talked like this. Made me feel like such a *perv. Maybe we should change the subject.

我的天啊。妮琪最討厭我討論像這樣的事。讓我覺得自己好變態。或許我們該換個話題。

Tiffany: I don't mind it.

我不介意。

Pat: You don't, do you?

妳不介意，是吧？

Tiffany: No. But then people were getting in fights in the parking lot at work and in the bathroom. And the boss called me into his office and tried to **pin it all on me**. So I accused him of *harassment. And then they fired me, sent me home and put me on some *meds.

不介意。不過後來大家開始在公司停車場和洗手間爭吵打架。老闆把我叫進他的辦公室，想把錯都怪在我頭上。我就指控他騷擾。他們後來炒我魷魚，把我送回家讓我吃藥。

*perv [pɚv] (n.) 性變態的人，色狼，即 pervert

*harassment [hɚˈræsmənt] (n.) 騷擾

*med (n.) （俚）藥物治療（常用複數），即 medication

Bradley Cooper

布萊德利庫柏

©blueathena / flickr.com

MP3 049

Actor Bradley Cooper was born on January 5, 1975 in Philadelphia and was raised [1]**Catholic** in a traditional Irish-Italian family. In 1997, he graduated with honors in English from Georgetown University. Not sure what to do with a liberal arts degree, he [2]**headed** to New York and completed an MFA at the Actors Studio Drama School. Cooper began his acting career in 1999 with a small role on HBO's *Sex and the City*, and landed the role of reporter Will Tippin in the TV spy drama *Alias* two years later.

Cooper's first big movie role came in 2005, when he was [3]**cast** in the popular comedy *Wedding Crashers*. At the time, Cooper was known mostly for playing nice guys like Tippin, but his character in *Crashers*, Zachary "Sack" Lodge, was more of a villain. Various movie roles followed, but it was *The Hangover* (2009), in which Cooper plays the [5]**foul-mouthed** best man Phil, which shot him to stardom. *People* magazine [4]**took notice**, naming Cooper its "Sexiest Man Alive" in 2011.

In 2012, Cooper starred opposite Jennifer Lawrence in the David O. Russell film, *Silver Linings Playbook*. He earned a best actor Oscar nomination for his portrayal of Pat Solitano, a [6]**bipolar** former teacher who wants to win his wife back. Cooper teamed up with Russell and Lawrence again in *American Hustle* (2013) and another Oscar nomination followed, this time for best supporting actor. Next up, Cooper is [7]**slated** to star as Navy SEAL Chris Kyle in the Clint Eastwood biopic *American Sniper*.

LANGUAGE GUIDE

graduate with honors 以優異成績畢業
名詞 honor 一般常作「榮譽、敬意」的意思，在這裡則代表「良好的成績」，graduate with honors 就是以優異的成績畢業，通常專指大學畢業。

liberal arts 通識教育
大專院校所提供的基礎教育，像是語言、哲學、文學或科學等一般知識，目的在於提升整體智性發展，訓練一般判斷和思考能力。而 liberal arts college 就是以人文科目為主的文學院。

VOCABULARY BANK

1) **Catholic** [ˈkæθlɪk] (a./n.) 天主教的；天主教徒
Poland is a Catholic country.
波蘭是天主教國家。

2) **head** [hɛd] (v.) 朝特定方向前往
Where are you headed?
你要往哪兒去？

3) **cast** [kæst] (v./n.) 選派演員（扮演角色）；
演員陣容，卡司
The actor is often cast as a criminal.
這位演員常演罪犯。

4) **take notice** [tek ˋnotɪs] (phr.) 注意，關注
Voters began to take notice of the candidate
after the speech.
選民在那場演說後開始注意到這位候選人。

進階字彙

5) **foul-mouthed** [ˈfaʊlˌmaʊðd] (a.) 口出惡言的
Nick learned how to swear from his foul-
mouthed father.
尼克從他滿嘴粗口的爸爸那裡學會罵髒話。

6) **bipolar** [baɪˋpolə] (a.) （患有）躁鬱症的，
bipolar disorder 即「躁鬱症」
At present, there is no cure for bipolar disorder.
目前還沒有治癒躁鬱症的方法。

7) **slate** [slet] (v.) 排定，預定（通常用被動式）
The rocket is slated for launch in June.
火箭預定會在六月發射。

男星布萊德利庫柏一九七五年一月五日生於費城，在傳統的天主教家庭長大，雙親分別為愛爾蘭裔和義大利裔。一九九七年，他以優等成績自喬治城大學英文系畢業。不確定拿人文學位要做什麼，他前往紐約，在演員工作坊戲劇學校修完藝術碩士（編註：MFA 即 Master of Fine Arts 的縮寫）。庫柏在一九九九年展開戲劇生涯，在 HBO 的《慾望城市》演一個小角色，兩年後獲得電視間諜劇《雙面女間諜》的記者威爾提平一角。

庫柏在二〇〇五年獲得第一個電影大角色，主演備受歡迎的喜劇片《婚禮終結者》。在當時，庫柏主要以演像提平的好人著稱，但他在《婚》片中的角色札克瑞「薩克」洛吉比較像反派。各種電影角色接踵而至，但讓他開始大放異采的是《醉後大丈夫》：庫柏在片中飾演說話粗俗的男儐相菲爾。《時人》雜誌注意到了，將庫柏列為二〇一一年「最性感的男人」。

二〇一二年，庫柏在大衛羅素的電影《派特的幸福劇本》和珍妮佛勞倫斯演對手戲。他詮釋曾任教師、一心想把妻子追回來的躁鬱症患者派特索利塔諾，獲得奧斯卡最佳男主角提名。庫柏和羅素及勞倫斯在《瞞天大佈局》（二〇一三）再次攜手合作，亦再獲奧斯卡提名——這一次是最佳男配角。接下來，庫柏預定要在克林伊斯威特執導的傳記電影《美國狙擊手》裡扮演海豹隊員克里斯凱爾。

LANGUAGE GUIDE

Navy SEAL
美國海軍海豹部隊員

Navy SEALs 全名為 U.S.
Navy Sea, Air, Land
Teams，為美國海軍的一
支特種部隊，任務包括非
常規作戰、國內
外防禦、反恐
及特殊偵察
等。

He's Just Not That Into You 《他其實沒那麼喜歡妳》

🎞 電影對白

安娜（Anna，史嘉莉喬韓森飾）到班（Ben，布萊德利庫柏飾）的律師事務所找他。班想拿份資料給她看，但卻怎麼也找不著。

Ben: I know it's here somewhere. I spoke to George Lane in Music, and he gave me this whole list of references for you.

我知道一定在這疊資料裡。我和音樂部的喬治連恩談過了，他給了我一票可讓妳參考的資料。

Anna: It's cool. You can call me when you find it.

沒關係。等你找到再打給我吧。

Ben: I swear I didn't *lure you here **under false pretenses.**

我發誓我沒有藉故把妳騙來這裡。

Anna: I know. But a girl can dream. You're obviously too good of a guy.

我知道。但女孩總有做夢的權利吧。你顯然是個大好人。

*lure [lʊr] (v.) 引誘

🎥 電影介紹

電影以女性在感情上常有的迷思起頭：當一個男人對一個女人越壞、越喜歡激怒她，就表示他其實很喜歡這女人。然而事實真是如此嗎？本片圍繞在幾位年輕女性的愛情故事上，藉由一段段互相交織的關係與遭遇來呈現愛情的消長和轉變。由珍妮佛安妮斯頓 (Jennifer Aniston)、茱兒芭莉摩 (Drew Barrymore)、班艾佛烈克 (Ben Affleck)、史嘉莉喬韓森 (Scarlett Johansson) 和布萊德利庫柏等數名好萊塢巨星聯合主演。

`MP3 051`

under false pretenses 找藉口，巧立名目

名詞 pretense [ˈpri.tɛns] 意為「藉口、虛假的理由」，而 under false pretenses 就表示假借名義去做某事，其實醉翁之意不在酒。

A: Why do you hate the Bush administration so much?

你為什麼這麼討厭布希政府？

B: Because they invaded Iraq **under false pretenses.**

因為他們藉故攻打伊拉克。

Wedding Crashers 《婚禮終結者》

🎥 電影介紹

約翰（John，歐文威爾森 (Owen Wilson) 飾）和傑瑞米（Jeremy，文斯范 (Vince Vaughn) 飾）這對哥倆好專辦離婚調停，兩人的是好是混進別人的婚禮白吃白喝兼把妹。這次財政部長要嫁女兒，兩人混進這場年度盛會，順利把到兩位伴娘，卻因此得罪其中一位伴娘的未婚夫薩克（Sack，布萊德利庫柏飾）……。

`MP3 052`

get dirt on sb. 挖人醜事

dirt 在此表示「丟臉或不堪的事情」，get dirt on（也常說為 dig up dirt on），就表示找出某人的醜事，讓他難堪。

A: Why is Sarah trying to **get dirt on** her husband?

莎拉幹嘛要挖她老公的瘡疤？

B: Her divorce lawyer told her to.

她的離婚律師要她這麼做。

🎞 電影對白

薩克懷疑約翰和傑瑞米謊報身分混進婚禮，因此打電話拜託友人找私家偵探調查這兩人的底細。

Sack: Hey, man, listen, do you remember that private detective we used to set up that fucking Shearson Lehman *prick?

嘿，老兄，聽著，你還記不記得我們之前找來整那個王八蛋雪森來曼的私家偵探？

Sack's friend: The big *sleazy Tommy Gufano. He's a *wop genius!

那個賤胚湯米葛分諾。他是個天才義大利佬！

Sack: Yes. I need you to **get** some **dirt on** these two guys, John and Jeremy Ryan.

沒錯，我要你挖出這兩個叫約翰跟傑瑞米萊恩的醜事。

*prick [prɪk] (n.) (口) 渾蛋（男子生殖器的俚俗說法）

*sleazy [ˈslizi] (a.) 低級的，奸詐的，卑劣的

*wop [wɑp] (n.) (口) 義大利佬（貶義）

The Hangover 《醉後大丈夫》

📽 電影介紹

在結婚的前兩天，道格（Doug，賈斯汀巴薩 (Justin Bartha) 飾）跟三位伴郎，也就是他的麻吉菲爾（Phil，布萊德利庫柏飾）和史都（Stu，艾德赫姆斯 (Ed Helms) 飾）以及道格未來的小舅子艾倫（Alan，查克葛里芬納奇 (Zach Galifianakis) 飾），四人開車到拉斯維加斯展開單身派對。結果三位伴郎隔天起來頭痛欲裂，完全記不起發生了甚麼事，而且新郎還不見了！眼看婚禮迫在眉睫，他們必須趕快想起前晚幹了什麼蠢事，且及時找到道格。然而，當他們一層層抽絲剝繭，釐清混亂後，才發現事情大條了……。

MP3 053

blow one's mind
使某人驚嘆不已，令某人大為驚奇

某事 blow one's mind，就表示某人對此事大感驚艷，與 blow sb. away 意思相同。

A: How did you like *The Sixth Sense*?
你覺得《靈異第六感》怎麼樣？

B: It was awesome. The ending totally **blew my mind**.
很棒。結尾令我大感意外。

🎞 電影對白

菲爾一行人開著車，要把老虎送回牠主人的身邊。這時艾倫突然問大家，哈雷彗星下次出現是什麼時候。

Phil: Who cares, man?
誰在意啊，老兄。

Alan: Do you know Stu?
你知道嗎，史都？

Stu: I don't think it's for like another sixty years or something.
我不認為會等上六十年之類的。

Alan: But it's not tonight, right?
不過，不會是今晚吧？

Stu: No. I don't think so.
不，我覺得不會。

Alan: But you don't know for sure? I have this cousin Marcus who saw one said it **blew his mind**. I want to make sure I never ever miss out on a Halley's *Comet.
但你不確定對吧？我有個表哥馬克斯他就看過，他說那景象讓人驚歎連連。我想確保我此生都不會錯過哈雷彗星。

*comet [ˋkɑmɪt] (n.) 彗星

Gossip Box
雙語都流利的性感男星

因《醉後大丈夫》而走紅的布萊德利庫柏，之前在法國參加記者會時，大家才驚訝地發現，原來他完全不需要翻譯隨行，就能以一口流利的法文對主持人的提問應答如流。事後他表示，其實他對法文產生興趣是從一部叫做《火戰車》(*Chariots of Fire*) 的電影開始，大學時期還遠赴南法留學，不到半年就能與當地人溝通無礙。沒想到布萊德利除了性感，還挺有語言天分的呢！

Silver Linings Playbook 《派特的幸福劇本》

🎥 電影介紹

派特（Pat，布萊德利庫柏）進精神病院八個月後終於出院回家與爸媽同住，他最想做的事就是與離異的妻子重修舊好。始終深信烏雲背後總會有一線光芒的派特不屈不撓，他不斷改變自己，努力讓自己成為妻子心目中的理想對象。就在此時，他認識了好友的寡婦小姨子蒂芬妮（Tiffany，珍妮佛勞倫斯 (Jennifer Lawrence) 飾），朝夕相處之下，兩人之間的關係開始產生了微妙的變化……。

🎬 電影對白

派特的母親朵洛莉絲（Dolores，賈姬威佛 (Jacki Weaver) 飾）來療養院接派特回家，派特希望母親能順路載他的病友丹尼（Danny，克里斯塔克 (Chris Tucker) 飾）一程。在車上，母親突然接到院方打來的電話，才知道丹尼根本不能出院。驚怒交加的朵洛莉絲打算調頭送丹尼回醫院。

Pat: Mom, just listen. Do not touch the steering wheel!

媽，聽我說。別動方向盤，放手！

Dolores: Pat, this whole thing was a mistake.

派特，這整件事都是個錯誤。

Pat: I'm sorry, Mom. You OK?

對不起，媽。妳還好嗎？

Dolores: I am **out on a limb** for you with the courts right now.

我在法庭上幫你背書已經很冒險了。

Danny: It's my fault. Pat didn't know. He's my friend, so he's *rooting for me. I'm having a disagreement with the hospital. We're working it out.

都是我的錯。派特他不知情。他是我的朋友，所以他支持我。我現在和院方有點爭執。但我們會解決的。

***root for sb.** (phr.) 聲援、支持某人

MP3 054

(go) out on a limb 冒險（做某事），遇到困難

名詞 limb 本意「樹枝」，(go) out on a limb 意指爬上小樹枝，上下不得的困境，就是指「做某事有風險，或是做起來有困難」；go out on a limb 也可用在提出與多數人不同的觀點，或是發表具爭議性的言論。

A: I'm going **out on a limb** recommending you for a position at our company.

推薦你來我們公司做事讓我很為難。

B: Don't worry. I won't let you down!

別擔心。我不會讓你失望的！

派特出院回到家中，告訴爸爸他打算重新追回他老婆 妮琪（Nikki），但爸爸卻想叫他死了這條心。

Pat Sr.: Listen, Patrick, she's gone. She's not around anymore. Nikki left.

聽著，派翠克，她走了。她已經不住這附近了。妮琪離開了。

Pat: What are you doing, Dad? You know what? *Excelsior. Excelsior.

爸，你這是在幹嘛？你知道嗎？我會精益求精。精益求精。

Pat Sr.: What does that mean?

這話什麼意思？

Pat: It means I'm gonna take this *negativity and use it as *fuel. I'm gonna find a **silver lining**. And that's no bullshit.

表示我會把負面情緒化為力量。我會找到一線生機。這不是在唬爛。

***excelsior** [ɪkˋsɛlsɪər] (n.) 精益求精，追求卓越

***negativity** [ˌnɛgˋtɪvəti] (n.) 負面情緒、態度

***fuel** [ˋfjuəl] (n.) 燃料

MP3 055

silver lining 曙光，一絲希望

silver lining 是指「烏雲周圍所透出的光線」，出自諺語 Every cloud has a silver lining.（烏雲背後總會有一線光芒），意指即便身處逆境，也總會有令人寬慰或值得期待的一面。這句話常用來鼓勵人要往好處想，不要放棄希望。

A: I just heard that I'm going to be laid off next month.

我剛聽說我下個月會被資遣。

B: Well, every cloud has a **silver lining**. You're always telling me how you want to go back to school.

呃，總會有好的一面的。你不是一直告訴我你很想回學校念書嗎。

Limitless 《藥命效應》

🎥 電影介紹

萎靡落魄的作家艾迪（Eddie，布萊德利庫柏飾）偶然拿到一種能在短時間內激發人腦未開發部分的神奇藥物——NZT，於是艾迪就靠著超乎常人的智慧與反應力名利雙收。然而艾迪很快就發覺竄紅崛起的負面代價，許多圖謀不軌的人紛紛鎖定他，意圖揭穿他成功背後的祕辛，而這靈藥的致命副作用也逐漸浮現……。

🎬 電影對白

吃下神奇藥物後，艾迪的感官變得超敏銳，觀察力也變得特別好，當房東太太對著他連珠砲似地謾罵時，他卻對這奇特的體驗感到新鮮，同時還發現房東太太包包裡放了一本法律教科書。房東太太察覺到他神態有異，於是便問他怎麼回事。

Eddie: You don't like me and I don't blame you. You see a self-defeating, energy-sucking piece of shit who's **sponging off** your husband. You're wishing I'd blow my brains out, but my existence shouldn't make you this upset. What is it?
妳不喜歡我，我不怪妳。在妳眼中我是個自暴自棄、壓榨妳老公的吸血鬼。妳巴不得我舉槍自盡，但我的存在應該不致於讓妳這麼不爽。所以到底是什麼原因？

Landlady: That's none of your business.
不關你的事。

Eddie: Something wrong at law school?
法學院出了點狀況嗎？

Landlady: How do you know I'm in law school?
你怎麼知道我在唸法學院？

MP3 056

sponge off sb. 佔某人便宜

sponge 原意為「吸取，吸收」，口語上則引申有「討得，揩油」的意思，例如形容賴在親戚或朋友家白吃白喝的人，就可以用這個字。

A: Has Steve found a job yet?
史蒂夫找到工作沒？

B: No. He's still living at home and **sponging off** his parents.
還沒。他還住在家裡吃父母的。

Christian Bale 克里斯汀貝爾

©cinemafestival / Shutterstock.com

MP3 057

One of the finest actors of his [1]**generation**, Christian Bale was born in Wales in 1974. At just 13 years of age, Bale was [2]**thrust** into the [3]**spotlight**, starring in Steven Spielberg's 1987 wartime drama *Empire of the Sun*. As Jim Graham, a boy struggling to survive in a Japanese-run POW camp during WWII, Bale showed great range for a child actor. And the same [4]**intensity** moviegoers first saw in Jim's performance is still there in Bale's roles today.

Although he's denied it, Bale has earned a [5]**reputation** for method acting, a technique where actors try to create in themselves the thoughts and feelings of their characters. During filming for *American Psycho* (2000), for example, Bale was so [11]**immersed** in his role as a [12]**serial** killer that he didn't [6]**associate** with the other cast members or crew. For Trevor Reznik, his food and sleep [7]**deprived** character in *The Machinist* (2004), Bale lost a shocking 63 pounds. [8]**Incredibly**, he then gained 100 pounds in six months to begin filming *Batman Begins* (2005), the first film in Christopher Nolan's acclaimed Batman trilogy.

In 2010, Bale won the best supporting actor Oscar for his portrayal of [9]**boxing** trainer Dicky Eklund in *The Fighter*. Then, in 2013, he received a best actor Oscar nomination for his role as [13]**con artist** Irving Rosenfeld in *American Hustle*. Outside of acting, Bale, a husband and father of two, is an active supporter of environmental causes. As for what's next, he's rumored to be the first choice to play Apple [10]**founder** Steve Jobs in an [14]**upcoming** biopic.

LANGUAGE GUIDE

POW camp 戰俘營
POW 為 prisoner of war 的縮寫。戰俘營就是用來拘禁戰爭時所俘虜到的敵方軍人。

VOCABULARY BANK

1) **generation** [ˌdʒɛnəˋreʃən] (n.) 代，世代
   We should all do our part to preserve the planet for future generations.
   我們應盡全力為後代子孫保護地球。

2) **thrust** [θrʌst] (v.) 用力推，伸展
   Reporters thrust microphones in front of the star.
   記者把麥克風塞到明星面前。

©s_bukley / Shutterstock.com

堪稱同世代頂尖男星之一的克里斯汀貝爾在一九七四年生於威爾斯。年僅十三歲時，貝爾便被推到聚光燈下，主演史蒂芬史匹柏一九八七年的戰爭片《太陽帝國》。貝爾飾演二次世界大戰期間於日本戰俘營奮鬥求生的男孩吉姆葛拉罕，展現了就童星而言無比精湛的演技。而影迷最初在吉姆身上看到的強烈情感，至今仍存在於貝爾扮演的所有角色中。

雖然自己否認，但貝爾已博得「方法派演技」的美名，這種技巧指演員努力設身處地，在自己內心營造角色的思想和情感。例如，在拍攝《美國殺人魔》（二〇〇〇）期間，貝爾完全融入連續殺人犯的角色，因而不和劇組其他演員或工作人員來往。為了在《迷魂殺陣》（二〇〇四）扮演飲食和睡眠雙雙被剝奪的崔佛雷茲尼克，貝爾令人咋舌地減了六十三磅。不可思議地，六個月後他又增重一百磅，開始拍攝《蝙蝠俠：開戰時刻》（二〇〇五），克里斯多福諾蘭廣獲好評的蝙蝠俠三部曲的第一部。

二〇一〇年，貝爾在《燃燒鬥魂》詮釋拳擊教練狄奇艾克倫德而贏得奧斯卡最佳男配角獎。接著，二〇一三年，他在《瞞天大佈局》中飾演騙徒厄文羅森菲德而獲奧斯卡最佳男主角提名。在演戲之外，身為人夫和兩個孩子的父親，貝爾是積極的環保運動支持者。至於他的下一步，據傳是在即將開拍的一部傳記電影中，飾演蘋果創辦人史提夫賈伯斯的首選。

SHOWBIZ WORD

method acting 方法派演技

方法派演技是俄國戲劇大師史坦尼斯拉夫斯基 (Constantin Stanislavski) 所提倡，屬於寫實主義的表演方式，名導演李史特拉斯堡 (Lee Strasberg) 深受影響，將此演繹方式引進美國。主張演員從觀察現實中著墨，揣摩現實生活，進而想像演繹角色的心理狀態，在投射出這樣心態下所會表現出的行為，不僅是單純的模仿肢體動作，需將自己的思想、情感及行為與角色完全融合。嚴格來說，演員不是在演繹角色而是完全全成為角色。擅長以此方式表演的演員如達斯汀霍夫曼 (Dustin Hoffman)、艾爾帕西諾 (Al Pacino) 和勞勃狄尼洛 (Robert De Niro) 等等。

VOCABULARY BANK

3) **spotlight** [ˋspɑtˏlaɪt] (n.) 聚光燈，the spotlight 常比喻為「公眾、媒體注意」
Since retiring, the politician has enjoyed life out of the spotlight.
自從退休後，這名政治家享受遠離媒體曝光的生活。

4) **intensity** [ɪnˋtɛnsətɪ] (n.)（情感、表現的）強度，強烈
The class was moved by the intensity of the poem.
這首詩的情感強烈的詩感動了全班。

5) **reputation** [ˏrɛpjəˋteʃən] (n.) 名譽，名聲
The scandal destroyed the senator's reputation.
醜聞事件毀了這位議員的名聲。

6) **associate** [əˋsoʃɪˏet] (v.) 往來，交際，交往
The politician was accused of associating with criminals.
這位政治人物被指控和罪犯來往。

7) **deprive** [dɪˋpraɪv] (v.) 剝奪，（使）缺乏
No child should be deprived of an education.
沒有任何孩子的受教權應該被剝奪。

8) **incredibly** [ɪnˋkrɛdəblɪ] (adv.) 不可思議地，非常地
That movie was incredibly boring.
這部電影非常無趣。

9) **boxing** [ˋbɑksɪŋ] (n.) 拳擊運動
Boxing is a dangerous sport.
拳擊是一項危險的運動。

10) **founder** [ˋfaʊndə] (n.) 創立者，創辦人
Jigoro Kano was the founder of judo.
嘉納治五郎是柔道的創始人。

進階字彙

11) **immerse** [ɪˋmɜs] (v.) 沉浸於
The best way to learn a language is to immerse yourself in it.
學習語言的最佳辦法就是沈浸其中。

12) **serial** [ˋsɪrɪəl] (a.) 連續的，一連串的，一系列的
There are no suspects yet in the serial killings.
這一連串的殺人案還沒找到任何嫌犯。

13) **con artist** [ˋkɑn ˋɑrtɪst] (n.) 騙子，也可以說 con man (n.) con 騙局
The old lady lost her life savings to a con artist.
那位老太太一生的積蓄都給騙子拿走了。

14) **upcoming** [ˋʌpˏkʌmɪŋ] (a) 即將來臨的
The coach assembled the team to talk about the upcoming game.
教練把隊伍集合起來討論即將來臨的比賽。

Batman Begins 《蝙蝠俠：開戰時刻》

電影介紹

這是由克里斯多福諾蘭所執導蝙蝠俠三部曲的首部曲。劇中描述布魯斯韋恩（Bruce Wayne，克里斯汀貝爾飾）如何從一個豪門貴公子成為正義蝙蝠俠。親眼目睹父母死亡的韋恩，對社會正義感到失望，決定用自己的方式來打擊毀滅高譚市的黑暗勢力。

MP3 059

rattle sb's cage 惹毛某人

你想想當你把籠子搖晃得咯咯作響，關在籠子裡的動物是不是會氣到抓狂？rattle sb's cage 就是指你做某事來惹惱別人。

A: Who **rattled Bob's cage**?
是誰把鮑伯惹毛啊？

B: I don't know. He's been in a bad mood all day.
我不知道，他一整天心情都不好。

電影對白

在車站，瑞秋（Rachel，凱蒂荷姆斯 (Katie Holmes) 飾），被黑幫老大費康尼（Falcone，湯姆威金森 (Tom Wilkinson) 飾）派來的兩名手下包夾。蝙蝠俠先將瑞秋身後的那個給解決了，另一個被嚇跑了。瑞秋正開心以為自己打跑了他們，一轉身卻被這個不知是敵是友的蝙蝠俠嚇到，便將原本拿來要對付壞人電擊棒攻擊蝙蝠俠，但似乎沒有什麼用⋯⋯。

Batman: Falcone sent them to kill you.

費科尼派他們來殺妳。

Rachel: Why?
為什麼？

Batman: You **rattled his cage**.
妳把他惹毛了。

The Dark Knight Rises 《黑暗騎士：黎明昇起》

電影對白

慈善舞會上，布魯斯韋恩將瑟琳娜（Selina，安海瑟薇 (Anne Hathaway) 飾）偷走的珍珠項鍊從她脖子上拿了回來，瑟琳娜親了他一下就消失不見，布魯斯走到門口，找幫他停車的泊車小弟準備離開。

Bruce Wayne: Must have lost my ticket.
我一定是把票弄丟了。

Valet: Your wife said you were taking a cab home.
您太太說您要坐計程車回家。

Bruce Wayne: My wife?
我太太？

[瑟琳娜將韋恩的車開走，後來司機阿福開車來接他]

Alfred: Just you, sir? Don't worry, Master Wayne. Takes a little time to **get back into the swing of things**.
就您一個人？別擔心，韋恩少爺。重返情場總得花點時間。

電影介紹

此片為《黑暗騎士：開戰時刻》(Batman Begins) 和《黑暗騎士》(The Dark Knight) 的續集，時間背景設定在《黑暗騎士》的八年後。蝙蝠俠因背負殺死丹維哈特的黑名而消失八年，布魯斯韋恩也將自己封閉在家裡。隨著末日化身班恩（Bane，湯姆哈迪 (Tom Hardy) 飾）的出現，蝙蝠俠決心再出江湖，拯救高譚市。

MP3 060

get (back) into the swing of things 進入狀況

swing 有「擺動」的意思，事情已經進入到可以正常擺動的狀態，就表示你適應的很好，融入其中。get in the swing of things 就是在形容「開始進入狀況」的狀態。

A: How are things going with your new job?
你的新工作怎麼樣？

B: Not bad. I'm still **getting into the swing of things**.
還可以，我還在進入狀況。

American Hustle 《瞞天大佈局》

Gossip Box

體重伸縮自如的貝爾

大家心目中的永遠的布魯斯韋恩——克里斯汀貝爾表示將不再續演蝙蝠俠，不曉得讓多少戲迷心碎。但了解的人都知道，拒絕被定型戲路，一向是貝爾的堅持，因此我們常看見貝爾為戲體重增增減減。這次在《瞞天大佈局》中變身成為一位胖到挺個大肚腩，還禿頭的中年大叔，任誰都不敢置信眼前這位就是那個帥氣的蝙蝠俠。不過這並不是貝爾的極限，最誇張的一次是在《迷魂殺陣》(*The Machinist*) 中扮演一位機械師，當時為了這個角色，貝爾瘦了近三十公斤，接著馬上接演《蝙蝠俠：開戰時刻》，又馬上增重大約三十公斤。

🎥 電影介紹

故事改編自七〇年代美國聯邦調查局備受爭議的「釣魚執法」真實案件。厄文（Irving，克里斯汀貝爾飾）與其情婦希妮（Sydney，化名為伊蒂絲（Edith），艾美亞當斯 (Amy Adams) 飾）是對手法高明的詐騙搭擋，在一次行動下被捕，為了能脫罪，被迫與 FBI 幹員瑞奇（Richie，布萊德利庫柏 (Bradley Cooper) 飾）聯手佈局暗中搜集政客關說收賄的罪證，企圖一舉揪出所有違法官員。只是厄文妻子羅莎琳（Rosalyn，珍妮佛勞倫斯 (Jennifer Lawrence) 飾）像顆不定時炸彈一樣，可能是造成整個行動失敗的原因！

🎬 電影對白

厄文和伊蒂絲中了瑞奇的詭計，騙局洩底，伊蒂絲因偽造身份進了看守所三天，瑞奇用盡各種說法要求伊蒂絲加入 FBI 的釣魚行動，現在換成說服厄文。只是瑞奇繞了一大圈，始終沒有說到重點。

Richie: My grandmother lived to be ninety-three years old and never lied in her life.

我外婆活到九十三歲，一輩子從沒撒過謊。

Irving: Congratulations!

真是恭喜你！

Richie: Thank you. I'm proud of that too. Does that make her another good person? Isn't that something to strive for?

謝謝，我也感到很驕傲。當一個像她一樣的好人，豈不是一件值得努力效法的事情嗎？

Irving: Why are you **breaking my balls**, huh? Get to the point.

你幹嘛一直挖苦我？長話短說。

MP3 061

break sb's balls
挖苦、嘮叨某人

在口語中，balls 又能指男性的睪丸，不過 break someone's balls 可不是在指身體上的攻擊喔，這個俚語通常是指調侃別人，或是對人碎碎念、嘮叨地責罵，或是指用言語欺負別人。bust sb's balls 也有相同的意思，而且更常用喔！

A: When are you gonna fix the faucet, Ralph?

你什麼時候才要修理水龍頭啊，拉爾夫？

B: Stop **breaking my balls**, Martha. I'll do it when I have time.

不要再碎碎念了，瑪莎。等我有時間就會去做。

A: Why were the other guys on the team all insulting me?

為什麼隊上所有人都在羞辱我？

B: They were just **busting your balls**. They always do that with the new guy.

他們只是在開你玩笑，他們總是這樣對待新進球員。

Terminator Salvation

《魔鬼終結者：未來救贖》

 電影介紹

劇情背景設定在二○一八年審判日後人類與天網間的戰爭，同時此部電影也特別注重人類與機器人的角色定位。被視作拯救未來希望的約翰康納（John Connor，克里斯汀貝爾飾）帶領人類對抗天網與其旗下的終結機器人，以保護人類存活下去。面對人類和機器人的混種人馬可仕（Marcus，山姆沃辛頓 (Sam Worthington) 飾），約翰康納的信念備受動搖，最後他決定與馬可仕聯手攻進天網軍團總部。只是在戰鬥中身受重傷的約翰康納，是如何存活下來，成為未來二○二九年反抗軍的首領？

電影對白

康納告訴指揮中心，情況不同了，他們要延後這次的攻擊行動，因為他有機會可以潛入天網拯救人質，但指揮中心卻不同意。

John Connor: Skynet has Kyle Reese.

天網抓到凱爾瑞斯。

General Ashdown: Then that is his fate.

那麼這是他的命。

John Connor: No, it's our fate. I have to save him. He is the key. The key to the future, to the past. Without him, we lose everything.

不，這是我們的命運。我必須去救他，他是關鍵，不論是對未來或過去都是，沒有他，我們會失去一切。

General Ashdown: No, you **stay the course**!

不行，你得照計劃行動。

John Connor: If we stay the course, we are dead! We are all dead!

如果我們照計劃進行，那麼我們必死無疑，我們全都死定了！

MP3_062

stay the course
堅持到底

這裡的 course 解釋為「方向、路線」，停留在相同的路線，stay the course 就是在說不管遇到任何的困難，也不會轉換方向，堅持下去。

A: How is your diet coming? Did you reach your goal?

減肥的狀況如何了？有沒有達到妳的目標？

B: Not yet, but I'm determined to **stay the course**.

還沒，但我決定堅持到底。

Gossip Box

最佳男女配角「鬥魂」全包辦

《燃燒鬥魂》中飾演吸毒酗酒的天才拳擊手的克里斯汀貝爾和拳王的媽媽梅莎莉里奧 (Melissa Leo) 橫掃奧斯卡與金球獎的最佳男女配角。貝爾不僅為了這個角色減重，和馬克華伯格還必須進行專業的拳擊練習，甚至邀請戲中真實人物──狄奇做拳擊指導，來協助電影拍攝。

The Fighter 《燃燒鬥魂》

🎥 電影介紹

改編自美國拳壇傳奇故事，描述狄奇與米奇這對個性與天份大相逕庭的兄弟，在職業拳壇的奮鬥史。擁有拳擊天份的狄奇（Dicky，克里斯汀貝爾飾）前途原本一片看好，卻因染上毒癮而自毀前程；米奇（Micky，馬克華伯格 (Mark Walberg) 飾）雖然努力不懈，卻始終交不出漂亮的成績單。出獄後的狄奇改過自新，重新接手米奇教練的一職，這對兄弟聯手搭擋，燃燒彼此的鬥魂，一路在拳壇闖出名號。

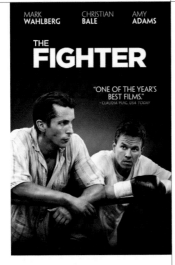

MARK WAHLBERG　CHRISTIAN BALE　AMY ADAMS

THE **FIGHTER**

"ONE OF THE YEAR'S BEST FILMS."
-CLAUDIA PUIG, USA TODAY

📼 電影對白

狄奇因放縱玩樂，錯過了訓練米奇拳擊的時間，遲到了將近三個小時。當他趕到練習場時，歐基夫（O'Keefe，米奇的另一個拳擊教練，同時也是名警官）很不高興，對他擺了臉色，但狄奇絲毫不覺得愧疚，還開歐基夫開玩笑。

O'Keefe: Better late than never.
遲到總比不到好。

Dicky: Oh, look! Detective's on the scene. Gonna **get to the bottom of** this. Figure this one out, huh?
你瞧，警探來到現場，將會查個水落石出，我們來辦案吧？

[狄奇模仿歐基夫的動作]

O'Keefe: Dick, you're an asshole.
狄奇，你真的有毛病。

`MP3 063`

get to the bottom of sth.
找出事情的真相

你想想整件事情被你翻到毫無保留，都見底了，還有什麼東西藏得住？get to the bottom of sth. 就是在說把事實真相搞清楚，查個水落石出，常用在警方調查案件方面。

A: Did you figure out why your car's making that funny noise?
你有找到你車子發出怪聲的原因嗎？

B: No, but my mechanic said he'd **get to the bottom of** it.
沒有，不過我的修車師傅說他會追查到底。

Equilibrium 《重裝任務》

📼 電影對白

普列頓察覺到他的夥伴派崔 (Partridge) 犯了感覺罪，決定前往荒原捕捉他。普列頓找到派崔時，他正在看一本書，他引用書本裡關於夢想的文字之後，問普列頓說他是不是也一樣會做夢。

John Preston: I'll do what I can to see they **go easy on** you.
我會設法請他們對你手下留情。

Partridge: We both know they never "go easy."
我們倆都知道他們從不會手下留情。

John Preston: Then, I'm sorry.
那麼我也只能說聲抱歉。

Partridge: No, you're not. You don't even know the meaning.
你才不覺得，你根本不明白什麼叫抱歉。

🎥 電影介紹

第三次世界大戰之後，情緒波動被視作戰亂禍源，所有公民每天服用藥物「普世寧」來控制情感，政府培養精良特警來捕捉拒用藥物的感覺犯。約翰普列頓（John Preston，克里斯汀貝爾飾）原本是冷酷無情的特警高層主管，某天打破藥瓶錯過服藥，意外重拾生命的熱情，爭取自由的鬥志，讓他決心推翻冷酷的政府。

EQUILIBRIUM

`MP3 063`

go easy on sb.
手下留情

這裡的 easy 不是指「簡單的」，而是「寬容的」。因此 go easy on 就是在說對人不要太狠，太不客氣。

A: Do you think the guy will get a long sentence?
你覺得那個人會被判重刑嗎？

B: Well, it's his first offence, so the judge will probably **go easy on** him.
嗯，這是他第一次犯罪，我想法官應該會對他手下求情。

Scarlett Johansson 史嘉莉喬韓森

©Helga Esteb / Shutterstock.com

Hollywood Walk of Fame
好萊塢星光大道

在好萊塢大道 (Hollywood Boulevard) 上的其中一段人行道，鑲有兩千顆星形的獎章來紀念對娛樂演藝事業有貢獻的名人。每個星星獎章下方會有得獎人貢獻領域的黃銅徽章，這個徽章分為五大類，分別為電視、電影、音樂、廣播和戲劇。

MP3 065

Scarlett Johansson was born in New York City on November 22, 1984 to a Danish father and American mother. When she expressed an interest in acting as a young child, her mother enrolled her in classes at the famous Lee Strasberg [1]**Institute** and took her to auditions all over Manhattan. Johansson made her stage debut in an off-Broadway production of *Sophistry* at the age of eight, and made her first film appearance in the box office flop *North* a year later.

After small roles in the crime drama *Just Cause* (1995) and romantic comedy *If Lucy Fell* (1996), Johansson began to receive [2]**critical** praise for her performances, first as a [7]**runaway** orphan in *Manny & Lo* (1996), and next as a [3]**disabled** girl in Robert Redford's *The Horse Whisperer* (1998). But it wasn't until she made the [4]**transition** from teen to adult roles that her career really [8]**took off**. In 2003, Johansson won a best actress BAFTA for her portrayal of a lonely young wife in *Lost in Translation*, as well as best actress BAFTA and Golden Globe nominations as a [5]**muse** to the Dutch painter Vermeer in *Girl with a Pearl Earring*.

Barely out of her teens, Johansson was becoming not just a Hollywood star, but one of its biggest sex symbols as well. No wonder Woody Allen, famous for casting beautiful women in his films, chose her to star in his 2005 thriller *Match Point*. The film, which ended a [6]**streak** of flops for Allen, led to further collaborations, including the 2008 critical and box office success *Vicky Christina Barcelona*. In 2012, Johansson received a star on the Hollywood Walk of Fame, confirming her A-list status.

©Helga Esteb / Shutterstock.com

史嘉莉喬韓森在一九八四年十一月二十二日生於紐約市，父母分別為丹麥人和美國人。小時候，她一展現對演戲的興趣，媽媽就讓她報名參加知名的李史特拉斯堡戲劇學院的課程，並帶她到曼哈頓各地試鏡。喬韓森八歲就在外百老匯戲劇《詭辯》獻出舞台處女秀，一年後首次登上大銀幕，演出票房失利的電影《北方》。

在犯罪電影《正當防衛》（一九九五）和浪漫喜劇《愛在布魯克林橋》（一九九六）演出小角色後，喬韓森的演出開始獲得好評，先是在《親親姊妹花》（一九九六）飾演逃亡的孤兒，接著是在羅勃瑞福導演的《輕聲細語》（一九九八）中扮演殘障女孩。但要等到她從青少女轉型為成人角色，她的演藝事業才真正起飛。二〇〇三年，喬韓森在《愛情不用翻譯》詮釋寂寞的年輕妻子，贏得英國電影與電視藝術學院 (BAFTA) 最佳女主角獎，同年又在《戴珍珠耳環的少女》飾演荷蘭畫家維梅爾的繆思女神，贏得 BAFTA 和金球獎最佳女主角雙料提名。

這時，才剛滿二十歲的喬韓森不僅躋身好萊塢明星之列，也成為性感女神。怪不得專挑美女擔綱演出聞名的伍迪艾倫，會欽點她主演二〇〇五年的驚悚片《愛情決勝點》。這部片為艾倫一連串票房慘澹的作品畫下句點，也促成兩人繼續合作，包括二〇〇八年叫好又叫座的《情遇巴塞隆納》。二〇一二年，喬韓森獲得好萊塢星光大道的星形獎章，更確定她一級女星的地位。

VOCABULARY BANK

1) **institute** [ˈɪnstɪˌtut] (n.) 學院，機構
Bradley works as a researcher at a scientific institute.
布萊德利在科學機構當研究員。

2) **critical** [ˈkrɪtɪkəl] (a.) 評論的，批評的
(n.) critic [ˈkrɪtɪk] 評論家，批評家
The band's first album was a critical success.
這個樂團的首張專輯受到好評。

3) **disabled** [dɪsˈebəld] (a./n.) 殘障的，殘廢的；殘障者
The school has a special program for disabled children.
這所學校對殘障學童設立專門課程。

4) **transition** [trænˈzɪʃən] (n.) 轉變，變革
The country made a smooth transition to a market economy.
這個國家順利轉型成市場經濟型態。

5) **muse** [mjuz] (n.) 繆思，（帶來靈感的）女神、人
The artist's lover was his muse for many years.
多年來，這位藝術家的愛人一直是他的繆思。

6) **streak** [strik] (n.) 連續的狀態
The team is on a five-game winning streak.
這支隊伍正處於五連勝狀態。

進階字彙

7) **runaway** [ˈrʌnəˌwe] (a./n.) 逃跑的；逃跑者
(phr.) run away [rʌn əˈwe] 逃跑
The charity runs a shelter for runaway children.
這個慈善機構為逃家的小孩開了一個收容所。

8) **take off** [tek ɔf] (phr.) 起飛，蔚為風潮，大受歡迎
The star's career took off when she was nominated for an Oscar.
那位明星在獲奧斯卡提名後星路大開。

SHOWBIZ WORDS

off-Broadway 外百老匯
泛指在曼哈頓百老匯戲院區 (Manhattan Broadway Theater District) 以外演出的小型專業戲劇，如上西城 (Upper West Side)、格林威治村 (Greenwich Village) 等地。外百老匯不管是製作成本、演員片酬、劇作家價碼、演出場地（99-500 個座位）等都比不上百老匯，表演內容的實驗性質濃厚。由於票價經濟實惠，而且品質仍然值得期待，因此能有一定票房。在外百老匯叫好叫座的戲劇也常有機會登上百老匯的舞台，如《歌舞線上》(A Chorus Line)、《上帝的魅力》(Godspell)、《吉屋出租》(Rent) 等。

flop 失敗的作品、演出
flop 有「倒下、落下」，引申出「失敗的作品或是演出」之意，故 box office flop 就是指票房極差的電影，critical flop 則是指評價很爛的作品。

A list 一線（明星）
A-list 指的是「一線（明星）」，用來表示好萊塢電影目前當紅，或是票房保證賣座的明星，這是好萊塢一位資深影劇記者詹姆斯烏爾姆 (James Ulmer) 以各項評比數據來衡量明星所做的排行，這個評比標準稱為烏爾姆量尺 (Ulmer Scale)，根據此評比列出的名單稱已成為好萊塢的票房選擇必看。當然，有一線就會有「二線」(B-list)，甚至有「三線」(C-list)，現今報章雜誌常說的「B 咖」概念便是由此而來的。最初烏爾姆量尺只有三個等級，但演藝圈其實還有許多比 C 咖行情更低的無名小卒，於是有人便創造出 D-list 來指那些名不經傳的超小牌演員。

史嘉莉喬韓森 *Scarlett Johansson*

Match Point 《愛情決勝點》

🎥 電影介紹

克里斯（Chris，強納森瑞斯梅爾 (Jonathan Rhys Meyers) 飾）原本是位平凡的網球教練，因緣際會之下認識了富家公子湯姆，還娶了她的妹妹克蘿伊（Chloe，艾蜜莉摩提默 (Emily Mortimer) 飾），等於拿到了通往財富和成功之門的金鑰。但他卻被湯姆美麗的未婚妻諾拉（Nola，史嘉莉喬韓森飾）給深深吸引，兩人的慾火一發不可收拾，諾拉甚至懷了他的孩子，克里斯該如何面對這一切？

MP3 067

make a pass at sb.
挑逗某人；吃某人豆腐

pass 是指「傳遞」，make a pass at sb. 就是指跟人家眉來眼去、眉目傳情，也能指勾引人家、挑逗別人的行為，像是毛手毛腳、吃人豆腐。

A: Why did you just slap that guy?
你為什麼甩那個男生一個耳光？

B: He **made a pass at** me!
他對我毛手毛腳！

🎞 電影對白

克蘿伊告訴克里斯，湯姆和諾菈邀請他們晚上一起去看電影，但她推掉了。

Chris: Oh.... But we have no plans. Well, no special plans.
是喔，但我們沒有安排啊，沒特別的計畫啦。

Chloe: I thought we said we'd stay in.
我想說我們說好要待在家。

Chris: Yeah, but it wasn't **written in stone**. We could've joined them.
是沒錯啦，但又沒硬性規定。跟他們去也無妨啊。

Chloe: We still can, if you'd prefer it.
如果你想去的話，我們還是可以去啊。

🎞 電影對白

諾拉告訴克里斯，克蘿伊非常喜歡他，一心想嫁給他。但克里斯擔心克蘿伊的媽媽 (Eleanor) 不會同意他們結婚。

Chris: I don't think her mother would approve of that either.
她媽媽應該也不會贊成。

Nola: No. No, it's different. I don't buy into Eleanor, and she knows it, but you......are being groomed. You mark my words. They almost died when they thought that Chloe had run off with some......guy that ran a gastro pub in the city. But you're gonna do very well for yourself, unless you blow it.
不，這不一樣。我根本不鳥艾莉娜，她心裡也有數。但你……已經被安排登堂入室，相信我的話。過去他們以為克蘿伊跟市區的一個美食酒吧老闆私奔的時候氣得要死。但你會過得非常好，除非你搞砸了。

Chris: And how am I going to blow it?
那我怎麼做會搞砸？

Nola: By **making a pass at me**.
跟我有一腿。

MP3 068

be written in stone 絕不動搖，不可改變

寫字在石頭上，想修改可沒這麼容易。be written in stone 引申出「已定案的、不可更改的」這樣的意思，但大部分使用在否定句。你也可以說 be carved in stone 或 be set in stone。

A: Would it be possible to make a few changes to the plan?
有可能將這計畫稍做更動嗎？

B: Sure. It's not **written in stone**.
可以啊，這並非不可改變的。

Vicky Christina Barcelona 《情遇巴塞隆納》

🎬 電影對白

安東尼奧邀請維琪和克莉絲汀娜一同到奧維多去度週末，想帶她們到那個小鎮晃晃，品嚐美食及美酒，甚至希望可以和她們兩個發生關係！

Vicky: Jesus, this guy doesn't **beat around the bush**. Look, señor, maybe in a different life.
天啊，這個傢伙講話真夠直接的。聽著，先生，也許下輩子吧！

Antonio: Why not? Life is short, life is dull, life is full of pain. This is a chance for something special.
為什麼不呢？人生苦短，生活無聊又痛苦，要把握機會來點特別的。

Vicky: Right. Who exactly are you?
最好是，你到底是誰啊？

Antonio: I am Juan Antonio. And you are…Vicky, and you are Cristina, right? Or is it the other way around?
我是安東尼奧，妳是……維琪，然後妳是克莉絲汀娜，對吧？還是剛好顛倒？

Christina: Yeah, that's right.
對，你沒說錯。

Vicky: It could be the other way around, because either of us will do to keep the bed warm. I get it.
不管是不是顛倒，只要跟你上床，是誰也沒差。我懂你的意思。

🎥 電影介紹

電影主軸在三個女人與一個男人的情愛糾葛。維琪（Vicky，蕾貝卡赫爾 (Rebecca Hall) 飾）是個有婚約且傳統的女孩，而克莉絲汀娜（Cristina，史嘉莉喬韓森飾）則是個浪漫、喜歡尋求刺激卻不懂自己想要什麼的人。在巴塞隆納旅行時，遇上了藝術家安東尼奧（Antonio，哈維爾巴登 (Javier Bardem) 飾）。維琪從一開始的排斥到後來的產生愛意；十分享受這段異國情慾關係的克莉絲汀娜，卻因安東尼奧前妻伊蓮娜（Elena，潘妮洛普克魯茲 (Penélope Cruz) 飾）的出現，開始對這段感情產生變化。

MP3_069

beat around the bush
拐彎抹角

bush 是指矮樹叢，這個諺語字面意思是「敲打樹叢的周邊」，不直接打樹叢只打樹叢的旁邊，beat around the bush 就是用來形容有人說話愛兜圈子、拐彎抹角，顧左右而言他就是不講重點。

A: Well, I didn't flunk the test.
呃，我考試沒被當。

B: Stop **beating around the bush**. What was your score?
別再顧左右而言他了。你到底幾分？

Gossip Box

大師心中的完美女神

伍迪艾倫當初要拍《愛情決勝點》時，欽點的女主角其實是凱特溫斯蕾 (Kate Winslet)，不過溫絲蕾婉拒了，這個好機會落入當時才二十一歲的史嘉莉手中。史嘉莉的表現頗受大導演的青睞，伍迪艾倫的英倫三部曲中，也因此有兩部是由她擔綱女主角，甚至還接著主演《情遇巴塞隆納》。伍迪艾倫形容史嘉莉是位幽默風趣、美麗性感兼具的完美女子，只要他的劇本裡有適合的角色，史嘉莉絕對是他的女主角首選！

©s_bukley / Shutterstock.com

The Nanny Diaries 《豪門褓母日記》

🎥 電影介紹

大學剛畢業的安妮（Annie，史嘉莉喬韓森飾），因緣際會之下到豪門家庭裡照料 X 太太（Mrs. X，蘿拉琳妮 (Laura Linney) 飾）四歲大的兒子。當褓母期間，安妮見識到上流社會光怪陸離的奇特行徑。X 太太甚至列出一堆家規要安妮遵守。安妮違反規定和帥哥鄰居哈佛型男（Harvard Hottie，克里斯伊凡 (Chris Evans) 飾）談戀愛，但紙包不住火，X 太太好像發現了⋯⋯，安妮接下來該怎麼辦？

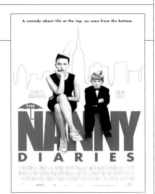

A comedy about life at the top, as seen from the bottom.

SCARLETT JOHANSSON · LAURA LINNEY

THE NANNY DIARIES

🎞 電影對白

決定要當褓母的安妮，準備搭好友琳妮特（Lynette，艾莉西亞凱斯 (Alicia Keys) 飾）的便車搬進上東區，琳妮特邊幫忙她將行李放上車，邊想勸退她。

Lynette: You know, my grandmother worked as a domestic so we wouldn't have to. And here you are, fresh out of college voluntarily taking a nanny gig.

妳知道嗎，我的祖母以前就是做傭人，我們才免於步入她的後塵。瞧妳，一個大學畢業的新鮮人，竟然自告奮勇要當褓母。

Annie: I told you, this is not a lifelong commitment. OK? It's just a way for me to **get my head together**. Besides, the money is great. I finally get to move to the city.

我說過了，我不會做一輩子，好嗎？我只是想理理頭緒。更何況，薪水也很不錯。我終於可以搬進城裡了。

Lynette: I'm moving to the city to go to grad school, not to be somebody's servant. Plus you know you're wrong, or you wouldn't be lying to your mother.

我搬進城裡是為了要唸研究所而不是要去做別人家的傭人。另外，我想妳也應該知道妳自己做錯了，否則妳不會對妳媽撒謊。

MP3 070

get one's head together 理清思緒

這個俚語是從嬉皮用語而來，這裡的 head 可以解釋為「想法」，get one's head together 把想法都整理好放在一起，就是在形容理清自己的態度，讓思緒更縝密，搞清楚自己的想法和方向。

A: Are you gonna start looking for another job right away?

你打算要馬上開始找其他工作嗎？

B: No. I'm gonna take some time off to **get my head together** first.

不，我打算先休息一段時間，釐清自己的方向。

Gossip Box

超辣女英雄

身材火辣、身手矯健的美女探員 —— 黑寡婦 —— 史嘉莉喬韓森，曾被評選為全球最性感美女的冠軍。雖然黑寡婦至今仍多以配角的身分現身電影，還沒有機會獨挑大樑，但喬韓森的演出，讓這號人物絲毫不失風采，完全不輸其他超級英雄。

© Jove Maegan / flickr.com

Iron Man 2 《鋼鐵人 2》

📽 電影對白

東尼和小辣椒（Pepper，葛妮絲派特洛 (Gwyneth Paltrow) 飾）一同前往摩納哥參加歷史方程式賽車活動。此時，東尼的私人助理娜塔莉（Natalie，史嘉莉喬韓森飾）已在會場上等待他們。

Tony: You look *fantastic.
妳看起來很美。

Natalie: Why, thank you very much.
哇，謝謝誇獎。

Tony: But that's *unprofessional. What's **on the docket**?
但當老闆的講那種話不成體統。接下來有什麼行程？

*fantastic [fæn`tæstɪk] (a.) 了不起的，極好的
*unprofessional [ˌʌnprə`fɛʃənəl] (a.) 違反職業道德的

📹 電影介紹

此部電影為《鋼鐵人》(Iron Man) 的續集，億萬富翁東尼史塔克 (Tony Stark，小勞勃道尼 (Robert Downey Jr.) 飾）為鋼鐵人的身份曝光後，美國政府堅持要東尼把鋼鐵衣這項革命性武器交給美國軍方。同時，一名來自過去史氏家族的神秘科學家伊凡萬科 (Ivan Vanko，米基洛克 (Mickey Rourke) 飾），也利用史氏工業技術來對付東尼。陷入危機的東尼，如何和他的新舊盟友一同抵抗企圖毀滅他及全人類的敵人。

MP3 071

on the docket 時間的安排

docket [`dɑkɪt] 有「（議會的）議事表，事項表」的意思，on the docket 原本的意思是「行程表上該做的事情」，而口語意思又如同 on the agenda。

A: What's **on the docket** for tonight?
今晚有什麼安排？

B: How about going out for dinner and a movie?
出去吃個晚餐、看場電影如何？

Hitchcock 《驚悚大師：希區考克》

📹 電影介紹

本齣電影是描述阿弗烈德希區考克 (Alfred Hitchcock，安東尼霍普金斯 (Anthony Hopkins) 飾）這位大導演在《驚魂夜》(Psycho) 拍攝期間的經歷。劇中的珍妮李 (Janet Leigh，史嘉莉喬韓森飾）和安東尼柏金斯是如何雀瓶中選得到男女主角？希區考克和妻子艾瑪 (Alma，海倫米蘭 (Helen Mirren) 飾）的感情，又激盪出多少創作的靈感？

MP3 072

tighten one's belt 縮衣節食

大家不知道有沒有吃撐了放鬆皮帶的經驗？反過來的，當飢腸轆轆時勒緊褲腰帶，或許會覺得沒那麼餓。當某人收入減少，無法「收支平衡」(make ends meet) 的時候，就可以說要 tighten one's belt，表示要開始「節約度日」了。

A: How are we going to make ends meet with just one income?
我們只有一份收入要怎麼達到收支平衡？

B: We're just going to have to **tighten our belts**.
我們必須要節省了。

📽 電影對白

希區考克決心要自己出資拍攝電影，開拍前，他的太太艾瑪列出了可以幫助節省費用的清單。

Alma: So, I've made a list of places where we can **tighten our belts**.
那麼，我列出了一些可以縮減開支的清單。

Hitchcock: Huh?
什麼？

Alma: We could all learn the art of self-restraint, couldn't we, Alfred?
我們都得學習自我節制這門藝術，是不是啊，阿弗烈德？

Hitchcock: Gardeners once a week? Weekends off for the driver? No, that's impossible. We'll have to find other places to cut.
園丁一週只來一趟？司機週末放假？不行，不可能，一定還有其他地方可以減少開銷的。

Joseph Gordon-Levitt 喬瑟夫高登李維

©Everett Collection / Shutterstock.com

SHOWBIZ WORD

made-for-TV movie 電視電影

也可稱做 TV movie。電視電影指的是由電視公司製作並播放，拍得像電影一樣的影片。這樣的「電影」並不會在戲院播放，只能電視上看到。made-for-TV movie 長度和一般電影差不多，製作成本通常比電影還低，但是比電視劇高。附帶一提，還有一種在拍攝完後，沒在電影院上映，卻直接出 DVD 的電影則稱做 made-for-DVD movie（也可叫 direct-to-DVD movie 或 straight-to-DVD movie）。

film noir 黑色電影

film noir 源自於法文，意思為 black film。這種電影類型大約是在一九四〇年代晚期在好萊塢發跡，屬於犯罪劇情片，片中內容的道德界定模糊，沒有絕對的是非對錯，風格大多陰暗且憤世嫉俗，背景常設定在犯罪叢生的低階社會。

MP3 073

Successfully making the transition from child star to [1]**legitimate** adult actor isn't easy. However, Joseph Gordon-Levitt, who starred in movies like *Angels in the Outfield* (1994) and the popular 90s NBC comedy series *Third Rock from the Sun as a kid*, has done just that. At 33 years of age, Gordon-Levitt is [2]**establishing** a reputation as an A-list actor with his [3]**subtle** yet [9]**edgy** performances.

Growing up in Los Angeles, Gordon-Levitt appeared in several TV commercials and made-for-TV movies before playing a young orphan in *Angels*. You might say show business is in his blood—his grandfather was an actor and director during Hollywood's Golden Age. After a successful [4]**run** on *Third Rock* as the [5]**alien** son Tommy, Gordon-Levitt entered Columbia University in 2000. He studied history, [6]**literature** and French, but the [7]**lure** of Hollywood proved too great, and he [8]**dropped out** in 2004 to return to acting.

Back in Hollywood, Gordon-Levitt's self-described strategy was to "be in good movies." Films like *Mysterious Skin* (2004), in which he played a gay [10]**prostitute**, and high school film noir *Brick* (2005) displayed his growth as an actor. And his performance in the [11]**offbeat** rom-com *(500) Days of Summer* (2009) earned him a Golden Globe nomination. Recently, Gordon-Levitt worked with director Christopher Nolan in the sci-fi thriller *Inception* (2010) opposite Leonardo DiCaprio, and in Nolan's final Batman movie, *The Dark Knight Rises*. He's also produced and directed several films—including *Don Jon*, which he also starred in—for his own production company, HitRecord.

©B612星球/flickr.com

要從童星成功轉型為像樣的成人演員並不容易。但小時候主演過《魔幻大聯盟》（一九九四）等電影和九〇年代備受歡迎 NBC 喜劇《笑星撞地球》的喬瑟夫高登李維辦到了。現年三十三歲的他，正以細膩又銳利的演技躋身 A 咖之列。

生長於洛杉磯的高登李維在《魔》片演孤兒之前，已於數支電視廣告和數部電視電影亮相。你或許可以說，他身體裡流著表演事業的血──他的祖父曾在好萊塢黃金時代身兼演員及導演。在《笑星撞地球》連續幾季演出外星人兒子湯米大放異彩之後，高登李維於二〇〇〇年進入哥倫比亞大學就讀。他修歷史、文學和法文，但好萊塢的誘惑實在太強烈，於是他在二〇〇四年休學，重回演藝圈。

回到好萊塢後，高登李維自己形容的策略是「拍好片。」諸如他在片中飾演同性戀男妓的《音速青春》（二〇〇四）和高中黑色電影《追兇》（二〇〇五）等電影，皆展現他在演技方面的成長。而他在非主流浪漫喜劇《戀夏 500 日》中的演出，更為他贏得金球獎提名。近期，高登李維和導演克里斯多福諾蘭合作，除了在科幻驚悚片《全面啟動》（二〇一〇）中與李奧納多狄卡皮歐演對手戲，亦參與諾蘭蝙蝠俠系列的最後一部曲《黑暗騎士：黎明昇起》。另外，他也為他自己的製片公司 HitRecord 製作、執導了數部電影，包括他主演的《超急情聖》。

SHOWBIZ WORD

Hollywood's Golden Age 好萊塢黃金時代

好萊塢的黃金時代，大約是在一九二〇年代晚期至一九六〇年代初，許多經典電影都是在那個年代產生，例如《亂世佳人》(Gone with the Wind)、《北非諜影》(Casablanca)、《梟巢喋血戰》(The Maltese Falcon)、《羅馬假期》(Roman Holiday)，還有希區考克的許多電影等等。聲效技術在二〇年代晚期首次加入電影當中，不僅無聲電影時代終結，同時也刺激了票房收入。

VOCABULARY BANK

1) **legitimate** [lɪˋdʒɪtəmet] (a.) 正統的，真正的
Several American presidents were legitimate war heroes.
好幾名美國總統都是真正的戰爭英雄。

2) **establish** [ɪˋstæblɪʃ] (v.) 創辦，建立
The university was established in 1926.
這所大學於一九二六年創立。

3) **subtle** [ˋsʌtəl] (a.) 微妙的，細微的
The coconut milk gave the curry a rich, subtle flavor.
椰奶為咖哩增添了濃郁又細微的味道。

4) **run** [rʌn] (n.) 連續的事（演出、成功，失敗等）
Cats had an 18-year run on Broadway.
《貓》劇在百老匯連續上演十八年。

5) **alien** [ˋeliən] (a./n.) 外星人（的）
The movie is about an alien ship that crashes on Earth.
這部電影是和外星人船艦撞上地球有關。

6) **literature** [ˋlɪtərətʃə] (n.) 文學，文學作品
(a.) literary [ˋlɪtəˌrɛri] 文學的，文藝的
Donna studied French literature in grad school.
多娜在研究所攻讀法國文學。

7) **lure** [lur] (n.) 誘惑物，魅力
The lure of easy money leads many people into a life of crime.
不勞而獲的誘惑使得許多人誤入歧途自毀前程。

8) **drop out (of)** [drɑp aut] (phr.) 輟學
My parents would kill me if I dropped out of school.
如果我輟學的話，我爸媽會宰了我。

進階字彙

9) **edgy** [ˋɛdʒi] (a.) 前衛的，不落俗套的
That theater shows edgy art films.
那間戲院播放前衛的藝術電影。

10) **prostitute** [ˋprɑstɪˌtut] (n.) 娼妓
(n.) prostitution [ˌprɑstɪˋtuʃn] 賣淫
Several prostitutes were arrested and taken to the police station.
數名妓女被逮捕並帶回警察局。

口語補充

11) **offbeat** [ˋɔfˋbit] (a.) 非主流的，非傳統的，奇特的
The actor is best known for playing offbeat characters.
這名演員以演出奇特角色而聞名。

(500) Days of Summer 《戀夏 500 日》

🎥 電影介紹

男孩湯姆（Tom，喬瑟夫高登李維飾）在第一次遇見女孩夏天（Summer，柔伊黛絲香奈 (Zooey Deschanel) 飾）的時候，便無可救藥的愛上了她。在擁有彼此的五百天裡，所有戀愛奇招都投注在這段感情中，與夏天在一起的點點滴滴全都在湯姆心中留下深深的愛戀痕跡，夏天是他這輩子認定的那個女孩。可是……夏天卻不認為這就是愛情，他們要如何面對五百天後嶄新的未來？

MP3 077

There are plenty of (other) fish in the sea. 天涯何處無芳草。

海裡面還有很多其他的魚，這個俚語跟我們中文所有說的「天涯何處無芳草」意思一樣，用來表示可供選擇的人或事還有很多，當別人遇到失敗的事情或是失戀時，就可以說這句話。口語上常會用縮寫，但是把 there are 縮寫念為 there're 並不好發音，因而通常會把句裡的 are 換成 is，變作 there's，雖然文法不對，不過在口語上還是會這樣使用。

A: Don't worry, Jessica. **There's plenty of fish in the sea**.
潔西卡，別擔心。天涯何處無芳草。

B: Yeah, but I'll never meet anybody like Rick again.
是沒錯，但我不會再遇到像瑞克這樣的人了。

🎬 電影對白

湯姆因為夏天要和他分手，整個人失魂落魄，一直在廚房砸盤子。他的好朋友們麥肯錫（McKenzie，傑弗利阿蘭德 (Geoffrey Arend) 飾）、保羅（Paul，馬修葛雷古柏勒 (Matthew Gray Gubler) 飾）和妹妹瑞秋（Rachel，克蘿伊摩蕾茲 (Chloë Grace Moretz) 飾）努力安慰他，試圖讓他恢復心情。

McKenzie: So you'll meet somebody new. Point is, you're the best guy I know. You'll get over her.
你會認識其他人。重點是，你是我認識中最棒的人，你會忘了她。

Paul: I think it's kind of like how they say. **There's plenty of other fish in the sea.**
就像大家說的，天涯何處無芳草。

Tom: No.
才不是。

Paul: They say that.
大家都這麼說啊。

Tom: Well, they're lying. I don't want to get over her. I want to get her back.
那他們都騙人。我不想忘記她，我要她回到我身邊。

Inception 《全面啟動》

🎥 電影介紹

柯比（Cobb，李奧納多 (Leonardo DiCaprio) 飾）和亞瑟（Arthur，喬瑟夫高登李維飾）是一組趁人熟睡，進入其潛意識偷取寶貴祕密的神偷團隊。這次他們接受齊藤（Saito，渡邊謙 (Ken Watanabe) 飾）的雇用，準備執行另一項新犯罪（不再是偷取想法的搶案，而是植入構想）。柯比尋找其他專家加入完成這項犯罪計劃，只是不論事先規劃地如何詳盡，總是會有個危險敵人來破壞，這使得柯比與夥伴們陷入危險之中。

🎬 電影對白

柯比為了讓費雪（Fischer，席尼墨菲 (Cillian Murphy) 飾）相信自己是要來保護他的夢不被別人入侵，以詭譎的天氣變化讓費雪起疑，造成夢境的晃動，使得和亞瑟在一起的艾莉雅德妮（Ariadne，艾倫佩姬 (Ellen Page) 飾）感到疑惑。

Arthur: Cobb is drawing Fischer's attention to the strangeness of the dream, which is making his subconscious look for the dreamer. For me. Quick, give me a kiss.
柯比讓費雪注意到夢境的怪異，讓他的潛意識來尋找做夢者，也就是我。趕快，親我一下。

[親了亞瑟後，環顧四周]

Ariadne: They're still looking at us.
他們還是在注意我們。

Arthur: Yeah, it was **worth a shot.**
沒錯，但值得一試。

The Dark Knight Rises 《黑暗騎士：黎明昇起》

📽 電影介紹

此片為《黑暗騎士：開戰時刻》(*Batman Begins*) 和《黑暗騎士》(*The Dark Knight*) 的續集，時間背景設定在《黑暗騎士》的八年後。蝙蝠俠因背負殺死哈維丹特的汙名而消失八年，布魯斯韋恩 (Bruce Wayne，克里斯汀貝爾 (Christian Bale) 飾) 也將自己封閉在家裡。隨著末日化身班恩 (Bane，湯姆哈迪 (Tom Hardy) 飾) 的出現，蝙蝠俠決心再出江湖，拯救高譚市。

MP3 077

take the fall 背黑鍋

fall 在口語中當名詞時，是指「被警察逮捕」，take the fall 原本也是這樣的意思，但後來也有為別人犯下的過錯或是罪行承擔責罰的意味，也就是替別人頂罪，可能是被抓，甚至是坐牢。

A: How come that dirty politician never gets punished for his crimes?
為什麼那名貪官從來不會因為他犯下的罪行而被處罰？

B: He always pays other people to **take the fall** for him.
他總是買通別人來替他背黑鍋。

MP3 076

worth a shot 值得一試

名詞 shot 有「嘗試、機會」的意思，worth a shot 就是指「某事／物值得一試」；而另一個常見的片語 give...a shot 就表示「嘗試…看看」。

A: Do you think I should try to borrow the money from Walter?
你覺得我該跟華特借這筆錢嗎？

B: Well, he may not have that much, but I guess it's **worth a shot**.
呃，他可能沒那麼多錢，不過還是值得一試吧。

🎞 電影對白

高譚市警探約翰布萊克 (John Blake，喬瑟夫高登李維飾) 前往布魯斯韋恩的宅邸。布萊克告訴韋恩，戈登局長在地下道追逐持槍犯時被攻擊，救出他時，他一直喃喃著什麼地下軍隊，還有一個叫班恩的面罩人。

Bruce Wayne: Shouldn't you be telling your superior officers?
這件事你不該向你上頭的長官報告嗎？

John Blake: They asked me if he saw any giant alligators. He needs you. He needs the Batman.
他們還問我局長會不會是看到了什麼大鱷魚才滿口胡言。他需要你，需要蝙蝠俠。

[……]

John Blake: I don't know why you **took the fall** for Dent's murder, but I'm still a believer in the Batman.
我不知道你為什麼要背下謀殺丹特這個黑鍋，但我始終相信蝙蝠俠。

Gossip Box

《全面啟動》讓喬瑟夫不奶油

還記得《全面啟動》中有一幕，喬瑟夫須在毫無重力的空間裡打鬥，沒想到那竟然不是動畫合成！為拍攝這一幕，製作團隊精心設計一個長超過三十公尺的通道，外面再由兩個巨大馬達旋轉操作，放眼望去的所有東西都在旋轉，光是要維持平衡都很困難，不過喬瑟夫親臨上陣，完全沒有用到替身演員，咬牙完成拍攝。而且為了能完美呈現這一個場景，喬瑟夫還特地練肌肉，擺脫從前純情小生形象。

50/50 《活個痛快》

電影介紹

IT TAKES A PAIR
TO BEAT THE ODDS.

50/50
SEPTEMBER 30

二十七歲的亞當 (Adam，喬瑟夫高登李維飾) 是為廣播電台企劃，不菸不酒無不良嗜好的他，居然被診斷出罹患癌症，這對他來說無非是晴天霹靂。抗癌治療中，在好友凱爾 (Kyle，賽斯羅根 (Seth Rogen) 飾)、母親以及凱薩琳醫師 (Katherine，安娜坎卓克 (Anna Kendrick) 飾) 的陪伴下，亞當體認出生命中最重要的東西，也決心不讓病魔打敗自己。

電影對白

亞當的父母和亞當在診療室等待羅斯醫生 (Dr. Ross) 的會診，以得知化療的結果。

Dr. Ross: Sorry to keep you folks waiting. Anyway, I'll **cut to the chase**. The cancer is not responding to the *chemo. As you can see, the tumor is continuing to grow here along the nerve. We have to remove it now, or we risk *metastasis.
抱歉讓你們久等了，那我就直說了。癌細胞對化療沒有反應，你可以看到，這裡的腫瘤沿著神經持續增生。[醫生指向 X 光片] 要馬上切除，否則可能會轉移。

Adam: OK, so what do we do?
好，那要怎麼做？

Dr. Ross: We need to operate. Now I've moved some things around and I can get you in this Thursday morning with Dr. Walderson. She's one of our finest *neurosurgeons.
一定要動手術，我已經把一些事情排開來，星期四早上請華德森醫師為你動刀。她是我們神經外科的權威。

*chemo [ˈkɛmo] (n.) 化學治療，為 chemotherapy 的縮寫

*metastasis [məˈtætəsɪs] (n.) 轉移

*neurosurgeon [ˈnʊroˌsɝdʒən] (n.) 神經外科醫師

MP3 078

cut to the chase
切入正題，進入重點

我們都知道 chase 有「追逐」的意思，那麼 cut to the chase 到底在說什麼？其實這個慣用語跟拍電影有很大的關係。電影動作片中，追逐戲通常是最精采、最重要的部分。當導演說 cut to the chase 就是在說把攝影鏡頭切換到追逐畫面。後來就引申出「直接切入主題，長話短說」的意思。

A: It's kind of a long story. Do you want me to start from the beginning?
這說來話長，你要我從頭說起嗎？

B: No, I'm kind of in a hurry. Just **cut to the chase**.
不，我有點趕，直接說重點吧！

MP3 079

off the hook 脫離苦海

hook [hʊk] 有掛鉤、吊鉤的意思，off the hook 是指從責任或危機中脫身，就像是已經上鉤的魚又順利脫逃一樣。let sb. off the hook 則有饒過某人、放過某人的意思。

A: Mom, I really don't want to babysit Joey. I'll miss the game on Saturday.
媽，我真的不想照顧喬依。這樣星期六會錯過球賽。

B: Good news—you're **off the hook**. Uncle Rick is taking him to the zoo.
好消息，你解脫了。瑞克叔叔要帶他去動物園。

A: I said I was sorry for forgetting your birthday. Don't you forgive me?
忘了妳的生日我已經向妳道過歉，妳不能原諒我嗎？

B: Ha! I'm not letting you **off the hook** so easily.
哈！我可不會那麼輕易饒過你。

Premium Rush 《超急快遞》

🎥 電影介紹

威力（Wilee，喬瑟夫高登李維飾）是紐約最快的單車快遞手。一天，一名女子指名要威力幫她送信，且需在限時的九十分鐘內送件完成，然而在這過程中，威力卻遭到警官鮑比蒙戴（Bobby Monday，麥克夏儂 (Michael Shannon) 飾）的瘋狂追逐，到底這封信裡藏著什麼天大的祕密？

MP3 080

one's number is up 氣數已盡，劫數難逃

相信大家一定都知道「氣數已盡」這個成語，相同意思的英文用語，也一樣是用數字來形容喔！這個俚語是從軍隊延伸出來的，「說人家的數字到了」就是再說「某人陣亡了」，這個 number 指的是士兵的代號數字，因此 sb.'s number is up 就是在形容某人快死了，或是說人家大難臨頭，要倒大楣了。

A: Wow, that was close! That car almost hit us.
哇，剛剛好險！那台車差點撞到我們。

B: Yeah. I thought **my number was up**.
對啊，我還以為我要死了。

📽 電影對白

威力出車禍的那一瞬間，突然想起女友凡妮莎（Vanessa，丹妮雅拉米瑞茲 (Dania Ramirez) 飾）之前曾問過自己，騎車總是不用煞車，難道自己都不怕會出事？

Vanessa: Aren't you afraid you're gonna get killed?
難道你都不怕被撞死嗎？

Wilee: Yeah, but if it comes, that's just gonna come out of nowhere. Am I afraid? Sure, but that's part of it, you know? There's no feeling like that.
會怕，但若真的發生，根本無從防範。會怕嗎？會啊，但這就是騎快車，沒別的感覺比得上。

Vanessa: When y**our number's up**, your number's up.
該來的就是會來。

Wilee: You could say that.
可以這麼說。

Don Jon 《超急情聖》

📽 電影對白

唐岡到處去跟人家打聽，終於知道芭芭拉的姓名，並在臉書上找到她，傳訊息邀約她共進午餐。一見面，芭芭拉就問他是從哪得知她的名字，因為她確信自己沒有說出來，唐岡一直狡辯說芭芭拉那晚喝醉，才會忘記自己有說。

Barbara: I had a few drinks the other night, so I may not have remembered telling you my first name, but I definitely did not tell you my last name.
那晚我確實有喝幾杯，我可能不記得我有說到我的名字，但一定沒告訴你我姓什麼。

Jonny: I'm telling you....
我跟妳講……

Barbara: Don't lie to me. Look, you don't know me, so I'm gonna let you **off the hook** this time. But trust me, in the future you'll be much happier if you always tell me the truth.
別騙我。聽著，你不認識我，所以這次我打算饒過你。但相信我，以後如果都對我說實話，你會更好過。

🎥 電影介紹

唐岡（Don Jon，喬瑟夫高登李維飾）對愛情動作片情有獨鍾，依賴色情網站給予他在現實生活得不到的快感；芭芭拉（Barbara，史嘉莉喬韓森 (Scarlett Johansson) 飾）沉迷於愛情電影，總期待電影中的浪漫愛情會出現在她身上。唐岡在遇見芭芭拉後，很快陷入戀情，但卻因芭芭拉不能忍受唐岡背著她上色情網站而畫下句號。隨著唐岡的同學伊絲特（Esther，茱莉安摩爾 (Julianne Moore) 飾）的出現，帶領著唐岡體會不同的愛情態度，唐岡會因而改變自己的愛情觀嗎？

Sandra Bullock 珊卓布拉克

SHOWBIZ WORD

audition 試演會

一般找工作要面試、筆試,而演藝工作則要透過 audition,也就是在主考官(一般是製作人、導演,或經紀公司主管)面前唱歌、跳舞或表演。影藝表演相關學校招生時,也會舉辦 audition。

在電影及電視界,一般會就已經決定好的劇本進行選角(casting),然後請屬意的人選透過攝影機試演,看看演員在螢幕上呈現的效果好不好,因此這個行業的 audition 也稱作 screen test(試鏡)。

megahit 熱賣大作

字首 mega- 可以表示「百萬倍」,也有「非常大的」的意思;hit 是名詞,意思為「成功、受歡迎的事物」。 megahit 就是指銷售量或是票房都超人氣的熱賣大作,尤指電影或是唱片等等。

其他表達「熱賣大作」的用法如下列:

- blockbuster 賣座電影
- smash hit 廣受歡迎的電視劇、產品
- bestseller 暢銷書、產品
- chartbuster 熱門唱片、歌曲

LANGUAGE GUIDE

為什麼紐約被稱作 the Big Apple?

紐約之所以被稱作 the Big Apple(大蘋果)的實際由來已不可考,根據紐約歷史學會資料顯示,紐約被稱為大蘋果應追溯至一九二一年《紐約晨報》(The New York Morning Telegraph)一位名為約翰費茲傑羅(John J. Fitzgerald)的賽馬專欄作家,約翰在賽馬場跟來自紐奧良的黑人馬伕聊天時,得知在他們眼中,紐約是個遍地黃金且充滿無限可能的地方,就像人人都想咬上一口的大蘋果。也有人說這是源自一九二〇至三〇年間的爵士樂用語,當年美國爵士樂大行其道,許多爵士樂手經常到各地巡迴演出,而樂手們一致公認紐約是待遇最好的城市,也就是最甜美多汁的大蘋果。

Academy Award winning actress Sandra Bullock was born on July 26, 1964. Her father, a U.S. Army [1]**serviceman**, and her mother, a German [2]**opera** singer, met in Germany, where Bullock spent most of her childhood. She [3]**accompanied** her mother on tours around Europe, getting her first taste of the stage by performing minor roles. Bullock returned to the U.S. for high school, and after completing a degree in drama at East Carolina University, she headed for the bright lights of the Big Apple.

In New York, Bullock attended auditions while tending bar and doing other odd jobs. After appearing in several small independent films, she got her break: a supporting role in the sci-fi [11]**flick** Demolition Man (1993). This led to her first starring role opposite Keanu Reeves in the megahit Speed (1994), and Bullock never looked back. Over her career, she has shown her acting [7]**prowess** in dramas like Crash (2004), and the ability to tickle our funny bones in comedies like Miss Congeniality (2000) and The Proposal (2009).

In 2010, Bullock won the best actress Oscar for her portrayal of the [8]**no-nonsense** football mom Leigh Anne Tuohy in The Blindside. She was nominated again in 2013 for her role as Dr. Ryan Stone in Gravity, which Variety magazine called "a one-woman show" because of Bullock's [9]**riveting** performance. Off the silver screen, Bullock has [4]**donated** over $4 million to the Red Cross for international [5]**disaster** relief, so our "Miss [10]**Congeniality**" should be considered for the title of "Miss [6]**Humanitarian**" as well!

©Andrea Raffin / Shutterstock.com

奧斯卡最佳女主角得主珊卓布拉克出生於一九六四年七月二十六日。她的父親原於美軍服役，母親則是德國歌劇歌手，兩人在德國相遇，布拉克的童年也大多在那裡度過。她陪伴母親巡迴歐洲，並初次登台演出小角色，之後回到美國讀高中，在東卡羅萊納大學完成戲劇學位後，前往五光十色的大蘋果紐約。

在紐約，布拉克一邊參加試鏡，一邊在酒吧當侍者也打其他零工。在幾部獨立小電影亮相後，好機會降臨：科幻片《超級戰警》（一九九三）的配角。這為她帶來第一個女主角，在超級賣座片《捍衛戰警》（一九九四）與基努李維演對手戲，從此布拉克不再回頭。在演藝生涯中，她已經於《衝擊效應》（二〇〇四）等劇情片展現精湛演技，也在《麻辣女王》（二〇〇〇）和《愛情限時簽》（二〇〇九）等喜劇展現逗我們發噱的能力。

二〇一〇年，布拉克在《攻其不備》飾演嚴肅的美式足球媽媽黎安，贏得奧斯卡最佳女主角獎。二〇一三年她再次以《地心引力》的蕾恩史東博士一角獲得提名，她引人入勝的演出使《綜藝》雜誌形容該片簡直就是她的「個人秀」。在銀幕之外，布拉克已經捐了超過四百萬美元給紅十字會進行國際賑災，因此我們的「麻辣女王」也該榮膺「慈善女王」的頭銜才是！

TONGUE-TIED NO MORE

never look back 魚躍龍門

當一個人越來越成功，地位越來越高，眼界越來越廣，看世界的角度和理解事物的方式都與過去不同，這就是 never look back 那種已經不再回頭看過去的自己是怎麼想的感覺。

A: I hear Paula is a successful author now.
我聽說寶拉現在是成功的作家。

B: Yeah. Since her first book was published, she's never looked back.
是啊。她的第一本書出版之後，就飛上枝頭做鳳凰了。

tickle one's funny bone 令人捧腹

大家應該都有發生過手肘撞到之後超麻超痠、哭笑不得的感覺，那根被撞到的肱骨因此被戲稱為 funny bone。tickle one's funny bone 的意思就是讓人得好笑。

A: Do you want to read the comic section?
你要看報紙的漫畫版嗎？

B: No thanks. None of the comics really tickle my funny bone.
謝了不必。那些漫畫都沒有讓我真的覺得好笑的。

VOCABULARY BANK

1) **serviceman** [ˋsɚvɪsmən] (n.) 軍人
Several servicemen were killed in the bomb attack.
在這次炸彈攻擊當中有數名軍人喪生。

2) **opera** [ˋɑprə] (n.) 歌劇
Did you enjoy the opera last night?
你喜歡昨晚的歌劇表演嗎？

3) **accompany** [əˋkʌmpənɪ] (v.) 陪同，伴隨
Children under twelve must be accompanied by an adult.
十二歲以下兒童必須有成人陪同。

4) **donate** [ˋdonet] (v.) 捐獻，捐贈
Michael donated some of his old clothes to charity.
麥可把他的一些舊衣服捐贈給慈善團體。

5) **disaster** [dɪˋzæstə] (n.) 災難，災害
Taiwan is frequently hit by natural disasters.
台灣很常受到天然災害侵襲。

6) **humanitarian** [hjuˏmænəˋtɛrɪən] (n./a.) 人道主義者，慈善家；人道的，慈善的
Mother Theresa was a great humanitarian.
泰瑞莎修女是一位偉大的慈善家。

進階字彙

7) **prowess** [ˋpraʊɪs] (n.) 傑出的能力
President Obama is known for his prowess as a public speaker.
美國總統歐巴馬以傑出的公開演說能力聞名。

8) **no-nonsense** [noˋnɑnsɛns] (a.) 正經的，直截了當的，講究實際的
A no-nonsense coach was hired to improve team discipline.
一位嚴肅的教練受聘加強那支球隊的紀律。

9) **riveting** [ˋrɪvɪtɪŋ] (a.) 吸引目光的，引人入勝的
The author's riveting novels brought him fame and fortune.
那位作家引人入勝的小說讓他名利雙收。

10) **congeniality** [kənˏdʒiniˋælɪtɪ] (n.) 意氣相投，選美界選的 Miss Congeniality 即為「最佳人緣獎」
The gentleman's club has an atmosphere of congeniality.
那紳士俱樂部的氣氛非常融洽。

口語補充

11) **flick** [flɪk] (n.) 電影
My girlfriend dragged me to see another chick flick last night.
我的女友昨晚拖著我又去看了一部女生才愛看的電影。

Gravity 《地心引力》

🎥 電影介紹

這是蕾恩史東博士（Dr. Ryan Stone，珊卓布拉克飾）第一次執行太空任務，卻不幸遇到災難，不但太空梭全毀、與地面斷訊，她和資深太空人麥特科沃斯基（Lieutenant Matt Kowalski，喬治克隆尼 (George Clooney) 飾）還被捲入黑暗之中。隨著氧氣和燃料逐漸耗盡，完全沒有獲救機會的他們，要如何自行找到回家的路？

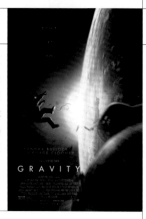

📽 電影對白

地球上方太空中一片寧靜祥和，史東博士專心於機具維修，太空人麥特悠閒地太空漫步。忽然，位於休斯頓的地面控制中心傳來事故消息。

Control: Explorer, this is Houston.
探索號，這裡是休斯頓。

Captain: Go ahead, Houston.
請說，休斯頓。

Control: NORAD reports a Russian satellite has incurred a missile strike. The impact has created a cloud of debris orbiting at twenty thousand miles per hour. Current debris orbit does not overlap with your trajectory. We'll **keep you posted** on any developments.
北美空防司令部說一架俄羅斯衛星遭到飛彈攻擊。造成的大量碎片以時速兩萬英里繞行地球。目前碎片的軌跡跟你們的軌道沒有重疊。有任何後續發展我們會隨時通知你們。

MP3 083

keep sb. posted 持續告知某人最新情況

post 這個字當動詞有「貼公告周知」的意思，因此 keep sb. posted 就代表讓某人一直持續得知最新消息，就像一直看到最新貼出來的公告一樣。

A: Has there been any change in your mother's condition?
你媽媽的狀況有什麼改變嗎？

B: No. But the doctor said he'd **keep me posted**.
沒有。不過醫生說他會持續讓我知道最新狀況。

📽 電影對白

史東博士和太空人麥特只差一點就要逃到中國太空站，為了讓史東博士更有生還的機會，麥特決定放手讓自己越漂越遠。

Dr. Stone: I'm gonna take the Soyuz and come get you.
我要開聯合號去救你。

Kowalski: No, you're not.
不行，妳不可以。

Dr. Stone: I'm coming to get you.
我要去救你。

Kowalski: No, I've got too much of **a head start** on you.
不行，我已經走太遠妳追不上了。

Dr. Stone: I'm coming to get you.
我要去救你。

Kowalski: I'm afraid **that ship already sailed**. Ryan, you're gonna have to learn to let go.
恐怕已經來不及了。蕾恩，妳一定要學會放手。

MP3 084

a head start 搶先起步（的優勢）

head start 是「提早起步」的意思。

A: It's not fair. You can run faster than me.
不公平。你跑得比我快。

B: OK, I'll give you **a head start** then.
好啦，那我讓你先起跑。

賽跑若是提前偷跑，就已經贏在起跑點，獲勝的機會當然大增。因此這句話也可以表示具有某種優勢，使人更容易成功。

A: Why are you looking for jobs now? You won't graduate for another few months.
你幹嘛現在就開始找工作？你還有好幾個月才畢業。

B: I want to get **a head start** in my career.
我希望我的職涯能早點開始。

電影對白

史東博士有機會逃上中國太空站，卻失去求生的意志，太空人麥特一直透過無線電鼓勵她，告訴她能夠利用中國太空站的救生船逃生，史東卻說喪氣話，表示她受訓開模擬器時每次都墜毀。

Kowalski: It's a simulator, that's what it's designed for.
那是模擬器，就是要拿來墜毀的。

Dr. Stone: Every time. I crashed it every time.
無一幸免。我每次都墜毀。

Kowalski: You point the damn thing at Earth. It's **not rocket science**. And by this time tomorrow, you're gonna be back in Lake Zurich with a hell of a story to tell.
妳只要把那鬼東西對準地球。這能夠有多難。等到明天此時，妳就回到蘇黎世湖，還有一個很刺激的故事可以講了。

©Everett Collection / Shutterstock.com

Gossip Box

最得觀眾緣的好萊塢女星

珊卓布拉克日前得到第四十屆「全美觀眾票選獎」的最收歡迎女影星、最受歡迎喜劇片女星等四大獎，成了典禮上的大贏家，謙虛的她一上台，除了感謝劇組團隊的辛勞，也特別提到養子路易斯，展現十足的親和力。

MP3 084

that ship has sailed 為時已晚

字面意思是「船已經開走了」，用來形容機會已經流失，或是某個狀況已成定局，不可能再改變。

A: I'm still hoping Sandy will take me back.
我還在盼望珊蒂會回心轉意跟我復合。

B: I hate to tell you, but **that ship's sailed**. She already has a new boyfriend.
我實在不想告訴你，但真的為時已晚了。她已經有新男友了。

MP3 085

not rocket science
不會很難

rocket science 是「太空火箭科學」，牽涉到艱深的數學、動力機械、天體物理，不是腦袋一般的大眾能理解的，因而引申為「需要超高智而才能完成的事」。這個詞在生活中最常出現的形式是 not rocket science，表示一件事「不會難到哪裡去」。

A: I can't figure out how to connect the DVD player to the TV.
我不知道要怎麼把 DVD 播放器接到電視上。

B: C'mon, man! It's not exactly **rocket science**.
老兄，拜託喔！這沒有那麼難吧。

©s_bukley / Shutterstock.com

The Proposal 《愛情限時簽》

📷 電影介紹

強悍的女主管瑪格麗特（Margaret，珊卓布拉克飾）是在美國工作的加拿大人，為了逃避居留權過期即將被遣送出境的命運，竟異想天開硬要他的助理安卓（Andrew，萊恩雷諾斯 (Ryan Reynolds) 飾）娶她為妻。如果想要通過移民官員的考試，這對共犯必須攜手到安卓在阿拉斯加的家，宣布他們的婚訊……。

MP3 086

with cherries on top 拜託求求你

冰淇淋或糕點上常會擠一坨鮮奶油，再放上鮮紅櫻桃作點綴，這種做法總是讓人心情愉悅。因此這個説法常出現在拜託別人幫忙，或是請求別人原諒的情境下。表達請求通常都會用 please 這個字，但光説一個 please 不夠，還想再加強語氣時，一般會在 please 前面加 pretty，還不夠就再加上 with cherries on top 或是 with sugar on top，變成 pretty please with cherries on top / with sugar on top。

A: Can I use the car tonight, Dad? Pretty please **with cherries on top**?
爸，我今晚可以開車嗎？拜託拜託求求你可以嗎？

B: Well, OK. But you have to be back before eleven.
這個嘛，好吧。但你要在十一點以前回來喔。

🎬 電影對白

魔鬼女主管瑪格麗特，拜託小助理安卓娶她，安卓馬上端起架子，嫌她不夠誠意，逼得瑪格麗特當街下跪，低聲下氣向他求婚。

Margaret: Sweet Andrew.
親愛的安卓。

Andrew: I'm listening.
我有在聽。

Margaret: Would you please, **with cherries on top**, marry me?
你能夠，拜託拜託求求你，跟我結婚嗎？

Andrew: OK. I don't appreciate the sarcasm, but I'll do it. See you at the airport tomorrow.
好吧。我不太喜歡那股反諷語氣，但我會娶妳，明天跟妳在機場見了。

The Blind Side 《攻其不備》

📷 電影介紹

出身問題家庭的麥可在寒冬夜裡被黎安（Leigh Anne Tuohy，珊卓布拉克飾）發現時已經無家可歸，她毫不猶豫邀請這位女兒的同學回家過夜，從此開啟了這位黑人貧苦少年跟這個富裕白人家庭的親密關係。

MP3 087

a-word A開頭的 (髒) 字

在電影對白中，爸爸開玩笑講粗話説出 ass（屁股）這個字，立刻被媽媽糾正：Don't use the a-word. 這裡的 a-word 就是 ass 這個字。其他的髒字也都可以比照辦理，當你不想講出某個髒字，只要説出字首字母再加上 -word 即可代替，例如 f-word 就是 fuck，n-word 就是 nigger，依此類推。

A: Why did Johnny get suspended?
為什麼強尼被留校察看？

B: He used the **f-word** in class.
他説了那個 F 開頭的髒字。

🎬 電影對白

黎安和她的丈夫尚恩 (Sean)，看完兒子 S.J. 的感恩節話劇表演，開車離開學校。S.J. 向經營墨西哥速食連鎖店的爸爸要兑餐券。

S.J.: Dad, I'm gonna need a few more of those free *quesadilla tickets.
老爸，我需要多拿幾張免費墨西哥起司薄餅兑換券。

Leigh Anne: And *where does the acorn fall?
他這是像到誰啊？

Sean: Hey, don't laugh too hard. The quesadilla saved our ass.
嘿，不要笑嘛。墨西哥起司薄餅他媽的養活我們一家人耶。

Leigh Anne: Don't use the **a-word**.
不要説髒話。

*****quesadilla** 在兩張玉米餅 (tortilla) 中間夾起司煎烤而成的墨西哥食物

*****where does the acorn fall** 原句為 The apple doesn't fall far from the tree.（蘋果只會掉在蘋果樹附近。）這裡則將 apple 替換為 acorn（橡實），都表示「有其父必有其子」的意思。

©Everett Collection / Shutterstock.com

28 Days 《28 天》

🎥 電影介紹

葛雯（Gwen，珊卓布拉克飾）的母親在她童年時就因酗酒而酒精中毒身亡，使她變成一個自我放逐、玩世不恭的人。一回她在姊姊的婚禮上喝醉後大鬧婚禮，還酒駕衝入民宅，最後被判進重建中心戒酒戒毒。在中心的這二十八天裡，她不但與裡面的人結為好友，還重新找回新自己的人生。

🎞 電影對白

這天葛雯的男朋友賈斯伯 (Jasper) 來到重建中心探望葛雯，在優美的湖光山色中向葛雯求婚，並拿出暗藏的香檳酒慶祝，沒想到葛雯竟把酒丟入湖中，賈斯伯對於葛雯的舉動大為吃驚，急忙探詢原因。

Gwen: Maybe there is something wrong with me.
也許我有毛病。

Jasper: Is that what they're telling you?
他們是這樣告訴妳的？

Gwen: No...yep. It is. I think they're right.
不是……沒錯。就是那樣。我覺得他們説得對。

Jasper: They're not. You're just **in a rut**. It happens to everyone.
他們錯了。妳只是因循常規。每個人都是這樣。

Gwen: No, there's an entire world of people who do everything right.
不是，多得是一堆正經生活的人。

MP3 088

in a rut 因循常規，一成不變

rut 原本字意是「（車子走過的）痕跡」，後來引申為「常規、慣例」routine，所以 in a rut 是形容某種狀況一直依循著既定的模式進行，多半是指工作或是生活一成不變。好比每天就只是下班回家，隔天睡醒再去上班，如此日復一日，你就可以用 My life is just in a rut. 來描述自己的生活。

A: All I ever do these days is prepare for the graduate school entrance exams.
我這些日子在做的只有準備研究所的入學考試。

B: You're really stuck **in a rut**. You need to take a break.
你真是了無生趣。你該休息一下了。

Gossip Box

珊姐幽默的致謝詞

珊卓布拉克因演出《攻其不備》而得到金球獎最佳女主角，上台領獎時，她的第一句話就是：Did I really earn this, or did I just wear you all down?（我究竟是真得獎了，還是大家都被我累垮了？）。wear down 這個術語常出現在比賽中，意思是磨損或削弱別人的力量，讓對方疲於奔命，也恰巧是《攻其不備》中的台詞之一，珊卓適時使用雙關語讓台下觀眾會心一笑，可見這位影后的反應有多快。

Johnny

強尼戴普

Depp

MP3 089

LANGUAGE GUIDE

Rolling Stones 滾石樂團

一九六二年成立至今的長青樂團 Rolling Stones 是一支英國搖滾樂團,被視為整個七○年代的音樂代表。這支「壞男孩團體」與當時同期的「好男孩團體」Beatles（披頭四）分庭抗禮,共同打破一直以來美國音樂引領全球的慣例,在美國掀起「英國瘋」。滾石樂團目前的成員為主唱米克傑格 (Mick Jagger),吉他手凱斯理查茲 (Keith Richards),貝斯手查理華茲 (Charlie Watts) 和鼓手羅尼伍德 (Ronnie Wood)。

Keith Richards

凱斯理查茲和米克傑格不僅是兒時玩伴,共同創團之後也是勇於嘗試各種音樂形式的創作搭檔,他們的作品融入非洲音樂、舞曲、龐克搖滾,對流行音樂極具貢獻。凱斯理的吉他技巧出神入化,曾被《滾石雜誌》選為史上百大經典吉他手的第十名,在荒唐排行榜上也不遑多讓,他一生不但差點被炸死、電死、燒死、謀殺、毒死、從樹上摔死,甚至被書壓死。常年吸毒的他甚至吸過他父親的骨灰（他捨不得把洒落桌面的少許骨灰掃到地上）!

這也就難怪強尼戴普會不止以凱斯理為範本塑造瘋癲史傑克船長的形象,更邀他在《神鬼奇航 3:世界的盡頭》(Pirates of the Caribbean: At World's End) 當中飾演史傑克的父親蒂格船長 (Captain Teague),成為當集宣傳上的賣點之一。

Johnny Depp was born in Kentucky on June 9, 1963 to an engineer and a waitress. He dropped out of high school to chase his dream of becoming a rock musician. In the early 1980s, however, he was introduced to Nicholas Cage, who encouraged him to pursue an acting career. Brief appearances in *A Nightmare on Elm Street* (1984) and *Platoon* (1986) led to a starring role on the popular 80s Fox TV series *21 Jump Street*. Although the show made Depp a teen idol, he rejected being turned into a "product," and quit the show to focus on films.

In 1990, Depp began his long collaboration with director Tim Burton in *Edward Scissorhands*, and the pair has gone on to make eight films [1]**to date**. *Scissorhands* and other Burton films like *Ed Wood* (1994), *Sleepy Hollow* (1999) and *Charlie and the Chocolate Factory* (2005) display Depp's talent for playing [9]**quirky** but [10]**charismatic** characters. Still, Depp's most [2]**celebrated** role, Captain Jack Sparrow in the wildly successful Pirates of the Caribbean franchise, best [11]**embodies** these [3]**traits**. In a [4]**nod** to his rock roots, Depp says he based his odd [5]**pirate** on [6]**legendary** Rolling Stones guitarist Keith Richards.

Outside of acting, Depp, a father of two, has owned a Paris restaurant as well as a [7]**vineyard** in southeastern France, and continues to make music. Although he has hinted at [8]**retirement** from acting, fans shouldn't be too worried. Depp is returning as Captain Jack Sparrow in the fifth *Pirates* movie in 2016.

1) **to date** [tu det] (phr.) 至今
The author's latest novel is his best work to date.
這位作家的最新小說是他至目前為止最好的作品。

2) **celebrated** [ˋsɛlə͵bretɪd] (a.) 著名的，馳名的
Mark Twain is one of America's most celebrated authors.
馬克吐溫是美國最知名的作家之一。

3) **trait** [tret] (n.) 特性，（人格）特質
Patience is one of Allen's best traits.
耐心是艾倫優點之一。

4) **nod** [nɑd] (n./v.) 點頭，致意，同意；點頭
In a nod to the locals, the star said a few words in their language.
為了向當地民眾致意，那位明星用他們的語言說了幾句話。

5) **pirate** [ˋpaɪrət] (n.) 海盜，盜版者
Many ships have been attacked by pirates in the Indian Ocean.
許多船隻在印度洋上遭海盜襲擊。

6) **legendary** [ˋlɛdʒən͵dɛri] (a.) 傳奇的，傳說的
The CEO's work ethic is legendary.
這位總裁工作上律己甚嚴，非常人所能及。

7) **vineyard** [ˋvɪnjəd] (n.) 葡萄園
The grapes at our vineyard are harvested by hand.
我們葡萄園的葡萄是以人工採收。

8) **retirement** [rɪˋtaɪrmənt] (n.) 退休
You should start saving for your retirement as early as possible.
你應該盡早開始為你的退休生活存錢。

進階字彙

9) **quirky** [ˋkwɝki] (a.) 獨樹一格的，不尋常的
Ned has a quirky sense of humor.
耐德的幽默感很詭異。

10) **charismatic** [͵kærɪzˋmætɪk] (a.) 有魅力的，有吸引力的
Churchill was a charismatic leader.
邱吉爾是很有魅力的領袖。

11) **embody** [ɪmˋbɑdi] (v.) 具體呈現，將…具體化
Parents should embody the values they want to teach their children.
父母教養子女應以身作則。

強尼戴普一九六三年六月九日出生於肯塔基州，雙親分別為工程師和侍者。他高中輟學，追求當搖滾樂手的夢想。但一九八〇年代初期，他被介紹給尼可拉斯凱吉，凱吉鼓勵他朝戲劇發展。在《半夜鬼上床》（一九八四）及《前進高棉》（一九八六）的驚鴻一瞥，讓他得以在備受歡迎的八〇年代福斯電視影集《龍虎少年隊》擔綱主角。雖然那部戲將戴普塑造成青少年偶像，但他拒絕被變作「商品」，遂辭演該劇而專注於電影。

一九九〇年，戴普以《剪刀手愛德華》開啟與提姆波頓導演的長期合作，這對搭檔至今一共拍了八部片。《剪刀手愛德華》和其他諸如《艾德伍德》（一九九四）、《沉睡谷》（一九九九）和《巧克力冒險工廠》（二〇〇五）等由波頓執導的電影，在在展現戴普詮釋怪異但迷人角色的天賦。儘管如此，最能體現上述特質的，莫過於戴普最知名的角色：廣獲成功的《神鬼奇航》系列裡的史傑克船長。為向他的搖滾根源致意，戴普表示，他在扮演這位怪異海盜時，主要在模仿滾石合唱團的傳奇吉他手凱斯理查茲。

在演戲之外，身為兩個孩子的父親，戴普分別在巴黎及法國東南部擁有一家餐廳和一座葡萄園，並持續創作音樂。雖然他已暗示要退出戲劇界，但影迷不必太擔心。戴普會在二〇一六年的《神鬼奇航》第五集，以史傑克船長之姿重返銀幕。

Charlie and the Chocolate Factory 《巧克力冒險工廠》

📽 電影介紹

巧克力製造商威力旺卡（Willy Wonka，強尼戴普飾）的工廠已近十五年未見有人進出，卻能不斷生產巧克力銷售全世界，現在他開放五個入內參觀的機會，分別由五個孩子獲得。他們進到工廠之後，會發現什麼驚人的秘密？

🎞 電影對白

跟著威力旺卡進入工廠的幸運兒，除了善良的貧窮男孩查理巴格特（Charlie Bucket），還有貪吃甜食的奧古塔斯格盧普（Augustus Gloop）、被寵壞的維露卡索爾特（Veruca Salt）、自以為聰明的麥克提維（Mike Teavee），和嚼口香糖冠軍紫羅蘭博雷加德（Violet Beauregarde）。參觀工廠時，紫羅蘭偷吃尚在研發階段的口香糖，結果變成一顆大藍莓。

Veruca Salt: Will Violet always be a blueberry?
紫羅蘭會永遠變成一顆藍莓嗎？

Willy Wonka: No…maybe…I don't know. That's what you get from chewing gum all day. It's disgusting.
不會吧……或許會……我不知道。一個人整天口香糖嚼不停就會變這樣。噁心死了。

Mike Teavee: If you hate gum so much, why do you make it?
你那麼恨口香糖，幹嘛還要製造？

Willy Wonka: Once again, you shouldn't mumble. It's starting to **bum me out**.
我說過了，不要一直咕噥著。我快要不高興了。

`MP3 091`

bum sb. out 讓某人討厭，讓人悲傷
這個俚語表示「令人討厭」，也有「讓人感到失望或沮喪」的意思。

A: Why is Todd so negative all the time? He's **bumming me out**.
塔德為什麼老是抱持那麼負面的態度？我被他煩死了。

B: Don't take it personally. That's just the way he is.
不要太往心裡去。他那人就是這樣。

A: God! It's been raining for two weeks straight!
天啊！已經連續下雨兩個星期了！

B: Yeah. I wish it would stop. It's really **bumming me out**.
對啊。真希望雨能停。我快悶出命來了。

🎞 電影對白

被當作壞核桃的維露卡掉進垃圾場之後，旺卡先生帶著剩下的麥克和查理一行人繼續參觀工廠。旺卡先生帶著剩下的麥克和查理一行人繼續參觀工廠，他們正要進入一座電梯。

Willy Wonka: The elevator's by far the most efficient way to get around the factory.
搭電梯是參觀工廠最快速的方法。

Mike Teavee: There can't be this many floors.
不可能有那麼多層樓。

Willy Wonka: How do you know, Mr. **Smarty-Pants**?
你又知道了，自以為是先生？

Gossip Box

怎麼穿都「型」？

帥氣的鬍鬚搭配超亂髮型、紫色墨鏡與帽子，這造型就是強尼戴普的正字標記，但大家可能沒注意到：他超愛穿破鞋！戴普日前上節目時，腳上穿的就是一雙原本是黑色，卻退色到近乎發白的舊皮鞋，依然迷倒一票粉絲，讓人直呼「好酷！」但不被明星光環迷惑的人亦所在多有，因此「最差穿著」名人榜上，戴普也常名列其中。

smarty-pants 自作聰明的人

smarty-pants 是指那種沒人問他也愛賣弄學問的人，但他其實沒那麼厲害，愛自作聰明的人。其他字眼如 smarty、smart aleck、know-it-all 都代表一樣的意思。

A: The people on this quiz show are so dumb!
參加這個搶答節目的人都好笨！

B: OK, **smarty-pants**. Why don't you sign up to be on the show then?
好啊，萬事通先生。那你怎麼不去報名參加上節目？

A: Your brother is such a smart aleck.
你的哥哥真是博學多聞。

B: Yeah. He's a real **know-it-all**.
是啊。他真的是個萬事通。

Alice in Wonderland 《魔境夢遊》

🎥 電影介紹

少女愛麗絲（Alice Kingsleigh，蜜雅娃絲柯斯卡 (Mia Wasikowska) 飾）跟著一隻怪兔子掉入兔子洞，來到一個異異的世界，並捲入壞心紅皇后與善良白皇后兩姐妹的戰爭。愛麗絲必須聯合瘋狂帽客（Mad Hatter，強尼戴普飾）等人除掉天魔，讓世界恢復秩序。

📰 電影對白

斷頭台上，劊子手想要摘掉瘋狂帽客的帽子。

Mad Hatter: I'd like to keep it on.
我想要戴著帽子。

Executioner: **Suit yourself**. As long as I can get at your neck.
隨便你。只要我能夠砍到你的脖子。

Suit yourself. 隨便你。

Suit yourself. 就是「你覺得高興就好，我不勉強你」的意思。

A: I don't think I'm going to the movie tonight.
今晚的電影我不想看。

B: OK, **suit yourself**. But it's supposed to be really good.
好，不勉強，不過這片應該很好看。

這句話另一個使用時機，是碰到一意孤行的人，你知道怎麼勸他都不會有用，就可以擺下這一句，表示「我管你去死」。

A: I know you don't want me to take a job in another city, but it's a great opportunity.
我知道你不想要我接下另一個城市的工作，但這是大好機會。

B: Fine! **Suit yourself**! I'm sure you'll meet someone new over there.
好！妳要去就去吧！想必妳到那邊一定會另結新歡。

Edward Scissorhands 《剪刀手愛德華》

🎥 電影介紹

愛德華（Edward，強尼戴普飾）是寂寞科學家創造的男孩，當愛德華的剪刀手要被換成正常手時，科學家心臟病發猝死。多年後，愛德華被帕戈博格斯（Peg Boggs）太太發現並將他帶回家。愛德華的剪刀手乍看之下很恐怖，卻能將花木修剪得非常漂亮，幫人修剪頭髮也得心應手。社區居民漸漸接納他，對他從恐懼轉為喜愛。而他也與寄宿家庭的女兒小金（Kim，薇諾娜瑞德 (Winona Ryder) 飾）墜入情網……。

🎞 電影對白

金和男友吉姆還有一個同學走在街上，看到附近庭院的樹叢都被愛德華雕塑成動物或人物的形狀。

Kim: I think they look weird. They **give me the creeps**.
我覺得看起來好怪。它們讓我心裡發毛。

Classmate: You should see the clown in front of Miss Peters' yard.
妳該去看看彼得太太院子前面的小丑。

MP3 094

give sb. the creeps
令人心裡毛毛的

感到恐懼時，往往會渾身不自在，好像有蟲在皮膚上爬似的，當你有這種感覺，就會說 sth. give me the creeps，也就是某樣東西「讓我寒毛直豎」，也可以說 give sb. the willies。

A: IThat old house **gives me the creeps**.
那間老屋讓我毛骨悚然。

B: Yeah. It looks like it's haunted.
對啊。看起來好像鬧鬼。

🎞 電影對白

晚餐時，收留愛德華的帕戈太太跟她的先生比爾在聊天。

Peg: Bill, you know what Edward was telling me? He had lunch at Jackie's today and she just had her kitchen completely redone.
比爾，你知道愛德華跟我說什麼嗎？他今天在潔姬家吃午飯，她剛剛重新翻修她的廚房。

Bill: I'll be darned.
真是不可思議。

Peg: New paint, new cabinets, new floors, a new microwave, new silent dishwasher....
新的粉刷、新櫥櫃、新地板，新的微波爐、新的靜音洗碗機……。

Bill: Isn't that wonderful?
太棒了不是嗎？

MP3 095

I'll be darned. 真是意想不到。

darn 是 damn（該下地獄的，在英文裡一般被視為粗話）的婉轉語，I'll be darned / damned. 這個句子可以用在兩種情況，一是表示「我完全沒料到。」但講這句話的人，有時是在表示諷刺，像電影對白中的比爾根本不關心鄰居廚房的事，他這樣說只是在配合太太，其實一點都不驚訝，另一方面他故意誇大語氣，也顯示他覺得這個話題有夠無聊。

A: Peter asked me to marry him. Can you believe it?
彼得求我嫁給他。你相信這種事嗎？

B: Well **I'll be darned**! What did you say?
我還真是想不到！那妳怎麼說？

另一種情況則是在拒絕做愚蠢的事。

A: Stella wants to get back together with you? Did you say yes?
史黛拉想跟你復合？你答應了嗎？

B: After she dumped me? No way! **I'll be damned** if I give her another chance.
在她把我甩了之後？當然不行！我發神經才會再給她一次機會。

Pirates of the Caribbean: *The Curse of the Black Pearl*

🎥 電影介紹

殖民地總督千金伊莉莎白（Elizabeth Swann，琪拉奈特莉 (Keira Knightley) 飾）小時候從小海盜威爾身上拾獲一枚鬼盜船金幣。伊麗莎白長大後，鬼盜船來襲，她持那枚金幣找船長巴伯沙（Captain Hector Barbossa，傑佛瑞洛許 (Geoffrey Rush) 飾）談判卻遭挾持，成為鐵匠的威爾（Will Turner，奧蘭多布魯 (Orlando Bloom) 飾）為拯救心上人，遂加入海盜船長史傑克（Captain Jack Sparrow，強尼戴普飾）追捕鬼盜船，沒想到鬼盜船上的海盜全都是殭屍……。

MP3 096

sticks and stones 不痛不癢

這句話原本是小孩的順口溜：Sticks and stones may break my bones, but words can never hurt me.（棍子和石頭或許還能打斷我的骨頭，拿話罵我可就傷不了我了。）大人會開玩笑地說 sticks and stones 來表示。當別人把你罵個狗血淋頭，但你根本不在乎時，就可以無所謂地說 sticks and stones，意思就是「你怎麼罵我都無所謂」。

A: I can't believe he called you an asshole. What did you say?
我不敢相信他罵你混蛋。你怎麼回他？

B: I just said "**Sticks and stones**, man, sticks and stones."
我只說「隨便你罵，老兄，我無所謂」。

📇 電影對白

史傑克船長救了意外落水的伊麗莎白一命，卻也因此被英軍上銬逮捕。史傑克船長挾持伊麗莎白，要回他的武器和帽子。他雙手被銬無法整理行裝，就叫被他抱在胸前的伊麗莎白幫他一把。

Captain Sparrow: Now if you'll be very kind. Easy on the goods, darling.
現在要麻煩妳了。手腳輕一點，寶貝。

Elizabeth: You're *despicable.
你太卑鄙了。

Captain Sparrow: **Sticks and stones**, love. I saved your life. You save mine. We're *square.
我無所謂，親愛的。我救妳一命，妳救我一命。我們扯平了。

*despicable [dɪ`spɪkəbəl] (a.) 卑劣的
*square [skwɛr] (a.) 扯平的

Gossip Box

大家可別看強尼戴普老愛在電影裡搞怪搞醜，他可是不折不扣的大帥哥，而且不止一次，是兩次（分別是在二〇〇三年及二〇〇九年）榮獲《時人》(People) 雜誌評選為世界上最性感男性！

©Entertainment Press / Shutterstock.com

©Stijn Vogels / flickr.com

Matt

麥特戴蒙

Damon

MP3 097

Matt Damon was born on October 8, 1970 in Cambridge, Massachusetts. He grew up near his friend and distant cousin Ben Affleck, and the pair acted in high school theater productions together. Damon began studying English at Harvard in 1988, but dropped out in his [1]**senior** year to move to Los Angeles and try an acting career.

In L.A., Damon and Affleck began writing a screenplay when they had trouble finding parts. After many [2]**rejections**, the two young actors talked a major studio into making *Good Will Hunting*, which was [3]**released** in 1997. The film, starring Damon as a math [4]**genius** from a rough Boston neighborhood and Affleck as his best friend, was a huge hit. The pair won the Oscar for best original screenplay, and Damon a best actor Oscar nomination, which [5]**launched** his career.

Following *Good Will Hunting*, Damon played another title character, this time in Steven Spielberg's WWII [6]**epic** *Saving Private Ryan* (1998). The new [10]**millennium** saw the rise of Damon as a big action star in the *Bourne Identity* (2002) and its two sequels. He also [7]**tackled** dramatic roles in *Syriana* (2005), *The Departed* (2006) and *Invictus* (2009), with his portrayal of South African rugby captain Francois Pienaar opposite Morgan Freeman's Nelson Mandela earning him a best supporting actor Oscar nomination.

Damon's recent projects include the sci-fi movie *Elysium* (2013) about a [11]**dystopian** future, and George Clooney's *Monuments Men* (2014), a drama about the [12]**Allied** effort to [8]**recover** precious artworks during WWII. Damon also has plans to return to his Boston roots as [9]**infamous** crime boss James "Whitey" Bulger in an upcoming film to be directed by his old [13]**buddy** Ben Affleck.

©Jaguar PS / Shutterstock.com

SHOWBIZ WORD

screenplay 電影劇本
play 當名詞時可指「戲劇，劇本」，而 screenplay 則專指電影或電視劇的劇本，也叫 script。劇本裡的台詞，英文則是説 line。

©Jaguar PS / Shutterstock.com

麥特戴蒙在一九七○年十月八日出生於麻州劍橋市。他和朋友兼遠親班艾佛列克一起長大，兩人也一起在高中話劇演出。戴蒙於一九八八年進入哈佛主修英文，但在大四那年輟學，搬到洛杉磯試圖開展演藝事業。

在洛杉磯，戴蒙和艾佛列克發現演出機會難尋，於是開始寫劇本。在多次遭拒之後，這兩位年輕演員說服一家大型電影公司拍攝《心靈捕手》（編註：Will Hunting 為麥特在本片的角色名），於一九九七年上映。該片由戴蒙飾演出身於波士頓一個危險社區的數學天才，艾佛列克飾演他最好的朋友，立刻造成轟動。這對搭檔贏得奧斯卡最佳原創劇本獎，戴蒙也獲得最佳男主角獎提名，就此展開影藝生涯。

在《心靈捕手》之後，戴蒙又演出一個被用作劇名的角色，這一次是在史蒂芬史匹柏執導的二次大戰史詩電影《搶救雷恩大兵》（一九九八）。新的千禧年，戴蒙搖身變成動作片巨星，演出《神鬼認證》（二○○二）和兩部續集。他也在《諜對諜》（二○○五）、《神鬼無間》（二○○六）和《打不倒的勇者》（二○○九）挑戰劇情片的角色；他在《打》片中飾演南非橄欖球隊長法蘭索爾皮納爾，與摩根弗里曼飾演的曼德拉演對手戲，贏得奧斯卡最佳男配角獎提名。

戴蒙近期的作品包括描述人類反烏托邦未來的科幻電影《極樂世界》（二○一三），以及喬治克隆尼的《大尋寶家》（二○一四）：描述同盟國在二次世界大戰期間努力尋回珍貴藝術品的電影。戴蒙也計畫回到波士頓老家，在老友班艾佛列克執導的新戲中飾演惡名昭彰的犯罪頭子詹姆斯「白毛」巴爾傑。

VOCABULARY BANK

1) **senior** [ˈsinjə] (a.) 高年級生的
Chuck got married in his senior year of high school.
查克高中三年級就結婚了。

2) **rejection** [rɪˈdʒɛkʃən] (n.) 拒絕，退回
I want to ask her out, but I'm afraid of rejection.
我想約她出來，但我怕被拒絕。

3) **release** [rɪˈlis] (v./n.) 發表，發行；發行的作品
The band will release their new album in July.
這樂團七月會發行他們的新專輯。

4) **genius** [ˈdʒinjəs] (n.) 天才，天賦
Mozart was a musical genius.
莫札特是音樂天才。

5) **launch** [lɑʊntʃ] (v.) 展開，發動
The singer is launching his tour next month.
那位歌手下個月將展開巡迴演唱。

6) **epic** [ˈɛpɪk] (n./a.) 史詩，史詩般的作品；史詩般的
That channel plays all the old Hollywood epics.
那個頻道專播好萊塢早期的史詩片。

7) **tackle** [ˈtækəl] (v.) 著手處理，對付
The government has promised to tackle inflation.
政府承諾要打擊通貨膨脹。

8) **recover** [rɪˈkʌvə] (v.) 取回，找回
The thieves were caught, but the stolen goods were never recovered.
小偷抓到了，但贓物永遠拿不回來了。

9) **infamous** [ˈɪnfəməs] (a.) 惡名昭彰的，聲名狼藉的
South Africa is infamous for its high crime rate.
南非的高犯罪率惡名遠播。

進階字彙

10) **millennium** [mɪˈlɛniəm] (n.) 千禧年，千年（複數為 millennia）
The year 2000 marked the beginning of the third millennium.
西元兩千年揭開了第三個千禧年的序幕。

11) **dystopian** [dɪsˈtopiən] (a.) 反烏托邦的
(n.) dystopia 反烏托邦（政治、經濟社會生活極糟的假想地）
George Orwell is most famous for his dystopian novel *1984*.
喬治歐威爾最出名的就是他的反烏托邦小說《1984》。

12) **Allied** [ˈælaɪd] (a.) （二次大戰中）同盟國的
The Battle of Okinawa was won by the Allied forces.
沖繩島一戰是由同盟國獲勝。

口語補充

13) **buddy** [ˈbʌdi] (n.) 好朋友，夥伴
Me and my buddies are going fishing this weekend.
我和我的哥兒們這週末要一起去釣魚。

Good Will Hunting

🎥 電影介紹

主角威爾（Will，麥特戴蒙飾）是個天才，兒時的創傷使他緊閉心門，選擇埋沒天賦，做著不起眼的工作渾噩度日。在麻省理工學院擔任清潔工時，威爾無意間解開藍伯教授（Lambeau，史戴倫始考斯佳 (Stellan Skarsgård) 飾）出給學生的數學難題，又剛好惹上一場官司，因此藍伯便向法官建議，要求威爾每週固定向他報到，一同研討數學，另一方面還得接受心理治療，作為免除責罰的條件。威爾在輔導過程中不但與心理治療師尚恩（Sean，羅賓威廉斯 (Robin Williams) 飾）成為莫逆之交，還找到了內心的平和及人生的方向。

🎞 電影對白

威爾正在向女友史蓋兒（Skylar，米妮瑞福 (Minnie Driver) 飾）解釋他的天賦是怎麼運作的。

Will: Beethoven, OK. He looked at a piano, and it just made sense to him. He could just play.
以貝多芬舉例好了。他看著鋼琴，就是那樣地理所當然。他就這麼會彈琴了。

Skylar: So what are you saying? You play the piano?
所以你是在說什麼？你會彈鋼琴？

Will: No, **not a lick**. I mean, I look at a piano, I see a bunch of keys, three *pedals, and a box of wood. But Beethoven, Mozart, they saw it, they could just play. I couldn't paint you a picture, I probably can't hit the ball out of Fenway, and I can't play the piano.
不，一點也不。我是說，當我看到鋼琴，我只看到一堆琴鍵、三個踏板，還有一個木箱。但對貝多芬、莫札特來說，他們看到鋼琴就會彈了。我不會畫畫，我大概也無法把球打出芬威球場，我也不會彈琴。

Skylar: But you can do my *o-chem paper in under an hour.
但你卻能在一小時內寫完我的有機化學報告。

Will: Right. Well, I mean when it came to stuff like that... I could always just play.
沒錯，我的意思是，當碰到這些事的時候……我就是會做。

*pedal [ˈpɛdəl] (n.) 腳踏板
*o-chem 全稱為 organic chemistry（有機化學）。

Gossip Box
天才不只是會演戲！

從小就是鄰居的麥特和班艾佛列克 (Ben Affleck)，是死忠兼換帖的好兄弟，兩人合力完成的《心靈捕手》劇本甚至獲得奧斯卡最佳原創劇本獎。這位在戲中的數學天才證明自己在現實生活中也是個天才，麥特絕對不甘於只是會演戲！麥特日前接受母校哈佛頒贈「哈佛藝術獎章」時，感歎地說，他當初為專心拍攝《印地安傳奇》(Geronimo: An American Legend) 而休學，以為可以藉著這部片大紅大紫，不料熬了五年才熬出頭，這次母校願意頒發這個獎項給他，也算是彌補了當初未完成學業的缺憾。

©Featureflash / Shutterstock.com

MP3 099

not a lick 一點也不
名詞 lick 可指「少量」，例如 a lick of... 就是指「少量的……」，而 not a lick 直譯為「連少量都沒有」，就表示「一點也不、完全沒有」的意思。

A: The police don't have any evidence against the suspect?
警方沒找到對嫌犯不利的證據嗎？

B: Nope. **Not a lick.**
沒。連個渣都沒有。

《心靈捕手》

🎬 電影對白

威爾帶史蓋兒給朋友們認識，大夥坐在店裡閒聊。

Morgan: Man, I can't believe you brought Skylar here when we**'re** all fucking **bombed** and been drinking. What the fuck is she gonna think about us?

老兄，我真不敢相信你在我們都喝醉的時候帶史蓋兒到這兒來。她會怎麼想我們？

Katharine: Howard, please, this is beneath you.

霍華，拜託，別作賤你自己。

Will: Yeah, Morgan, it's a real *rarity that we'd be out drinking.

對啦，摩根，我們真的「很少」出來喝啦。

*rarity [ˋrɛrətɪ] (n.) 稀少，罕見

MP3 100

be bombed 喝得爛醉

bombed 跟 loaded、smashed 和 wasted 都是爛醉的意思，也可以用來形容嗑藥後很 high 的感覺（high 在口語中指嗑藥後神智恍惚的狀態）。口語上用來形容「酒醉」的字有很多，例如有點醉意，但還不到不省人事的地步，這種「微醺」的狀態，就可以用 tipsy 來表示。

A: Is it true that you got **bombed** at the bar last night?
你昨晚真的在酒吧喝到爛醉喔？

B: No way! I was just tipsy.
哪有！我只是有點茫茫而已。

若是要講「爛醉」，除了 bombed，還可以用 plastered、tanked、sloshed、hammered 和 shit-faced 等形容詞。

A: How come you took a taxi home last night?
你昨晚為什麼是叫計程車回家？

B: I got **tanked** at the party.
我在派對上喝很醉。

We Bought a Zoo《我們買了動物園》

🎥 電影介紹

班傑明密（Benjamin Mee，麥特戴蒙飾）原是一名媒體工作者，因生活遭逢變故，於是舉家搬到位於鄉村的廢棄動物園重新開始。他們打算重新開幕動物園，在學習打理動物園的同時，這家人與動物和他人之間的關係也有了不同的發展。

MP3 101

jump the gun 操之過急，太早行動

賽跑時，起跑前通常會先鳴槍，表示比賽開始。還沒鳴槍就先起跑，就是「搶先行動，偷跑」的意思。

A: I'm thinking of asking Becky to marry me.
我在考慮向貝琪求婚。

B: Whoa! Don't **jump the gun**. You've only known her for a month.
哇！不要操之過急。你才認識她一個月而已。

🎬 電影對白

房仲業者史蒂文斯 (Stevens) 帶班傑明去看房子，班傑明一看到動物園的房子就很喜歡，立刻決定要搬來這裡。

Mr. Stevens: Right now, I think we're **jumping the gun**.
我覺得我們現在好像操之過急了。

Benjamin Mee: This is exactly what we've been looking for.
這完完全全就是我們想找的房子。

Mr. Stevens: Uh...let's not *get ahead of ourselves. Let's just take it all in first. Don't take a gift that's not given to you yet now.
呃，我們還是不要太倉促了。我們先全盤了解一下。不要連禮物都還沒送你就急著拿啊。

*get ahead of oneself (phr.)（某人）行動太快，操之過急

Rounders 《賭王之王》

🎥 電影介紹

向來以賭博為生的麥克（Mike，麥特戴蒙飾）經歷一次慘敗後，決心脫離賭博生涯，再也不涉足賭場。雖然他慢慢步上正軌，卻覺得這條路遠不及撲克牌局驚險刺激。某次他剛出獄的好友沃爾（Worm，艾得華諾頓（Edward Norton）飾）欠下高利貸，麥克便重操舊業，企圖在最短的時間內籌到一萬五千美金，否則兩人小命就要不保了……

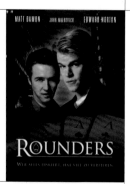

MP3 102

before you know it 很快就會……

這個片語字面上的意思是「在你知道之前」，其實就是指「很快，馬上」的意思。

A: You're not gonna be at the mall all day are you?
你不會在購物中心待上一整天吧？

B: No. I'll be back **before you know** it.
不會。我很快就會回來了。

MATT DAMON

©Ritu Manoj Jethani / Shutterstock.com

🎬 電影對白

經過一次慘敗後，麥克決心戒賭，任勞任怨地開卡車還債來賺取學費。直到老友沃爾出獄，麥克平靜的生活又起波瀾。沃爾極力邀約他一起和他搭檔，重出江湖。

Mike: No, man. I'm off it.
不要，老兄。我不玩了。

Worm: What are you? You're getting cold cards?
你怎麼了？你手氣不好嗎？

Mike: No, man. I mean I quit.
不是。我洗手不幹了。

Worm: What? Are you shitting on me?
什麼？你在唬爛我嗎？

Mike: No, man. I got **cleaned out**.
不是。我輸慘了。

🎬 電影對白

麥克在牌局中精心策劃，企圖引誘泰迪（Teddy，約翰麥可維奇（John Malkovich）飾）上鉤，將泰迪桌上的賭注通通占為己有。不過，畢竟薑是老的辣，麥克反被泰迪將了一軍，瞬間輸光所有積蓄，此刻心情就像從山峰跌落谷底，友人柯尼許（Knish，約翰特圖羅（John Turturro）飾）前來安慰他。

Knish: Want some?
要抽口大麻嗎？

Mike: No. I'm *down to the felt, Knish. I lost everything. Man, I lost my *tuition.
不用。我完蛋了，柯尼許。我輸光了。天啊，我把學費輸光了。

Knish: It happens to everyone. Time to time, everyone *goes bust. You'll back in the game **before you know it**.
每個人都會碰到。時不時，大家都會輸得很慘。很快你就會回到賭桌上的。

Mike: No, man, I'm done. I'm out of it.
不，老兄，我不玩了。我要收手。

*down to the felt 這句話是梭哈的術語，意指「輸光所有的錢」。
*tuition [tu`ɪʃən] (n.) 學費
*go bust [go bʌst] (phr.) 破產

MP3 103

clean out 被洗劫一空

字面上是「被洗得一乾二淨」，用在賭博上，就是「輸個精光」的意思。因此不論你是因為輸錢，還是運氣不好遭小偷、被搶劫等等，若是身上財物分文不剩，這句話就派上用場了。

A: Did you have a good divorce lawyer?
你有找到好的離婚律師嗎？

B: I wish. My wife **cleaned** me **out**.
真希望有找到。我老婆把我身上的錢都挖走了。

這句話還可以用在別的地方，例如用來表示「掃貨，搶購一空」。

A: It says on the news there's a typhoon coming.
新聞說有颱風要來了。

B: Then we better go shopping before the supermarket gets **cleaned out**.
那我們最好趕在超市被搶購一空前去採買。

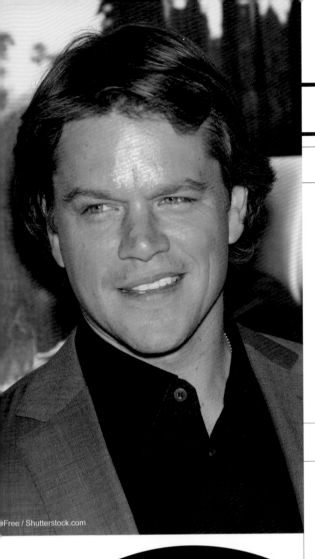

©Free / Shutterstock.com

The Departed 《神鬼無間》

📽 電影介紹

改編自港片《無間道》。描述警方與黑道互相安插臥底到對方手下進行滲透,比利寇提根(Billy Costigan,李奧納多狄卡皮歐(Leonardo DiCaprio)飾)是警方派去黑道的臥底,而柯林蘇利凡(Colin Sullivan,麥特戴蒙飾)則是黑道佈署在警方中的奸細,隨著雙方的鬥爭白熱化,這兩位具有雙重身分的要角內心也產生了重大轉變,除面對抉擇善惡的掙扎,還要擔心自己的身分會否曝光……the departed 直譯為「死者」,depart 也有「背離」的引申義,與原港片的「無間」一詞有相似的意境。

🎞 電影對白

柯林和另一名探員同時出現在犯罪現場勘察。

Detective: I'd appreciate it if you got out of my crime scene.
如果你離開我的犯罪現場,我會很感激。

Colin: This is my crime scene, but **knock yourself out.**
這是我的現場才對,不過你自便吧。

Knock yourself out.
請自便。

這句話與 Be my guest. 類似,都是請人家自便的意思,差別在於 Knock yourself out. 比較沒那麼客氣,通常是在兩人熟識,或是當你不是很在意對方要幹嘛的時候使用。

A: Do you mind if I eat the last slice of pizza?
你介意我吃掉最後一片披薩嗎?

B: No. **Knock yourself out.**
不會啊。請便。

©Joe Seer / Shutterstock.com

Gossip Box

麥特?柏格?傻傻分不清楚

好萊塢有很多長像神似的明星,麥特戴蒙和馬克華柏格就是個好例子。據說有位女性素人某日在街上巧遇馬克華柏格(Mark Wahlberg),開心地大叫:「麥特戴蒙!」並上前要求合照,回去還將照片傳上網,炫耀自己遇到了麥特,結果被眼尖的網友糾正,女孩才尷尬地發現自己認錯人了。這段對話內容後來被轉貼至馬克華柏格的臉書上,幽默的他不但一點也不介意,反倒自嘲地說:「很接近那啦!」不知各位讀者是否也覺得這兩位明星有幾分相似呢?

©Ji buKley / Shutterstock.com
©Everett Collection / Shutterstock.com

Angelina 安潔莉娜裘莉 Jolie

Award-winning actress, [1]**tireless** human rights [2]**advocate**, sex symbol, mother—these are just a few ways to describe Angelina Jolie. Born in Los Angeles in 1975, Jolie enrolled in the Lee Strasberg Institute, where she studied method acting, at age 11. Jolie admits to being a troubled teen, engaging in drug use and self-harm, and she had a difficult relationship with her father, actor Jon Voigt. She even quit acting at 14, [3]**opting** to model and [4]**explore** other interests.

[5]**Eventually**, though, Jolie would return to acting. Her first major movie role was as the [6]**gifted** computer [7]**hacker** Kate "[8]**Acid** Burn" Lilly in *Hackers* (1995). Other early credits include a young New York cop opposite Denzel Washington in *The Bone Collector* (1999) and the mental patient Lisa Rowe in *Girl, Interrupted* (1999), for which Jolie won the best supporting actress Oscar. But it was her role as an English [11]**archeologist** in 2001's *Lara Croft: Tomb Raider* and its 2003 sequel, *The Cradle of Life*, that brought Jolie international [10]**fame** made her one of Hollywood's highest-paid actresses.

Jolie fell in love with [9]**co-star** Brad Pitt on the set of *Mr. & Mrs. Smith* in 2005, and the couple, known as "Brangelina" in the [12]**tabloids**, has been together ever since. While not married—they did get in engaged in 2012—the pair has six children, including three they've adopted together. Jolie is also known for her human rights work, which includes serving as goodwill ambassador for the UN Refugee Agency for over a decade.

©rocor / flickr.com

SHOWBIZ WORD

sex symbol 性感偶像

sex symbol 這個字眼最早出現在一九五〇年帶中期，代表對大眾具有性吸引力的名人，經常以票選排名的形式出現在時尚、八卦雜誌當中。一開始都是電影明星，但隨著時代演進，現在包括樂團歌手、模特兒、運動員，甚至政治人物都可能入列。不過 sex symbol 最著名的例子是瑪麗蓮夢露 (Marilyn Monroe)，她甚至被 BBC（英國國家廣播公司）評為永不隕落的好萊塢性感偶像。

credit 作品

credit 在文中的定義是指一個人參與過的作品（影視、舞台等）。這個字的另一個定義是「工作貢獻」，也就是個人及團體在整個製作過程中參與的內容。為了幫每一個曾經投入的人力留下工作紀錄，電影、電視節目最後會將演員和所有工作人員列出（複數形 credits），以表彰所有人的貢獻。

©Kris Olin / flickr.com

獲獎女星、堅持不懈的人權鬥士、性感偶像、母親──這些尚不足以形容安潔莉娜裘莉。一九七五年生於洛杉磯的她，年僅十一歲就進入李史特拉斯堡學院學習方法演技。她自承在青少年時期備受毒品與自殘的困擾，與父親演員強沃特的關係也不和睦。她甚至在十四歲時放棄演戲，選擇當模特兒和探索其他興趣。

不過，裘莉終究還是回到演藝圈。她的第一個電影要角是在《網路駭客》（一九九五）中飾演天賦異稟的電腦駭客凱特「強酸腐蝕」莉莉。她的其他早期作品包括在《人骨拼圖》（一九九九）飾演年輕紐約警察與丹佐華盛頓演對手戲，以及在《女生向前走》（一九九九）的精神病患麗莎羅威──並因此贏得奧斯卡最佳女配角獎。但讓裘莉揚名國際、且成為好萊塢片酬最高女星之一的，是二〇〇一年《古墓奇兵》及二〇〇三年續集《古墓奇兵：風起雲湧》當中的英國考古學家一角。

裘莉在二〇〇五年《史密斯任務》的片場與同片男星布萊特彼特陷入愛河，從此，這對被小報暱稱為「布裘戀」的佳偶就形影不離了。雖然沒有結婚──但在二〇一二年訂婚──兩人共有六個小孩，包括一起領養的三個。裘莉也以人權工作聞名，包括為聯合國難民署擔任超過十年的親善大使。

LANGUAGE GUIDE

Lee Strasberg Institute 史特拉斯堡戲劇電影學院

全名為 Lee Strasberg Theatre and Film Institute，分別於紐約曼哈頓及加州好萊塢開設學校，由演技名師李史特拉斯堡創立於一九六九年，旨在推廣及教授方法演技 (method acting)。這所學校作育英才無數，除了裘莉之外，勞伯狄尼洛 (Robert De Niro)、史嘉莉喬韓森 (Scarlett Johansson)、李小龍之子李國豪 (Brandon Lee) 等都是著名校友。

goodwill ambassado 親善大使

親善大使是一種榮譽職位，經常由社會名流或特定領域名人出任，代表某個團體（如慈善、商業）出訪他國進行宣傳，或是駐留在其他國家實際參與該團體的活動。另外一類帶有官方色彩的親善大使，是幫某個地區（國家、城市）進行國對國、城市對城市的文化交流。親善大使雖然有「大使」二字，但大多不具外交豁免權。

UN Refugee Agency 聯合國難民署

refugee 讀作 [ˌrɛfjʊˈdʒi] 意思為「難民」；agency 則表示（政府機構的）局、署、處等。UN Refugee Agency 是指「聯合國難民署」，全名為 Office of the United Nations High Commissioner for Refugees（縮寫 UNHCR），成立於一九五〇年，總部設於瑞士日內瓦，旨在救援並保護全球各地難民，成立迄今已幫助數千萬難民，因其貢獻卓越於一九五四年及一九八一年兩度獲得諾貝爾和平獎。

VOCABULARY BANK

1) **tireless** [ˈtaɪəlɪs] (a.) 孜孜不倦的，不屈不撓的
The police have been tireless in their search for the murderer.
警方一直鍥而不捨地追查殺人犯。

2) **advocate** [ˈædvəkɪt / ˈædvəˌket] (n./v.) 提倡者，擁護者；提倡，擁護
The new media law has been criticized by free speech advocates.
新的大眾傳媒法受到自由言論提倡者的抨擊。

3) **opt** [ɑpt] (v.) 選擇，挑選
The couple opted to rent a movie instead of going out.
這對情侶選擇租一部電影而不出門。

4) **explore** [ɪkˈsplor] (v.) 探索，瞭解，探究
You should explore your options before you choose a major.
你應該先探索有哪些選擇，然後再選擇主修課程。

5) **eventually** [ɪˈvɛntʃuəli] (adv.) 最後，終究
(a.) eventual
Allen and Grace plan to get married and have children eventually.
艾倫和葛麗絲打算最後還是要結婚生子。

6) **gifted** [ˈɡɪftɪd] (a.) 有天賦的
My brother is more athletically gifted than I am.
我的哥哥比我更有運動天賦。

7) **hacker** [ˈhækə] (n.) 電腦駭客
The hacker was arrested for breaking into a government computer system.
該名駭客因侵入政府電腦系統被捕。

8) **acid** [ˈæsɪd] (n.)〔化〕酸，尖刻
Vinegar contains a mild acid.
醋中含有弱酸。

9) **co-star** [ˈkoˌstɑr] (n./v.) 合演者；合演，亦作「costar」
Humphrey Bogart and Ingrid Bergman were co-stars in *Casablanca*.
亨佛瑞鮑嘉和英格麗褒曼共同主演《北非諜影》。

10) **fame** [fem] (n.) 聲望，名聲
The actress moved to Hollywood in search of fame and fortune.
那名女演員搬到好萊塢追求名利。

進階字彙

11) **archeologist** [ˌɑrkiˈɑlədʒɪst] (n.) 考古學家
Angkor Wat was discovered by a French archeologist in 1860.
吳哥窟是在一八六〇年由一位法國考古學家發現。

12) **tabloid** [ˈtæblɔɪd] (n.) 小報，八卦報
Don't believe everything you read in the tabloids.
小報上看到的事情不能盡信。

Lara Croft: Tomb Raider 《古墓奇兵》

🎥 電影介紹

四十八小時後，五千年一次的九星連環天象即將再現，只要將分成兩塊的「光之三角」合璧，加上一具神秘古鐘，即能打開時空之門，獲得無上力量。蘿拉卡夫特（Lara Croft，安潔莉娜裘莉飾）在考古學家父親遺物中找到古鐘，卻因此成為光明會這個邪惡團體的追殺對象。蘿拉必須搶在光明會之前找齊「光之三角」，才能拯救宇宙。

MP3 107

make a mental note 記在腦子裡

make a note 是「寫筆記」，把筆記寫在腦子 (mental) 裡，自然是要記牢等一下要做的事情，或是把某件事記在心上。

A: You know that Mother's Day is coming up soon, right?
你知道母親節快到了吧？

B: Thanks for reminding me. I'll **make a mental note** to send her flowers.
謝謝你提醒我，我一定會記得送花給她。

©Featureflash / Shutterstock.com

📽 電影對白

蘿拉的古鐘被光明會奪走，她趕緊前往藏有第一塊「光之三角」的吳哥窟密室，光明會更要用古鐘開啟第一個鑰匙，蘿拉發現他們找到的是掩人耳目的假鑰匙，趕緊出面制止，但光明會的領袖鮑威爾（Manfred Powell，伊恩葛林 (Iain Glen) 飾）不相信。

Lara: I need you to get the piece so I can steal it from you later.
我需要你們取得那塊「光之三角」，我才能從你們手上偷過來。

Manfred Powell: You're bluffing. Julius, **make a mental note**: kill Miss Croft if she attempts any such thing.
妳是在唬人。朱立斯，不要忘記這件事：如果卡夫特小姐輕舉妄動就殺了她。

Julius: Yes, sir, Mr. Powell.
沒問題，長官，鮑威爾先生。

📽 電影對白

鮑威爾覺得蘿拉不可能那麼好心幫忙，根本是想製造機會騙走他手上的古鐘。

Manfred Powell: Lady Croft, tell me, is there a good reason why I kept you alive?
卡夫特女爵，請告訴我，有什麼好理由讓我饒妳一命？

Lara: Yes. That is not the true eye.
有。那不是真的光明之眼。

Manfred Powell: This is the true eye.
這是真的光明之眼。

Lara: It's not, actually. It's a mirror image.
事實上不是。那是一個鏡像。

Manfred Powell: Miss Croft, I think you're trying to cheat me out of my little **ray of sunshine**.
卡夫特小姐，我覺得妳只是想騙走我心愛的東西。

MP3 108

a ray of sunshine 一縷陽光

a ray of sunshine 是指為生活帶來一點樂趣，或在環境艱困時帶來希望的人事物，也可以用諷刺語氣表示。

A: Are you looking forward to seeing your grandson?
是不是很期待可以見到你的孫子啊？

B: Of course. He's my **ray of sunshine**.
當然，他是我的開心果。

Gossip Box

巨星情侶魅力無法擋

因拍攝《史密斯任務》(*Mr. and Mrs. Smith*)，而和布萊德比特 (Brad Pitt) 傳出戀情，交往至今近十年，兩人的感情一直是娛樂媒體追逐的焦點。雖然兩人還未結婚，但已有了六個孩子，感情穩定，甚至還有傳兩人將再度聯手搭擋拍電影。

媒體在報導超級名人情侶檔，但每次都要把兩個人的名字寫出來實在很麻煩，乾脆創一個字來當作代稱。Brangelina 就是將布萊德比特 (Brad Pitt) 與安潔莉娜裘莉 (Angelina Jolie) 的姓名首字結合。以下是其他例子：

- **Tomkat 湯凱戀**

  Tom Cruise + Katie Holmes，即阿湯哥及前阿湯嫂凱蒂

- **Billary 比拉戀**

  Bill Clinton + Hillary Clinton，前美國總統柯林頓及夫人希拉蕊

- **Zanessa 柴妮莎戀**

  Zac Efron + Vanessa Hudgens，柴克艾弗隆及前女友凡妮莎哈金絲

- **Bennifer 班妮佛戀**

  Ben Affleck + Jennifer Garner / Jennifer Lopez，班艾佛烈克跟現任妻子珍妮佛加納，以及舊愛珍妮佛羅培茲。剛好前後兩任都叫 Jennifer，因此現在跟老婆珍妮佛加納這段便被稱做 Bennifer 2

©Northfoto / Shutterstock.com

Girl, Interrupted
《女生向前走》

📽 電影介紹

個性叛逆的蘇珊娜（Susanna，薇諾娜瑞德 (Winona Ryder) 飾）因太過特立獨行竟被診斷為精神分裂，送進精神病院，因此結識個性直率的麗莎（Lisa，安潔莉娜裘莉飾），及一群獨特的女孩。她們在護士薇樂莉（Valerie，琥碧戈柏 (Whoopie Goldberg) 飾）的幫助下，終於找回全新的人生。

🎞 電影對白

精神病院中，黛西（Daisy，布蘭妮墨菲 (Brittany Murphy) 飾）與蘇珊娜、麗莎聊到上廁所時旁邊有看護監視的感受。

Daisy: Which do you like better? Taking a dump alone or with Valerie watching?

妳們比較喜歡哪個？單獨拉屎，還是有薇樂莉在旁邊看？

Susanna: Alone

自己啦。

Daisy: Everyone likes to be alone when it comes out. I like to be alone when it goes in. To me, the cafeteria is like being with twenty girls all at once **taking a dump**.

拉出來的時候大家都喜歡自己一個人。吃進去的時候我喜歡獨自一人。對我而言，大食堂就跟二十個女生擠在一起大便沒兩樣。

MP3 109

take a dump 拉屎

相信不必說大家也看得出來這句話有點粗魯，但這部電影裡都是瘋子，說話不顧旁人眼光也就不足為奇了。意思和 take a dump 相近，但更粗俗、更髒的還有 take a shit 和 take a crap。

A: Why is the dog being punished?

狗狗為什麼被處罰？

B: He **took a dump** on the carpet.

因為牠在毯子上拉屎。

Salt 《特務間諜》

🎥 電影介紹

伊芙莎特（Evelyn Salt，安潔莉娜裘莉飾）遭北韓逮捕刑求，在男友麥克（Mike Krause，奧格斯特帝爾（August Diehl）飾）極力營救下終於獲救，她在答應男友求婚時，向他坦誠自己是美國中央情報局（CIA）的探員。結婚兩週年當天，伊芙莎特遭誣陷為俄國臥底刺客，逃回家發現丈夫麥克也被綁架。莎特要如何救出麥克並證明自己的清白？

🎞️ 電影對白

伊芙審訊一名自首的俄羅斯臥底，沒想到他反倒指證伊芙其實是潛伏在美國的俄羅斯間諜。走出審問間的伊芙，立刻要求泰德（Ted，李佛薛伯（Liev Schreiber）飾）讓她打電話給她的老公，只是電話一直沒回應，這讓伊芙緊張了起來。

Ted Winter: Look, Ev, try to stay calm.

聽著，伊芙，試著冷靜下來。

Evelyn Salt: I'm not a goddamn Russian spy.

我不是什麼天殺的俄羅斯間諜。

Ted Winter: I didn't say you were. Let's go to my office, we can **sort this out**.

我沒說妳是。一起去我的辦公室，我們可以解決這個問題。

Peabody: No, no. We gotta go to a secure location. Now.

不，不。我們得去安全的地方。現在。

Ted Winter: All right. Doesn't get any more secure than this. Ev? Five minutes.

好吧。沒地方比這裡更安全了。伊芙？五分鐘就好。

MP3 110

sort sth. out 解決問題

sort 當動詞有「依照分類挑出、整理」，或是在「心中理出頭緒」。當我們說 sort sth. out 時，就是把一堆東西「分類擺好」，或是電影對白中的意思「把某個問題搞清楚，找出解決方案」。

A: Jack and Karen are having problems in their marriage.

傑克和凱倫的婚姻出現了一些問題。

B: Maybe a marriage counselor can help them **sort** their problems **out**.

也許找婚姻咨詢師可以幫他們找出問題。

Gossip Box

學人精退散！

二○○四年奧斯卡影后莎莉賽隆（Charlize Theron）收服同屆奧斯卡影帝——浪子西恩潘（Sean Penn），成為最新的銀幕情侶！但這干裘莉什麼事？

據說啊，裘莉為此氣壞了，因為她覺得賽隆一整個是在抄襲她的路線：同為奧斯卡影后、戲路類似、都為聯合國效力、也跟她一樣收養小孩。現在又跟超高知名度的好萊塢壞男孩湊成一對。再這樣下去，以後她跟布萊得比特的新聞還有誰要看啊！？

Changeling 《陌生的孩子》

電影介紹

職業婦女克麗絲汀柯林斯（Christine Collins，安潔莉娜裘莉飾）獨立撫養兒子華特 (Walter)。為了養家，她這個週末必須加班，讓年僅九歲的兒子單獨看家，沒想到下班回來卻發現兒子失蹤了。她請求洛杉磯警方協尋，經過八個月的漫長等待，盼來的卻是一個假冒的孩子和一場災難……。

電影對白

克麗絲汀終於結束加班，急著要在天黑之前趕回家，卻被主管班哈里斯（Ben Harris，法蘭克伍德 (Frank Wood) 飾）叫住，只為了當面誇獎她的工作表現。

Mr. Harriss: Christine. Good, I was hoping to catch you. Look, I've been following your work reports, and I just want to let you know that I am very impressed. When I first suggested hiring female supervisors, my superiors weren't *big on the idea. But you have **held your own** as well as any of your male counterparts.

克麗絲汀。太好了，我想要找妳聊聊。聽著，我一直有在注意妳的工作報告，我只是想讓妳知道我很欣賞。我一開始提議雇用女性主管時，我的上司不太喜歡這個點子。但妳已經證明自己的能力不遜於其他男性主管。

Christine Collins: Thank you, Mr. Harris.

謝謝你，哈里斯先生。

*big on (phr.) 熱衷於，特別喜歡

MP3 111

hold one's own 能夠勝任、應付

這個片語表示一個人有能力處理身邊的事情或面對挑戰。

A: Are you worried that Billy will get bullied at school?

你有擔心比利在學校會被欺負嗎？

B: No. He can **hold his own** in a fight.

不擔心，打架他應付得來。

電影對白

克麗絲汀回到家發現兒子不見了，附近到處找都一無所獲，只能打電話報警。沒想到警方卻說政策規定失蹤不滿二十四小時不能啟動協尋，還暗示孩子是因為家庭有問題才會逃家。

Police: Look, 99 times out of 100, the kid shows up by morning. We don't have the resources to go chasing every kid who runs off with his pals.

聽著，一百次裡有九十九個孩子天亮就回家了。我們沒有人力去把每個和朋友到處亂跑的孩子追回來。

Christine Collins: No, no, no. No, that's not Walter. He doesn't do that.

不，不，不。不對，那不是華特。他不會這樣做。

Police: **With all due respect**, ma'am, every parent who calls says the same thing.

我無意冒犯，女士，每個打來的爸媽都這樣說。

MP3 112

with all due respect 無意冒犯

這句話字面上的意思是「我很尊重你」，經常用於句首，表示接下來要說的話或許會讓對方不爽，因此先行致意。

A: I think it's wrong for parents to spank their children.

我認為父母打小孩是不對的。

B: **With all due respect**, I disagree.

我無意冒犯，但我不認同。

©Featureflash / Shutterstock.com

Meryl Street 梅莉史翠普

©Featureflash / shutterstock.com

MP3 113

On March 2, 2011, Meryl Streep arrived at the White House for a date with President Obama, who presented her with the National Medal of Arts, the country's highest honor for artists. And no wonder—during her [1]**remarkable** five decade career, which includes roles in film, television and theater, she's received more Oscar and Golden Globe nominations than any other actor. Streep is widely regarded as the greatest living actress, as well as one of the greatest of all time.

Born in New Jersey in 1949, Streep joined the drama club in high school, and later studied drama at Vassar College and earned an MFA from the Yale School of Drama. She made her Broadway debut after graduating in 1975, and her film debut two years later in *Julia*. Streep was next picked by Robert De Niro, who had seen her in a play in New York, to appear with him the *The Deer Hunter* (1978). Although her role as Linda was small, her [2]**striking** performance as a soldier's [3]**fiancée** won her a best supporting actress Oscar nomination. This led to supporting roles in more big movies, including 1977's *Manhattan* and *Kramer vs. Kramer*, for which she won her first Oscar.

The 1980s saw Streep moving into leading roles, most [4]**notably** Polish [7]**holocaust** survivor Sophie in *Sophie's Choice* (1982), which won her a best actress Oscar. The versatile actress also showed a [8]**knack** for comedy, [9]**wowing** critics in *Postcards from the Edge* (1990) and later in the smash hit *The Devil Wears Prada* (2006). Most recently, Streep received a Grammy nomination for her singing in *Mamma Mia!* (2008) and a third Oscar for her portrayal of Margaret Thatcher in *The Iron Lady* (2011). Streep is now 65, and [5]**fortunately** for movie audiences, she has no plans to [6]**retire** anytime soon.

LANGUAGE GUIDE

National Medal of Arts
美國國家藝術獎

此獎項由美國國會於一九八四年所創，旨在表彰對藝術有貢獻的人，授獎人是由國家藝術基金（National Endowment for the Arts，簡稱 NEA）選出，頒獎人為當任美國總統。除了梅莉史翠普外，資深演員艾爾帕西諾 (Al Pacino) 也曾獲頒此獎。

二〇一一年三月二日，梅莉史翠普抵達白宮和歐巴馬總統會面，總統頒給她國家藝術勳章，美國授予藝術工作者的最高榮耀。而這一點也不奇怪——在她五十年的演藝生涯，包括在電影、電視和劇場的角色，她獲得的奧斯卡及金球獎提名比任何演員都多。史翠普被公認為當今世上最傑出的女演員，也是史上最傑出的女星之一。

一九四九年生於紐澤西州的史翠普在高中加入戲劇社，後來則在法薩爾大學主修戲劇，並拿到耶魯大學戲劇學院的藝術碩士。她在一九七五年畢業後首度於百老匯登台，電影處女秀則是兩年後的《茱莉亞》。接下來史翠普在紐約演出戲劇時，獲得羅勃狄尼洛青睞，選中她和他演出《越戰獵鹿人》（一九七八）。雖然她演的琳達只是個小角色，但她詮釋士兵未婚妻的生動演技仍為她贏得奧斯卡最佳女配角提名。這為她爭取到更多強片配角的角色，包括一九七七年的《曼哈頓》和《克拉瑪對克拉瑪》，後者更讓她贏得第一座奧斯卡獎。

一九八〇年代，史翠普晉升主角，最著名的是在《蘇菲亞的選擇》（一九八二）中飾演納粹大屠殺的波蘭籍生還者蘇菲亞，贏得奧斯卡最佳女主角。這位多才多藝的女演員也展現喜劇天分，以《來自邊緣的明信片》（一九九〇）和之後的賣座鉅片《穿著 Prada 的惡魔》（二〇〇六）驚艷眾影評。近年來，史翠普先是在《媽媽咪呀！》（二〇〇八）一展歌喉，獲得葛萊美獎提名，後於《鐵娘子》（二〇一一）詮釋柴契爾夫人，贏得第三座奧斯卡小金人。史翠普現年六十五歲，而值得電影觀眾稱幸的是，她近期還沒有退休的計畫。

VOCABULARY BANK

1）**remarkable** [rɪˋmɑrkəbəl] (a.) 非凡的，特別的
Swimming with dolphins was a remarkable experience.
和海豚一起游泳是個非常特別的經驗。

2）**striking** [ˋstraɪkɪŋ] (a.) 引人注目的
The artist likes to use striking colors in his paintings.
那位畫家作畫喜歡用搶眼的色彩。

3）**fiancée** [ˌfiɑnˋse] (n.) 未婚妻，fiancé 即「未婚夫」
Steven and his fiancée have been engaged for nearly a year.
史帝分和他的未婚妻已經訂婚將近一年了。

4）**notably** [ˋnotəbli] (adv.) 尤其，特別
There have been many layoffs, most notably in the manufacturing sector.
近來發生許多資遣的狀況，特別是在製造部門。

5）**fortunately** [ˋfɔrtʃənɪtli] (adv.) 幸運地，僥倖地
(a.) fortunate
Fortunately, the weather was perfect during our vacation.
好險我們去度假的時候天氣很好。

6）**retire** [rɪˋtaɪr] (v.) 退休
We plan on moving to Florida after we retire.
我們計畫退休後搬到佛羅里達州。

進階字彙

7）**holocaust** [ˋhɑlə͵kɔst] (n.) 大屠殺（尤指二次大戰時納粹對其他人種的屠殺）
Over six million Jews were killed in the Holocaust.
在二戰大屠殺時死了六百萬以上的猶太人。

8）**knack** [næk] (n.) 本領，訣竅
Daniel has a knack for finding simple solutions to complicated problems.
丹尼爾有本事可以找出複雜問題的簡單解決方法。

口語補充

9）**wow** [wau] (v.) 使（人）稱讚、贊嘆
The magician wowed the audience with his magic tricks.
魔術師的魔術戲法驚艷了全場觀眾。

The Devil Wears Prada 《穿著 Prada 的惡魔》

📹 電影介紹

安德莉亞（Andrea，安海瑟薇 (Anne Hathaway) 飾）是擁有漂亮學歷的社會新鮮人，一心想進入知名雜誌社擔任記者。為獲得媒體工作的資歷，她應徵成為時尚雜誌的編輯助理。對時尚一竅不通的安德莉亞必須達到惡魔總編米蘭達（Miranda，梅莉史翠普飾）種種無理的要求，還得忍受來自各方的冷嘲熱諷。然而就在她的工作漸有起色，開始受到肯定時，即將崩解的感情生活和人際關係也讓她思索起這一切的意義，使她明白，自己終究得在這份華麗工作與人生初衷之間做出抉擇。

MP3 115

reach for the stars 追求遠大目標

「摘下天上的星星」是件不可能的任務，因此英文就用 reach for the stars 表示想要達成一件難以達成，甚至近乎不可能的事情，也可以說 reach for the moon。

A: Did your parents have anything to do with your success?
你的成功與你父母有任何關係嗎？

B: Yes. They always encouraged me to **reach for the stars**.
有的。他們總是鼓勵我要追求遠大目標。

Gossip Box

什麼都會演，什麼都不奇怪！

被譽為「地表最強女演員」的梅姨，日前上美國知名主持人艾倫狄珍妮 (Ellen DeGeneres) 的訪談節目時，應觀眾來信要求，現場來了段即興表演，分別用性感的語調、一位正在分娩女子的方式以及青少年的方式，讀出主持人所提供的文稿，惟妙惟肖的演技獲得眾人讚賞，成為 YouTube 點閱率相當高的片段。

🎞 電影對白

米蘭達一進公司就先抱怨（Emily，艾蜜莉布朗特 (Emily Blunt) 飾）辦事不牢靠，然後開始對她喋喋不休地交辦事情。

Miranda: I don't understand why it's so difficult to confirm appointments.
我從來不知道確認預約這件事情有這麼難。

Emily: I'm so sorry, Miranda. I actually did confirm....
我很抱歉，米蘭達。我昨天真的有先確認……。

Miranda: Details of your *incompetence do not interest me. Tell Simone I won't approve that girl she sent me for the Brazilian *layout. Tell Richard I saw the pictures he sent for that feature on female *paratroopers and they're all so deeply unattractive. Is it impossible to find a lovely, slender female paratrooper? Am I **reaching for the stars** here? Not really.
妳辦事無能的細節我沒興趣聽。告訴席夢，我不喜歡她在巴西版裡用的女模。告訴理查我看過他送來的女傘兵專題照片，全都不能看，一點都不吸引人。難道沒辦法找到可愛又苗條的女傘兵嗎？還是我太強人所難？不是吧。

*incomepetence
[ɪn`kɑmpətəns] (n.) 無能，不稱職
*layout [`le.aʊt] (n.)（書籍、廣告等的）版面設計，版面編排
*paratrooper [`pærə.trupə] (n.) 傘兵

Doubt 《誘惑》

🎬 電影對白

米蘭達正在和編輯們討論當季服裝的搭配重點，不過編輯提出的構想都讓她不滿意，於是米蘭達自己挑了一件粉紅色蓬裙洋裝，詢問助手奈吉（Nigel，史丹利圖奇（Stanley Tucci）飾）有什麼想法。

Nigel: You know me. Give me a full *ballerina skirt and a *hint of *salon, and I'm *on board.

你懂我的，只要有芭蕾蓬裙和一點奢華風我就覺得 OK 了。

Miranda: But do you think it's too much like....

不過那似乎太像……。

Nigel: Like the Lacroix from July? I thought that, but no, not with the right *accessories.

和 Lacroix 七月的風格太接近？我本來這麼想，但加上正確的配件就不會。

Miranda: Where are the belts for this dress?

配這件洋裝的皮帶在哪裡？

[編輯手忙腳亂地找出可搭配的兩條腰帶]

Miranda: Why is no one ready?

為什麼就是沒人先準備好？

Editor: Here. It's **a tough call**. They're so different.

在這裡。實在很難決定，兩條皮帶風格完全不同。

*ballerina [ˌbæləˈrinə] (n.) 芭蕾舞女演員
*hint [hɪnt] (n.) 少許，微量
*salon [səˈlɑn] (n.) 高級精品店
*on board (phr.) 贊成
*accessory [ækˈsɛsəri] (n.) 配件

MP3 116

tough call 令人難以抉擇的事物

call 在此當名詞，表「決定」，原為運動比賽時裁判的「判決」之意。tough call 就代表令人猶豫不決、難以下決定的難題。

A: We're not sure whether we should buy an apartment or just rent.

我們還不確定要買公寓，還是用租的就好。

B: Yeah. That's always a **tough call**.

對啊，這總是很難做的決定。

📷 電影介紹

安修女（Sister Aloysius Beauvier，梅莉史翠普飾）是一位極度保守的教會學校校長，她的教區督導佛林神父（Father Brendan Flynn，菲力普塞默諾曼夫（Philip Seymour Hoffman）飾）卻是一位主張開放的神職人員。兩人之間看似以一位學童的福祉為賭注的鬥爭，究竟孰是孰非，讓捲入其中的詹修女（Sister James，艾美亞當斯（Amy Adams）飾）非常困惑。

🎬 電影對白

安修女找來米勒太太，打算告訴她神父與她兒子可能有染的事情。

Sister Beauvier: I am concerned about the relationship between Father Flynn and your son.

我很擔心你兒子和菲琳神父之間的關係。

Mrs. Miller: You don't say. Concerned. What do you mean, concerned?

是哦。擔心，你說的擔心是指什麼？

Sister Beauvier: That it may not be right.

這關係或許不大對。

Mrs. Miller: Well, there's something wrong with everybody, and their soul gotta be forgiven.

這個嘛，每個人都不完美，但他們的靈魂都會得到寬恕。

MP3 117

You don't say. 真的假的，是哦

不了解這個俚語的人，初聽到這句話可能會誤以為對方很沒禮貌，怎麼叫人「不要說話」。其實這句話有兩種意思，一是當對方告訴你某件事情時，你感到有點詫異（但並非不相信對方的話），或是想表示「我聽到了」，這時就可說 You don't say，像是我們中文常說的「真的假的？」「是喔」。

A: I heard that Bill and Suzie are having a baby.

我聽說比爾和蘇西有寶寶了。

B: You don't say.

是喔。

另一個情形是，當對方說了一件大家早就知道的事，你也可以諷刺地說這句話，中文類似於「那還用說？」

A: If you're trying to lose weight, you shouldn't eat that cupcake.

如果想減肥的話，妳就不該吃那個杯子蛋糕。

B: You don't say....

還用你說……。

Mamma Mia! 《媽媽咪亞！》

📹 電影介紹

多娜（Donna，梅莉史翠普飾）與女兒蘇菲（Sophie，亞曼達賽佛芮 (Amanda Seyfried) 飾）在希臘共同經營一間民宿。即將結婚的蘇菲無意間看到媽媽的日記，發現她曾與三位男士有過舊情，其中一位很可能就是她的親生父親，於是蘇菲便偷偷邀請這三個男人來島上參加婚禮，希望搞清楚究竟哪一位才是自己的生父。

🎬 電影對白

蘇菲的姊妹淘麗莎 (Lisa) 和艾莉 (Ali) 在婚禮前夕去找蘇菲，好久不見的三人非常開心。

Sophie: I'm getting married tomorrow. I'm so glad you're here, because I have a secret and I can't tell anybody else.

我明天就要結婚了。真高興妳們能來，因為我有個無法跟其他人說的祕密。

Lisa: Sophie, you're **knocked up**?

蘇菲，妳該不會是「中獎」了吧？

Sophie: No! No! No! I've invited my dad to my wedding.

不！不！不！我邀請我爸來參加我的婚禮。

Lisa: You're joking!

妳騙人！

Ali: You found him at least?

妳終於找到他了？

Sophie: No! No, no, no, no, not exactly.

不，也不算啦。

MP3 118

be knocked up
懷孕

knock sb. up 在俚語中表示「讓某人懷孕」，因此要形容某個女生不小心「中獎」，就可以說 be knocked up。

A: Do you know why Sam is marrying Ellen?

你知道山姆為什麼要娶愛倫嗎？

B: Yeah—because he **knocked her up**.

我知道，因為他把她肚子搞大了。

🎬 電影對白

多娜和她的老友蘿西 (Rosie)、坦雅 (Tanya)，因為蘇菲的婚禮而齊聚一堂，看見已亭亭玉立的蘇菲，兩人開始和多娜聊起蘇菲來。

Rosie: She's a **chip off the old block**!

她真是你的翻版啊！

Donna: If she were more like me, she wouldn't be getting married at 20.

如果她再像我一點的話，她就不會二十歲結婚了。

Tanya: Or married at all!

或是根本不會結婚！

MP3 119

chip off the old block
酷似父母的人

從一大塊東西掉出的小碎片，其外觀和性質當然與原來相去不遠。因此英文就用這句話來表示做子女的跟爸媽很像，也就是「有其父(母)必有其子(女)」。

A: Wow, Bill looks just like his father!

哇，比爾長得跟他爸真像！

B: Yep. He's a **chip off the old block**.

對啊。簡直就是一個模子刻出來的。

Gossip Box

演而優則「唱」的梅姨

梅莉史翠普堪稱是好萊塢獲獎最多的女星，然而她的能耐還不止於此。在《媽媽咪亞！》中，她不但一展歌喉，同時還得爬上爬下、邊唱邊跳。她打趣地說：「我那二十幾歲的孩子看到我在片中穿著工人服唱唱跳跳，簡直丟臉到想鑽進地洞裡去咧！」

The Iron Lady 《鐵娘子》

電影介紹

此為英國史上唯一的女首相 —— 柴契爾夫人 (Margaret Thatcher) 的傳記電影，描述這位鐵娘子老年時在家中整理亡夫遺物時，開始憶起自己年輕時所發生的種種，包括如何與丈夫相遇、涉足政壇、當選保守黨黨魁、經歷戰爭……到罹患老人癡呆症。本片除了讓觀眾得以一窺這位女強人的生平事蹟，還能瞭解英國近代各個重要歷史事件，而梅莉史翠普入木三分的演技更是本片的最大亮點。

電影對白

阿根廷大舉入侵福克蘭群島，聲稱自己握有該地主權。美國國務卿因此前來與柴契爾會晤，詢問柴契爾夫人是否真要為了宣示主權，出兵遠在英國好幾千哩外的福克蘭群島。

U.S. Secretary of State: So you are proposing to go to war over these islands. They're thousands of miles away, a handful of citizens, politically and economically insignificant, if you'll excuse me.
所以您打算要出兵這些島嶼。它們在好幾千哩之外，島民人數寥寥無幾，在政治和經濟上也沒什麼重要性，請容我這麼說。

Thatcher: Just like Hawaii, I imagine.
我想，就像夏威夷吧。

U.S. Secretary of State: I'm sorry?
不好意思，您說什麼？

Thatcher: 1941, when Japan attacked Pearl Harbor. Did America **go cap in hand** and ask Tojo for a peaceful *negotiation of terms? Did she turn her back on her own citizens there because the islands were thousands of miles from mainland United States? No, no, no! We will stand on principle or we shall not stand at all.
一九四一年，當日本偷襲珍珠港的時候。美國人有低聲下氣地向東條英機談判求和嗎？有棄自己的子民於不顧，就因為那裡離美國本土好幾千哩遠嗎？沒有，並沒有！我們要堅守原則，否則就無立足之地了。

*negotiation [nɪˌɡoʃiˋeʃən] (n.) 協商，談判

MP3 120

go/come cap in hand
大低聲下氣（討取）

人們對人說話時常會脫帽以表尊重，乞丐在行乞時也常會用手捧著帽子，請人把捐贈的東西丟進帽子裡。這個片語就是由這兩個情境而來的，表示低聲下氣、卑微地乞求別人。go / come cap in hand 為英國慣用說法，美國則比較常說 go / come hat in hand。

A: Maybe you parents will lend you the money.
或許你爸媽會借你這筆錢。

B: There's no way I'm **going to my parents hat in hand** asking for money.
我絕對不會低聲下氣去向我爸媽要錢。

A: Why did you forgive Brett for insulting you like that?
布瑞特那樣羞辱你，你怎麼會原諒他？

B: Well, he **came to me hat in hand** and apologized.
嗯，因為他低聲下氣來向我道歉。

©Featureflash / shutterstock.com

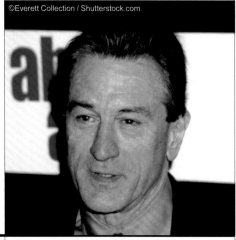

©Everett Collection / Shutterstock.com

LANGUAGE GUIDE

Stella Adler Studio of Acting
史黛拉愛德勒戲劇工作坊

演員暨導演的史黛拉愛德勒 (Stella Adler, 1919-1992) 於一九四〇年代開始從事戲劇教學，並在一九四九年成立自己的工作坊，數十年教學不懈，一九八五年更在洛杉磯成立了史黛拉愛德樂戲劇學院暨劇場 (Stella Adler Academy and Theatre)。這所學校除了教授舞台表演技巧，也開設聲音表情及演説、舞台化妝等專業課程，除了本文的勞勃狄尼洛、哈維凱托，馬龍白蘭度 (Marlon Brando) 也是她的得意門生。

Martin Scorsese 馬丁史柯西斯

導演馬丁史柯西斯被視為電影史上最具影響力的導演之一，不但編、導、演、製作全方位從事電影創作獲獎無數，也志願投入電影保存工作。

年輕的馬丁史柯西斯與勞勃狄尼洛

Robert De Niro 勞勃狄尼洛

MP3 121

Born in New York's Greenwich Village in 1943, Robert De Niro was [1]**brought up** by his mother in the Little Italy neighborhood of Lower Manhattan after his parents, both artists, divorced in 1945. De Niro's father, who lived nearby, often took him to the movies, and he liked to impress his mother by [2]**imitating** the actors he saw when he returned home. De Niro made his first stage appearance at the age of ten, playing the [3]**Cowardly** Lion in a local production of *The Wizard of Oz*. Although he joined a gang in his teens—he was known as "Bobby Milk" for his pale [4]**complexion**—his interest in acting saved him from a life of crime.

After dropping out of high school to study at the famous Stella Adler Studio of Acting, De Niro began his career with roles in early Brian De Palma films like *The Wedding Party* (1963) and *Greetings* (1968). His career took off when he was chosen by Martin Scorsese to appear opposite Harvey Keitel in the 1973 crime drama *Mean Streets*. De Niro's [5]**intense** portrayal of the [6]**reckless** gambler Johnny Boy won him the role of the young Vito Corleone in *The Godfather Part II* (1974), a performance that earned him his first Academy Award, for Best Supporting Actor.

In 1976, De Niro continued his collaboration with Scorsese, playing the [8]**psychotic** Travis Bickle in *Taxi Driver*, widely [7]**acknowledged** as one of the best films of all time. The [9]**duo** would go on to make many more films together, including *Raging Bull* (1980), which won the actor his second Academy Award, this time for Best Actor, *Goodfellas* (1990) and *Casino* (1995). More recently, De Niro has found success in comedies like the box office hit *Meet the Parents* (2000) and its sequels, and even as a director with *The Good Shepherd* (2006), a spy drama starring Matt Damon and Angelina Jolie.

©cinemafestival / Shutterstock.com

勞勃狄尼洛於一九四三年在紐約格林威治村出生，同為藝術家的雙親一九四五年離婚之後，他便在母親撫養之下於曼哈頓的小義大利地區長大。住在附近的父親常帶他去看電影，而他回到家便喜歡模仿他看到的演員來贏得媽媽讚賞。狄尼洛十歲時首次登台亮相，在當地演出的《綠野仙蹤》裡扮演膽小的獅子。雖然青少年時曾加入幫派——他因皮膚白而被稱為「牛奶鮑比」——但他對演戲的興趣讓他免於誤入歧途。

在高中輟學、進入知名的史黛拉愛德勒戲劇工作坊研習後，狄尼洛以接演早期布萊恩狄帕馬電影的角色展開演藝生涯，比如《婚宴》（一九六三）和《祝福》（一九六八）。當他被馬丁史柯西斯挑中，在一九七三年犯罪電影《殘酷大街》與哈維凱托演對手戲，他的事業就此展翅高飛。狄尼洛在片中把魯莽的賭客強尼男孩演得活靈活現，為他贏得《教父第二集》（一九七四）中年輕的維托柯里昂一角，這次演出更讓他榮獲他的第一座奧斯卡獎：最佳男配角。

一九七六年，狄尼洛繼續和史柯西斯合作，在公認史上最佳電影之一的《計程車司機》中飾演精神病患崔維畢可。這對搭檔繼續攜手拍攝多部電影，包括為他贏得第二座奧斯卡獎的《蠻牛》（一九八〇）——這一次是最佳男主角，以及《四海好傢伙》（一九九〇）和《賭國風雲》（一九九五）。近年來，狄尼洛也在諸如賣座片《門當父不對》和其續集等喜劇大放異彩，甚至當起導演執導《特務風雲》（二〇〇六）：麥特戴蒙和安潔莉娜裘莉領銜主演的間諜劇。

LANGUAGE GUIDE

Brian De Palma 布萊恩狄帕馬

導演布萊恩狄帕馬縱橫影壇四十年，最擅長處理犯罪及驚悚電影，叫好又叫座的作品包括凱文科斯納 (Kevin Costner) 主演的《鐵面無私》(The Untouchables)、湯姆克魯斯 (Tom Cruise) 主演的《不可能的任務》(Mission: Impossible) 以及二〇一四年重拍一九七六年的同名經典驚悚作品《魔女嘉莉》(Carrie)。

©Featureflash / Shutterstock.com

VOCABULARY BANK

1) **bring up** [brɪŋ ʌp] (phr.) 撫養，養育
Catherine was brought up by her grandparents.
凱瑟琳是由祖父母撫養長大。

2) **imitate** [ˈɪməˌtet] (v.) 模仿，仿效
Larry is good at imitating foreign accents.
賴瑞很會模仿外國口音。

3) **cowardly** [kauədli] (adv.) 膽小的，怯懦的
The cowardly robber only targeted women.
那個癟三搶匪只挑女性下手。

4) **complexion** [kəmˈplɛkʃən] (n.) 膚色，氣色
Maria has a dark complexion.
瑪麗亞的膚色較深。

5) **intense** [ɪnˈtɛns] (a.) （感情）激烈的，強烈的
The actor is good at expressing intense emotions.
這名演員擅長表現強烈的情感。

6) **reckless** [ˈrɛklɪs] (a.) 魯莽的，不顧後果的，危險的
The man was found guilty of reckless driving.
該名男子被判危險駕駛的罪名。

7) **acknowledge** [əkˈnɑlɪdʒ] (v.) 承認，認可
The historian is acknowledged as an expert in his field.
這名歷史學家在該領域當中被視為專家。

進階字彙

8) **psychotic** [saɪˈkɑtɪk] (a.) 有精神病的
The prison has a special ward for psychotic prisoners.
這所監獄有專門關精神病囚犯的牢房。

9) **duo** [ˈduo] (n.) 二人組
Simon and Garfunkel were a popular folk duo.
賽門與葛芬科是很受歡迎的民謠雙人團體。

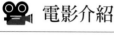

The Godfather Part II
《教父 2》

🎥 電影介紹

本片由兩條故事線交織而成，主線是第二代教父麥可科里昂（艾爾帕西諾 (Al Pacino) 飾演），穿插第一代教父維托柯里昂（Vito Corleone，勞勃狄尼洛飾演）在紐約發跡後回鄉報殺父之仇的故事。父親為了家庭、親友成為黑道，兒子想由黑漂白卻家破人亡，形成強烈的對比。

🎞 電影對白

年輕的維托跟合夥行竊的朋友被角頭老大費努奇 (Fanucci) 強收保護費，兩個朋友都傾向乖乖交錢，但維托獨排眾議，出面與費努奇幹旋。

Vito Corleone: I'm short of money right now. I've been out of work...so just give me a little time. You understand, don't you?

我現在缺錢。我失業一陣子了……請多我一點時間。你能了解的，對吧？

Fanucci: You've got balls, young man! How come I never heard of you before? You've got a lot of guts. I'll find you some work for good money. **No hard feelings**, right? If I can help you, let me know.

你有種，年輕人！我之前怎麼都沒聽説過你這號人物？你的膽子很大。我會幫你物色賺大錢的工作。不傷和氣，對吧？有什麼要我幫忙的，儘管告訴我。

MP3 123

no hard feelings 不傷和氣

hard feeling 就是「不爽」。這個詞經常為複數，用在否定句。跟人説 No hard feelings? 表示之前彼此曾發生不愉快，吵架不會説什麼好聽話嘛；no hard feelings 就是跟人家爭執過後，確認彼此不傷和氣，不開心的事情就別往心裡去了。

A: I'm really sorry for all those things I said. **No hard feelings**, right?

我對於自己説過的話感到很抱歉。不傷和氣吧？

B: I'm sorry for what I said too. **No hard feelings**.

我也對我説的話感到抱歉，我們就當沒事了吧。

Gossip Box

銀幕硬漢竟是俗辣？

好萊塢最近流行拍老先生電影，像是《一路玩到掛》(The Bucket List) 這種，勞勃狄尼洛跟席維斯史特龍 (Sylvester Stallone) 也在二〇一三年合拍拳擊片《進擊的大佬》(Grudge Match)。他告訴史特龍：Listen, Sly...I had a bad rib injury not long ago that I'm still nursing, so please—don't hurt me!（聽著，老史……我不久以前肋骨嚴重受傷，現在還在療養，所以拜託——不要傷到我！）但其實全片都是用替身，只有兩場戲要他們自己打，史特龍從頭到尾小心翼翼，拍完還問候對手肋骨的傷還好吧？沒想到勞勃狄尼洛竟然説：I never had a rib injury—I just told you that so you wouldn't kill me!（我的肋骨其實沒受傷——我那樣説你才不會殺了我！）

Analyze That 《老大靠邊閃：歪打正著》

🎥 電影介紹

黑手黨老大維迪（Vitti，勞勃迪尼洛飾）刑期即將屆滿出獄之時突然發瘋。FBI 探員於是找來他入獄前的精神科醫師班索貝爾（Ben Sobel，比利克里斯托 (Billy Crystal) 飾），索貝爾非常不願意再跟這個黑手黨老大攪和在一起，但事與願違，而硬把兩人湊在一起的結果，就是小衝突不斷，大爭執不停⋯⋯。

🎬 電影對白

維迪在監獄中跟囚犯們一起觀賞電視劇《小凱撒》(*Little Caesar*)：劇中角頭老大凱撒 (Caesar) 正在揪出內賊，而且覺得達克斯 (Ducks) 嫌疑最大。

Ducks: What is so hard to understand here? You said yourself Peezee was a mamaluke and he couldn't be trusted. Now all of a sudden you **got a soft spot for** this guy.

有這麼難懂嗎？你自己也說過皮茲是個笨蛋，不能相信他。現在你忽然就喜歡他了。

Caesar: I just don't think it was him.

我就是覺得不會是他幹的。

Ducks: OK, I'll buy it. If not Peezee, then who? Who? Tell me.

好，我接受。如果不是皮茲，那是誰？誰？告訴我。

Caesar: I think it was you, Ducks.

我認為是你，達克斯。

MP3 124

have a soft spot for someone
喜愛（某人）

soft spot 指的是「特別親切的感覺」，因此當你對一個人有好感，或是有點喜歡，就可以用 have a soft spot for someone 來形容對他的感覺。

A: You **have a soft spot for** Billy, don't you?

你喜歡比利，對吧？

B: No, I don't. I just don't think it's fair to accuse him of cheating without proof.

我沒有。我只是認為沒有證據就指控他作弊是不公平的。

🎬 電影對白

受制於 FBI 的規定，維迪必須住在班索貝爾家，他的太太蘿拉（Laura，麗莎庫卓 (Lisa Kudrow) 飾）大為光火，找索貝爾私下理論，維迪卻大搖大擺跑來要咖啡。

Vitti: Somebody said something about coffee.

剛剛有人提到咖啡。

Laura: Oh yeah, that was you. You said you wanted some.

對喔，就是你嘛。你說要來些咖啡的。

Vitti: So, **what's the holdup**?

那還等什麼？

Laura: Ben, why don't you make your friend some coffee? I'm gonna take a long bath. And hopefully drown.

班，你何不泡杯咖啡給你朋友？我要去好好洗個澡，希望能淹死。

MP3 125

What's the holdup?
何事耽擱？

holdup 是指事情進行到一半停下來，進度受阻。所以問人 What's the holdup? 就表示你覺得進度被對方拖延了。這句話超級適用於你在等人開始做一件事，卻看他拖拖拉拉一直不動手，這時就可以丟給他一句 What's the holdup?

A: Can you wait for me ten more minutes?

你可以再等我十分鐘嗎？

B: **What's the holdup**? I'm in a hurry.

你拖拖拉拉是在幹嘛？我很趕耶。

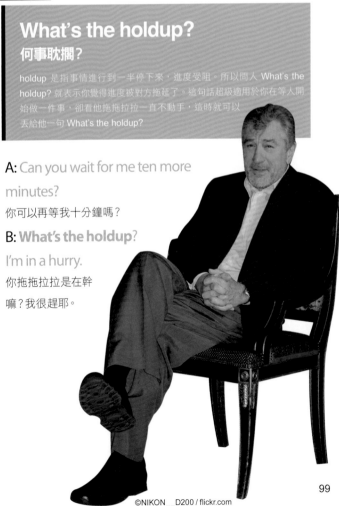

The Good Shepherd 《特務風雲：中情局誕生秘辛》

🎥 電影介紹

第二次世界大戰即將開打，以威廉蘇利文將軍（General William Sullivan，勞勃迪尼洛飾）為首的美國軍方人士，透過耶魯、哈佛大學秘密兄弟會，吸納如愛德華威爾森（Edward Wilson，麥特戴蒙（Matt Damon）飾）這類白種男性精英進行諜報訓練，成為中央情報局 (CIA) 的濫觴。

🎞 電影對白

二戰結束，愛德華結束情報工作回國。某一天，當初吸納他的蘇利文將軍又跑來他家。

General Sullivan: Well, while everybody has been feeling good about themselves, the Soviets, without firing a shot have taken over half the World. They're **breathing down our necks**. They'll be in our backyard before you know it.
哎，正當大家志得意滿的同時（編註：指美國戰勝），蘇聯不費一槍一彈就佔領半個世界。他們正對我們虎視眈眈。一不留神他們就要跑到我們後院了。

MP3 126

breathe down one's neck 緊盯某人

若能感覺到某人在你的脖子後面呼吸，那人肯定跟你貼得超近，美語中即以這句表示「緊盯某人」，若是用在工作場合中，則可表示「嚴密監督某人」。

A: Why didn't the suspect try to get rid of the evidence?
那名嫌犯為什麼沒把證據給摧毀？

B: Because the police were **breathing down his neck**.
因為警察正緊盯著他。

A: Your boss is a real control freak.
你的老闆真是一個控制狂。

B: Yeah. It's impossible to get anything done with him **breathing down my neck** all the time.
是啊。他一天到晚緊迫盯人，哪能做事啊。

🎞 電影對白

蘇利文將軍病入膏肓來日無多，他臨走之前告訴愛德華要注意身邊所有的人，誰都不能相信。

General Sullivan: I love this country.
我愛這個國家。

Edward Wilson: We all do, sir. We all do.
我們都愛，長官。我們都愛。

General Sullivan: No matter what anyone tells you, there'll be no one you can really trust. I'm afraid **when all said and done** we're all just clerks too.
不管別人跟你說什麼，沒有一個能夠百分之百相信。恐怕到頭來，你我都只是小囉嘍。

MP3 127

when all said and done 畢竟，總之

這句話是在做總結，字面上表示「說到頭來，做到最後」，也就是「畢竟，總之」的意思。

A: Why did everybody get so depressed when our team lost the match?
我們的球隊輸了大家幹嘛難過成這樣？

B: Good question. **When all is said and done**, it's just a game.
好問題。不過就是球賽罷了。

©Featureflash / Shutterstock.com

©betto rodrigues / Shutterstock.com

電影對白

蘇利文將軍認為不受國家控制卻法力無邊的秘密組織，一定會對國家造成危害，必須回歸體制，成立受國家管控的部門。

General Sullivan: I'm concerned that too much power will end up in the hands of too few. It's always in someone's best interest to promote enemies, real or imagined. I see this as America's eyes and ears. I don't want it to become its heart and soul. So I told the President, for this to work there's going to have to be some kind of civilian oversight.

我擔心過大的權力最後會落入極少數人手裡。總是有些人為了一己私利塑造敵人，不管是真敵人還是假想敵。我把這個部門視為美國的探查世界的耳目。我不希望它反過來控制國家的命脈和靈魂。因此我告訴總統，這一切唯有透過某種公民監督才行得通。

Edward Wilson: Oversight? How can you have a covert organization if you have people **looking over your shoulder**?

監督？如果工作時有人在背後探頭探腦，要怎麼建立秘密組織？

`MP3 128`

look over one's shoulder
緊密監視；提心吊膽

字面上的意思是「越過肩膀看另一邊」，如果是別人從你背後往前看，那就表示這個人在你身後緊盯著你，意思跟前面的 breathe down one's neck 相同。

A: Why did you decide to move out?
你為什麼要搬出來住？

B: My parents were always **looking over my shoulder**.
我爸媽之前老是對我緊迫盯人。

若是你轉頭看肩膀後面，那就是覺得背後有威脅，表示「提心吊膽」。

A: Why did the criminal turn himself in to the police?
那個罪犯為什麼跑去找警察自首？

B: He was tired of always having to **look over his shoulder**.
他受夠了整天提心吊膽的生活。

Amy 艾美亞當斯
Adams

SHOWBIZ WORD

musical theater 音樂劇

musical theater 是一種結合歌舞及話劇的表演形式，所演出的音樂劇作品就是 musical。雖然 musical 與 opera（歌劇）都以歌唱為主要抒發形式，但兩者還是有差別：opera 是從頭唱到尾，中間都不講話，而且演員不像 musical 那樣載歌載舞、蹦蹦跳跳。本書提到的《奧克拉荷馬！》(Oklahoma!)、《悲慘世界》(Les Misérables) 都屬於 musical。

dinner theater 餐廳秀

這是一種結合餐廳、酒吧與劇場，讓觀眾一邊吃飯、小酌，一邊看秀的娛樂形式，提供的表演經常是舞台表演（如脫口秀）、舞台劇或音樂劇。這種餐廳於一九七〇年代在美國盛極一時，現在已較不流行。

live-action/animated film
真人動畫電影

在過去，live-action film（真人演出、非動畫電影）與 animated film（動畫電影）是相對的兩種影片拍攝形式，但隨著科技進步，真人演出已經透過各種電腦拍攝技術與動畫結合了，而這種形式的電影就稱為 live-action/animated film。

number   曲目，音樂片段

number 是指音樂劇、歌劇當中的一支歌曲、一段舞蹈或一首樂曲。

Born into an American military family in Italy on August 20, 1974, Amy Adams moved from base to base until her family settled in Colorado when she was eight. She danced [1]**ballet** and sang in the [2]**choir** during her high school years, but turned her attention to musical theater after graduating. She was performing at a dinner theater in Minneapolis when she made her movie debut in *Drop Dead Gorgeous* (1999). Co-star Kirstie Alley (of *Cheers* fame) encouraged her to move to Hollywood and pursue an acting career.

Adams gained wider exposure as Brenda Strong, Leonardo DiCaprio's love interest in Steven Spielberg's *Catch Me If You Can* (2002). Her real breakthrough, though, would come later in the independent film *Junebug* (2005). Adams' cheerful, [3]**pregnant** wife in *Junebug* [8]**garnered** much [4]**critical** praise, leading to bigger roles like Princess Giselle in Disney's live-action/animated *Enchanted* (2007). As Giselle, she got to [5]**show off** her [6]**vocal** skills in numbers like "Happy Working Song," which she later sang live at the Oscars.

Adams next delivered two [7]**memorable** performances opposite Meryl Streep, first as a young nun in *Doubt* (2008), which earned her an Oscar nomination for best supporting actress—one of five in her career thus far, and next in *Julie & Julia* (2009). Since then, she's had her choice of roles. 2013 in particular was a banner year for Adams, who appeared in three hit movies: *Man of Steel, American Hustle* and *Her*. It's safe to say that we'll be seeing a lot more of this talented actress in the future!

©Everett Collection / Shutterstock.com

©Featureflash / Shutterstock.com

VOCABULARY BANK

1) **ballet** [bæˋle] (n.) 芭蕾舞，芭蕾舞團
Peter dreams of becoming a ballet dancer.
彼得夢想成為一名芭蕾舞者。

2) **choir** [kwaɪr] (n.) 合唱團，唱詩班
Dorothy sang in her high school choir.
桃樂絲高中的時候參加學校合唱團。

3) **pregnant** [ˋprɛgnənt] (a.) 懷孕的
The woman is pregnant with twins.
那個婦女懷了雙胞胎。

4) **critical** [ˋkrɪtɪkəl] (a.) 評論的，批評的
The band's first album was a financial and critical success.
這個樂團的首張專輯叫好又叫座。

5) **show off** [ʃo ɔf] (phr.) 炫耀，愛表現
Jimmy is always showing off in front of his classmates.
吉米老愛在班上同學面前賣弄。

6) **vocal** [ˋvokəl] (a.) 聲音的，歌唱的
It takes years of vocal training to become an opera singer.
要經過多年的聲樂訓練才能成為歌劇演員。

7) **memorable** [ˋmɛmərəbəl] (a.) 難忘的，值得懷念的
The singer gave a memorable performance at the charity concert.
這歌手在慈善演唱會的表演很令人難忘。

進階字彙

8) **garner** [ˋgɑrnə] (v.) 贏得，獲得
The author's latest novel has garnered several awards.
這位作家的最新小說已經獲得不少獎項。

TONGUE-TIED NO MORE

banner year 豐收年

banner [ˋbænə] 當名詞時是「代表旗幟」或「橫條大標語」，也是網頁上方大大橫擺的廣告位置，當形容詞則表示「傑出的」。當我們說某一年是某人／機構的 banner year，就表示那一年表現不只是 OK 而已，還非常出色，有突破性的表現。
A: How are your investments doing this year?
你今年的投資表現如何？
B: Great! It's been a banner year for the stock market.
非常棒！今年股市真是大豐收。

it's safe to say (that) 可以很篤定地說

safe 是「安全的」，當一個人說的話用 safe 來形容，表示他說的絕不誇張，有憑有據，絕不會被打槍。
A: Business has been really bad this year.
今年的生意真的很差。
B: Yeah. I think it's safe to say we won't be getting a Christmas bonus.
是啊。看來我能很篤定地說，我們今年不會有年終獎金了。

一九七四年八月二十日出生於義大利，來自美國軍人家庭的艾美亞當斯，從小隨著全家搬來搬去，不斷更換軍事基地，直到八歲全家定居科羅拉多州為止。她在中學時期跳芭蕾、參加合唱團，但注意力在畢業後轉向音樂劇。她在明尼亞波利一間餐廳秀劇院演出期間，於《美麗擠出來》（一九九九）獻出電影處女秀。同劇女星克莉絲蒂艾莉（以《歡樂酒店》成名）鼓勵她移居好萊塢發展戲劇事業。

亞當斯在史蒂芬史匹柏的《神鬼交鋒》（二○○二）中飾演李奧納多狄卡皮歐的戀愛對象布蘭達史強，打開知名度。但她真正的突破是拜之後接演的獨立電影《妙媳婦見公婆》（二○○五）所賜。她在片中飾演快樂的孕妻，廣獲好評，也為她帶來更大的角色，例如迪士尼真人動畫片《曼哈頓奇緣》（二○○七）中的吉賽兒公主。扮演吉賽兒，她得以在《快樂工作歌》等樂曲中展現歌唱技巧，她後來也在奧斯卡頒獎典禮現場獻唱這首歌。

接下來亞當斯有兩次令人難忘的演出，都是與梅莉史翠普同場飆戲：首先是《誘惑》（二○○八）的年輕修女，此角為她贏得奧斯卡最佳女配角提名——她至今共獲五次；再來是《美味關係》（二○○九）。此後，她可以自己選角色了。對亞當斯來說，二○一三年尤其是豐收的一年，她一共主演三部賣座片：《超人：鋼鐵英雄》、《瞞天大佈局》和《雲端情人》。很篤定的是：未來我們將會很常見到這位天才女星！

艾美亞當斯

Amy Adams

Catch Me if You Can 《神鬼交鋒》

📷 電影介紹

法蘭克（Frank，李奧納多狄卡皮歐 (Leonardo DiCaprio) 飾）原本有個幸福美滿的家庭，後來家道中落，父母離婚，法蘭克受不了打擊而離家出走，並以偽造支票的方式換取金錢花用，沒想到因此發了一筆橫財，也成了聯邦調查局追捕的對象。查緝的主要負責人是卡爾（Carl，湯姆漢克 (Tom Hanks) 飾），兩人就在這一追一逃的過程中，產生惺惺相惜的情感……。

MP3 131

hit the jackpot 中大獎

jackpot [ˋdʒæk͵pɑt] 是「梭哈等賭博遊戲中所累積的最大賭注、獎金或比賽中的頭獎」，hit the jackpot 就是「中大獎、大獲全勝」的意思。

A: How can Allen afford to buy a new house?
艾倫怎麼買得起新房子？

B: He bought a lottery ticket and **hit the jackpot**.
他買了一張彩券，結果中了頭彩。

🎞 電影對白

法蘭克愛上一位護士布蘭達（Brenda，艾美亞當斯飾），於是開始冒充醫生，和布蘭達在同一家醫院工作。兩人的感情突飛猛進，法蘭克決定到布蘭達家會見她的父母。為討好布蘭達的律師父親，他又謊稱自己是南加大法學院的畢業生。

Frank: Before I went to medical school, I passed the bar in California. I practiced law for one year. Then I decided why not try my hand at *pediatrics?
在我去上醫學院之前，我通過加州的律師資格。我執業了一年。然後，我決定何不試試看小兒科呢？

Brenda: You're just full of surprises.
你總是給人意外驚喜。

Brenda's mom: Oh, my. A doctor and a lawyer. Well, I'd say that Brenda **hit the jackpot**.
喔，老天。又是醫生又是律師。嗯，我該說布蘭達釣到大金龜了。

*pediatrics [͵pidɪˋætrɪks] 小兒科

Julie & Julia 《美味關係》

🎞 電影對白

茉莉不敢吃蛋也不敢碰蛋，但是今天的料理要用到蛋，所以找了好友莎拉 (Sarah) 來幫忙。

Sarah: "Immediately and gently push the white over with a wooden spoon for two to three seconds." Immediately.
「迅速而輕柔的用木匙把蛋白推過去，拌兩三秒。」要迅速。

Julie: Eww…disgusting.
噁……好噁心。

Sarah: Oh, maybe the eggs aren't fresh. Julia says the eggs have to be fresh.
喔，或許是蛋不新鮮。茉莉亞書上說蛋要新鮮。

Julie: They are fresh.
蛋很新鮮。

Sarah: OK. You don't have to **bite my head off**. I'm just quoting Julia.
好啦。妳不必兇我。我只是引述茉莉亞的話。

📷 電影介紹

茉莉（Julie，艾美亞當斯飾）是個不快樂的女性上班族，為了尋找生活寄託，決定將六〇年代電視名廚茉莉亞（Julia，梅莉史翠普 (Meryl Streep) 飾）所寫的法式料理食譜從頭到尾做一遍，並將過程記錄在網誌上。

MP3 132

bite sb's head off 對某人兇巴巴

當有人心情不好，隨便跟他說一句話就像鬥雞一樣，跟你嗆聲準備吵架，這樣的行為就可以用 bite sb's head off 來形容。

A: It looks like Ellen's in a bad mood today.
看起來艾倫今天心情很差。

B: Yeah. I asked her if something was wrong and she **bit my head off**.
對啊。我問她是不是有什麼不對勁，她還兇了我一頓。

📽 電影介紹

改編自美國拳壇傳奇故事，描述狄奇與米奇這對兄弟在職業拳壇的奮鬥史。擁有拳擊天份的狄奇（Dicky，克里斯汀貝爾 (Christian Bale) 飾）前途原本一片看好，卻因染上毒癮而自毀前程；米奇（Micky，馬克華伯格 (Mark Wahlberg) 飾）雖努力不懈，卻始終交不出漂亮的成績單。出獄後的狄奇改過自新，重新接掌擔任米奇的教練一職，這對兄弟聯手搭檔，燃燒彼此的鬥魂，一路過關斬將。

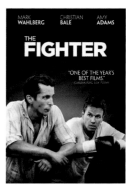

🎞 電影對白

米奇帶女友夏琳（Charlene，艾美亞當斯飾）到高級區去看了一部不像他們會看的電影，米奇在看電影時頻打瞌睡，夏琳對這部片也興趣缺缺。於是夏琳質問他，他是不是有女朋友，才刻意帶她來這麼遠的地方約會。

Charlene: What's going on? You got a girlfriend or something? You hiding me from her?

到底怎麼了？你是不是有女朋友還是什麼的？背著她偷偷跟我約會？

Micky: I don't have a girlfriend, all right? I...I like you. I came here 'cause I don't wanna show my face in Lowell. I told everybody I was gonna win that fight and get **back on track**.

我真的沒有女朋友，好不好？我……很喜歡妳。會帶妳來這裡是因為我不想被熟人看到，我告訴大家這場拳擊我會贏還會重回拳壇。

`MP3 133`

back on track 重回正軌

track 是指「軌道」，on track 就是在軌道上跑，路線和目標都很清楚。back on track 用來表示原本遭遇困境，就像火車脫軌跑不動，之後重整旗鼓再出發，讓一切回歸正常，就可說 get back on track。

A: How is your project coming along?

你的計劃進行得如何？

B: I was behind schedule for a while, but now it's **back on track**.

我之前進度有點落後，但現在已經重新上軌道了。

American Hustle 《瞞天大佈局》

電影介紹

故事改編自七〇年代美國聯邦調查局備受爭議的「釣魚執法」真實案件。厄文（Irving，克里斯汀貝爾飾）與情婦希妮（Sydney，化名為伊蒂絲（Edith），艾美亞當斯飾）是對手法高明的詐騙搭擋，在一次行動下被捕，為了能脫罪，被迫與 FBI 幹員瑞奇（Richie，布萊德利庫柏（Bradley Cooper）飾）合作，設局蒐集政客關說收賄的罪證，企圖一舉揪出所有違法官員。只是厄文的妻子羅莎琳（Rosalyn，珍妮佛勞倫斯（Jennifer Lawrence）飾）像顆不定時炸彈一樣，可能是造成整個行動失敗的原因！

MP3 134

go all the way
發生關係，上床

all the way 表示從起點到終點走完全程。親密關係包括牽牽小手、親親抱抱，到最後發生性關係，口語中會以 go all the way 來表示達到最終階段，也就是「上床」了。

A: How long did you and Cindy go out before you **went all the way**?
你跟辛蒂約會多久才上床？

B: About a month.
大概一個月。

電影對白

瑞奇曾和伊蒂絲有過約定，要真正相愛且了解對方之後才能發生關係。但現在在伊蒂絲房裡的瑞奇已慾火焚身，剎也剎不住。

Edith: I am not gonna **go all the way** until we do it for real, remember?
我不會跟你上床，除非我們真的要在一起，記得嗎？

Richie: I wanna do it now!
我現在就想要！

Edith: That's what we agreed on, all right? So, we're not gonna do that, all right?
我們之前講好了，好嗎？所以我們現在還不可以，好嗎？

Gossip Box

**艾美和珍妮佛女女激吻
超吸睛**

藉著在《瞞天大佈局》中的精湛演出，艾美亞當斯一舉奪下金球獎最佳喜劇女演員。在片中飾演小三的她徹底惹怒了正宮珍妮佛勞倫斯，沒想到珍妮佛「宣示主權」的方式竟是對她來一記激吻！這血脈賁張的一幕令觀眾印象深刻。事後艾美在受訪時表示，這橋段其實是導演建議的，不過她也樂在其中，因為珍妮佛實在是太可愛了！

Doubt 《誘惑》

🎥 電影介紹

安修女（Sister Aloysius Beauvier，梅莉史翠普飾）是一位極度保守的教會學校校長，她的教區督導佛林神父（Father Brendan Flynn，菲力普塞默諾曼夫（Philip Seymour Hoffman）飾）卻是一位主張開放的神職人員。兩人之間看似以一位學童的福祉為賭注的鬥爭，究竟孰是孰非，讓捲入其中的詹修女（Sister James，艾美亞當斯飾）非常困惑。

MP3 135

up to no good 心術不正

up to 是「在幹嘛」，好比問人 What are you up to? 就只是想知道「你在幹嘛？」但說 up to something 表示「謀劃」，就帶有負面意味，例如：I think she's up to something.（我覺得她心懷不軌。）當我們說某人做壞事，或是計劃要做壞事時，就可以說他 up to no good。

A: What are those boys doing over there in the parking lot?

那幾個男孩在停車場那邊幹嘛？

B: I don't know, but it looks like they're **up to no good**.

不知道。但看來他們似乎要搞鬼。

📽 電影對白

詹修女是年輕的新進教師。校長安修女跑來她的教室講台翻箱倒櫃，從抽屜裡拿出一幅教宗的錶框黑白照。

Sister Aloysius Beauvier: You should frame something. Put it up on the blackboard. Put the pope up.

妳應該找個東西裱起來。把它掛在黑板上。就掛教宗這張吧。

Sister James: That's the wrong pope. He's deceased.

但妳弄錯教宗了。他已經過世了。

Sister Aloysius Beauvier: I don't care what pope it is. Use the glass to see behind you. Children should think you have eyes in the back of your head.

我才不管這是哪個教宗。用裱框的玻璃看後面。孩子們應該要覺得妳腦袋後面有長眼睛。

Sister James: Wouldn't that be a little frightening?

那樣不會有點嚇人嗎？

Sister Aloysius Beauvier: Only to the ones who are **up to no good**.

只有心懷不軌的人才會被嚇到。

📽 電影對白

詹修女向安修女告密，懷疑佛林神父與一位男童之間有不正當的關係。安修女把佛林神父找來對質，佛林神父的解釋非常合理，還說如果不相信他的話，安修女大可找學生指導員麥昆先生 (Mr. McGuinn) 求證。

Sister James: What a relief. That explains everything. Thanks be to God. Look, Sister, it was all a mistake.

真是鬆了一口氣。一切真相大白了。感謝上帝。看吧，安修女，全都是一場誤會。

Sister Aloysius Beauvier: And if I talk to Mr. McGuinn?

如果我找麥昆先生來談一談呢？

Father Brendan Flynn: Talk to him, **by all means**. But now that the boy's secret's out, I'm gonna have to remove him from the altar boys. That's what I was trying to avoid.

找他談，沒問題。但現在那孩子的秘密曝光了，我必須將他從輔祭男童除名。這正是我一直想避免的。

MP3 136

by all means 當然，沒問題

這個片語可以單獨當一個句子，也可放在句尾，表示接受別人的提議或請求，也就是「沒問題」的意思。

A: May I borrow your pen?

我可以借你的筆嗎？

B: **By all means**.

當然囉。

Robert Downey, Jr. 小勞勃道尼

©s_bukley / Shutterstock.com

Born in Manhattan on April 4, 1965 to an underground director and an actress, Robert Downey, Jr. made his film debut at the age of five, playing a puppy in his father's comedy *Pound*. He continued performing in his father's films into his teenage years, when he also spent summers [8]**honing** his acting skills at a performing arts camp in the Catskills. When his parents divorced in 1978, Downey moved to California with his father, but later dropped out of high school and returned to New York to pursue his acting career.

Downey appeared in several off-Broadway productions and joined the cast of *Saturday Night Live*, but headed back to California to play James Spader's [10]**sidekick** in the 1985 drama *Tuff Turf*. He soon found himself [1]**running with** the Brat Pack, playing a school [2]**bully** in *Weird Science* (1985) and his first leading role opposite Molly Ringwald in *The Pick-up Artist* (1987). That same year, Downey won acclaim for his portrayal of Julian Wells, a rich boy [3]**addicted** to drugs in *Less Than Zero*. This led to bigger roles in bigger movies—he costarred with Mel Gibson in the action comedy *Air America* (1990), and his performance as Charlie Chaplin in *Chaplin* (1992) won him a best actor Oscar nomination.

[4]**Unfortunately**, Downey began to [9]**reprise** his *Less Than Zero* role in real life in the mid-90s, developing a drug habit that [5]**threatened** to end his career. But after he finally kicked his habit, he made a huge [6]**comeback**. 2008's *Iron Man*, in which he plays the title character, was a critical and box office smash, and his role as an Australian actor in *Tropic Thunder* that same year won him another Oscar nomination. Since then, Downey's name has been a [7]**guarantee** of box office success, whether as Tony Stark in other Marvel movies or Sherlock Holmes in Guy Ritchie's Holmes movies.

LANGUAGE GUIDE

Marvel Comics 驚奇漫畫

驚奇漫畫於一九三九年成立，最早叫做 Timely Comics，後經過數次更名，現在母公司為驚奇娛樂 (Marvel Entertainment)，並棣屬於華特迪士尼公司 (Walt Disney Company) 底下。公司的幾名漫畫家像是史丹李 (Stan Lee)、傑克科比 (Jack Kirby)、史帝夫迪特科 (Steve Ditko) 共同創造出多位耳熟能詳的美國超級英雄，除了電影《復仇者聯盟》(*The Avengers*) 裡的主角，還包括蜘蛛人 (Spider-Man)、X 戰警 (X-Men)、驚奇四超人 (Fantastic Four) 及夜魔俠 (Daredevil) 等。

小勞勃道尼在一九六五年四月四日出生於曼哈頓，爸媽分別為非主流導演和演員的他，五歲就獻出電影處女秀，在父親執導的喜劇《動物收容所》裡演一隻小狗。他繼續在父親的電影裡演出到青少年階段，那時他也花了好幾個暑假到卡茲奇山的表演藝術營磨鍊演技。一九七八年爸媽離婚後，道尼同父親遷居加州，但後來自高中輟學，回紐約追求演藝事業。

道尼在數部外百老匯歌舞劇登台，並加入《週六夜現場》的劇組，但隨後重回加州，在一九八五年的劇情片《火爆小子》飾演詹姆士史派德的搭擋。不久他開始與「新鼠黨」同進同出，先是在《摩登褓姆》（一九八五）演校園惡霸，後於《泡妞專家》（一九八七）首次擔綱主角，與莫莉琳華演對手戲。同年，道尼在《零下的激情》詮釋有毒癮的富家子弟朱利安威爾斯，大獲好評。這為他帶來更大製作電影裡更重要的角色——他與梅爾吉伯遜共同主演喜劇《飛離航道》（一九九〇），而他在《卓別林與他的情人》（一九九二）化身為查理卓別林的演出，更為他贏得奧斯卡最佳男主角提名。

不幸的是，一九九〇年代中期，道尼開始將他在《零下的激情》的角色搬進現實生活，染上差點斷送演藝生命的吸毒惡習。但他在終於戒除毒癮後，成功東山再起。二〇〇八年，他主演的《鋼鐵人》叫好又叫座；而同年他在《開麥拉驚魂》詮釋的澳洲演員一角，又為他贏得奧斯卡提名。自此，小勞勃道尼的名字儼然成為票房保證，無論是在其他漫威漫畫改編的電影扮演東尼史塔克，或在蓋瑞奇執導的福爾摩斯電影扮演夏洛克福爾摩斯，皆締造佳績。

TONGUE-TIED NO MORE

kick...habit 戒除…習慣

kick 有「踢、踹」的意思，kick...habit 也就是把某種習慣給踢走，是在形容要擺脫某種壞習慣，像是抽菸、吸毒等，把它戒除。

A: Have you kicked your smoking habit yet?
你戒菸了沒？
B: No, not yet. It's a hard habit to kick.
不，還沒有，這習慣很難戒。

VOCABULARY BANK

1) **run with** [rʌn wɪθ] 結交，和⋯鬼混
Mike ran with a bad crowd in high school.
麥克高中時交了一群壞朋友。

2) **bully** [ˋbʊli] (n.) 惡霸
That bully always steals my lunch money.
那個惡霸總是把我的午餐錢給偷走。

3) **addicted** [əˋdɪktɪd] (a.) 上癮的，入迷的
Samantha is addicted to chocolate.
莎曼莎對巧克力上癮。

4) **unfortunately** [ʌnˋfɔrtʃənɪtli] (adv.) 遺憾地，可惜
Unfortunately, I won't have time to do any sightseeing while I'm in Paris.
很可惜，我在巴黎不會有時間觀光。

5) **threaten** [ˋθrɛt(ə)n] (v.) （構成）威脅
The athlete's injury could threaten his career.
這位運動員的傷勢可能危及他的運動生涯。

6) **comeback** [ˋkʌm͵bæk] (n.) 東山再起，再度走紅
Miniskirts are making a comeback this year.
今年又開始流行迷你裙了。

7) **guarantee** [͵gærənˋti] (n.) 保證，保證書
These days, a college degree is no guarantee of a good career.
現在這個時代，大學學歷已經不再是事業成功的保證。

進階字彙

8) **hone** [hon] (v.) 磨鍊
Patrick is going to a cram school to hone his math skills.
派崔克去補習班加強他的數學。

9) **reprise** [rɪˋpriz] (v.) 重複（表演）
The actor reprised his role in the sequel.
那個演員在續集中再度飾演他的角色。

口語補充

10) **sidekick** [ˋsaɪd͵kɪk] (n.) 跟班，伙伴
Robin is Batman's sidekick.
羅賓是蝙蝠俠的伙伴。

SHOWBIZ WORD

smash 熱門作品

smash 在口語中的意思是「轟動一時的、極為成功的」；當名詞的 smash 就是 smash hit 的縮寫，用來表示造成轟動的電影、戲劇，歌曲等作品，box office smash 就是指票房極佳的電影。

Iron Man 《鋼鐵人》

🎥 電影介紹

東尼史塔克（Tony Stark，小勞勃道尼飾），美國政府頂尖武器承包商「史氏工業」的總裁，也是一位發明家。在阿富汗時，東尼被一群暴徒綁架，為求活只好服從暴徒首領之命，為其打造破壞力極大的毀滅性武器，並偷偷為自己發明一套鋼鐵衣以逃回美國。回國後的東尼，決定要為史氏工業轉型造福人類，卻被最高執行長施奧比（Obadiah Stane，傑夫布里吉（Jeff Bridges）飾）百般阻撓。助理小辣椒波茲（Pepper Potts，葛妮絲派特洛（Gwyneth Paltrow）飾）及值得信任的羅德（Rhodey，泰倫斯霍華（Terrence Howard）飾）要如何幫助東尼保護世界？

🎞 電影對白

東尼請小辣椒去入侵他辦公室裡面的主機，拿出最近的運貨資料，打算用此來阻止施奧比的黑箱交易，並找出他們交易的武器加以摧毀。小辣椒拒絕他，還說要辭職。

Tony: You stood by my side all these years while I reaped the benefits of destruction. Now that I'm trying to protect the people I've put **in harm's way**, you're going to walk out?
我賣武器賺錢那麼多年，妳一直都在我身邊。現在我想要保護因我受害的人民，妳卻要離我而去？

Pepper: You're going to kill yourself, Tony. I'm not going to be a part of it.
東尼，你會把你自己給害死。我不想參與在其中。

MP3 139

in harm's way 造成傷害

in harm's way 這個片語意思是造成傷害或是指危險的情形。相反地，out of harm's way 就是遠離傷害、很安全的意思。

A: Why are you against having a gun at home to protect yourself?
家裡有槍能保護自己，你為什麼反對？

B: I think having a gun in the house would put my kids **in harm's way**.
我覺得家裡有槍會對我的小孩造成危險。

Iron Man 2 《鋼鐵人 2》

🎥 電影介紹

為《鋼鐵人》的續集，億萬富翁東尼史塔克為鋼鐵人的身份曝光後，美國政府堅持要東尼把鋼鐵衣這項革命性武器交給美國軍方。同時，一名來自過去史氏家族的神秘科學家伊凡萬科（Ivan Vanko，米基洛克（Mickey Rourke）飾），也利用史氏工業技術來對付東尼。陷入危機的東尼，要如何和他的新舊盟友一同抵抗企圖毀滅他及全人類的敵人？

🎞 電影對白

東尼要和羅德（Rhodey，唐奇鐸（Don Cheadle）飾）聯手對抗萬科控制的鋼鐵士兵，他們的對策是要衝往制高點然後把最強的大砲武器帶往山脊，結果兩人都往那前進，羅德告訴東尼他的意思是由他前往制高點。

Tony: You have a big gun. You are not the big gun.
你是有一支大砲但你不是最猛的。

Rhodey: Tony, don't be jealous.
東尼，別嫉妒我。

Tony: No. It's subtle, all the **bells and whistles**.
才不是，你可真低調，全身掛得五四三。

Rhodey: Yeah. It's called being a badass.
對啊，我這才叫是狠角色。

Tony: Fine. All right. You go up top. I'll draw them in.
好吧，好吧，你去制高點，我把它們引來。

Gossip Box

好萊塢東山再起傳奇

什麼，鋼鐵人曾經墮落？！小勞勃道尼曾有過一段荒唐的歲月，年輕沉迷於吸毒，甚至被送進牢裡勒戒，差點把自己美好的演藝生涯給斷送掉。戒毒後的他，因接演《鋼鐵人》系列電影，這名風趣幽默的超級英雄，人氣旺不僅僅只是電影人物本身，連帶小勞勃道尼的聲勢也水漲船高，鋼鐵人形象深植人心。

©muliertenebrae / flickr.com

MP3 140

bells and whistles
花俏的配備

在英文中看到 bells and whistles 如果直接翻成「鈴鐺和口哨」，那可就糗大了！這個片語是形容你在機器或裝置上，額外裝一些花俏且引人注目的功能、配備，但卻不太必要，有時候帶有貶抑的意味。

A: Why was your new car so expensive?

你的新車怎麼這麼貴啊？

B: It came with all the latest **bells and whistles**.

還外加一些最新的配備啊。

Iron Man 3 《鋼鐵人 3》

🎥 電影介紹

此為《鋼鐵人》和《鋼鐵人 2》的續作，由原班人馬再次演出。這一次東尼要面對的是自己的心。在經歷過復仇者聯盟事件後，東尼深受打擊，因為擁有鋼鐵衣並不代表就能打贏世界上所有的敵人，於是東尼像發了狂的製造鋼鐵衣，脫下鋼鐵衣的自己還剩下什麼？東尼要如何突破心魔，並擊敗這一連串毀滅自己的主謀？

🎬 電影對白

東尼發現電視上出現的滿大人 (Mandarin) 只是齊禮安（Killian，蓋皮爾斯 (Guy Pearce) 飾）找的替身，他才是主導這整個一切的背後主使者。

Killian : You have met him, I *assume?

我猜你見過他了？

Tony: Yeah, *Sir Lawrence Oblivion.

沒錯，好偉大的演員啊！

Killian: I know he's a little **over the top** sometimes. It's not entirely my fault. He's a stage actor. They say his Lear was the *toast of Croydon, wherever that is. Anyway, the point is ever since that big dude with the hammer fell out of the sky, *subtlety's kind of had its day.

我知道他有時會太入戲，但這不完全是我的錯。他是舞台劇的演員，大家都說他因為演李爾王而成為克羅伊登的大紅人，也不知道那是什麼鬼地方。反正，我要說的是，自從那個拿著錘子的大漢（編註：意指索爾）從天而降之後，就沒人吃含蓄這套了。

*assume [ə`sum] (v.) 以為，認為

*Sir Lawrence Oblivion 利用二十世紀最受尊敬的舞台演員——勞倫斯奧立佛爵士 (Sir Lawrence Olivier) 來開的玩笑

*toast [tost] (n.) 受歡迎的人（事）

*subtlety [`sʌtəltɪ] (n.) 含蓄，微妙之處

MP3 141

over the top
太誇張了，太驚人了

這個說法可以是正面或負面的意思。正面是描述某事或動作很驚人。負面則是形容某件事情或動作太過極端，或是花了過多時間精力做了某事情，不大合宜。

A: How did you like the movie?

你覺得那部電影怎樣？

B: It wasn't bad, but the ending was a little **over the top**.

不差，但是結尾有點太誇張了。

Zodiac 《索命黃道帶》

📽 電影介紹

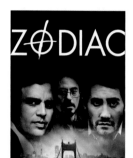

改編自舊金山的真實連續殺人案件，故事描述一個瘋狂殺人魔「黃道帶殺手」在犯案前後總是會寫信給媒體，說明犯案動機及暗示後續行動，並附上其設定的神祕密碼。玩弄警方於股掌之間，也搞的全國人民不得安寧。至今榮逍遙法外，行蹤成謎。

保羅艾利（Paul Avery，小勞勃道尼飾）是報社的犯罪新聞記者，羅伯特格雷史密斯（Robert Graysmith，傑克葛倫霍（Jake Gyllenhaal）飾）則是報社中的政治漫畫家，他們倆與警察大衛托斯奇（David Toschi，馬克魯法洛（Mark Ruffalo）飾）為追捕黃道帶殺手越陷越深，而這個恐怖殺人狂不斷留下線索，埋藏在他們的生活底下，危及他們的安全。

🎞 電影對白

黃道帶殺人魔信上指名報社一定要在八月一日前將他寄來的密碼刊登在頭版上，否則將會大開殺戒。因為這份密碼也有寄給其他兩間報社，於是記者們開始討論出現在信中的簽名符號，以及是否要報導。

Paul: Is it me, or does that look like a gunsight?
是我自己的感覺，還是這上頭的符號看起來像個槍的瞄準眼？

Thieriot: Today's August first. He wants his code in the afternoon edition.
今天是八月一日。他要求把密碼登在我們今天的晚報。

Hyman: If the *Examiner* doesn't **have the balls to** run it, we *scoop the Bay.
如果《舊金山觀察家報》沒種刊登，我們就拿到灣區的獨家報導了。

*scoop [skup] (n.)（第一手，內幕）消息，新聞，細節；獨家、搶先報導

MP3 140

have the balls (to) 有膽去做

ball 意思是球，口語中也能指睪丸，也就是男人的象徵，因此用 ball 來形容男子氣概。have balls 就表示有膽量、有勇氣，也就等同於中文的「有種」，因此 have the balls to 就是指很有膽量要去做某件事情。

A: I think I'm gonna go over and ask that girl for her number.
我決定要走過去跟那個女生要電話。

B: Ha-ha. I bet you don't **have the balls to** do it.
哈哈，我覺得你一定不敢。

Sherlock Holmes

📽 電影介紹

片中柯南道爾筆下的經典人物被以不同的方式呈現，福爾摩斯（Sherlock Holmes，小勞勃道尼飾）和華生（John Watson，裘德洛（Jude Law）飾）面臨一系列新的挑戰，《福爾摩斯：詭影遊戲》（Sherlock Holmes: A Game of Shadows）為此的續作。辦案能力無人能敵的福爾摩斯將和他的醫生搭檔華生，一同揭露一場可能會璀毀全英國的致命陰謀。

Gossip Box

聽老婆嘴，大富貴

道尼的人生開始出現轉機，跟他身邊的這位 Mrs. Downey 有很大的關係。不過在認識現任太太蘇珊道尼（Susan Downey）之前，道尼曾有過一段婚姻，只是結婚生子對於當時沉淪於毒品的年輕道尼，沒有起太大的效用，最後離婚收場。就在人生一度留校察看的道尼，遇見他人生中的那個「對的人」，也就是蘇珊，為了她不再碰毒品，並且和她共組家庭，找到人生的目標，走回正軌，小勞勃道尼就此重生。

福爾摩斯》

🎬 電影對白

華生和瑪莉 (Mary) 去找福爾摩斯，一上樓卻發現他吊在天花板上。瑪麗嚇到了，但華生倒是挺了解他，知道他不可能自殺，於是用枴杖戳醒他。原來他在找布雷伍德 (Blackwood) 沒被絞死的原因，沒想到這樣的姿勢挺舒適的，他竟睡著了。

Holmes: *[to Mary]* Good afternoon, dear.
[對瑪莉說] 午安，親愛的。

Watson: Get on with it, Holmes.
趕快繼續說，福爾摩斯。

Holmes: Well, cleverly concealed in the hangman's knot was a hook...oh, my, I think my legs have fallen asleep. I should probably come down.
嗯，劊子手的繩結裡巧妙地藏了個鉤子……哦，天啊，我的腳都麻了，該下來了。

Mary: John, shouldn't we help him down?
華生，我們不幫他下來嗎？

Watson: No, no, I hate to cut him off midstream. Carry on.
不，不，我不喜歡中途打斷他，請繼續。

---

get on with (it)
繼續做某件事情

這邊的 get on 和 go on 的意思很接近，都是指「持續進行」，get on with (it) 就是在說「給時間繼續做某件事情」；當使用在祈使句時，則是指「趕快去做某件事情」。

A: Stop playing video games and **get on with** your homework!
不要再打電動了，趕快去寫功課！

B: OK, Dad. Just let me finish this game.
好啦，爸，就讓我打完這一局嘛。

Due Date 《臨門湊一腳》

🎥 電影介紹

彼得海曼（Peter Highman，小勞勃道尼飾）為了陪老婆待產，準備搭機回家。只是一切計畫都因遇上一名一心只想成為演員的男子伊森崔布雷（Ethan Tremblay，查克葛里芬納奇 (Zach Galifianakis) 飾），而全部搞砸。先是兩人被趕下飛機，列入拒載黑名單，再來是彼得的行李、皮夾和護照，所有行囊全都給飛機載走。毫無退路的他，只好和伊森同行。沒想到，這趟變調的旅程在不知不覺中改變他們的人生……。

🎬 電影對白

彼得覺得伊森根本取藝名的必要，覺得他很蠢，因為他又不是真正的演員。伊森非常不服氣。

Ethan: Give me a scene.
給我個場景。

Peter: OK, I'm Julia Roberts. We are engaged to be married. You have terminal cancer. **Break the news** to me.
好吧，假如我是茱莉亞羅伯茲。我們已經訂婚了，但你被查出是癌症末期。你要怎麼告訴我？

Ethan: Julia Roberts, as you know, we are engaged to be married. I have terminal cancer.
茱莉亞羅伯茲，如妳所知我們要結婚了，不過我癌症末期。

Peter: Awful
爛死了。

break the news (to sb.) 把消息告訴別人

break the news 可不是在說把新聞給打破喔，它的意思是把重要的消息告訴別人，通常是指不好的消息。

A: What's the worst part about being a surgeon?
當外科醫生最難的部分是什麼？

B: Breaking the news to patients' families when they don't make it.
向家屬公布病患的死訊。

©s_bukley / Shutterstock.com

Jake Gyllenhaal 傑克葛倫霍

©Everett Collection / Shutterstock.com

LANGUAGE GUIDE

Gulf War 波斯灣戰爭

發生於一九九〇年至一九九一年，起因為伊拉克與科威特兩國發生領土、石油等利益糾紛，伊拉克大舉入侵科威特。由於該區位處歐亞交界，戰火可能波及整個中東區域，甚至引發世界大戰，因此聯合國安全理事會強勢介入，要求伊拉克部隊撤出科威特，同時這場戰役也是美國繼越戰後第一次主導的大規模戰爭，最後伊拉克無條件投降，美國的國際地位也因此更為穩固。

Scott Fischer 史考特費雪

生於一九五五年，自十四歲受到啟發後開始愛上登山，並於一九八四年成立 Mountain Madness 登山公司，帶領登山隊征服各世界高峰，成為美國知名登山響導。一九九六年，當費雪第五度攀登聖母峰時，因為過晚攻頂，下山時遇到大風雪而不幸罹難，震驚美國登山界。

MP3 145

Jake Gyllenhaal was born in Los Angeles on December 19, 1980. Considering that his father is a Hollywood director, his mother a [1]**producer** and screenwriter, and his older sister Maggie an actress, it's not surprising that Gyllenhaal, who grew up on movie [2]**sets**, would choose an acting career himself. His first screen appearance came in 1991, when he played Billy Crystal's son in the hit comedy *City Slickers*. His parents, however, [3]**forbid** him from taking any roles that would require him to be away from home for long periods.

In 1998, Gyllenhaal enrolled in Columbia University, his mother's [7]**alma mater**, and studied Eastern religions and [4]**philosophy** for two years before dropping out to focus on acting. His breakout performance in *October Sky* (1999), about a young man in West Virginia who dreams of winning a science scholarship, was followed by the [8]**cult** favorite *Donnie Darko* (2001). Next, after almost winning the lead in *Spider-Man 2*, Gyllenhaal played a student fighting to survive an environmental disaster in *The Day After Tomorrow* (2004), a role that [5]**inspired** his [9]**ongoing** interest in environmental causes.

2005 saw Gyllenhaal star as a [6]**frustrated** Marine during the Gulf War in *Jarhead*, and as a gay cowboy in Ang Lee's acclaimed drama *Brokeback Mountain*. The latter role earned him an Oscar nomination for best supporting actor. Gyllenhaal has since delivered strong lead performances in 2007's *Zodiac* and *Rendition*, and opposite Anne Hathaway in 2010's *Love and Other Drugs*. In 2015, Gyllenhaal will tackle another mountain in *Everest*, in which he'll play famous climber and guide Scott Fischer.

©Everett Collection / Shutterstock.com

傑克葛倫霍在一九八〇年十二月十九日生於洛杉磯。考慮到他的父親是好萊塢導演、母親是製作人和編劇、姐姐瑪姬是演員,在攝影棚長大的葛倫霍也選擇演戲這條路並不意外。他在一九九一年獻出大銀幕處女秀,在賣座喜劇《城市鄉巴佬》飾演比利克里斯托的兒子。但他爸媽禁止他接演需要長時間離家的角色。

一九九八年,葛倫霍進入母親的母校哥倫比亞大學就讀,主修東方宗教與哲學,但在兩年後休學,專心演戲。他先在《十月的天空》(一九九九)有突破性的演出:西維吉尼亞州一個夢想贏得科學獎學金的年輕人,接著主演小眾經典《怵目驚魂二十八天》(二〇〇一)。接下來,在與《蜘蛛人》第二集男主角失之交臂後,葛倫霍於《明天過後》(二〇〇四)飾演在一場環境浩劫中奮力求生的學生,這個角色也激發他對環保議題持續關注。

二〇〇五年,葛倫霍先後在《鍋蓋頭》和李安廣獲好評的劇情片《斷背山》中飾演波斯灣戰爭期間備受挫折的海軍陸戰隊員和同性戀牛仔。後者為他贏得奧斯卡最佳男配角提名。此後葛倫霍無論在二〇〇七年的《索命黃道帶》和《關鍵危機》擔綱主角,以及在二〇一〇年的《愛情藥不藥》與安海瑟威演對手戲,都有亮眼表現。二〇一五年,葛倫霍將在《聖母峰》再攻一座山,飾演知名登山好手兼嚮導史考特費雪。

MP3 146

VOCABULARY BANK

1) **producer** [prəˋdusə] (n.) 製作人,製片
Steven Spielberg is famous as both a director and producer.
史蒂芬史匹柏是著名的導演兼製作人。

2) **set** [sɛt] (n.) 攝影棚,攝影場
The director called for quiet on the set.
導演要求在攝影棚裡要保持肅靜。

3) **forbid** [fɚˋbɪd] (v.) 禁止,不許
Sam's parents forbid him to play video games.
山姆的父母不准他玩電玩遊戲。

4) **philosophy** [fɪˋlɑsəfɪ] (n.) 哲學,生活的信條(或態度)
There aren't many career options for philosophy majors.
主修哲學的人沒有很多工作機會。

5) **inspire** [ɪnˋspaɪr] (v.) 賦予⋯靈感,激勵
The novel was inspired by the author's childhood experiences.
作者的童年經驗是這部小說的靈感來源。

6) **frustrated** [ˋfrʌstretɪd] (a.) 有挫折感的,洩氣的
The coach feels frustrated about the team's poor
教練對球隊表現不佳感到挫折。

進階字彙

7) **alma mater** [ˋɑlmə ˋmɑtɚ] (phr.) 母校
The businessman donated millions to his alma mater.
這位商人捐贈了數百萬元給他的母校。

8) **cult** [kʌlt] (a.) 小眾的,非主流但有忠實粉絲的
The Rocky Horror Picture Show is a cult classic.
《洛基恐怖秀》是一部經典小眾電影。

9) **ongoing** [ˋɑnˏgoɪŋ] (a.) 進行中的,持續的
Many have lost their jobs in the ongoing financial crisis.
許多人在持續的金融危機中失業了。

Jake Gyllenhaal 傑克葛倫霍

The Day After Tomorrow 《明天過後》

📷 電影介紹

氣候學家傑克霍爾（Jack Hall，丹尼斯奎德 (Dennis Quaid) 飾）發現溫室效應最終會造成地球急速凍結，雖然曾警告政府，卻沒被採信。大自然的反撲來得如此迅速，而傑克的兒子山姆（Sam，傑克葛倫霍飾）被困在重災區紐約，傑克決定冒險前往紐約，展開危險的救援行動。

MP3 150

jump to conclusions 妄下定論

省略所有的過程和細節，直接看結果，這樣很容易會評斷錯誤喔！jump to conclusions 就是在形容這樣妄下定論的情形。

A: I saw Ken in a restaurant with some woman. I think he's cheating on his wife.
我看到肯和其他女人在餐廳用餐，我覺得他一定是外遇了。

B: Hey, you shouldn't **jump to conclusions**. They may just be friends.
嘿，你不要妄下定論。他們説不定只是朋友。

🎬 電影對白

傑克因為山姆的微積分期末考被當感到相當失望，山姆説考砸的原因是他在腦中解出了所有答案，但沒寫出答題過程，雖然向教授解釋過了，但還是沒用。

Jack: Ridiculous. How can he fail you for being smarter than he is?
太荒謬了，怎麼可以因為你比他聰明而把你當掉？

Sam: That's what I said.
我也是這麼説。

Jack: You did? How'd he take it?
你有説哦？他有什麼反應？

Sam: He *flunked me, remember?
他不是把我當掉了嗎？

Jack: Oh, yeah. Sam, I'm sorry. **I jumped to conclusions**.
喔，對。山姆，我很抱歉，我不該妄下定論。

*flunk [flʌŋk] (v.) （把學生）當掉；通不過（考試）

Brokeback Mountain 《斷背山》

📷 電影介紹

在六○年代保守的懷俄明州，同性戀牛仔，傑克（Jack，傑克葛倫霍飾）和艾尼斯（Ennis，希斯萊傑 (Heath Ledger) 飾）不斷抑制對對方的情感，表面維持大家眼中正常的生活。他們倆人能夠抵擋這些壓力，勇敢地相愛嗎？

🎬 電影對白

這是離開斷背山後，傑克和艾尼斯第一次相會。他們到旅館去度過激情的一夜，以消這四年的相思之情。

Jack: Four years. Damn!
媽的，都四年了！

Ennis: Yeah, four years. Didn't think I'd hear from you again. I figured you were sore from that punch.
是啊，已經四年了。沒想到你還會跟我聯絡，我以為那一拳把你氣死了。

Jack: That next summer, I drove back up to Brokeback. Talked to Aguirre about a job, and he told me you hadn't been back, so I left. Went down to Texas for rodeoing. That's how I met Lureen. Made two thousand dollars that year, bull riding. Nearly starved. Lureen's old man makes serious money, farm machine business. Of course he **hates my guts**, though.
第二年的夏天我有開車回斷背山，找安奎爾要工作，他跟我説你沒回去，所以我就走了。後來我就去德州參加牛仔大賽，在那裡認識了蘿琳。一整年參加騎牛賽才賺兩千塊，幾乎快餓死。蘿琳她老爸在賣農用機器，很賺錢的，所以當然非常討厭我。

End of Watch 《火線赤子情》

Gossip Box

斷背山上的風采

與已故男星希斯萊傑合演的《斷背山》，讓傑克葛倫霍的演藝事業爬上高峰。兩人出色的演技將壓抑的同性愛戀完美詮釋，電影叫好叫座之餘，也讓傑克正式躍進「演技派男演員」的行列，兩人在片中精湛的演出，讓他們倆分別入圍奧斯卡最佳男主角及男配角獎，雖然兩人都與小金人失之交臂，卻因此片而結下深厚的情誼，傑克甚至成為希斯女兒的乾爹呢！

©Everett Collection / Shutterstock.com

📷 電影介紹

巡邏警員布萊恩泰勒（Brian Taylor，傑克葛倫霍飾）和麥克札瓦拉（Mike Zavala，麥可潘納 (Michael Peña) 飾），不僅是一對好搭檔也是好兄弟，兩人在全美治安最不安定的洛杉磯南區執勤，不論是直搗毒窟、處理家庭暴力案件，還是火場搶救，兩人都是義無反顧，出生入死。本片亦利用警察胸前的微型攝影機，原形呈現執勤畫面，讓觀眾親臨火線，身歷其境感受警員執行任務的危險。

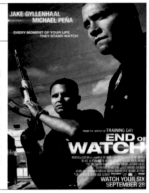

🎬 電影對白

布萊恩跟麥克提起，他正在用簡訊傳情的女子很聰明，是位流體液壓系統碩士，麥克就開始調侃他。

Mike: I wouldn't *brag about that, dude. That she has a Master's degree in *fluid *hydraulics.
這沒什麼好誇耀的兄弟。說她是流體力學碩士。

Brian: I date all these girls, man. They're **smoking hot**.
老兄，我和很多女孩約過會，她們都超辣的。

Mike: Yeah, your little fucking *badge bunnies.
是啦，就是那些有戀警情節的女孩嘛！

Brian: I **get laid** without a badge, thank you very much.
我要上床才不用警徽，真是非常感激你！

*brag [bræg] (v.) 吹牛，自誇

*fluid [ˋfluɪd] (n.) 流體，液體

*hydraulics [haɪˋdrɔlɪks] (n.) 水力學

*badge [bædʒ] (n.) 徽章，標誌，badge bunny 意即「迷戀警察的女生」

MP3 151

hate sb's guts 非常討厭某人

當我們非常討厭一個人的時候，中文會說恨之入骨。英文可就不一樣囉。gut 有「腸子」或「內臟」的意思，hate sb's guts 討厭你討厭到連你的腸子內臟都討厭，看來是真的恨你入骨啊！

A: Do you get along with your stepfather?
你和你的繼父相處得融洽嗎？

B: No way. I **hate his guts**.
一點都不好，我超討厭他。

A: Did you see the dress Jennifer Lopez wore on *Idol* last night?
你有看到珍妮佛羅培茲昨晚在《超級偶像》的穿的洋裝嗎？

B: Yeah. She was **smoking hot**!
有啊，她超辣的！

get laid 跟人上床

這個 laid 為 lay 的過去式，在口語中 lay 還有「躺臥」(lie) 的意思，get laid （給人弄躺著）就引申出和別人發生關係的意思，也就是上床的口語說法。

MP3 152

smoking hot 性感火辣的女生

smoking hot 就是形容身材「辣到冒煙」、超性感、超有魅力的火辣女子。

A: Do you think I should wear this outfit to the party?
你覺得我穿這套去參加派對怎麼樣？

B: No. You'll never **get laid** looking like that.
不要吧，妳這個樣子不會有人想跟妳上床。

Love And Other Drugs 《愛情藥不藥》

🎬 電影對白

傑米帶梅姬一同前往芝加哥參加醫學會議，會場的對面正好在有帕金森氏症病友的分享會。傑米在會上遇見一名男子，他的太太也得帕金森氏症，傑米問他有沒有什麼好的建議可以分享。

Man: You don't need my advice.
你不需要我的建議。

Jamie: Come on. I'm very trainable.
好嘛，我很受教的。

Man: My advice is to go upstairs, pack your bags, and leave a nice note. Find yourself a healthy woman. I love my wife. I do. But I wouldn't do it over again. The thing nobody tells you, this disease will steal everything you love in her. Her body, her smile, her mind. Sooner or later, she'll lose motor control. Eventually, she won't even be able to dress herself. Then, the fun really begins. Cleaning up her shit, frozen face, *dementia. It's not a disease, it's a Russian novel…. Look, I'm sorry. I'm **out of line**. Hang in there.
我的建議就是上樓去收拾行李，留張字條，去找個健康的女人。我很愛我太太，很愛。但我沒辦法再這樣一次。沒有人會告訴你的是，這種病會奪走你所愛她的一切，她的身體、她的笑容、她的心智。遲早她的身體會不聽使喚，最後連自己穿衣服都沒辦法。接著樂趣真的來了，你還得幫她清理大便，表情僵硬、癡呆。這不是疾病，這跟俄羅斯小說一樣悲慘……。噢，抱歉，我太過火了，你要加油。

*dementia [dɪˋmɛnʃə] (n.) 癡呆

MP3 147

out of line 太過火，有失分寸
這裡的 line 有底線、界線的意思。英文中 out of line（在底線之外） 就是用來形容做事或說話超越人家忍受範圍，太過頭了，沒有拿捏好分寸。

A: My supervisor keeps making rude comments about my weight.
我的主管一直對於我的體重有很輕蔑的評論。

B: That's way **out of line**. You should tell the boss.
這樣太超過了，你應該要告訴你的老闆。

📷 電影介紹

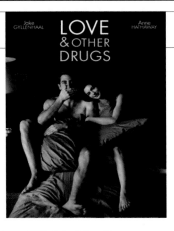

迷人又帥氣的傑米（Jamie，傑克葛倫霍飾）是個藥商業務，有當他碰見美麗的梅姬（Maggie，安海瑟薇 (Anne Hathaway) 飾）時，完全為她所傾倒。但梅姬因罹患帕金森氏症，不願被感情細綁，在傑米的堅持之下，梅姬逐漸軟化，他倆的感情日漸穩定。只是當傑米開始積極設法治好梅姬。他們甜美的生活開始產生壓力，也讓兩人關係緊繃。他們最後能一起突破難關？還是此各分東西呢？

Gossip Box

二度戀上安海瑟薇

我們都知道傑克葛倫霍第一次「遇見」安海瑟薇，是相戀在《斷背山》，不過那時的安海瑟薇只是傑克掩飾性傾向的煙霧彈，終於兩人又能在《愛情藥不藥》中再續銀幕前緣！《愛情藥不藥》有多場令人血脈賁張的親熱床戲，裸身上陣的兩人倒是一點都不尷尬。兩人的速配指數超高，在安海瑟薇結婚前，甚至有許多戲迷期待他們能假戲真做，跳出銀幕，成為真正的情侶呢！

Source Code 《啟動原始碼》

📽 電影介紹

美軍上尉史蒂文斯（Stevens，傑克葛倫霍飾）執行「腦波原始碼」特殊實驗任務，想找出芝加哥火車爆炸案的真凶。任務中，他被植入遇難者史恩的腦裡，以史恩之軀重返爆炸前的黃金八分鐘，透過景象還原來追捕這名炸彈客以阻擋下一波連續攻擊。就在快要破案之時，卻發現自己與史恩友人克莉絲汀（Christina，蜜雪兒摩納漢 (Michelle Monaghan) 飾）動了真情，他企圖在這個時空之下，阻止爆炸事件的發生來拯救她，史蒂文斯能如願嗎？

MP3 148

(not)sweat the small stuff
（別）大驚小怪

你有沒有發現緊張或惱怒時都會滿頭大汗啊？sweat 除了有流汗的意思，也能指焦慮、煩惱，「Don't sweat the small stuff.」就是叫人不要為了小事抓狂。

🎞 電影對白

因火車誤點，坐在史蒂文斯和克莉絲汀娜隔壁座位的男子開始有些不耐煩。

Man: What's so damn hard about it? I run a business, OK? Everything moves on time or people get fired. That's the way it works in the real world. Ten minutes.
到底是什麼搞不定，我是開公司的，好嗎？員工要是不準時就會被開除。真實世界就是這樣。已經十分鐘了。

Stevens: Hey, buddy? **Don't sweat the small stuff**. You'll drown.
嘿，老兄，別為了小事心浮氣躁，你會受不了。

Man: Thank you for that moment of Zen, but nobody was talking to you.
謝謝你的禪理開示，但沒人在和你說話。

A: Peter never puts the toilet seat down when he's finished!
彼得上完廁所從不把馬桶座給放下！

B: You shouldn't **sweat the small stuff**. It'll just drive you crazy.
別太大驚小怪了，這樣只會把你自己給逼瘋。

Prisoners 《私法爭鋒》

📽 電影介紹

凱勒多佛（Keller Dover，休傑克曼 (Hugh Jackman) 飾）的六歲女兒安娜跟朋友喬伊一起失蹤了，負責偵辦此案的警探洛基（Loki，傑克葛倫霍飾）逮捕了最有嫌疑的弱智兒艾利克斯瓊斯（Alex Jones，保羅丹諾 (Paul Dano) 飾），卻因證據不足而釋放他。隨著黃金時間一點一滴的過去，心急如焚的凱勒會做出怎樣瘋狂的行為來拯救自己的女兒？

MP3 149

keep one's word 說話算話，遵守諾言

這裡的 word 是表示「你說過的話」，keep one's word 維持某人說過的話，意思就是在叫人要遵守承諾、要說話算話。如果要說別人黃牛、說話不算話的時候，英文就可以說 break one's word。

A: Are you sure George is coming to pick us up?
你確定喬治要來接我們嗎？

B: Don't worry, he'll be here soon. He always **keeps his word**.
別擔心，他很快就來了。他每次都說到做到。

🎞 電影對白

艾利克斯不見蹤影，洛基找了卻什麼也找不到，於是他跑去向原本答應會安排人手監督的警長理論。但警長卻把責任推回給他，因為洛基認為艾力克斯應該是無辜的。

Captain: Look, I don't have money in the budget for watching innocent people.
是沒錯，但我想你說他是無辜的。而且我以為你說昨天晚上的那個人才是我們要找的人。聽著，我沒有這麼多預算去監視一些無辜的人。

Loki: You said to me that you'd put him under surveillance.
可是你告訴我你會安排人監視他。

Captain: What do you want me to say?
那你還要我說什麼？

Loki: You gonna **keep your word**? You could have just given me a call, because I would have been there all night.
你要說話算話啊？哪怕你就是撥通電話告訴我，我也會整晚待在那裡。

119

Kate Winslet 凱特溫斯蕾

Kate Winslet 凱特溫斯蕾

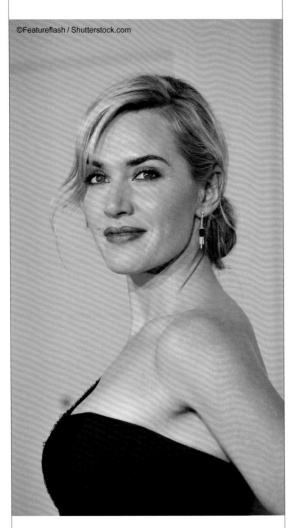

©Featureflash / Shutterstock.com

MP3 153

5) **Arguably** the finest British actress of her generation, Kate Winslet was born in Berkshire, England on October 5, 1975. She began taking acting classes at age 11, and made her first TV appearance a year later, in a breakfast cereal commercial. The director praised Winslet, describing her as a 1)**natural**. As a teenager, she acted in BBC TV shows and made her film debut in Peter Jackson's *Heavenly Creatures* (1994), earning critical praise for her portrayal of Juliet Hulme, a girl who 6)**conspires** to murder the mother of her best friend.

In 1995, Winslet landed a key supporting role in Ang Lee's 2)**adaptation** of Jane Austen's novel *Sense and Sensibility*. But her breakout performance would come next alongside Leonardo DiCaprio in *Titanic* (1997). Winslet fought hard for the female lead role, even calling director James Cameron daily to say, "I'm Rose! I don't know why you're even seeing anyone else." Her 3)**persistence** 7)**paid off**, and *Titanic* became one of the biggest blockbusters of all time. Instead of making more big Hollywood movies, Winslet began to choose roles she found more interesting, appearing in a string of art-house films like *Quills* (2000), *Eternal Sunshine of the Spotless Mind* (2004) and *Little Children* (2006).

But this career direction also paid off. In 2008, Winslet won a best actress Golden Globe for her performance opposite DiCaprio in *Revolutionary Road* and a best actress Oscar for her portrayal of an 8)**illiterate** Nazi guard in *The Reader*. In addition, at age 33, she had become the youngest actress ever to receive six Academy Award nominations. Given Winslet's talent and 4)**dedication**, her seventh Oscar nomination can't be far off.

VOCABULARY BANK

1) **natural** [ˈnætʃərəl] (n.) 有某種天生才能的人
Michael is a natural at basketball.
麥可天生就會打籃球。

2) **adaptation** [ˌædæpˈteʃən] (n.) 改編，改寫
The director is working on an adaptation of *Macbeth*.
這導演正在拍攝一部改編自《馬克白》的電影。

堪稱同世代最佳英國女演員的凱特溫斯蕾，一九七五年十月五日生於英國柏克夏。她從十一歲開始上戲劇課，一年後以一支早餐麥片廣告片首度於電視亮相。導演對溫斯蕾讚不絕口，形容她是天生的演員。青少年時期，她在 BBC 電視節目中演出，也在彼得傑克遜的《夢幻天堂》（一九九四）獻出電影處女秀，飾演同謀殺害最好朋友母親的少女茱莉葉休姆，大獲好評。

一九九五年，溫斯蕾在李安改編的珍奧斯汀小說《感性與理性》中演出重要配角。但她的突破性演出是與李奧納多狄卡皮歐攜手演出《鐵達尼號》（一九九七）。溫斯蕾非常努力才爭取到女主角，甚至每天打電話給導演詹姆士克麥隆說：「我就是蘿絲！我不明白你為什麼還要看別人。」她的堅持獲得回饋，《鐵達尼號》也成為史上最賣座的鉅片之一。但此後溫斯蕾並未接演更多好萊塢大片，反倒開始挑選她覺得比較有趣的角色，主演一連串的藝術電影，例如《性書狂人》（二〇〇〇）、《王牌冤家》（二〇〇四）和《身為人母》（二〇〇六）。

但這個事業方向也給了她回報。二〇〇八年，溫斯蕾在《真愛旅程》和狄卡皮歐演對手戲贏得金球獎最佳女主角，又於《為愛朗讀》詮釋不識字的納粹衛兵，拿下奧斯卡最佳女主角獎。另外，三十三歲時，她成為史上最年輕獲得六次奧斯卡提名的女演員。以溫斯蕾的天分和投入，她的第七次奧斯卡提名指日可待。

SHOWBIZ WORD

blockbuster 賣座強片

blockbuster 這個字源自二次世界大戰，指的是一種威力強大能將敵方陣營摧毀的巨型炸彈，後來引申表示「賣座電影」，且多半是耗費鉅資拍攝而成，知名的 DVD 出租業者百視達就是用 Blockbuster 這個字當作店名。除了電影，blockbuster 也能用來表示大受歡迎的影集或小說。

art-house film 藝術片

亦可作 art film。這種類型的電影常以讚頌美學與藝術為由，且實驗性質較高，並不是一般符合大眾口味的商業片。播放這種類型電影的電影院可稱做 art house。

MP3 154

VOCABULARY BANK

3) **persistence** [ˌpɚˋsɪstəns] (n.) 堅持，固執
Learning to play an instrument takes persistence and patience.
學習演奏樂器需要堅持和耐心。

4) **dedication** [ˌdɛdɪˋkeʃən] (n.) 投入，專注
Thanks to your dedication, we were able to finish the project on time.
多虧你的投入，我們才能準時完成這項專案。

進階字彙

5) **arguably** [ˋɑrgjʊəblɪ] (adv.) 可說是⋯
That restaurant has arguably the best sushi in town.
這間餐廳的壽司可說是城裡最好吃的。

6) **conspire** [kənˋspaɪr] (v.) 密謀，同謀
The military officers were arrested for conspiring against the government.
那幫密謀推翻政府的軍官全都被逮捕了。

7) **pay off** [pe ɔf] (phr.) 得到好結果，取得成功
I hope all our hard work pays off.
我希望我們一切的努力會有好結果。

8) **illiterate** [ɪˋlɪtərɪt] (a./n.) 文盲的；文盲
Over half the population of Cambodia is illiterate.
柬埔寨有超過一半的人口是文盲。

Kate Winslet 凱特溫斯蕾

Revolutionary Road 《真愛旅程》

📹 電影介紹

愛波（April，凱特溫絲蕾飾）和法蘭克（Frank，李奧納多狄卡皮歐 (Leonardo DiCaprio) 飾）這對夫妻一向自視甚高，認為自己與眾不同。為了不像其他人為了家庭放棄夢想，愛波提出放棄這裡，前往巴黎闖天下的計劃。不計代價逃離平庸的愛波和為維持現有一切而不斷妥協的法蘭克，為了實現這個夢，夫妻兩人把自己逼到臨界點，他們的婚姻搖搖欲墜。

MP3 155

get/have cold feet 臨陣脫逃

想像自己站在台前準備對眾人演講時，那種從腳發冷的緊張，有一種想逃走的感覺。get/have cold feet 得了冷腳，就是在說原本決定好要去做一件重要的事，結果當真的要去做之前，突然膽怯、退縮了

A: Did you **get cold feet** before you got married?
妳結婚前有臨陣退縮嗎？

B: No, but my fiancé did.
沒有，但是我的未婚夫有。

Gossip Box

與李奧納多跳脫愛情的 love

《真愛旅程》是李奧納多和凱特溫絲蕾相隔十一年，繼《鐵達尼號》之後，再次攜手演出的作品。因《鐵達尼號》結下情緣的兩人，感情甚好，不過倆人都公開表示過，兩人之間是屬於純友誼，絲毫沒有男女情感。溫絲蕾因《真愛旅程》奪得金球獎影后時，第一個擁抱的也是坐在身旁的李奧納多，甚至在真誠地在台上說：「Leo, I love you so much.」，將他視為自己生命中極為重要的人之一。就連溫絲蕾三度嫁作人妻，低調舉辦婚禮時，還找來李奧納多牽自己步紅毯，不難看出他們的交情有多深厚！

🎞 電影對白

法蘭克向房東海倫夫婦以及他們個性有點歇斯底里的兒子約翰（John，麥克夏儂 (Michael Shannon) 飾）宣布因為愛波懷孕，遠赴巴黎的計劃有了變數。約翰非常不諒解，認為有小孩只是藉口。法蘭克告訴他要養得起才能生，他們應該留在這裡給小孩安穩的生活。

John: OK, OK. It's a question of money. Money's a good reason. But it's hardly ever the real reason. What's the real reason? Wife talk you out of it or what? Little woman decide she isn't quite ready to quit playing house? No, no, that's not it. I can tell. She looks too *tough and *adequate as hell. OK, then. It must've been you. What happened?
好吧，好吧，跟錢有關，錢真是個好理由，但很少是真正的理由。真正的原因是什麼？你老婆說服你不要去嗎？小女人想繼續扮家家酒？不，不對，不是這樣。我看得出來，她太堅強，她很行。那麼就一定是你不想去，怎麼了？

Helen: John, please. You're being very rude.
約翰，拜託別這樣，這樣很失禮。

John: No, no. What happened, Frank? You **get cold feet**? You decide you're better off here after all?
才不會。到底發生什麼事，法蘭克？你想臨陣脫逃？你還是覺得留在這裡比較好？

*tough [tʌf] (a.) 堅強的，強悍的
*adequate [ˋædəkwɪt] (a.) 勝任的，適當的

©s_bukley / Shutterstock.com

Titanic 《鐵達尼號》

電影介紹

夢之船鐵達尼號在一九一四年舉目之下啟航，展開史上最令人嘆息的死亡處女旅程。傑克（Jack，李奧納多狄卡皮歐飾）一個四海為家的男子，因賭贏船票而搭上鐵達尼號。在一日偶然解救甲板上要跳船自盡的富家少女蘿絲（Rose，凱特溫絲蕾飾），兩人展開一段甜美的愛情。只是隨著冰山浩劫的來襲，這段淒美的愛情終將永遠沉在大西洋底下……。

MP3 156

at the top of one's lungs
非常大聲

lung 的意思是「肺」，說話前先把氣都吸得快滿到肺部頂端，就表示你要用盡全力大吼，at the top of one's lungs 就是在形容非常大聲說話，聲嘶力竭的大吼。

A: Casey was screaming **at the top of her lungs** for the whole concert.
凱西整場演唱會都超級大聲尖叫。

B: No wonder she lost her voice!
難怪她失聲了！

MP3 157

be no picnic
不輕鬆，不中意

你想想你都出外郊遊了，卻不能野餐，是不是很煞風景，一點都不好玩。be no picnic 就是在形容不輕鬆愉快的事情。

A: It must be hard raising two kids on your own.
獨自扶養兩個孩子一定很辛苦。

B: Yep. Being a single parent **is no picnic**.
是啊，當個單親父母可一點都不輕鬆。

電影對白

蘿絲去找傑克，除了要為那晚在甲板上的救命之恩表示感激以外，也謝謝他的保密。傑克反問她，究竟是為了什麼事情想不開。

Rose: It was everything. It was my whole world and all the people in it. And the *inertia of my life, plunging ahead, and me, powerless to stop it.
是所有事情，我周圍的整個世界以及我身邊所有的人。慣性的生活不斷地往前走，而我卻無力能阻止。

[蘿絲將手上的戒指秀給傑克看]

Jack: God, look at that thing. You'd have gone straight to the bottom.
我的老天啊，看看這東西，一定會讓妳沉到海底。

Rose: 500 invitations have gone out. All of Philadelphia society will be there. And all the while, I feel I'm...standing in the middle of a crowded room...screaming **at the top of my lungs**, and no one even looks up.
五百張請帖已經發出去了，所以費城的名流人士都會到。然而我一直覺得自己站在擁擠人群的房間裡，聲嘶力竭地吶喊，卻沒人理會。

*inertia [ɪn`ɝʃə] (n.) 慣性，維持現狀

電影對白

參加晚宴後的傑克用盡方法想再看見蘿絲，但都被阻擋，傑克於是躲在甲板上，等待蘿絲的出現。看到蘿絲一行人，傑克趁機將蘿絲帶進甲板的房間裡。

Rose: Jack, this is impossible. I can't see you.
傑克，這樣行不通，我不能再見你了。

Jack: I need to talk to you.
我有話跟你說。

Rose: No, Jack. No. Jack, I'm engaged. I'm marrying Cal. I love Cal.
不行，傑克，不能這樣。傑克，我已經訂婚了，我要嫁給卡爾，我愛他。

Jack: Rose, you**'re no picnic**, all right? You're a *spoiled little *brat, even. But under that, you're the most amazingly, *astounding, wonderful girl...woman that I've ever known.
蘿絲，妳不是很好相處，好嗎？妳甚至是個嬌縱的小公主。但內心裡，妳是我見過最迷人、最脫俗、最棒的女孩……不，女人。

*spoiled [spɔɪld] (a.) 被寵壞的
*brat [bræt] (n.) 淘氣鬼，小鬼
*astounding [ə`staʊndɪŋ] (a.) 令人驚艷的，令人驚奇的

Eternal Sunshine of the Spotless Mind 《王牌冤家》

電影介紹

喬爾（Joel，金凱瑞 (Jim Carrey) 飾）發現自己的女友克蕾婷（Clementine，凱特絲蕾飾）到「忘情診所」去消除跟自己有關的所有回憶。一氣之下的喬爾夜決定要去把克蕾婷忘掉。但刪除記憶手術的過程，是要把那些即將刪除的過往重新體驗一次。喬爾突然發現他不想丟棄這些真摯動人的過往，只是上了手術台的他，該如何拯救呢？

電影對白

克蕾婷因為喬爾説自己人很好，就像她名字的原意一樣（編註：clemency 意思是「仁慈、寬厚」），而大發雷霆。

Clementine: Now I'm nice? Oh, God, don't you know any other adjectives? I don't need nice. I don't need myself to be it and I don't need anybody to be it at me.

我人很好？天哪，你沒別的形容詞了嗎？我不想當好人，沒這個必要，別人也不需要對我好。

Joel: OK, OK.

好吧，好吧。

[過了一會兒]

Clementine: Joel. It's Joel, right? I'm sorry I yelled at you. I'm a little **out of sorts** today.

喬爾，你叫喬爾，對吧？我很抱歉對你大吼大叫，我今天心情不太好。

MP3 158

out of sorts 心情不好；身體不適

sort 除了有「種類」的意思，也能當「性格、性質」。在原本的性格之外，那你可能有點失常囉，out of sorts 就是在説人家有點煩躁、心情不好，也能指身體狀況不好。

A: You look a little **out of sorts**.

你看起來心情不太好。

B: Yeah, I've been in a bad mood all day.

對阿，已經鬱悶一整天了。

A: You look a little pale. Are you getting sick.

你臉色有點蒼白，是不是感冒了？

B: Maybe. I have been **out of sorts** for a day or two.

可能吧，我已經不舒服一兩天了。

Labor Day

MP3 160

in good hands 被照顧的很好

英文中用 in good hands（在很好的手中）來形容某人事物被照顧、保護的很好，也有很安全的意思。你也可以説 in safe hands。

A: Be sure and take good care of my cat.

一定要好好照顧我的貓。

B: Don't worry. Fluffy is **in good hands** with me.

不用擔心，小毛會被我照顧得很好。

The Reader 《為愛朗讀》

🎥 電影介紹

麥克（Michael，雷夫范恩斯 (Ralph Fiennes)、年少時由大衛克勞斯 (David Kross) 飾）十五歲時曾和漢娜（Hanna，凱特溫斯蕾飾）有過一段難以忘懷的忘年之戀。漢娜喜歡麥可念各式各樣的名著故事給他聽，麥可則對於漢娜的成熟魅力難以自拔，兩人同時沈溺在歡愉的性愛關係。只是某天當漢娜不告而別，兩人的再次重逢卻是在法庭上……。

MP3 159

hold oneself together
維持情緒平穩

hold 有「撐住」的意思，把自己撐住不崩潰，就表示你努力維持某個狀態，hold oneself together 就是形容人努力維持理智，不讓自己的情緒失控。

A: How did you manage to **hold yourself together** after the divorce?
你離婚後是怎樣讓自己不崩潰的？
B: Well, I had a lot of support from my family and friends.
嗯，我的家人和朋友給我很大的支持。

🎬 電影對白

麥克得知坐牢超過二十年的漢娜即將出獄，女子監獄的管理者露易絲布倫納 (Louisa Brenner) 告訴麥可，漢娜無依無靠，沒有親人也沒有朋友，他是唯一和他有聯繫的人。麥克於是前往漢娜監禁的女子監獄，一到門口，露易絲已在門口等他，引領他進去找漢娜。

Louisa Brenner: I'm Louisa Brenner. Good morning.
我是露易絲布倫納，早安。

Michael: How do you do.
妳好。

Louisa Brenner: We were expecting you earlier. I should warn you, for a long time Hanna **held herself together**. She was very *purposeful. In the last few years, she's different. She's let herself go. I'm taking you straight to the *canteen. They've just finished their lunch.
我們以為你會早點到。進去之前我先跟你說，多年以來，漢娜一直都很堅強，她有很強的韌性。但這幾年她變了，變得放棄自己。我會直接帶你到餐廳，她們剛吃完午餐。

*purposeful [`pɝpəsfəl] (a.) 有決心的
*canteen [kæn`tin] (n.)（醫院、學校等）餐廳

《一日一生》

🎬 電影對白

回到艾黛兒家後，法蘭克表示自己只是想找個地方躲一下，讓他受傷的腿能休息，到晚上就會離開，而且絕對不會傷害他們。但艾黛兒不相信他。

Adele: I'm stronger than you think.
我比你想像中的堅強。

Frank: I don't doubt that.
我不懷疑。

Adele: And I won't let anything happen to my son.
而且我不會允許我兒子發生任何事。

Frank: He's **in good hands**.
他現在很安全。

🎥 電影介紹

與兒子亨利（Henry，蓋特林葛里菲斯 (Gattlin Griffith) 飾，成年後由陶比麥奎爾 (Tobey Maguire) 飾）相依為命的艾黛兒（Adele，凱特溫絲蕾飾），離婚後始終走不出陰影。在勞動節假期前夕，艾黛兒與亨利到賣場去，遇見了法蘭克（Frank，喬許布洛林 (Josh Brolin) 飾），在他的半威嚇半強迫之下，只好帶他回家。接下來這有如命中註定的勞動節假期幾天發生的所有事情，改變了他們的一生。

125

Emma Watson 艾瑪華森

©Featureflash / Shutterstock.com

才貌兼備的新一代女神

看著《哈利波特》中的妙麗越變越美，令人感到驚艷之餘，這位英國美女的聲勢也水漲船高。除了在電影中挑戰各種性格及造型迥異的角色，讓人看到她對演藝工作的敬業與努力外，很多粉絲更欣賞她的多才多藝。她不但能說一口流利的法文，還會寫詩、作畫，也曾替環保時尚品牌 People Tree 作設計，並受邀擔任 Wonderland Magazine 的客座時尚編輯。熱愛瑜珈的她最近還拿到了專業瑜珈教師執照。如此才貌兼備（而且是演藝圈中難得沒崩壞的童星），也無怪乎大家把她奉為新一代的好萊塢女神了。

MP3 161

"Has anyone seen a [4]**toad**? A boy named Neville's lost one." With these words, spoken by the [5]**aspiring** [1]**witch** Hermione Granger in *Harry Potter and the Philosopher's Stone* (2001), the world was introduced to actress Emma Watson, then just 10 years old. Over the course of the eight Harry Potter films, audiences have watched Watson grow into a beautiful, confident young woman—one with a bright future in acting ahead of her.

Watson was born in Paris on April 15, 1990 to two English lawyers. Her parents divorced when she was five, and she moved to England with her mother. Watson attended a part-time theater school in Oxford, appearing in several plays before her teacher [2]**recommended** her to casting [3]**agents**. After eight auditions, Watson was cast in the first Harry Potter movie as Hermione. And as quick as you can say "Leviosa!," Watson was a child star. During her decade as Hermione, the young actress earned over £10 million, and plenty of critical praise as well.

Watson's first non-Potter role was as an aspiring actress in the BBC film *Ballet Shoes* (2007). And since the Harry Potter franchise ended in 2011, she's starred in the teen drama *The Perks of Being a Wallflower* (2012) and opposite Russell Crowe and Jennifer Connelly in the [6]**biblical** epic *Noah* (2014). In addition to acting, Watson made her successful modeling debut for Burberry in 2009, and was the face of Lancôme in 2011. She's even found time to complete a degree in English (not witchcraft, sadly) at Brown University, proving this beauty has brains, too.

「有沒有人看到一隻蟾蜍？有個叫奈威的男孩弄丟了一隻。」在《哈利波特：神秘的魔法石》（二○○一）中，由一心想成為女巫的妙麗格蘭傑所說的這句話，讓全世界第一次認識到當時年僅十歲的女演員艾瑪華森。隨著八部哈利波特電影，觀眾已見證妙麗出落成亭亭玉立、充滿自信的年輕女性——前方的演藝生涯前途無量。

華森於一九九○年四月十五日在巴黎出生，雙親都是英國律師。爸媽在她五歲時離婚，而她和媽媽一起移居英國。華森在牛津參加一所非全天候的戲劇學校，演出數齣話劇後，由老師推薦給星探。經過八次試鏡，華森獲得《哈利波特》第一集的妙麗一角。就跟你說「啦唯啊薩」的速度一樣快，華森已成為家喻戶曉的童星。在飾演妙麗的十年間，這位妙齡女星賺進超過一千萬英鎊，也贏得如潮佳評。

華森第一個哈利波特以外的角色是 BBC 影集《芭蕾舞鞋》（二○○七）中一位想成為演員的女孩。而自從哈利波特系列在二○一一年落幕，她已主演青少年劇《壁花男孩》（二○一二），並於聖經史詩電影《諾亞方舟》（二○一四）和羅素克洛及珍妮佛康納莉演對手戲。除了戲劇，華森也在二○○九年為巴寶莉獻出成功的模特兒處女秀，也在二○一一年成為蘭蔻化粧品代言人。她甚至騰出時間完成學業，取得布朗大學英文學士（不是巫術，真遺憾），證明這位美女也是有大腦的。

LANGUAGE GUIDE

是 LeviOsa，不是 LeviosA

Leviosa 是《哈利波特》裡的一句咒語，可以凌空移動物品。榮恩在課堂上練習時一直不斷復誦這個咒語，試著讓桌上的羽毛飛起來，但卻一點動靜也沒有。一旁的妙麗看不下去，糾正起他的發音：「是 leviOsa，不是 leviosA」（重音在 O 而非 A），讓榮恩當場模掉，而這一幕也成了《哈利波特》第一集中令人印象深刻的經典畫面。

VOCABULARY BANK

1) **witch** [wɪtʃ] (n.) 女巫，巫婆，witchcraft 即「巫術，魔法」
Carrie dressed up as a witch for Halloween.
凱莉萬聖節時打扮成女巫。

2) **recommend** [ˌrɛkə`mɛnd] (v.) 推薦
Can you recommend a good lasagna recipe?
你可以推薦一個不錯的千層麵食譜嗎？

3) **agent** [`edʒənt] (n.) 經紀人，代理人
The real estate agent showed us several houses in the area.
房屋仲介帶我們去看這區的幾間房子。

進階字彙

4) **toad** [tod] (n.) 蟾蜍，癩蛤蟆
Toads are generally larger than frogs.
蟾蜍通常比青蛙來得大。

5) **aspiring** [ə`spaɪrɪŋ] (a.) 有志氣的，有抱負的，有意成為…的
Most aspiring authors never get their books published.
有志成為作家的人幾乎都無法讓他們的書出版。

6) **biblical** [`bɪblɪkəl] (a.) （常為大寫）聖經的，聖經中的
We plan to give our children biblical names.
我們打算給孩子取聖經上的名字。

Harry Potter and the Prisoner of Azkaban

《哈利波特：阿茲卡班的逃犯》

🎥 電影介紹

哈利波特系列的第三集。神祕的殺人犯天狼星（Sirius Black，蓋瑞歐德曼 (Gary Oldman) 飾）從阿茲卡班監獄逃跑了，魔法學校霍格華茲為此嚴陣以待，加派許多會懾人魂魄的催狂魔來守衛校園，然而這些理應要保護學生的催狂魔竟成了哈利波特（Harry Potter，丹尼爾雷德克里夫 (Daniel Radcliffe) 飾）難以擺脫的夢魘，而天狼星神祕的過去也隨著劇情發展逐漸揭露⋯⋯。

MP3 163

in a heartbeat 立刻，一下子

心臟跳動一下只要不到一秒鐘的時間，因此 heartbeat 就引申為「短暫、快速」的意思，in a heartbeat 就是「一下子，馬上」。

A: My company wants to transfer me to Paris, but I'm not sure I want to go.
我公司想派我去巴黎，但我還不確定自己是否想要去。

B: Really? I'd go **in a heartbeat**!
真的嗎？要是我會馬上就去耶。

🎬 電影對白

榮恩（Ron，魯伯特葛林 (Rupert Grint) 飾）和哈利、妙麗（Hermione，艾瑪華森飾）正在想辦法營救即將被處死的鷹馬巴嘴，家鼠斑斑突然咬了榮恩一口，趁榮恩手一鬆便逃走了，榮恩連忙去追斑斑，不料突然又衝出一隻狗靈咬住榮恩的腿拖行不放，後來榮恩總算成功掙脫，卻受了嚴重的腿傷。

Hermione: Ow! That looks really painful.
噢！看起來真的很痛。

Ron: So painful. They...they might chop it.
超痛的。他們⋯⋯他們可能會切斷我的腳。

Hermione: I'm sure Madame Pomfrey can fix it **in a heartbeat**.
我保證龐芮夫人一下子就能醫好它。

Ron: It's too late. It's ruined. It'll have to be chopped off.
太遲了。我的腿已經廢了。我要截肢了

Gossip Box

妙麗居然愛馬份？

在《哈利波特》中與榮恩湊對的艾瑪，沒想到卻坦承當初她愛的是演哈利死對頭馬份的湯姆費爾頓 (Tom Felton)，不過她也笑說當時只是純純的愛，兩人至今還是相當要好的朋友，說起這段往事還會哈哈大笑呢！

Harry Potter and the Order of the Phoenix

🎥 電影介紹

哈利波特系列第五集。黑魔王佛地魔回來了，但是魔法部只想粉飾太平，刻意忽略這個事實，甚至認為霍格華茲校長鄧不利多（Dumbledore，邁可坎邦 (Michael Gambon) 飾）是要用此謠言消滅魔法部長夫子（Cornelius Fudge，羅伯特哈迪 (Robert Hardy) 飾）的權威，夫子因此派了桃樂絲恩不理居（Dolores Umbridge，伊美黛史道頓 (Imelda Staunton) 飾）擔任黑魔法防禦術的新教授，隨時監控校長校集這些小魔法師的一舉一動。

🎞 電影對白

哈利在鳳凰會看到妙麗和榮恩後，責怪他們怎麼沒寫信告訴他有關鳳凰會的事。

Ron: We wanted to write, mate. Really, we did. Only….

我們很想寫信，兄弟。真的，我們想。只是……。

Harry: Only what?

只是什麼？

Hermione: Only Dumbledore made us swear not to tell you anything.

只是鄧不利多要我們發誓不能告訴你。

Harry: Dumbledore said that? But why would he **keep me in the dark**? Maybe I could help.

鄧不利多這麼說？但他幹嘛瞞著我？搞不好我能幫忙啊。

🎞 電影對白

因遭受催狂魔攻擊，哈利不得已在麻瓜（也就是表哥達利）前施展魔法，遭到霍格華茲開除，也讓他深陷致命危機。為了安全起見，教授們把哈利接到鳳凰會總部，抵達時榮恩和妙麗也在那裡。

Harry: So what is this place?

這究竟是哪裡？

Ron: Headquarters.

是總部。

Hermione: Of the Order of the Phoenix. It's a secret society. Dumbledore formed it back when they first fought **You-Know-Who**.

鳳凰會的總部，它是個祕密社團。鄧不利多當年第一次對抗「那個人」時創立的。

MP3 164

you-know-who 你知道的那個人

在哈利波特系列中，佛地魔（Lord Voldemort）的名字是個禁忌，大家能不提就不提，迫不得已也只會用 You-Know-Who 或 He-Who-Must-Not-Be-Named（那個不能指名道姓的人）帶過。通常當你不想說出那人的名字，而大家其實都知道你在說誰的時候，就可以用 you-know-who 來代替。

A: Brenda isn't still going out with **you-know-who** is she?

布蘭達不會還有跟「那個人」約會吧？

B: Unfortunately, yes.

很可惜，他們還在一起。

MP3 165

keep sb. in the dark 把某人蒙在鼓裡

in the dark 意思是「完全不曉得」、「被蒙在鼓裡」。當你發現自己什麼狀況都搞不清楚，完全沒被告知時，可以說 I'm completely in the dark.（我什麼都不知道）。若是故意「把某人」蒙在鼓裡，就是 keep sb. in the dark。

A: Her husband didn't tell her that he lost his job?

她老公沒跟她說他失業了嗎？

B: No. He **kept her in the dark** for months.

沒有。他瞞了她好幾個月。

Harry Potter *and the Goblet of Fire*

《哈利波特：火盃的考驗》

 電影介紹

為哈利波特系列第四集。本學期剛開學，各學院就緊鑼密鼓地為「三巫鬥法大賽」作準備。按照往例，三位參賽者必須年滿十七歲且由「火盃」遴選指定。然而年僅十四的哈利竟意外獲選，成為第四位參賽者，遭受眾人質疑的他只好硬著頭皮應戰。沒想到原來這一切的背後隱藏著要置他於死的重大陰謀，哈利能夠順利挺過這次考驗嗎？

電影對白

妙麗告訴榮恩自己已有一同出席舞會的舞伴，也就是高年級的級長西追（Cedric Diggory，羅伯派汀森 (Robert Pattinson) 飾）。榮恩像打翻醋子一樣，語帶嘲諷地説西追是在利用她，而且對她來説年紀太老了，讓妙麗聽了非常生氣。

Hermione: You know the solution then don't you.
那你現在知道該怎麼辦了吧。

General Ashdown: Then that is his fate.
那麼這是他的命。

Ron: Go on.
請説啊。

Hermione: Next time there's a ball pluck up the courage and ask me before somebody else does, and not **as a last resort**.
下次有舞會的時候，記得鼓起勇氣在別人邀請我前先約我，而不是把我當成最後的選擇。

©Flywithinsun / flickr.com

Gossip Box

資優生妙麗銀幕大解放

以妙麗一角深植人心的艾瑪華森在《星光大盜》中一改端莊形象，不但抽菸、嗑藥、行竊，連穿著都極盡風騷，大露事業線。她在採訪中表示，自己接演這個角色是為了走出《哈利波特》給她的形象包袱，同時也想讓影迷見識到不一樣的她。從她的敬業精神和可塑性看來，這位小妮子還真是天生吃這行飯的料呢！

MP3 166

as a last resort
當作最後的手段、不得已的下策

resort 在此為「手段、依靠」的意思，last resort 就是指已經用盡其他辦法都無效，最後迫不得已所採取的「終極手段」。

A: Are the doctors considering an operation to remove the brain tumor?
醫師們有考慮開刀拿掉腦瘤嗎？

B: Yes, but only **as a last resort**.
有，不過那是最後手段。

MP3 168

take a stand
站出來（發表意見、力挺或反對）

stand 作名詞時有「立場、態度」的意思，因此 take a stand 就是「表達立場」，後面常接介系詞 on、for 或 against。for 表示「支持、力挺某立場」；against 則是指「採取反對立場」；on 單純是表達對某議題表態的介系詞，可表支持也能表反對。

A: Do you like the president?
你喜歡現任總統嗎？

B: He's OK, but I wish he would **take a stand** on important issues.
還可以，但我希望他能針對重大議題作出表態。

A: Why did you vote for that candidate?
你為什麼投給那位候選人？

B: Because he **took a stand** against racism.
因為他站出來反對種族歧視。

The Bling Ring 《星光大盜》

🎥 電影介紹

一群住在洛杉磯高級地區的驕縱青少年，某天突發奇想去偷好萊塢明星的家，妮琪 (Nicki，艾瑪華森飾) 和友人們先是到芭黎絲希爾頓 (Paris Hilton) 的豪宅搶了一票，由於一切來得過於輕易，於是便食髓知味，繼續對其他好萊塢名人下手行竊。雖然犯下竊盜罪，這夥年輕人中仍有人因此聲名大噪，成為公眾偶像。導演科波拉希望能藉此片帶大家一窺上流社會那種紙醉金迷、奢華成性的作風，同時也點出年輕一代價值觀扭曲的問題。

🎞 電影對白

記者凱特 (Kate) 繼續訪問妮琪：

Kate: What's your goal or life plan if you have one?

如果妳有人生目標或計畫的話，那會是什麼？

Nicki: I do, I think my journey is to be a leader and push for peace and for the health of our planet.

我有啊，我想我在人生的旅途上會是個領導者，促進和平與地球的健康。

Shannon: Nicki has expressed to me a lot of her *humanitarianism.

妮奇向我傳達過很多她的人道情懷。

Nicki: It's my main goal. God didn't give me these talents and what I look like to sit around and just be a model or famous. I want to do something people notice, that's why I'm studying business, so I can be a leader and **take a stand** for people.

這是我的主要目標。上帝賜給我這些才能和美貌，不是只為了坐在那邊當個模特兒或名人。我想做點人們看得到的事，這就是我為什麼要讀商的原因，這樣我才能成為一位領導者，站出來支持民眾。

*humanitarianism [ˈbɪblɪkəl] (n.) 人道主義，博愛精神

🎞 電影對白

闖空門事件曝光後，記者到妮琪家採訪，問及她與友人莎曼珊 (Samantha，塔莎法蜜嘉 (Taissa Farmiga) 飾) 是怎麼認識的。

Nicki: The reason we related so well is my dad is a recovering alcoholic and Sam's mom is….

我們會這麼這麼要好的原因是我爸是個復原中的酒鬼，而小珊的媽媽是個……。

Laurie: A practicing….

是個不折不扣的……。

Nicki: A practicing drug addict and alcoholic and our moms became best friends and….

一個不折不扣的毒蟲和酒鬼，而且咱們媽媽又成為最好的朋友。

Laurie: And then she **went off the deep end**, she was on the verge….

然後她就失控了，她整個快要……。

Nicki: Please!

拜託別插話！

MP3 167

go off the deep end
抓狂，失控，精神崩潰

這個片語來自游泳時的情境，通常游泳的人會先從水深較淺處下水，不會貿然躍下深處。只有在情急或亂了方寸的情況下，才有可能直接從深處入水。因此這個片語就是在形容某人處於極度失控或是精神不穩定的狀況。

©Flywithinsun / flickr.com

A: What did she do when she found out her boyfriend was cheating on her?

當她發現男友不忠時，她做了什麼？

B: She totally **went off the deep end**.

她完全抓狂了。

A: How is Mark doing these days?

馬克最近好嗎？

B: He really **went off the deep end** after the divorce, but he's much better now.

他離婚後簡直是大崩潰，不過現在好多了。

Julia Roberts 茱莉亞羅勃茲

©Featureflash / Shutterstock.com

TONGUE-TIED-NO-MORE

get...rolling 使⋯開始，著手進行⋯

球賽開球時，球才會開始滾動，這個片語就是用動詞「滾動」(roll) 來表達讓事情開始運作的意思。

A: Should we start the meeting? It's almost 10:00.
我們要開會了嗎？快十點了。
B: Yes, let's get things rolling. We have a lot to cover.
好，我們趕快開始吧。有很多事情要討論。

a heart of gold 心腸好

金色常給人高尚和珍貴的感覺，因此英文就用「一顆金色的心」來形容人心地善良，待人和氣，有著高尚的品格。

A: What does Ted see in Lydia? She's so ugly.
泰德到底看上莉德亞什麼？她那麼醜。
B: She may not be pretty, but she has a heart of gold.
她或許不漂亮，不過她心腸很好啊。

MP3 169

Known for her long red [1]**curls** and bright smile, Julia Roberts is one of Hollywood's biggest stars. She made her big screen debut in *Satisfaction* (1988) at the age of 19, and over the years her movies have [2]**brought in** close to $4 billion worldwide—not bad for a little girl from Georgia who wanted to be a [3]**veterinarian** when she grew up. Her appearance in the indie comedy *Mystic Pizza* (1988) **got** her career **rolling**, and her portrayal of a young bride in *Steel Magnolias* the following year won her a Golden Globe Award and an Oscar nomination, both for best supporting actress.

Roberts' breakthrough role came in 1990, when she played opposite Richard Gere as a [10]**hooker** with **a heart of gold** in *Pretty Woman*. Six other actresses, including Meg Ryan and Daryl Hannah, [4]**turned down** the part, and Roberts' fee was only $300,000, but it's hard to imagine a better star-making role. [5]**Building on** this success, Roberts starred in thrillers like *The Pelican Brief* (1993), and rom-coms like *My Best Friend's Wedding* (1997) and *Notting Hill* (1999). Then, in 2000, she won the best actress Oscar playing the title character in *Erin Brokovich*, a [6]**determined** single mom who takes on a large power company that's polluting the environment.

[7]**Subsequently**, Roberts appeared in the hit crime comedies *Ocean's Eleven* (2001) and *Ocean's Twelve* (2004), starred in the film adaption of Elizabeth Gilbert's [9]**memoir**, *Eat Pray Love* (2010), and won another Oscar nomination playing Meryl Streep's daughter in *August: Osage County* (2013). Recently, however, Roberts has focused more on raising her three children. She reports they're just [8]**figuring out** what the world already knows: their mom is a real star.

VOCABULARY BANK

1) **curl** [kɜ] (n.) 捲髮
Are Jennifer's curls natural?
珍妮佛是自然捲嗎？

2) **bring in** [brɪŋ ɪn] (phr.)（使）賺的，創造（收入、利潤等）
Steven's job doesn't bring in enough to support his family.
史帝芬的工作收入不足以養家為口。

3) **veterinarian** [ˌvɛtərəˋnɛrɪən] (n.) 獸醫，一般簡稱為 vet
When are you taking Fluffy to the vet?
你什麼時候要帶毛毛去看獸醫？

4) **turn down** [tɜn daʊn] (phr.) 拒絕
I asked Danielle out, but she turned me down.
我有約丹妮兒出去，但她拒絕了。

5) **build on** [bɪld ɑn] (phr.) 以為⋯基礎
The millionaire's success was built on hard work and determination.
努力和決心是那位富豪成功的基石。

6) **determined** [dɪˋtɜmɪnd] (a.) 有決心的
I'm determined to finish writing this report before I go home.
我下定決心寫完這份報告才能回家。

7) **subsequently** [ˋsʌbsɪkwəntəli] (adv.) 其後，接著
The virus appeared last year and subsequently spread to the whole country.
病毒從去年開始出現，然後擴散到全國。

8) **figure out** [ˋfɪgjə aʊt] (phr.) 搞懂
I can't figure out how he does that magic trick.
我搞不懂他那個魔術是怎麼變的。

進階字彙

9) **memoir** [ˋmɛmwɑr] (n.) 回憶錄，傳記
The man wrote a memoir about his famous brother.
這名男子寫了一本回憶錄透露他那個名人兄弟的故事。

口語補充

10) **hooker** [ˋhʊkə] (n.) 娼妓
The mayor was caught sleeping with a hooker.
那位市長嫖妓被抓到。

以一頭紅色長捲髮和燦爛笑容聞名的茱莉亞羅勃茲是好萊塢當紅巨星之一。她十九歲時以《豪放四俏妞》（一九八八）獻出大銀幕處女秀，而這麼多年下來，她的電影已在世界各地創造近四十億美元的票房──對一個來自喬治亞州、長大後想當獸醫的小女孩來說還不賴。她在獨立製片喜劇《現代灰姑娘》（一九八八）的演出帶動她的演藝事業，而次年她在《鋼木蘭》飾演年輕新娘，為她一舉贏得金球獎最佳女配角獎，以及奧斯卡最佳女配角提名。

羅勃茲的突破性角色在一九九○年來到，她在《麻雀變鳳凰》中飾演心地善良的娼妓，和李察吉爾演對手戲。包括梅格萊恩和戴露漢娜在內等六位女演員皆婉拒該角，而羅勃茲的片酬僅三十萬美元，但很難想到比這更出色的造星角色了。以此次成就為基礎，羅勃茲先後主演《絕對機密》（一九九三）等驚悚片和《新娘不是我》（一九九七）及《新娘百分百》（一九九九）等愛情喜劇。接下來，二○○○年，她在《永不妥協》飾演片名角色艾琳布羅克維齊：一位意志堅強的單親媽媽，挑戰一家污染環境的大型電力公司，贏得奧斯卡最佳女主角獎。

隨後，羅勃茲擔綱賣座犯罪喜劇片《瞞天過海》（二○○一）及其續集《瞞天過海二：長驅直入》（二○○四）、主演伊麗莎白吉爾伯特回憶錄的電影版《享受吧！一個人的旅行》（二○一○），復於《八月心風暴》（二○一三）飾演梅莉史翠普的女兒，再次贏得奧斯卡提名。不過，近年來羅勃茲的生活重心主要在養育三個孩子上。她說，他們才剛剛理解與世皆知的事實：她們的媽媽是名副其實的巨星。

Erin Brockovich 《永不妥協》

🎥 電影介紹

改編自美國真實事件，艾琳（Erin，茱莉亞羅伯茲飾）是一位單親媽媽，帶著三個年幼的孩子，沒錢也沒工作。艾琳發生車禍意外後，律師艾德（Ed，亞伯芬尼（Albert Finney）飾）未能替她爭取到賠償金，於是她便強迫艾德雇用她為事務所僱員，後來艾琳因這份工作而意外發現電力公司造成公用水污染的問題，便決定挺身而出，查明真相。

MP3 171

you bet 的確，當然，沒問題

bet 是「下賭注」的意思，You bet. 即等於 You can bet money on that.（你可以把錢下注在上面），言下之意就是說很有把握。另一個使用情境則是在回應別人的要求或謝意，等於中文的「沒問題，不客氣」。

A: If he asked you out, would you say yes?
如果他約妳出去，妳會答應嗎？

B: **You bet!**
當然囉！

A: Could you help me move the couch?
你可以幫我搬這張沙發嗎？

B: **You bet!**
沒問題！

A: Thanks for giving me a ride.
謝謝你載我一程。

B: **You bet!**
不客氣。

🎞 電影對白

艾琳為了調查電力公司水污染一事，去訪查與太平洋電信公司 (PG&E) 有接觸的相關當事人多娜（Donna）。

Erin: I'm sorry. I just don't see why you're *corresponding with PG&E about your medical problems in the first place.
不好意思。我還是不懂妳當初為什麼要針對妳的醫療紀錄和 PG&E 通信。

Donna: Well, they paid for the doctor's visit.
這個嘛，他們有幫我付醫療費用。

Erin: They did?
他們有喔？

Donna: You bet. Paid for a checkup for the whole family. And not like with insurance where you pay and a year goes by and maybe you see some money. They just took care of it just like that. We never even saw a bill.
沒錯。他們幫我們全家支付健康檢查的費用。而且不像保險公司那樣，要先自己付錢，然後一年後或許你可以拿回來一些。他們就直接處理好。我們連賬單也沒看過。

Erin: Wow. Why'd they do that?
哇。他們幹嘛這樣做？

Donna: Because of the *chromium
因為鉻吧。

*correspond [ˌkɔrəˈspɑnd] (v.) 通信
*chromium [ˈkromiəm] (n.) 鉻

Gossip Box

鳳凰女代言魔術胸罩？

茱莉亞羅伯茲在《永不妥協》中飾演見義勇為的辣媽，讓她一舉拿下奧斯卡影后。應導演要求，她在戲中除了要替小孩餵奶，且為了凸顯角色性格，還得打扮得花枝招展，甚至穿上魔術胸罩。許多女性當時看了這部片以後，爭相詢問茱莉亞穿的是哪個品牌的魔術胸罩，意外替該內衣廠商帶來商機。

電影對白

隔壁鄰居喬治（George）好心幫艾琳帶了一天小孩。對男人還留有恐懼的她卻對他不假辭色，拒人於千里之外。

Erin: This isn't gonna get you laid, you know. *[to her daughter]* Get in bed.

你休想因此就能跟我上床。*[跟女兒說]* 去睡覺。

George: Oh, that's good, 'cause I don't find you attractive, either.

那很好，因為我也不覺得妳有魅力。

Erin: Well, good. Then we're even.

很好。那我們算扯平了。

George: Right. So we don't have to worry about that. I'm glad that we **got that out of the way.**

沒錯。所以我們不用去擔心那檔事。我很高興我們說清楚講明白了。

Erin: I feel much better.

那我就放心了。

George: I do, too. Really, seriously. Because now I can just look after the kids and not worry about you coming on to me all the time.

我也是。真的，老實說。因為我現在可以放心幫妳帶小孩，而不用老是擔心妳對我投懷送抱。

©Diagonal Uno / flickr.com

電影對白

艾琳在路上冒失的車輛攔腰撞上，她因此找了律師艾德，告上法院。對方律師仗著自己的當事人是懸壺濟世的醫師，暗指艾琳自己開車製造假事故，真詐財。

Erin: I was pulling out real slow, and **out of nowhere**, his Jaguar comes racing around the corner like a bat outta hell....

我當時車子剛開動，而他的捷豹車，不知從哪兒冒出來，瘋了似地疾駛出了巷口……

Lawyer: So you must've been feeling pretty desperate that afternoon.

妳那天下午想必相當走投無路吧。

Erin: What's your point?

你的重點是？

Lawyer: Broke, three kids, no job. A doctor in a Jaguar must've looked like a pretty good meal ticket.

沒錢、有三個小孩又失業。一個開著捷豹的醫生，看起來一定很像是飯票。

Erin: What? Hey! He hit me.

什麼？嘿！是他開車撞我的。

Lawyer: So you say.

那是妳說的。

MP3 172

get sth. out of the way
大功告成，放下心中的大石

in the way 是指「擋在路上」，常用來比喻「障礙」；反過來說，out of the way 便是指「不會礙事，沒有障礙」，感覺像是一路暢通。get sth. out of the way 就是形容好不容易完成了一件困難或不討喜的事，終於可以告一段落的意思。

A: How about seeing that new Tom Cruise movie tonight?

今晚去看湯姆克魯斯的新電影如何？

B: Sure, but I have to **get** my homework **out of the way** first.

好啊，但我得先把我的回家作業搞定。

A: I finally went and apologized to Margaret.

我後來終於去和瑪格莉特道了歉。

B: Good. Now that you **got that out of the way,** I hope you two can be friends again.

很好。既然你們已經把話說清楚了，我希望你們可以再做朋友。

A: Your leg is bleeding! What happened?

你的腿在流血！怎麼回事？

B: A dog just appeared **out of nowhere** and bit me.

剛有隻狗突然衝出來咬我。

MP3 173

out of nowhere
不知怎地

nowhere 表「不知名的地方」，out of nowhere 就是指「莫名其妙出現，不知道從哪裡突然冒出來的」。

135

Valentine's Day 《情人節快樂》

 電影介紹

由茱莉亞羅勃茲、潔西卡艾芭 (Jessica Alba)、布萊德利庫柏 (Bradley Cooper)、安海瑟薇 (Anne Hathaway)、艾希頓庫奇 (Ashton Kutcher)……等好萊塢眾星主演的一部浪漫喜劇。背景設定在洛杉磯，以交錯糾葛的故事線，述說一群人在情人節這天個自經歷的浪漫故事，也讓他們找到愛情的真諦。

電影對白

飛機上，空服員送來心型糖果，祝福每位乘客情人節快樂。善於觀察的女軍官凱特（Kate，茱莉亞羅勃茲飾）發現霍頓（Holden，布萊德利庫柏飾）對於心型糖果似乎有些排斥……。

Kate: Why do you hate heart-shaped candy?
你為什麼討厭心型糖果？

Holden: I think it's because it reminds me that this is Valentine's Day, and I'm recently single. We weren't **on the same page**.
我想是因為那會提醒我今天是情人節，而且我最近單身。我們倆完全沒默契。

Kate: Sorry
我很遺憾。

Holden: It's OK. It's over.
沒關係，都過去了。

MP3 174

on the same page
看法、見解一致

「在同一頁」，意思就是兩人的見解／看法一致、有共識，或是彼此擁有相同的訊息。

A: I think lowering prices would be the best way to increase sales.
我認為降價是促進銷售最好的辦法。

B: Good, then we're **on the same page**.
很好，那我們看法一致。

Gossip Box

影后過招

在《八月心風暴》中討論度最高、最獲影評讚賞的場景，莫過於梅莉嗑藥後在飯桌上以尖酸言語挑釁眾人的演出，隨後茱莉亞羅伯茲奮身撲倒梅姨，試圖搶走她手中的藥，此舉更掀起了另一波高潮。拍攝前，茱莉亞很擔心自己會弄傷梅姨，但敬業的梅姨鼓勵她釋放所有的情緒，放膽地演，於是兩人的敬業就促成了這場充滿張力的完美演出。

August: Osage County 《八月心風暴》

📽️ 電影介紹

薇歐拉（Violet，梅莉史翠普 (Meryl Streep) 飾）是一位染有毒癮且尖酸暴躁的母親，在丈夫不幸溺斃，長年在外的子女們紛紛趕回位於奧克拉荷馬州歐賽奇郡的老家喪命。原本相處就有問題的一家人再度聚首，所有心結、仇恨一次爆發，他們該如何處理這場家庭風暴？

🎬 電影對白

芭芭拉（Barbara，茱莉亞羅伯茲飾）和老公比爾（Bill，伊旺麥奎格 (Ewan McGregor) 飾）在前往娘家的途中下車休息，聊到芭芭拉的媽媽曾經因為天氣熱還不開冷氣，把鸚鵡給活活熱死的事。

Barbara: Goddamn, it's hot
天殺的，天氣真熱。

Bill: Suppose your mom's turned on the air conditioner?
妳覺得妳媽有開冷氣嗎？

Barbara: You kidding? Remember the *parakeets?
你在開玩笑嗎？還記不記得虎斑鸚鵡？

Bill: The parakeets?
虎斑鸚鵡？

Barbara: I didn't tell you about the parakeets? She got a parakeet, for some insane reason and the little fucker *croaked after two days. So she went to the pet store and **raised hell**, and they gave her another one. That one died after a day.
我沒告訴過你虎斑鸚鵡的事？她買了一隻虎斑鸚鵡，不知道怎麼搞的，那個小傢伙兩天後就掛了。所以她就去寵物店大吵大鬧，他們又給了她一隻。結果那隻一天後也死了。

*parakeet [ˋpærəkit] (n.) 虎斑鸚鵡，小鸚鵡
*croak [krok] (v.)（口）死掉

MP3 175

raise hell 大吵大鬧，撒野

形容大聲抱怨、大吵大鬧，通常是為了爭取某些事物，或是要對方答應某些事情，也可代表「放肆撒野」的意思。

©Everett Collection / Shutterstock.com

A: How did you finally get them to give you a refund?
妳最後是怎麼讓他們退錢給妳的？

B: I called Customer Service and **raised hell**.
我打電話去客服部大吵大鬧。

A: Where are the boys tonight?
兒子們今晚在哪裡？

B: Probably out **raising hell**.
大概在外頭撒野吧。

🎬 電影對白

芭芭拉和比爾為了孩子的教養問題起爭執，後來還扯到比爾有外遇這件事，兩人的爭吵越演越烈，不可開交，最後比爾撂下狠話。

Bill: You're thoughtful, Barbara, but you're not open. You're passionate, but you're hard. You're a good, decent, funny, wonderful woman, and I love you, but you're a **pain in the ass**!
妳很體貼，芭芭拉，但妳不夠坦誠。妳很熱情，卻又難相處。妳是個善良、正派、風趣又好得沒話說的女人，我也愛妳，但妳真是個討厭鬼！

MP3 176

pain in the ass 令人感到痛苦的人事物

被討厭的人或事所困擾，是否就像屁股長痔瘡一樣，令人坐立難安，有如芒刺在背？ pain in the ass 正是用來形容令人討厭的東西，較為文雅的說法為 pain in the neck。

A: God! The boss is driving me crazy.
天哪！我老闆快把我逼瘋了。

B: Yeah. He's a real **pain in the ass**.
對呀。他根本就是個討厭鬼。

國賓看電影

APP各平台版本免費下載中！

支援 iOS/Windows Phone/Android

iOS

 **ANDROID**

 **Windows Phone**

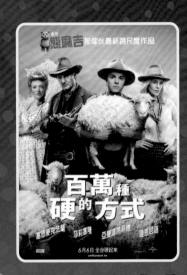

明日邊界
5/30(五)上映

百萬種硬的方式
6/6(五)上映

當我們混在一起
6/13(五)~6/15(日)口碑場
6/20(五)正式上映

變形金剛4：絕跡重生
6/26(四)上映

馴龍高手2
7/4(五)上映

猩球崛起:黎明的進擊
7/16(三)上映

威秀影城
LIVE CONCERT

Open your Mind. Shake your body. Wave your hand. Shock your ear.
Wide your eye. Power is on. Just enjoy it. We will Rock you.

VIESHOW
CINEMAS

威秀影城帶您前進全世界
海外演唱會零秒差LIVE直播，影廳就是你的

搖滾區！

國家圖書館出版品預行編目 (CIP) 資料

好萊塢 A 咖教你電影英文 Film Everything：EZ TALK 總編嚴選特刊 /
EZ叢書館編輯部作. -- 初版. -- 台北市：日月文化, 2014.06
160 面 ; 21x28 公分
ISBN 978-986-248-388-6(平裝附光碟片)
1. 英語 2. 讀本
805.18   103007786

EZ 叢書館

好萊塢 A 咖教你電影英文 Film Everything：EZ TALK 總編嚴選特刊

作　　者：EZ TALK編輯部
編　　審：Judd Piggott
筆　　者：Judd Piggott、Jacob Roth
譯　　者：洪世民
編　　輯：陳思容、韋孟岑
責任編輯：黃鈺琦
封面設計：楊意雯
版型設計：管仕豪
內頁排版：楊意雯、蔡修芳
錄音後製：純粹錄音後製有限公司
錄 音 員：Michael Tennant 、Meilee Saccenti

發 行 人：洪祺祥
第二編輯部
總編輯顧問：陳思容
法律顧問：建大法律事務所
財務顧問：高威會計師事務所

出　　版：日月文化出版股份有限公司
製　　作：EZ 叢書館
地　　址：台北市大安區信義路三段 151 號 8 樓
電　　話：(02) 2708-5509
傳　　真：(02) 2708-6157
網　　址：www.ezbooks.com.tw
客服信箱：service@heliopolis.com.tw

總 經 銷：聯合發行股份有限公司
電　　話：(02) 2917-8022
傳　　真：(02) 2915-7212
印　　刷：科樂印刷事業股份有限公司
初　　版：2014年6月
初版三刷：2015年3月
定　　價：350元
I S B N：978-986-248-388-6

封面圖權（依名字開頭字母順序）：
Cate Blanchett: Helga Esteb / Shutterstock.com
Emma Watson: Flywithinsun / flickr.com
Hugh Jackamn: s_bukley / Shutterstock.com
Leonardo DiCaprio: 達志 UPI
Robert Downey Jr.: lev radin / Shutterstock.com
Scarlett Johansson: Helga Esteb / Shutterstock.com